The Viana Memoirs
Vol. II

The Journey

by
L. Katherine Dailey

Edit et Cetera Ltd.
www.familybookhouse.com
Member: Colorado Independent Publishers Asso.

The Journey *is wholly and completely a work of fiction. Any similarity between characters and persons living or dead is purely coincidental. While some locations are real, they are used fictionally within this context.*

Cover Photo by Angel Malave
Taken at Wellington Lake, Colorado, USA
Models: Scott and Hayley Suderman
Cover Design: Linda Lane

ISBN: 0-9769989-7-1

DEDICATION

Dedicated to my sister, Shelley Carmichael. Your fascination with horses and genuine love of nature contributed greatly to the development of the character, Alexandra. Thank you for sharing your knowledge and experience.

ACKNOWLEDGMENTS

Thank you to all my family, especially my parents, Mary Jo and Charles Betts, and Lois and Neil Dailey. Your never-ending reassurance always motivates me!

With particular recognition to my husband, Michael. Because of your confidence in me, I can believe in success.

Randy Finley, Mount Baker Vineyards, Eberson, Washington, USA.

Larry Ross, Scott Creek World Grand Champion Miniature Horses, Salem, Oregon, USA.

And most important of all, to Linda Lane, my editor, for your expertise and countless laborious hours. Because of you, this story is exceptional. Thank you!

Finally, my appreciation goes out to all my readers. Your interest in clean, yet fun, stories is an inspiration.

Chapter One

Footsteps intruded upon the stillness of Simone's bed-chamber. She was startled out of a restless sleep.

Her husband stood beside her bed. He held a finger before his lips and beckoned her to follow him. For a moment she hesitated. Rarely did she venture outside her bedchamber at night.

Taking her hand, he pulled her along the shadow-cloaked corridor. In silence they passed several oil lamps burning low. Shadows stretched like crooked fingers across textured walls dulled to a curry yellow by the lamplight.

She looked down. They both walked barefooted. He, however, wore his outdoor wrap. She shivered in the thin night-shirt that served her well under her coverlet but proved woe-fully inadequate in the drafty hallway.

Somewhere between her still-drowsy state and her husband's recent peculiar behavior, she felt a growing sense of foreboding. For the first time since their wedding eight years before, she knew fear in his presence. Was it for her own safe-ty? Or was her alarm in behalf of him?

He halted at a closed door. Before turning the curve of the handle, he placed a tiny brass saucer over the lamp flame near-est them on the wall. The deepening shadows enfolded her, and she shuddered. In haste, he pushed the door inward, nudg-ing her into the dark parlor.

Moonlight filtered through the tall leaded-glass window on the opposite side of the large room. His warm hand gripped her cold one. They crossed the thick wool rug toward the window half draped by a heavy red curtain. Easing it aside, he motioned for her to peer out at the courtyard washed in moonlight. Between the stone carvings and the flower gardens, two figures stood talking.

The full moon played hide-and-seek behind a gauze of clouds and for a moment lit up the men's features. She recognized the taller, Pashur, her husband's closest general, who had served him for the past eight years.

Though their features were clear, their words were muffled through the glass. Simone strained to understand them, but could only shake her head.

She peered up at her husband. Worry lines furrowed his forehead. He raised one fist to his lips. The thick gold of the signet ring flashed in the moonlight.

Moments later, he motioned her back to the bedchamber in the same silent manner. He lit a single lamp, and her marble dressing table glowed in the soft light. She watched his reflection in the tall, gold-framed mirror hanging above it. He turned and stepped toward her.

Eyes burdened with pain now stared at her. And her anxiety escalated.

In some inexplicable way, he had changed in the previous weeks. A stranger peered out from the familiar dark eyes, once lustrous and abounding with life, but now dreary. His gaunt face seemed to grow paler each day. In mere weeks, he appeared to have aged a dozen years. Even the strength in his touch had waned. He was withdrawing into a seclusion from which even she—with all her exuberance and laughter—had been unable to draw him.

"Did you recognize those men?" he asked in a language that was all but unheard in the European nations that lay to the northwest.

"Only Pashur," she replied in the same tongue. "Of what were they speaking?"

He looked away. "Conspiracy. The other man is Addon, the leader of a powerful revolutionary group. They have been meeting in secret every night for the past week. And now they convene right under my nose. In the courtyard of my very castle!"

"You need not be concerned." Simone raised her chin. "One word from you will silence them—all of them."

His eyes squeezed shut as though her words had stabbed him. "Not when my generals are against me."

"Sabiir, you are a mighty king with a strong military. Rulers from surrounding nations shudder before your army. You are victorious in all your campaigns, and your people cherish you. They would never allow injury to you."

As though burdened with a weight too heavy to carry, his eyelids opened slowly. Through his dull gaze, he studied her face. "In your eyes I have always found strength and loyalty." He looked away. "I will be leaving you soon."

"You will be back. You have always returned to me." When he did not respond, she added, "Or I will accompany you."

Taking both her hands, he pressed them against his lips. But his eyes hardened. "This time it is a place from which I shall never return. I must face it alone; no army before me, no subjects to back me; even you—my sweet and trusted companion—cannot follow me."

"What are you saying?"

"I am faced with my most formidable enemy—one I cannot defeat. I am dying, Simone."

She pulled her hands from his and turned away. Chills skirted her body. In her heart she had known, but to hear it from him—in his own voice—was to be run through with a dagger.

He had faced death many times. And each time he had prepared for battle, she had prepared to face life without him. But he had cheated death. He had always returned the victor. Even now, a strange semblance of his past strength filled his eyes and his voice. She turned back, her countenance falling.

He lifted her chin. She straightened her back to stand tall.

"You were always strong. And you will be strong now." His approving nod reassured her despite his frightening words.

He dropped to his knees and placed his cheek against her belly, which had grown ever rounder over the past several weeks. She coiled his hair, the color of pitch, around her fingertips. A quick thrust from within her abdomen was followed by his sad smile.

"I may not live to meet my child. He will carry my name and be heir to my throne. When he is old enough and strong enough, the people will be told of him." He groaned, pushing himself to a standing position; her hands flew to cover the sorrow in her face. "I erred when I spoke to Pashur of my illness," he said, stepping away. "Now he seeks to use my death to his advantage the moment I am gone. But you will be the key to the throne. Follow my orders, and all will be right again in time."

"Tell me what I am to do."

"Upon his birth, the child will be given to Rios, who will conceal him. Rios was loyal to my father. He tutored me from the time I was an infant. My father entrusted both my education and upbringing to his care. Rios taught me to be more than a king. He taught me to be a *leader.* And he has been loyal to me all my life. He will teach my son of his lineage, of his responsibilities to this people."

"How am I to hide such a thing as the impending birth of a child?" she protested. "Already my servants know of it. I'm certain Pashur knows of it, also, at this late hour."

"I trust you to find a way to protect our child."

"He will have me executed."

"Indeed, Pashur is not a man to be trusted. However, he will not be your executioner. He will treat you with respect and dignity after I am gone. Yes, he will put you under guard, but he will not harm you. Of this I am confident because of the manner in which he has dealt with our enemies. You are not his enemy."

"Perhaps not, but I carry his enemy."

"That is the reason the child must escape."

Pulling an object from his pocket and the signet ring from his hand, he placed both in her palm, wrapping her fingers around them.

"Now listen carefully to what I tell you."

Weeks later, a rare drizzling rain cooled the arid region.

A woman, cloaked and hooded, kept to the shadows in the wee hours before daybreak. Making her way against the protection of the low structures along the empty stone street, she reached a darkened doorway underneath a simple sign that advertised the town's glazier. She slipped inside.

In the dimness, her footfall brought forth a man from the rear of the shop. Reaching up, the woman pulled back the black hood.

"Your Highness!" The man dropped to one knee. "The king sent word that he would be sending a servant."

"I had to be satisfied in the knowledge that these items have reached your hands." From underneath the cloak she produced the two objects the king had given her and a small scroll. "The future of this kingdom has been entrusted to your care." Her gaze upon him was stern.

"I will not rest until it has been accomplished. You have my word of honor, Your Highness."

Chapter Two
Twenty-three Years Later

"Alexandra."

Olivia Winterfield leaned forward to kiss the air beside Alexandra Viana's cheek. Neither her gloved hands, one of which grasped a closed parasol, nor her own cheek made contact with the young woman.

"Mrs. Winterfield, you look as radiant as the day." Alexandra stepped back to shade her eyes from the glaring sun. A moment later, she found herself wrapped in the embrace of the woman's husband.

He drew her to an arm's length, his grasp gentle on her shoulders. "Alexandra, you've grown up." His smile warmed her heart.

"Mr. Winterfield, how good to see you again."

"Now let me hear that in French. We must abandon our English for the next two weeks."

"*Monsieur, c'est un vrai plaisir de vous revoir.*"

"Ah, yes, and it's also my true pleasure to see you again. I'll have no worries about your ability to make yourself understood during our travels."

"I can't believe it's been two years since our families have been together."

"Yes, the wedding was the last time," he said.

"I hear from my sister that Andrew is treating her like a princess."

"Jessica deserves no less," Richard Winterfield said.

"And your son's conduct can only be credited to the fine example he had in his father."

"Ah, your own father has raised yet *another* princess." He patted her cheek and stepped over to greet her mother.

Alexandra turned to the young woman she spied from the corner of her eye. "Catherine!" They embraced, Catherine rocking her in her arms.

"Alex, to be with you again is heaven itself. I've so missed your company."

Despite the brilliance of the sun that kept them both squinting, Alexandra could detect the familiar sparkle in her friend's brown eyes. Thinking her a bit plain of face upon their first meeting three years earlier when Catherine was seventeen, Alexandra saw that she had matured into an attractive young woman. The freckles sprinkled across her nose were muted by a dusting of powder, and her rose petal lips blossomed into a welcoming smile.

"And John, how good to see you, as well." Catherine stepped up to Alexandra's slender eighteen-year-old brother to offer a quick embrace. John gave her shoulder a light pat and mumbled her name in return. "You're looking more like your father every day." She stared up into his face. "You must've grown six inches!"

John's height swallowed up Catherine's small form. She linked one arm each with him and Alexandra, and the three fell in line behind their parents. The group strolled toward the café where they would share lunch.

"I've heard so much about France, in particular Bordeaux." Alexandra's mother, Angela, turned toward Olivia. "How kind of you to extend the invitation so we could accompany you on the tour."

"I think, Richard," her father said, "that I've overestimated my abilities with the construction of the house. I didn't realize what such an undertaking would entail. And I blame *you*."

Alexandra stifled a grin. She could hear in his voice a note of feigned agitation and knew he was grinning too.

"I was obviously suffering from a mental disorder of some type when I made the decision to begin construction," he continued. "And you, a man who attempted the very feat himself years ago, failed to stop me from proceeding! Richard, how could you treat your oldest friend in such a manner?"

"We must learn from our own mistakes, John. How inconsiderate it would have been had I withheld from you a valuable learning experience."

The two men laughed heartily.

After a light lunch, the party hastened to their château, traveling by coach in the warm open air. Catherine, Alexandra, and young John occupied a coach separate from their parents.

The rainy season of southwestern France had ended in recent days as the short but glorious spring erupted. Lush landscapes and rivers full from the wet winter stretched across the countryside. To the south, the grand Pyrenees Mountains shared the spring run-off with the smaller foothills and valleys below. The timing had been perfect—before the hot, dry summer had begun its reign in this region of France.

Alexandra removed her bonnet and shook out her tawny locks. She splayed her long hair with her fingers and let it spill over the side of the coach as she tossed her head back. The sweet scents of spring filled her senses.

"Ah, can you not smell romance in the air, Catherine?" she asked in French. "Earlier you said you've missed my companionship, but I contend that you have not missed me as you say, for Grace writes that you've been preoccupied with the company of a handsome gentleman."

The petite blonde sat up straight, a blush overtaking her cheeks as she flicked a quick glance behind her at John.

Alexandra's brother had taken a seat, not inside the carriage with the two ladies, but beside the coachman. And Alexandra knew his reasoning. Her brother loved horses perhaps even more than she herself did. He had not yet succeeded in commandeering the reins but had already engaged the man in conversation about the two black beauties pulling the coach in a gentle trot.

"Yes, we've been spending much time together," Catherine whispered, turning back to Alexandra.

"My sister's letter didn't reveal much about him, not even his name. Only that she had played a part in furthering your acquaintance." Alexandra smiled. "Why does that not surprise me?"

"I'm grateful for Grace," said Catherine. "She misses you and Jessica so much. Since I have always longed for a sister of my own, the two of us seem to fill a void in each other's lives—though I do not see her as often as I'd like. She keeps quite busy with Stephen's firm and in the legalities of your father's estate, but we meet each month in town for tea. A few months ago she surprised me with two unexpected guests—two gentlemen. One was Stephen—"

"And the other a tall, handsome stranger with black curls and emerald eyes," Alexandra said, completing her sentence. Leaning forward, she whispered in French. "He took your hand to his lips and looked into your eyes as the room around you faded into shadows. But it was his smile that left you awestruck, for it revealed..." She paused and then said in English, "...a chunk of spinach nestled between his two front teeth!"

Catherine tossed her head back and laughed out loud.

Alexandra joined in the laughter until tears rolled from the corners of her eyes.

"Seriously, Alex," Catherine said between giggles.

"I'm sorry. Please do tell me about him," Alexandra pleaded while blotting her tears with the lace cuff of her sleeve. "I want to know everything!"

"He's not dark in tone, and his eyes are hazel. He's tall and broad, and his hair is dusty blonde. He wears round-rimmed spectacles. And...he despises spinach."

Alexandra laughed once again.

"I have to admit," Catherine continued, "he's not a stranger, either. His family has been acquainted with mine for generations. He's very sociable and seems to enjoy the company of old and young alike. We became friendly a few years ago at the ball we attended while your family was in Kent, do you remember? But we lost contact after that—until recently, that is. Anyway, he claims an acquaintance, not only with your oldest sister, but with you as well, Alex."

Alexandra's eyebrows twisted. She tried to recall meeting a man of his description.

Her friend provided the final clue. "He's an architect and travels quite a bit."

"Oh...yes," stated Alexandra, a sudden image flashing through her mind. Though trying to hide it, she felt a frown overcome her face. "Gregory Westcliffe, I presume."

"None other." A perky smile played on Catherine's lips.

"Mr. Westcliffe is..." Alexandra struggled to find the right words for the young architect who had of late become employed by her father. "He is, indeed, socially adept."

Catherine looked puzzled by the comment.

"Is not Bordeaux simply breathtaking?" Alexandra said, looking away in an attempt to hide her astonishment over Catherine's news.

"Did you hear, Alex? Mother is planning a summer ball."

Alexandra was grateful for Catherine's apparent notice of her hint to change the subject.

"She's often away traveling with Roman," Catherine continued, "but she'll be home nearly the entire summer. The ball is to be held the fifteenth of July. Already we've begun the preparations."

"That is exciting news, Catherine. I'm sure it'll be a glorious event, considering the beauty of the manor."

Alexandra closed her eyes to bathe in the warmth of the sunlight. She opened them again and laughed to herself to find her brother now in full control of the horses.

On the morning of their departure from Bordeaux, a soft knock occurred on Alexandra's door. She opened it to find Catherine.

"I have good tidings, Alex." She bounced on her toes.

"Tell me!"

"We'll be stopping in Amboise, where we'll be meeting up with Roman. He's to accompany us to Paris!"

"Is that so?" Alexandra frowned.

She did not know what her reaction should be. Roman Winterfield, Catherine's infamous older brother, sparked dread in her heart. She had not heard his name in almost two years. At once she wondered what havoc he had been wreaking during his travels. A man of remarkable good looks who had managed to remain unmarried despite his great wealth, he was the most conceited person she had ever met. His goal in life seemed to focus on making the women of London pawns in his manipulative games.

As the primary buyer in his family's import business, Roman traveled both the continent and the Orient in search of the unique and the extraordinary, maintaining an air of intrigue by his long absences and unannounced appearances at a smattering of London's social gatherings. One of the last times Alexandra had seen him, he was swarmed by young ladies who swooned at the slightest glance from him.

She shook her head at the memory. What a pity that a handsome face and lofty position seemed to be the only prerequisites for the empty young ladies of his acquaintance.

Perhaps, however, she was being too quick to judge him. Just prior to her sister's marriage to his brother, Roman had condescended in a most dramatic way, apologizing to Jessica for the mistreatment he had bestowed upon her. He even defended their father in a confrontation with his own peers.

"Is that so?" she repeated. Beyond that, she could not think of another response to her friend's announcement.

Late afternoon found the travelers at an inn situated in the center of the small town of Amboise. Weary from the journey, Catherine's parents sent her to retrieve her brother while they rested and bathed before dinner. The families would reconvene at the little café two doors down.

Alexandra accompanied Catherine, and they waited in the carriage outside a quaint potter's shop, where Roman Winterfield had instructed that one of their party meet him. His telegram stated that he would conclude his business call at five o'clock.

After waiting a while in the heat of the late afternoon, Alexandra inquired of the coachman, "Excuse me, but do you have the time?"

"Thirty minutes past five."

"Thank you."

How typical of Roman Winterfield—a man completely unconcerned about inconveniencing others! Yet pity the person that kept *him* waiting.

Catherine seemed content in allowing her brother all the time he desired; Alexandra, on the other hand, grew more impatient by the moment. They were all tired from the journey, and her stomach was demanding sustenance. She stood to step down from the carriage.

"Where are you going?" Catherine asked.

"To retrieve your brother."

Concern flashed over Catherine's expression. Alexandra knew she would never have given thought to interrupting his business meeting.

Alexandra walked the stone path to the entrance of the shop. She did not imagine Roman would recognize her anyway. How could he recall someone he had never noticed? Assuming he would mistake her for a customer, she intended to check the progress of the transaction, whatever that might be.

A tiny bell on the door announced her entry. Stepping into a small and dusty room filled with shelves covered by various forms of pottery, baskets, and iron- and glass-work, she heard the voices of two men near the rear of the store. She wound her way among the shelving, peeking her head around the last row. The two men, conversing in French, took no note of her.

She stopped and gazed at the profile of Roman Winterfield. His strong nose and chin complimented ebony eyes and hair. Yes, indeed, his was a handsome face, perhaps even more so than she had remembered.

While the two spoke, her attention was drawn to several lovely blown-glass vases on a nearby shelf. A swirled pattern of translucent blue made them glow in a shard of light streaming through the window.

"I'll give you two francs each for the baskets, and that's my final offer." Even in French, Roman dominated the conversation.

Alexandra looked beyond the two men at perhaps a dozen handsome baskets. Each had been woven onto an ornate iron frame, complete with curled legs and a bowed lid, secured in the front by an attractive twisted iron latch. They appeared more like treasure chests than baskets. A clever design, she mused—both lovely and practical.

"Are those the items over which you are debating?" Alexandra asked in French, stepping from behind the row of shelving and startling the two men. She nodded toward the baskets.

The shop owner looked at her and then back at Roman.

Roman offered no greeting, but only glared at her. Sensing his annoyance, Alexandra stood firm, head up and hands clasped behind her. She tilted her head toward Roman, awaiting a reply.

"*Monsieur* LaRon," Roman said with a scowl, "may I introduce to you Miss Alexandra Viana. She is..."

Shocking! He remembered her after all. His pause told her he was groping for some way to explain their relationship.

"...an associate of mine."

Of course, he had to keep it formal. Far be it for the lofty Roman Winterfield to introduce someone of her standing as an acquaintance, a relative, or worse yet, a friend. She had to agree that "associate" was a good choice. Yes, it was what she would have preferred.

"I am pleased to meet you, *Monsieur* LaRon," Alexandra stated in perfect French, extending a hand to him.

He took it in greeting.

"*Monsieur* Winterfield will give you five francs each for the baskets *if* you would be willing to include these six vases at no additional cost." She held a palm out toward the exquisite glass containers.

Roman's eyes bulged at the offer.

The man's smile broadened. "It's a deal!" He extended his hand to Roman. "After all, *Monsieur* Winterfield, a man of your integrity would not retract an offer made by one of your own associates, I'm sure."

Alexandra smiled. Roman's nostrils flared, his glare intense upon her. He took the hand of *Monsieur* LaRon in a firm shake.

"Good then," stated Alexandra. "We'll send someone for the items in…" She looked back to Roman in question.

"In a week," he said through clenched teeth, his dark eyes attempting to burn a hole through her.

"In a week," she said to the shop owner. "Be certain to pack them carefully, *Monsieur*. They must survive the trip across the Channel, you know." She smiled at the two, turned, and left the shop.

Several paces outside, she was stopped by the voice of Roman Winterfield, who hastened behind her.

"Why did you do that?" he demanded in English.

She turned back to face him. "Perhaps, Mr. Winterfield, you had not noticed the heavy dust that has collected upon those vases. It's obvious they've been sitting untouched for months, if not years. The people of this town are likely in no position to afford such a luxury. They require practicality in a container. Therefore, the vases, lovely as they are, are worthless to them—and to *Monsieur* LaRon. He will never sell them here. However, your father will be able to sell one of those vases in London for the price you just paid for *five* of the baskets. *Monsieur* LaRon receives twice the price for the baskets and frees up valuable space where the vases sit, Winterfield Imports gains a profit of more than one hundred percent, and you retain a client. Everyone comes out a winner. By the way, it's a pleasure to see you again, Mr. Winterfield."

She spun on her heel and retreated to the carriage.

Colorful flower boxes decorated the windows of the town's lone café, and round river rocks dotted the property. Green vines sporting tiny purple buds wandered up the trunks of the many trees shading the small structure. Steep-pitched and in the shape of an 'A,' the roof of the foyer reached the ground on either side of the entry door. Inside, a surprising number of patrons could be seated in the quiet and clean dining areas. Adding to its warm atmosphere, a stone fireplace dominated one full wall.

The Vianas and Winterfields sat in a private, yet spacious room. Large windows overlooked the gardens. Two oil lamps cast a warm glow upon the long table in the middle of the room. Alexandra admired a heavy German cuckoo clock as it chirped the arrival of the six o'clock hour.

"Roman, how good to see you once again," her father said, shaking his hand.

"I'm pleased to be in your company, John. It has been far too long." He turned to Angela. "It's my delight to see you again, as well, Madam."

Pleased that the once-unbearable Roman had at least retained his respect for her father, Alexandra could not quite suppress her surprise that the man had somehow gained a few manners during his travels. *Perhaps he purchased them. An expensive commodity, no doubt, but well worth the cost*, she mused, trying to wipe the smirk from her lips.

"Roman," she heard Richard say in a low tone while listening to her father and brother conversing. "I picked up an interesting tidbit while in town the other day. Do you recall the legend about the Desert Ice?"

Alexandra turned her attention to the Winterfield's conversation. What was Desert Ice?

"Of course. The Arabian diamond that disappeared some years back," Roman answered.

"Along with a signet ring," Richard replied. "Talk of them has resurfaced among certain of our business associates."

"That seems to happen from time to time."

"You realize what it means, don't you?" Richard prodded.

Roman didn't answer.

Pretending to be attuned to her father's conversation, Alexandra shifted her gaze discreetly to Roman Winterfield's face. It held the appearance of vague indifference.

"It means neither has yet been discovered," Richard continued, leaning forward.

"Or they're no more than what you said before—a legend," Roman replied and turned his attention to the menu.

"It's no coincidence that the two pieces went missing at the same time. Call me ridiculous if you must, but thoughts of those pieces have remained in the back of my mind since I first heard of them several years ago. You mark my word, Roman. *Someone's* got them. And someday they're going to materialize."

"Perhaps. But I prefer to focus my attention on the tangible, the here and now, like this meal. What do you think of the roast lamb and carrots?"

Richard abandoned the subject, also turning to the menu.

Desert Ice…signet ring…Alexandra mused over them in silence, wondering if her father had ever heard of them. She laughed to herself. Even if he had, of what interest would they be to him? The one gem that held any regard in his eyes now rested securely upon her mother's finger—the ruby wedding ring—the gem that had brought her family back together.

Alexandra looked with affection upon her father. She admired him above all other men. He had labored all his life to support their family, and yet had somehow managed to maintain a youthful look. She saw him as he always appeared to her—vigorous and handsome despite bits of gray threading now through his sandy hair.

Her mother was likewise ageless. The inner strength and integrity she possessed—the likely source of her outward grace—was a rare treasure in any person. The two were a perfect match, if ever there could be such a thing.

Not long ago, she envisioned as her own husband the proverbial handsome stranger who would fall in love with her and whisk her away to an enchanting land where he would cherish and adore her forever. Such daydreams were the product of a fanciful imagination spurred on by her treasured fairy stories. If such a prince of a man did exist, he would likely be the catch of some other young lady before she even learned of his existence.

Besides, Alexandra desired much more now. She would settle for no less than a man of deep insight and intriguing interests. Of course, romance would also be a necessity, one that would not fade with the passing of years.

She studied her parents as they conversed, knowing full well that her hopes had shifted from one fairy story to another. In all actuality, neither one seemed to be any more realistic than the other. What were the odds of her finding a man with even a fraction of her father's qualities?

Yet her sisters, Grace and Jessica, seemed to have found such rare men. Perhaps another Stephen Sutton or Andrew Winterfield existed out there somewhere.

Alexandra was content in waiting.

Lost in her reverie, she was slow to sense the weight of someone's stare from across the table. She glanced over to meet the eyes of Roman Winterfield. He looked away. Certain he was still angry with her for her intrusion at the potter's shop, she shrugged and struck up a conversation with Catherine.

Half an hour after the order had been placed, the waiter entered the room; trailing behind him came a timid-appearing young lady who appeared no older than fifteen. The two, especially the girl, struggled with heavy trays of food and drinks. The man set his tray on an empty table and beckoned to the girl, who, Alexandra reasoned, must have been his daughter, receiving some training in the family trade. The girl stepped up close to the corner of the table between Richard Winterfield and Roman, who had seated himself at the head of the table.

Across from where they stood, Alexandra watched as the waiter removed plates, bowls, and glasses from the tray the girl was holding.

"You're sure to enjoy the roasted lamb," the waiter said in melodious French, placing a steaming plate before Angela

Viana. "And you, Madam," he said, addressing Olivia, "will fall in love with the rosemary potatoes. Excellent choice." Taking other plates from the tray the girl was balancing, he chatted on. "My wife delights in nothing more than cooking for others."

Richard Winterfield sniffed and smiled. "Everything looks and smells delicious."

When Alexandra looked again at the girl's tray, just two dishes remained, one on each end. Tilting her head to one side, Alexandra noted the position of the girl's hands. They sat close together underneath its center.

As the girl's father leaned over to lift the plate nearest Richard, Alexandra pushed herself from her chair. Before she could sound a warning, the plate was lifted. The tray tipped off balance, sending the last steaming bowl to the edge. She watched in horror as the bowl flipped upside down, splashing onto the lap of Roman Winterfield! Trying to steady the heavy tray, the girl instead upset a glass of wine on the table. It, too, doused Roman, followed by the tray.

Alexandra froze, standing part way from her chair. For the slightest moment, utter silence washed the room as all stared wide-eyed at the mess covering the impeccable Roman. The girl's hands rose to cover her mouth, terror in the young eyes.

Roman's arms flew heavenward. He reeled from the steaming bath of stew and looked down on the red wine stain on his white shirt. Jumping to his feet, he let three French words boom from his throat. "Stupid, clumsy wretch!"

The waiter grabbed for a cloth. The girl burst into tears and fled from the room.

Alexandra ran after the girl. Rounding the end of the table, she glared up at Roman Winterfield. "It was not her fault. Can't you see she's just learning?" She hastened from the room and found the girl, who stood weeping just outside the doorway.

She heard the waiter apologizing while attempting to clean Roman's shirt and trousers. Through the open doorway,

Alexandra saw Roman glance her way as she consoled the frightened girl.

Roman's anger was palpable. *He must have gotten a bargain on those manners.*

Chapter Three

The following morning had not come soon enough in Alexandra's opinion. With the shaky start to their holiday, she assumed that what remained could only get better. The families had started just after daybreak for the lengthy trip to Paris, the Vianas in one coach and the Winterfield's ahead of them in the other.

The sound of her parents' conversation faded to a drone as she stared out toward the passing landscape.

"Alex, you seem distressed," her mother said several miles into the journey.

"Oh?" Alexandra pulled her gaze from the window, realizing she had not even noticed the countryside. "I suppose you're right, Mother. Papa, may I ask you something?"

"Of course."

"There's a situation that's bothering me. I'm not quite certain how to handle it." She looked at her brother on the seat beside her. His eyebrows rose with curiosity. "This does not concern you, John."

"Oh, but if it bothers my sister, it does," he teased.

"Well, I suppose you'll find out soon enough." She looked back at her parents. "Papa, it seems Catherine is...well...she's being courted by Gregory Westcliffe."

"Westcliffe!" her brother exclaimed, sliding to the edge of his seat. "What kind of game is he playing?"

"You've noticed it, too." Alexandra's brow puckered.

"I'd have to be blind not to see it!"

"John, calm yourself," their mother reprimanded. "See what?"

"Have you never watched Westcliffe when Alexandra's around?" Young John implored both their parents. "The man's an absolute maniac. He drops his work—whatever he's doing—to ogle her. He doesn't even try to cover it. And here he's been courting *Catherine*? That's disgusting."

"Thank heaven someone else has taken note," Alexandra said. "I was beginning to think it was me."

"His contract will be terminated the minute I return to the island," their father said.

"That may be the worst thing you can do, John," his wife argued. "Remember...he lives in London, where Alex will be for the summer. At least working on the island, he'll be away from there."

"Thank you all for your concern," Alexandra added, "but my worry is with Catherine. How do I notify her of his behavior without offending her? She's quite attracted to the man."

"How long has their relationship been in progress?" her father asked.

"Just a few months from what she's told me. And several of those weeks he's been away from her at our construction site."

"Perhaps you needn't say a word to her," her father suggested. "My advice to you is to give it time. A relationship with his likes shouldn't last."

"Poor Catherine," Alexandra said. "She's of the sweetest demeanor."

"I don't know how she or Andrew turned out so well, living in the same household as that brother of theirs," young John mumbled under his breath.

"Except for last evening's outburst," observed their father, "Roman seems to have made remarkable progress in his attitude since our reunion with his family three years ago."

"I've never found anything unpleasant in his tone," said Angela. "His reaction to the girl appeared to come from surprise, and its seeming harshness was unintentional, I'm sure."

Alexandra recalled the first time her mother had ever met Roman—Jessica's engagement party, which was after some drastic changes had already taken place. "Don't be so quick to sing his praises," she argued. "Although the defense he gave in your behalf on the night of the ball was noble, Papa, I feel any kindness in his mannerisms is a thin façade. His true character came through in his words to the girl."

"Alex, I'm surprised at you," her father reproved. "You've always been one to defend the good in others, little as that may be at times. If this is a façade, as you claim, then it goes well with him that he's putting forth such an effort; for he made no such attempt upon our first meeting him. Therefore, any endeavor on his part must be due to a genuine desire to improve."

Alexandra dropped her head in shame.

"After all," her father continued, "no man is perfect. He lived as a selfish being for nearly thirty years. One cannot expect immediate results without an occasional slip. Would it not be wise to give the man some credit?"

"I suppose only time will tell with him, as well," Alexandra muttered.

Perhaps she was being a bit harsh. Yet she felt justified to some extent, considering the man's history of verbal assaults upon Jessica and his disdainful treatment toward other members of her family. However, he *had* apologized later. Perhaps she was being defensive for her sister, not to mention the young lady in the café.

She and her sisters had been left with a bitter taste regarding Roman—none of them would deny that. Time alone would tell whether the infamous Winterfield brother had indeed changed.

Meanwhile, the families would be spending several days in Paris before she would return to Kent with Catherine and her parents. Her own parents would be rendezvousing with Jessica and Andrew in Germany.

Alexandra found relief in that Paris was a large city. Surely, she would not often be in the presence of Roman Winterfield.

The first full day in Paris, the two families separated. The Vianas eagerly explored the city with its charming shops and tailored parks. They wandered through a museum and visited with craftsmen selling their wares on the sidewalks.

A cool, heavy downpour had chased those on the streets inside for a brief time, but a few brave souls—the Vianas among them—continued their expeditions in the rain. Alexandra smiled at several couples snuggled under large umbrellas as they sauntered through the streets in quiet conversation, seemingly oblivious to the spring downpour.

Three years prior, her sister Jessica had written flowery letters during her visit to Paris, extolling the magnificence of France. Yet so many of its sights defied description, and, indeed, Alexandra often found herself speechless—in both English *and* French.

The following day the party of eight regrouped for a tour of the Museum of French History at Versailles. Invited to embark on the jaunt alongside Catherine, Alexandra discovered she would also be riding in the same carriage as Mrs. Winterfield and Roman.

Her first inclination was to decline, but Catherine's woeful look following her hesitation when invited pained her. She had not the heart to disappoint her friend. To her pleasant surprise, she and Catherine enjoyed private conversation while the other two busied themselves with discussions of their own.

Lined in perfect rows of leafy trees, the avenue leading to the Palace whispered to Alexandra a fore gleam of the extravagance that lay ahead.

"Oh, look!" Alexandra cried out, unable to repress the outburst as two large buildings came into view. "Not in a thousand years could I imagine living amidst such luxury."

"The dreams of the peasantry," Roman mumbled. Alexandra, astonished by such insensitivity, looked over just as he rolled his eyes toward his mother. A moment later, his gaze fixed squarely upon Alexandra's. "Those are the *stables*. What…is the sun in your eyes so you can't see the enormous structure beyond?"

A garbled snicker seeped from Olivia's throat.

Heat rushed to Alexandra's face as she turned away. In an instant she wished she could disappear. Why had she not followed her instincts and stayed in the carriage with her own family?

"Alex," Cȧtherine said, patting her arm, "it's an innocent mistake." She cast a look of disapproval toward her brother. "I did the same upon visiting here for the first time. Besides, the royal horses here lived better than many of the nobility elsewhere. You should see the courtyards in those stables, the stone archways and the impressive columns. There are fireplaces throughout—for the horses! I know of many a statesman who live quite comfortably in such arrangements."

"Thank you," Alexandra said in a whisper. Her heart began to calm; she could again enjoy the beauty of their surroundings. Though she felt Roman's gaze upon her, she did not dare look again in his direction.

Soon, when the buildings of the palace in all their grandeur splayed out before their carriage, Alexandra said not a word—nothing of the grand windows stacked two stories high, twin wings protruding to either side of them. As the carriage rolled onto the wide cobblestone courtyard, she kept silent over the immense statue of a warrior upon his horse, weathered green and scowling down at her from a pedestal, itself twice her height. She stifled her excitement upon exiting the carriage to be standing in the place of past generations of kings.

It was only when her mother came up beside her and took her arm that she felt she could again speak with ease. Once inside the stone walls, Alexandra did her best to avoid Roman's company.

Their party joined several others to form a modest group for a tour. Their guide, a Frenchman, appeared not much older than Alexandra herself. She watched with awe as he gave their group a brief history of the Palace, telling of its humble beginnings as a hunting lodge. He spoke with conviction and enthusiasm. How did a man of his youthful years possess such composure and knowledge?

After they began their excursion, Alexandra often felt the nearness of Roman. However, he did not attempt to speak with her. Each time, she was able to find an object of interest to pull her away.

Once, while admiring the view from a window, she overheard him talking with his mother. Of course, all in the vicinity would have had no trouble hearing his strong voice echoing throughout the chamber. He seemed to make no effort to subdue his tone, even speaking in French.

"Mother, look at this tapestry. It's quite amusing."

Olivia stepped over to study the subject. "Oh, yes. The plaque reads Louis XIV overthrowing Dunkirk. Beautiful handiwork, would you not say?"

By this time, the French tour guide had stationed himself right alongside Roman.

"It's not the handiwork I find objectionable," Roman said.

"Then what?" Olivia asked.

"Mother, can you be so blinded? He did not win Dunkirk; he purchased it—from the English, no less."

"Very astute of you," the young Frenchman spoke up. "An unfortunate aspect of many rulers—French or otherwise—is their tendency to overstate their victories."

"Overstatement is an *under*statement, would you not say?" Roman huffed. "More like an outright lie! You mislead your visitors."

"You got ahead of the tour," stated the young man. "I was about to explain the tapestry to the group."

"I should hope so," Roman said, tossing his head aside and walking into the adjoining Salon.

Alexandra smiled at the guide with as much apology as she could muster.

Soon they had ascended the King's Staircase to the second-story apartments.

"Such extravagance," Alexandra's mother whispered, coming up beside her. "I've not seen anything so elaborate in all the castles of Europe your father and I have toured." The others were scattered about the area, viewing various chambers.

"And did you hear what our guide said about the lifestyle within these walls?" Alexandra asked, while they strolled toward what appeared to be a hallway entrance. "Such an odd, ritualistic culture. Five thousand nobles centered on the attention from and approval of the royalty. They rarely left the confines of the compound!"

"Yes, a prison of sorts, but they had everything at their fingertips. What more could they have asked for?" her mother inquired.

"Individualism. Accomplishment. Purpose. Call me insane, but life in the impoverished countryside would've been paradise by comparison."

At that moment, they rounded a bright corner and stepped into what Alexandra could see only as excessive waste. Yet, she stood in awe. Stretching before her in intimidating beauty glowed a long hallway. Sunlight flooded in from high windows lining one entire wall. As if that were not enough, the opposite side boasted a complete covering of mirrors in arched bays. Two rows of chandeliers dropped like enormous crystal spiders from an arched ceiling crafted with colorful murals and carved golden framework, while intricate statues, like fancy little soldiers, embraced still more crystal fixtures at the perimeters the full length of the hall.

Alexandra stepped onto the polished parquet flooring, following their French guide. She looked up and all around as she walked. With its mirrors on her left, reflecting the windows, and the view of the expansive gardens to her right, the experience seemed like stepping into an enchanted storybook.

The Frenchman's voice surrounded her in echoes. "The Galerie des Glaces was Louis' prize. Two hundred forty-six feet of richness and splendor that brought admiration from French and foreigners alike."

The others in their party entered the grand hall behind them, and Alexandra heard her own gasps echoing in the corridor.

She and her mother advanced to the end of the hall.

"You may have noted the compelling murals gracing the ceiling," their guide was saying. "Most every piece of furnishing and decoration in the Palace was at one time pillaged and stolen. Almost all has now been repurchased. But the one thing the thieves could not take away was the murals. The most interesting of all is the one that shows Louis XVI crossing the Rhine, being depicted as Apollo."

Alexandra shot a glance her mother's direction. "The audacity…," she said in a sharp whisper, "…to depict oneself as a god! Mother, all this pomp…for what? The honor and glory of men? Just what is the purpose in all this grandeur?"

"Humans are impelled to worship," her mother responded in a subtle tone. "When ignorant of the reality, they make gods of themselves."

"Yes, but who would do such a thing?"

Just then, Roman entered the hall with his mother. His first reaction was to glance at his own reflection. Alexandra dropped her head in embarrassment for her entire party.

"Ah, the Hall of Mirrors," he said in a voice that ricocheted the full length of the room. "Imagine waking to this sight every morning, Mother, knowing it was all for you and created by you."

Alexandra watched him peruse the hall, apparently more interested in his own image than any masterpiece in the room.

Yes, she knew of at least one person who was all too happy in making a god of himself.

Chapter Four

The following day, Alexandra stayed behind while the rest of the party agreed to embark on various tours without her. They arranged to meet at Le Figaro Café at four o'clock for a light meal.

She remained at the château until late morning, lounging and strolling the grounds.

Adding to her pleasure was to at last have found some time to compose a letter to Jessica. She would send it along with her parents.

> My Dear Sister,
>
> I hope this letter finds you well.
>
> How I am loving France as you did. It is just as you depicted it three years ago. The beauty here is incomparable.
>
> No doubt you will soon hear that we have had a surprise guest along these few days. He is none other than your brother-in-law, Roman. I know you have not had the pleasure of being in his company these two years, Jessie, and, although I was fostering the hope that he had continued to improve in his behavior, I am sorry to report that I find him much the way he was upon our first acquaintance with him in Kent. His arrogance and heartless mannerisms have returned with even greater force, I believe.

However, he does show respect toward our father and mother, for which I am grateful. Yet, I am afraid that his behavior toward me is much the same as in the past. And poor Catherine puts forth such effort to capture his notice, yet he rarely bestows upon her so much as a glance.

Yes, Roman Winterfield remains obstinate and self-centered. I am sorry to bear a poor report after we all had such high hopes, but that is how it is. Please spare your husband these gruesome details, as I do not wish to discourage him.

On a lighter note, I find that France is graced with many handsome faces. No, I have not been whisked away; nor am I likely to be, for our jaunt through France will be of short duration. However, I met a rather intriguing young man at the Palace yesterday. As he guided our tour of the mansion, I noticed that he stayed rather near me, addressing me once in private conversation. And so there it is—the shortest romance in all of France's history, consisting of but a few moments. Yet I know you will be happy to hear of its end, as you are always my protective shield. Do not concern yourself over me, sister dear, for I have learned well from you to be cautious.

It has been a pleasure becoming reacquainted with Catherine. The more we know of each other, the more we find in common. She, John, and I have enjoyed each other's company exceedingly, though I find myself quite eager to escape the association of her repulsive brother.

I will release you to your tour of Germany, but wished that you know I am thinking of you. Please take care and do come to see me this summer in Kent if you are able. Your presence will make my visit complete.

Oh, yes, Mrs. Winterfield will be throwing a summer ball on the fifteenth of July. Please promise me you'll put forth your best effort to attend. And give my love to Andrew.

Yours, Alexandra

After completion of the letter, she pulled a bonnet over her head and grabbed an umbrella. Passing her parents' room, she slid the letter beneath the door, lest she forget about it later, and headed out for a leisurely afternoon.

The quiet solitude of a nearby park drew her in. Watching children race one another while their parents picnicked underneath large shade trees, she pretended to be a resident rather than a tourist. Other young ones laughed, leaping from shore to shore over a meandering brook. It tumbled over rocks and passed under the arches of several stone bridges throughout the park. Still other children followed tiny paper boats teetering along with the flow of the water.

Devouring the sweet scents of the flowering bushes, she listened with contentment to the songs of the birds. The air was filled with pink and white petals that the breezes plucked from the surrounding trees. They drifted to the ground in gentle silence, as though decorating the winding footpaths for a wedding. A nearby musician practiced on a mandolin, oblivious to her presence.

More than a little saddened when the hour arrived to meet her party for dinner, she returned to her role as tourist. The following day, her final one in Paris, would be spent touring a museum with Catherine; then they would depart for London.

She stopped to savor one last moment, imprinting the image of the park and its peace in her memory. Perhaps she could return again someday, but it would be a different season, a different song in the air. Although the aroma would no doubt prove just as alluring, it, too, would be different from this one glorious day.

As she turned to leave, she ran headlong into a man.

"I'm so sorry," she blurted in English. When she recognized him as the young tour guide from the Palace, she repeated herself in French.

"Please forgive me," he replied in his appealing accent. "I saw you here and have been building the courage to approach you. You are not leaving?"

"Yes, I must meet my party soon," she responded.

"Then allow me to escort you." He held an arm out.

Surely there could be no harm in walking with him the short distance to the café.

"Where in France are you from?" he asked as they strolled.

She wrinkled her brow. Had he not heard her first response in English? "I am not from France, but England."

"I am surprised. Your French—it is perfect."

"*Merci.*"

"I enjoyed the tour yesterday at the Palace," he said.

"As did I," she responded, thinking his comment a bit odd. How was their tour different from any other he had given?

"So you took pleasure in my company."

"Well...I appreciated and was surprised by your degree of knowledge."

"The party you were with is your family, yes?"

"We are two families traveling together."

"So, the tall, dark-haired man—he is not your brother?"

"No," Alexandra answered, becoming uncomfortable with his questioning. Where was this leading?

"Ah, a man of his looks must certainly be married."

Alexandra forced the air from her chest, her eyes wide in astonishment. "No. He is single."

"As are you?"

"That is a personal matter, Sir."

"You know," he stated, looking over at her, "such beautiful eyes as yours are to be found nowhere else in Paris."

"Excuse me, but a gentleman such as you would understand were I to wish to conclude my walk alone."

"Please forgive me. I meant no harm. You cannot continue unescorted. I will remain silent."

Alexandra's brow furrowed as she quickened the pace, her eyes straight ahead.

As they walked, a light drizzle began. The man asked for the umbrella she had been carrying, opening it to shelter them both. The wet streets reflected the shop windows and hanging flower baskets dangling from the streetlamps.

Soon they approached the familiar blue awning of LeFigaro's and stepped underneath. She smiled with politeness and thanked him as he pulled the umbrella closed.

"May I call on you tomorrow?" he asked, handing it to her.

"Thank you, but I will be returning to England soon, and my calendar is full. I appreciate your kindness."

"In that case, it was a pleasure," he said, taking her hand to his lips.

Stepping through the door of the café, she turned to watch as he disappeared into the rain. She was glad to see him go, sorry only for the fact that he had intruded upon what would have been a pleasant stroll in the rain.

She turned to find an equally disturbing scene. Standing behind her was Roman Winterfield.

"I see you've made a new friend," he said. "Wasn't that the guide from the Palace yesterday?"

"Yes," she stated, looking about to find none of her family in the café. "Where are the others?"

"I don't know. They left word that they would not be available for dinner."

Alexandra's first thought was to turn and dash out into the rain herself; but before she could take a step, Roman said, "Since we're here..." he hesitated just long enough for her to imagine what was on his mind, "...perhaps we could dine together."

Desperate to think of a way out, she surprised herself when the words that came forth were, "Very well." She was certain his invitation was for one of two reasons: out of obligation at finding themselves alone without their party or because it was his desire to reprimand her for interfering in his dealings with the shop owner and the baskets and for standing up to him when he had scolded the girl in the restaurant.

The image of the young Frenchman entered her mind. She wondered at her choice; perhaps dining with the impertinent Frenchman would have proved the safer decision.

The two were escorted to a quaint covered patio close to the street. A short iron fence adorned with colorful flower boxes framed it. The rain had begun to subside.

As she waited for him to pull her chair out for her, she determined to make the best of her situation. She had been taught since childhood to look for the good in others. Had her father not always said that all humans were God's creatures? Thus all possessed His qualities in *some* way, and to unearth them often only required a soft dusting of the fingertips, the way an archeologist would coax a valuable artifact from the soil. But the harder-packed clay might require a stiff-bristled brush. An archeologist must choose his tools with precision, her father would say, so as not to cause damage to the artifact.

Looking at her dinner partner, she prepared herself for the challenge.

He remained silent. It was obvious she was correct in her first assumption for his dining with her. She decided to try and venture into a conversation. "Did you enjoy your day, Mr. Winterfield?"

"Yes." He ended it quickly.

"And how are your parents enjoying Paris?" She offered another attempt.

"They have been here many times before."

She nodded, looking away.

The waiter approached to explain the menu and to offer a choice of wines. After his departure, the pair sat in silence for a few moments. Alexandra chose to remain on the subject of his family since it seemed the only possible topic they had in common.

"No doubt you miss your brother," she said. "I hear it has been many months since you last saw each other."

"Yes, I miss him very much." He again extinguished their conversation, crossing his arms over his chest.

She sighed, not yet prepared to concede. This one would require a chisel. After all, they could not sit in silence for an hour. However, to push too far could result in a verbal assault such as her sister experienced several times when conversing with the man. She proceeded with caution.

"Mr. Winterfield, I have heard of the many lands which you have been favored to explore. Most only dream of visiting such places. You are very fortunate in your situation."

"Fortunate?" He shot his usual glare at her. "Fortune had nothing to do with it. I have *labored* for Winterfield Imports all my adult life."

At least she had drawn out of him a heartfelt expression. She continued with the topic and kept her tone mild. "Do you not feel, Mr. Winterfield, that a man's family situation and conditions in life have a great bearing on his future prospects of fortune and social standing?"

How could he argue the point? The answer was obvious.

"A man can be and do anything he likes if he is determined."

Alexandra wondered who and what Roman Winterfield would have been had he been born into an impoverished family—had he not been handed an aristocratic lifestyle, a higher education, and an unlimited selection of vocations?

She thought for a moment. What would an archeologist use if a chisel failed him? Perhaps dynamite was in order. She proceeded. "I have heard the tale of an old man who once lived in this town...long ago." She prepared the explosive. "He was a beggar on this very street."

Roman rolled his eyes. "There is no excuse for a man to stoop to such a level. It is a shameful thing."

"Nonetheless, there he sat, day after day, year after year, in the rain and in the stifling heat."

Roman turned his head away, forcing a long sigh from his throat.

She pressed forward. "Many would pass him. Some would toss a coin or two into his ragged hat. Most appeared oblivious to his condition. Boys would at times throw stones at him and chase him away for a while. But later he would return."

Roman turned back to face her. She looked for some response in his eyes. They stared at her, cold and unchanged, but at least he appeared to be listening.

"No doubt he faced the darkness and the cold winters... alone." She set the fuse. "He was not a handsome man. His face was partially disfigured from an injury he had sustained years before." She paused to ignite it. Her words came slow and soft. "Most did not realize that he had been *deaf* since birth."

His arms dropped to his side and he shifted in his chair. Ah, he was becoming uncomfortable. He looked down and then back up at her again. "The man had two good hands, did he not?"

"No doubt."

"And his legs...he had two healthy legs and a strong back, did he not? And did he not also have a reasoning mind?"

"I've not heard otherwise," was her gentle response.

Roman leaned forward. "Then he could have been a craftsman of any kind or a farmer and grown his own food. He could have been a philosopher...or a teacher. There remains no excuse for the man." He leaned back against his chair, his arms settling over his chest again.

"Perhaps not," she said. The waiter interrupted to present the bottle of wine. Roman placed the order for their meal. After the waiter took his leave, Alexandra continued. "One morning the man was found...dead on the side of the road."

"One less burden on society," he muttered under his breath.

This was the expected response, and Alexandra remained unaffected by it. Instead, she persisted. "A few of the townspeople began to inquire about the man. What they discovered was truly disturbing. It seems that decades earlier, while still a young man, the beggar had run into a burning building to rescue a small child. Long minutes later, he emerged with her. She was unscathed. However, he had been burned, which had left his face badly disfigured." Now for the detonation. "And it had also rendered him blind in both eyes—a fact that had escaped the knowledge of the people in general."

Roman looked back at her, and she thought she caught a glimpse of sympathy in the dark eyes of her dinner partner. He sat in silence for a moment while Alexandra sipped the red drink.

"Excellent choice, Mr. Winterfield. You obviously know much about wine."

"So the man was deaf from birth? And now was blinded as well?"

She nodded. "No matter. He is dead now."

Roman's head turned aside, his brow wrinkled, as he looked at the floor.

"So you see, Mr. Winterfield, while not condoning laziness, there are many circumstances that go undetected by those on the outside and even more unforeseen occurrences that could, indeed, hinder a person from realizing his dreams."

His gaze remained downcast. At last he looked up at her. "Point well taken, Miss Viana."

He seemed to turn out one surprise after another. The instrument of choice had fulfilled its commission, just as her father had said. Perhaps Roman Winterfield was human after all.

However, Alexandra was disappointed to find that, not only had the ice not been broken, it appeared to have not so much as a chip. Try as she might, the remainder of their conversation was choppy and uneasy, and much of the meal was spent in silence. What a shame that a man of such extensive travels and experiences had so little to share. Being in his company even caused the flavorful food to taste a bit bland.

Near the conclusion of their meal, a violinist playing a sweet love ballad approached their table. As she enjoyed the melody, Alexandra gazed at the Winterfield son across from her. Here sat a most handsome man, almost perfect in features and physique. Although in the shadows his hair appeared black, in the sunlight she could detect hints of deep auburn woven throughout the dark waves. His dusky eyes were deep-set and his jaw strong. He was not identical to his twin, Andrew, but they possessed uncanny similarities and were equal in their good looks.

44

He was the only man to Alexandra's knowledge whose very name was found in the word 'Romance.' Yet, it was obvious he possessed neither the means nor the desire to please any woman. What a shame. Amused by the irony of it all, she smiled and finished her meal.

With their final day in Paris upon them, Alexandra wanted to tour the Louvre with Catherine, fulfilling a lifelong dream. The remaining members of their party had planned other activities.

Prior to their outings, Angela and Alexandra made time for a brief stroll together in the gardens of their little château.

"Mother, I'm brimming with excitement—and a bit of jealousy, I must admit—over your upcoming tour of Germany with Jessica and Andrew."

"As this time in Paris, it will be over far too quickly. I'm afraid much of my time then and when we return to Scotland will be spent in worry."

"Whatever about, Mother?"

"Alex, I must warn you that Grace looks forward to your visit for more than one reason. She wrote before we left Scotland to say she wants you to become better acquainted with her brother-in-law."

"I rather expected that. Though I've met him only once, I've heard Preston Sutton is an intriguing man. And you know Grace. I'm afraid even marriage and motherhood haven't dampened her zeal for matchmaking."

"I'll not have my youngest daughter put at peril."

"You're far too concerned, Mother. Mr. Sutton poses no such danger from what I recall."

"Promise me you'll tread carefully while in Kent this summer," her mother pleaded.

"Please don't worry. I'm keen to my sister's plots. She'll not catch me with my guard down. I know Grace has nothing but my best interests at heart."

"Your sister is a fine young woman and a caring mother, but although she seems to be somewhat particular in her own associates, she at times is not as scrupulous in designing romance between her friends. Perhaps I'll have her father talk to her again."

"Thank you, Mother, but that won't be necessary. I feel I'm capable of dealing with the situation." She chuckled. "On another note, I meant to inquire of you last evening the reason that the family changed the dinner engagement and did not meet at LeFigaro as we had planned."

"Because we received word from Roman that the two of you had met up and would be unable to meet us at LeFigaro. His instructions were that we should eat at the château rather than travel the distance to dine there. Why? Where did you eat?"

"LeFigaro!"

Chapter Five

Upon returning to the château, Alexandra was met by Catherine in the lobby. "Alex, I hope you don't mind, but my brother has asked to join us on our outing to the museum. Would it be alright with you?"

Alexandra wrinkled her brow. "I believe France is a free country. He may go wherever he chooses."

Why would Roman want to join them? And why had he arranged for the two of them to dine alone the previous evening? He had scarcely spoken to her during the meal. She knew better than to think he was a man who suffered from timidity. Were there something he wished to speak to her about, she felt certain he would have no trouble expressing himself. Why had he not broached the subject during their meal?

Alexandra shook it off, confident that Roman Winterfield would make his concern known.

Try as she might to overcome it, Alexandra found herself uneasy during the carriage ride to the museum. She sat beside Catherine, Roman on the seat opposite them, his arm outstretched across its back. She tried not to look his way, but when she did, his eyes remained fixed on the landscape. He said not a word and appeared to be uninterested in their conversation.

"Oh, how I'll miss this city!" Catherine sighed. "What a glorious time we've had together, Alex."

"Indeed."

"You, in particular, will be returning home with some fond memories of a handsome Frenchman, *oui*?" She nudged Alexandra, giggling.

"Catherine, it was nothing...really."

"I don't believe you. But if you insist, then let us focus on *future* attractions."

"What are you talking about?"

"Preston Sutton, that's what. I can see him now—sick with excitement over the return of the captivating Alexandra Viana. You'll be the most beautiful lady at the ball, Alex. Indeed, in all of Kent. Any man who does not melt at the sight of you is either blind or married."

"Catherine, please stop," Alexandra said under her breath, heat rushing to her face.

Catherine only laughed.

Alexandra shaded her face and turned away. From the corner of her eye, she could see Roman. He appeared to have taken no note of their conversation.

She breathed a sigh of relief.

The three separated just after beginning the tour of the museum.

Awestruck by the famous artwork gracing the walls of the magnificent structure, Alexandra admired works from grand murals to intricate sculptures, from the life-sized images of men and great beasts to delicate flowers and fruits. What an array of the creative talents had been collected and displayed! She imagined Jessica's reaction to these very masterpieces while touring the museum three years earlier.

A small glass case in one of the rooms captured her attention. She moved toward it. Others were drawn to it as well. Through the crowd she could see Catherine admiring a piece on the wall.

Within the display case, Alexandra discovered several colorful sea creatures, fresh and perfect in shape. How had they been preserved? She studied them closer, wandering around the cube to view them from every angle.

"They're made of glass," said a voice, deep and very near. She jumped to find Roman leaning over her.

"My apologies." He stepped back. "I had no intention of startling you."

"They can't be glass," she said, focusing again on the case. "You see there—the tiny fins on the fishes; the ribbons of tentacles on that jellyfish. Look closer. They must be real."

"Ah, but they are not. It's an ancient tradition, dating back to fifteenth century Bohemia. The Blaschka family began as jewelers and glassmakers. In recent times, Leopold Blaschka began using his unique talent for the design of these marine animals. I had the privilege of meeting the man myself. Today we see them as art, but in actuality, their original purpose was in the teaching of science. Among his supporters are professors, collectors, philosophers, even princes... I'm sorry."

"They're magnificent. Why do you apologize?"

They stepped away from the display, strolling toward the doorway.

"Many mistake my fascination over man's creativity for arrogance because of the knowledge I possess."

Indeed, Alexandra recalled the embarrassing exhibition he and his mother displayed at the Palace two days before.

"Perhaps it's not your knowledge as much as it is your address," she offered in a helpful tone.

"My address?" He stopped short.

"Well..." she said, wondering about the wisdom in continuing, "...yes. Your air and tone betray the impression of...the arrogance you mentioned." What could it hurt? His expression remained calm, so she continued. "Your voice is almost always devoid of any warmth at all. If you'll pardon my saying so, it's not unlike your mother's." She wanted to back away and run, not relishing the idea of meeting again with the glare she had experienced in the pottery shop. But he gave way to no such expression.

"I see." He looked straight ahead, clasping his hands behind his back.

"Isolation, such as that your life demands, is harmful to a man, I believe," she suggested. "Perhaps a bit more variety in female influence would prove beneficial."

A smug grin took over his face. "And you were considering that possibly *you* could assist in this matter of 'female influence'?"

"I was," she turned around and he followed her gaze, "in fact, thinking of your sister."

His smile dissipated.

"In my opinion," she continued, "Catherine is one of the finest examples of a caring and compassionate lady I know." The dainty young woman remained oblivious to their gazes. "And I believe she has long desired attention from you," she added. "Over the years she has forced herself to be satisfied with the fleeting glimpses and rare words you direct her way, but, really, she is deserving of much more."

"It would seem, Miss Viana, that you pride yourself on prying into the personal affairs of others." His usual irritation returned. Like the difference between a pail of fresh rain water that sparkles from the sun and dances in reflection of life and a solid block of ice, cold and hard, she noted a distinct change in his eyes. "I see my sister when I can. I'm sure she is aware of my deep feelings for her."

"Forgive me, Mr. Winterfield, but it was a sincere observation on my part. And if you will excuse the intrusion, I must contradict your assessment. How can one have genuine love for one of whom they know little? For instance, how much do you know of Catherine's current studies?" She knew his answer, which was, of course, no answer at all. "Or were you aware that her favorite game is chess? Or that her passion is horses?"

"That I do know." Roman defended himself, pointing at her.

"And did you know she is being courted by a man?" His lips parted as if to speak, but no words followed. In his narrowing eyes, she sensed anger and knew full well she was treading on dangerous ground. But she pressed on, fearing she would never have another opportunity to bring the subject to light and feeling it was of extreme importance to her friend. "Yes, Mr. Winterfield, she is of age now. Has that escaped your notice? I understand the man is an acquaintance of yours—Mr. Gregory Westcliffe."

Roman's glare left her to focus on his sister across the room and then settled back on Alexandra. The muscles in his jaw tightened, his lips pursing. But he said nothing. Instead, he exhaled through flared nostrils, whipped his head aside, and walked away.

She watched him go. What exactly had his anger meant? Was it because a man almost ten years his sister's senior had shown interest in her, a young woman who was still a child in her brother's eyes? Or was it his instinct to protect her, no matter the man? Could it be jealousy that first his brother, and now his sister, had found love, while he, Roman, remained unmarried? She dismissed the last thought. For a certainty he could court any woman of his choice. She and her sisters had seen firsthand how women too numerous to count had swooned over the handsome and mysterious Winterfield son.

Whatever the reason for his reaction, she recalled that he was no man with which to trifle. And she feared she had pushed him too far.

He joined her and Catherine in the carriage heading back to the château, but rode as he had when they came—in complete silence.

When she awoke the following morning, Alexandra learned that Roman had already left to resume his work in Europe. A farewell message had been relayed to the Viana family through his parents.

On the ship back to England, Alexandra leaned over the railing. She watched the churning waters of the channel below.

Pondering her encounters with Roman Winterfield, she thought she had more than once heard sincerity, even kindness in his voice. *Point well taken, Miss Viana,* he had replied in response to her story about the beggar. *They are made of glass* was his soft comment behind her at the museum. *Many mistake my fascination for arrogance.*

Perhaps she had been wrong. It now seemed she had indeed, found in him an appreciation and deep interest in a variety of subjects. And had she not even seen him smile—several times, in fact—a gesture, which, just two years previous, she thought would have cracked the stone face?

Yet, she had also seen vestiges of the arrogant Roman Winterfield who had belittled and humiliated the Viana family on several past occasions. And though not a serious reason for complaint, she still wondered at his unexpected arrangement for the two of them to dine alone. As he had offered no explanation—and, in fact, said almost nothing during the entire meal—he seemed intent on keeping the purpose a secret.

Her thoughts returned to the letter she had written to Jessica, the one now en route with her parents. After her encounter with the intrusive Frenchman and her dinner with Roman Winterfield, Alexandra had intended to redraft the letter. But she had missed the opportunity. No matter. Her sister should arrive in Kent within the month. An update could be made at that time.

Chapter Six

For a brief moment, Jessica Winterfield considered the beautiful woman holding her father's arm. Even after two years, she could scarcely believe the mother she had thought dead for so many years was not only alive, but now very much a part of her life and touring with her and Andrew in Germany.

The four of them stood in a courtyard under the shadow of a medieval castle, side-by-side in a half circle, gazing up at the immense structure.

"My goodness, Father, you have set your standards very high for the Viana residence," she said, shaking her head in astonishment.

Having entered via the gatehouse, which was larger than the cottage in which Jessica and her sisters had grown up, they stood surrounded from behind by a section of an enormous oval stone wall and ahead by the intimidating castle itself. Two of the three wings were visible from their vantage point and stood perpendicular to each other.

"How did you ever choose Reiswyk as your model?" Andrew asked of his wife's parents.

"I first saw its depiction in a wood carving in London," replied Angela, her gaze moving to a watchtower jutting up from the encircling wall where it curved to disappear behind the castle.

"You'll recall," Jessica's father stated, "that while the two of you were honeymooning in Ireland, the remaining Vianas toured Germany. We visited many magnificent castles. However, we experienced difficulty seeing past the elaborate murals, gold carvings, and polished marble to appreciate the structural design of the buildings. The majority, beautiful as they were, lacked practicality. The oversized rooms seemed cold and unusable. They were museums, not homes. We could not envision our family living in such a palace, exciting as they were to visit." John scanned the fortress before him. "Reiswyk was different. While majestic to be sure, its wings offer roomy seclusion and cozy comfort. Shall we begin? You'll see for yourselves why we chose it."

They entered the structure through a prominent round tower in front. Leaded-glass windows encircled them and reached the solid coned ceiling two stories above. A magnificent tile mosaic graced the floor in a soothing swirled pattern.

"We, too, have designed a mosaic for the entrance hall of our castle," explained Angela, "but ours will be a glorious mountain scene. Muir Ceann is what we have named the house," she said, taking Jessica's elbow. "It's Gaelic for 'island home.' However, I'm not proficient in the language. That's the best I can decipher. We like the sound of it anyway."

"I think that's beautiful," Jessica replied.

The party stepped into a receiving hall where the shaded windows allowed enough light to see numerous fraying tapestries strewn about on the walls. They were met by a frail-looking gentleman, who explained in German that several areas of the castle were under restoration; however, they were welcome to tour the remainder of the house.

He strolled with them, explaining that the fortress was built in the eleventh century and was home to several successive royal families. The name came from the second family, Duke Karl Von Reiswyk.

Jessica was fascinated with the history of the structure. It had succumbed to fire during the Thirty Years War in the seventeenth century and was restored by the last Duke to have resided in the great castle. However, it had been neglected after his death, hence the restoration now well underway.

The foursome and a group of others moved through the great vestibule toward the large banquet hall at the rear of the main wing. Light from six enormous windows, stretching from the floor to the full height of the ceiling two stories above, welcomed them. Jessica wandered over to peer out at the landscape. Far below, a thick canopy of forest nestled like a sprawling carpet where the cliff gave way to a wide, peaceful valley.

Jessica had been so immersed in the view that she did not hear her father's footsteps. His voice startled her.

"Amazing view, is it not? This castle, as all others, was strategically placed and designed for the greatest military protection. Many of the castles we visited include complete arsenals and clever defense mechanisms. You could say they were built for the battle."

"It's a relief to know that Muir Ceann will be a place of peace and contentment," she said, "not for the *de*struction of enemies, but for the *con*struction of families. But must it be so large, Father? I cannot picture the Vianas in such an immense house. Why, we could go for days and never see one another."

Her father smiled. "I failed to mention that our home will be scaled down. Your mother and I want it large enough to house five growing families and afford them all privacy, as well as togetherness. You must realize it won't be too long before both Alex and John will be starting families of their own."

"It's hard to imagine John as the head of his own family. I've barely come to terms with the fact that I have a younger brother, and here he is approaching manhood."

"I, too, am still in awe of our good fortune in finding him and your mother. After all our years of believing her to be drowned and not even knowing of his existence, I want this home to be a celebration of their return and our completion as a family."

Jessica looked up and saw moisture glisten in his eyes. She patted his arm and nodded, blinking several times to keep her own tears from rolling down her cheeks.

The two wandered outside to a small courtyard. Closing her eyes, she bathed her face in the warmth of the sun and listened to the chirping of birds hidden in the forest.

"I certainly hope our castle can be one of peace, as you say, Jessica," her father stated.

"I have no doubt of that, Father," she said, her eyes still closed. "Andrew is becoming more and more comfortable in his work on the island. Have you noticed that he's happy spending less time on his ships? And already Grace and Stephen are beginning their plans to move there. Everett will not be four years of age when they will settle in at Muir Ceann." Jessica thought of her energetic two-year-old nephew. She pictured his bouncy blonde curls and happy blue eyes. "How he must have grown since I last saw him."

"And with the arrival of *your* little one this November, Muir Ceann will be well on its way, as you say, to the construction of the family."

"So why then would you concern yourself at this early stage that it may not be one of peace, Father? Your grandchildren will be raised in a loving atmosphere." She saw a troubled look in his eyes.

"Jessica, when I learned of the mutual interest developing between you and Andrew, I must admit to being unprepared for such a prospect. Oh, I had known all along that you would not remain a child forever. I would have to let you go in time, but I ignored the signs when I saw them. It was a most difficult time for me."

Her heart tugged at her. Although unable now to comprehend the emotions involved in watching one's children grow only to give them to the world, she herself would one day face that very situation with the child growing in her womb.

"And if I had few signs of *your* feelings," he continued, "I had none at all from Grace. Your mother and I had dined several times with Stephen Sutton and corresponded at length regarding our legal matters. All the while we were unaware that the two had been exchanging letters for months by that time." John gave way to a little laugh, but Jessica sensed it was humility rather than humor that had prompted it. "Up to that point I thought I knew my daughters better than anyone. I suppose some secrets will always exist between parent and child."

"I'm sorry we were not more open with you, Father."

He put an arm around her shoulders. "Don't be so, Daughter. Your courtships corresponded to a rather hectic time in all our lives. However, I'm determined to put forth my greatest effort to be more cognizant of your younger sister and brother. It's not my intent to overprotect, but simply to guide them."

"As you did with me, Father. But you still haven't explained why you would have any reason to be concerned about our family." Jessica arched her eyebrows in the same manner she had often seen him do over the years.

"Perhaps my concern is a bit premature, but I've noticed some signs of interest on the part of a certain young man toward your sister although I feel she is mostly oblivious to them." Then he uttered under his breath, "But perhaps she chooses ignorance in this instance."

"I believe I know of the man to whom you're referring." Jessica smiled, recalling Alexandra's recent letter in which she had mentioned the handsome Frenchman.

"I'm afraid not, Jessica." Amusement filled his eyes. "The man I speak of would not bring such a pleasing smile to your face. He's the reason for the concern I mentioned before."

"Alex is twenty-two now and has matured so much since I left home. I believe the trials our family experienced three years ago affected her in many positive ways. The dreamy-eyed, naïve girl I used to know has given way to a self-confident and poised young woman, don't you think? Oh, she still possesses that air of innocence to a degree, and I hope that will stay with her." She hesitated. "I trust Alex to make a wise decision in the man she marries."

Jessica's heart was warmed by thoughts of her sister. Alexandra had a way of dealing with others in subtle ways, always careful not to overstep the boundary of kindness. In that way she wished she was more like her.

"The man I speak of is your brother-in-law."

"*What*?" Before she could stop herself, she burst out in laughter and only regained composure when she noticed no smile on his face. She covered her mouth. "You can't be serious, Father. Roman Winterfield would not recognize true beauty or real sense in a woman were it a brick wall in his path!"

"Sometimes our own biased opinions blind us to the truth." She felt the gentle chastisement in her father's words.

"Father, if you had read the letter Alex wrote while in France with you and Roman, you would have no doubt as to her opinion of him."

"Perhaps. But that letter does not reflect Roman's opinion of Alexandra."

Jessica wrinkled her brow.

"Your mother noticed his glances, as well," he said, "and he arranged for the two of them to dine alone two nights before our departure. He also invited himself to join her and Catherine on their outing the final day."

"But, Father, Alex's letter said he had reverted to his former course. It would seem that, from Alex's viewpoint, any noble traits once seen in Roman Winterfield were short-lived."

"On the contrary, your mother and I noticed marked improvements in his personality, or at least definite efforts in that direction."

"Well," Jessica stated, confident of her own opinion of Andrew's brother, "I suppose time will reveal what is in both their hearts." She knew Roman would be unable to keep up the charade with which he had apparently outfitted himself for her parents' sake.

But why would he care to impress them?

"If he *is* interested in her," her father said, "then we've not seen the last of Roman Winterfield." He winked and walked back inside, leaving her alone with her thoughts—thoughts with which she would rather not be alone.

Chapter Seven

Catherine Winterfield tucked the letter into her pocket, excused herself, and hastened up the stairs. Alexandra watched with curiosity, wondering what was so important inside that envelope the servant had handed her friend upon their return to Kent.

Several hours later, after they had time to unpack, Catherine invited Alexandra and John to the stables. Alexandra could barely contain her eagerness to venture onto the Winterfield grounds.

"I can't tell you how happy I am to host two guests who appreciate my horses as much as I do," Catherine said as the trio crossed the courtyard to the stables. "You can ride Sampson, John. He's high-spirited, so I only let experienced riders take him. You and I can ride Cinnamon and Willoughby, Alex. Duchess likes to follow along...I hope you don't mind. Her foal is due in a few weeks, so her exercise has lessened a bit as of late. Sampson's the sire, you know. Duchess is Roman's horse, though he takes little interest in her." Catherine talked on about the horses as they saddled them, and soon the four horses with three riders trotted along a quiet road through the magnificent forests of the Winterfield estate.

Stopping at the edge of a clearing, they looked out across a sea of grass sprinkled with wildflowers. One lone tree stood tall near the center, its branches reaching into the pale blue of the sky.

"Sometimes I bring the horses here to graze." Catherine leaned forward to pat Cinnamon's neck.

"Are there any streams or boulders hiding in this meadow?" John asked.

"Just a tree stump there to the west side," she pointed. "Otherwise it's very even, very flat." A broad smile overtook her face. "Why, John? Would you like to run him?"

Alexandra watched excitement rise in Catherine's face while John turned the horse, scanning the meadow. She deciphered his thoughts at once when he cast his brown eyes back toward Catherine.

"Go," she said, "but keep to the edge of the forest."

John called out a sharp command, cracking the reins. Sampson, who had been restless during the slow ride, shot into a run like a bullet from a gun barrel. Dust kicked up in clouds from beneath the thunderous hooves.

The remaining horses tossed their heads. Alexandra's steed took several steps backward. She held him tight and watched with excitement as her brother leaned parallel with the horse's stretched neck, urging the animal ahead, reins held short and loose. His dark hair stood out against the horse's bay coat.

Catherine's horse whinnied and turned in a circle as John rounded the first corner far on the opposite end of the meadow.

"Excellent rider!" Catherine exclaimed. "No one besides me has ever run that horse. Your brother is quite adept with him. Look at Sampson. He's beautiful. It's as if his hooves don't even touch the ground. The Thoroughbred in him truly shows his elegance when he's in a run, don't you think?"

The two grinned with excitement as the sleek bay shrunk with the distance, turned and raced along the forest edge, took the final corner, and began the return toward them. The patterned beat of the heavy hooves grew louder and louder.

"I was thrilled to discover how much John loves horses," Alexandra said. "We hold so many things in common."

"He's very handsome, Alex," Catherine said. "And I adore his accent. Fully Irish in an English family."

"It took me some time to adjust to that I must admit," she said with a laugh. "And my mother with her Spanish accent. Our household is certainly unique."

"I'm amazed at John's likeness to your father. And he's a good man, like your father—like all of you. Fortunate the woman to capture his heart."

John slowed the horse to a canter and then a trot as he approached. Sampson's nostrils flared from heavy breaths. The horse fought the restraint to slow the pace. Tossing his head back, he finally yielded to the strong grip on the reins. Beads of perspiration trickled from under the saddle and over the sleek body. John was also panting from the exhilarating ride. "Magnificent creature!" he exclaimed.

"The two of you make quite the pair," complimented Catherine. "Take him out any time you like, John. You needn't ask."

Near sunset they rounded a corner on their way back toward the house. A series of small brick buildings surrounded by row upon row of cultivated plants came into view.

"Is that a vineyard?" John asked.

"It is," replied Catherine. "The Winterfield estate produces its own wine, and of very fine quality, indeed. The vineyard was already established, though much smaller, when Father purchased the property. He simply changed the name. It operates independently of Father's business. A full staff is housed right here on the property."

"Do you know any of the staff?" John asked.

"No, I can't say that I do. One or two are usually on hand to serve wine when we host social gatherings, but I've not conversed with any of them. I'm sure they wouldn't recognize me were we ever to meet."

"Too bad," he said.

"Why?"

"Just a passing thought."

"I know you like a book, John," said Alexandra. "He'd love to get his hands into that soil," she added to Catherine.

"So we have a gardener in our midst?" she asked.

"And a very eager one at that," Alexandra added.

As they passed, a young man in the distance stood up from his work among the vines. He rested one elbow on the fencing. The brim of a worn leather hat shadowed his dark complexion. Long white sleeves, rolled just above his wrists, billowed in the breeze.

He studied the group on the horses, listening to the drone of their distant voices. They seemed to take no note of his presence. After they had passed, he leaned over to resume his digging.

Chapter Eight

Following dinner, Alexandra and Catherine settled onto the sofa while Richard Winterfield challenged young John to a game of billiards.

"Catherine," Alexandra said in a quiet tone, "I hope you'll forgive the intrusion, but I couldn't help notice that since our first meeting in France, you've scarcely mentioned Mr. Westcliffe's name in conversation." She recalled it was she herself who broached the subject even then.

Catherine's pale brown eyes looked away.

"It's said that the lips speak out of the heart's abundance," Alexandra pressed. "The reverse could be said, as well—out of the heart's emptiness, the lips remain silent."

"I compliment you on your observation, Alex. However, your conclusion could not be further from the truth. He has been very much on my mind."

"But is he in your heart?"

"I've come to realize that Gregory Westcliffe is a very commanding sort. If not obliged upon his outright requests, he resorts to more devious measures to have things his way. My absence from him, coupled with the opportunity to associate with your family, has opened my eyes. He is a very manipulative man."

"Catherine, for a certainty such a man can't be an agreeable suitor for a woman of integrity such as you. I'm thankful you've realized his character."

Catherine leaned her head back on the soft leather of the sofa and peered up at the ceiling, the wisp of a smile appearing on her lips. "It's as though I've been in a fog these past months. Gregory Westcliffe is..." She paused, her gaze still fixed on the ceiling. "...one of the most handsome men of my acquaintance. Most women melt at a mere glance from him. They become putty in his hands. Men and women alike accommodate his every wish and command." She sat up to face Alexandra again. "Yet it is *I* who has captured his fancy! I still find it difficult to believe. Men of his sort don't often look my way, Alex."

Alexandra frowned. How a person could employ his good looks to manipulate others was something she would never understand. Yet, she had seen it more than once.

"But he will not allow me to mention our courtship to our parents."

"*What*?" Alexandra glanced toward Catherine's father, who was intent on the game and his conversation with John. "Your parents know nothing of this courtship, Catherine?" Her words were a sharp whisper.

"No. Because the Westcliffes and the Winterfields have a long history of marriage alliances, he says both our parents will be ecstatic. He'd like to surprise them when the time is right. So for now we meet in secret, and his letters come anonymously."

"I can't believe this!"

"Yet during my holiday in France," Catherine continued, "I came to see past his handsome features and charisma and have realized that I do not know this man at all. I cannot know him, for he becomes whatever and whoever the situation demands."

"You must terminate this relationship at once, Catherine," Alexandra warned.

"I can't do that, Alex. He's right. Our parents would be thrilled. I see it as a matter of family responsibility. Given time, perhaps I'll come to love him. Besides," she hesitated but her gaze did not leave Alexandra's, "I fear it's too late." Catherine glanced over at the two men, who were too engrossed in their game to notice her pull a letter from her pocket. She handed it to Alexandra, who hid it on her lap as she read it.

> Catherine,
>
> I am afraid my work at the Viana estate will require my absence from London for several more weeks. However, I have heard about and plan to return for the Winterfield Ball. I find myself restless with excitement, for I have an important matter to discuss with you that very evening, one I am sure will bring great joy to family and society alike.
>
> Yours, G.W.

Alexandra shook her head at the absence of any sentiment at all in his words.

"He's going to propose marriage the night of the ball, Alex."

"You can't do this, Catherine! If you were aware of his behavior—"

"I don't want to know. Everything will be all right, you'll see. My family will be very pleased." Catherine took the letter and left Alexandra to join the men at the table.

"I understand John has obtained work for the summer." It was Alexandra's sister Grace who broached the subject of their brother as they strolled a London street. "Oh, look at this hat. Catherine, I could just see you wearing it while paying calls."

"It is beautiful," their young friend said, admiring it through the shop window.

"Yes, Grace, he'll be lending a hand at the Winterfield vineyard," Alexandra said of their brother as they moved on.

"At the mortification of my father, might I add," said Catherine. "To have his guest performing work on his property is unthinkable."

"But John managed to persuade him somehow," Alexandra added. "After a few days in the company of Catherine and me, he was in need of something more interesting to keep him occupied."

"And he loves the garden from what I understand," Grace said. "I wish I would've known him better before I ran off and married."

"He does love the garden—second only to horses."

"And he comes home in the evening with such enthusiasm," Catherine said. "We've learned so much about the techniques they're using and the vines, haven't we, Alex?"

"We have. He also tells us much about his supervisor, a man as devoted to the work as is John. So knowledgeable, John reports, though he's only about five years John's elder. Apparently he's been working for the Winterfield's about as long."

"How did he gain so much knowledge in just five years?" Grace wanted to know.

"John hasn't learned that yet," Catherine said. "Antoine Aramis is a man of few words about himself."

"Ah, he's of French descent." Grace's eyebrows arched.

"Of that John's certain. His accent is very heavy. John mimics him at times," Alexandra said, laughing. "He's beginning to take on his style of dress, as well. He leaves every morning in a worn leather hat Mr. Aramis loaned him. And he insists that John wear only white cotton shirts—says it protects his arms from cuts, the sun, and insects, and keeps him from perspiring."

"Mr. Aramis sounds promising...for someone," Grace said. "What does he like to do with his free time?"

"John can't seem to get much more information from him, only that he likes to spend it in the museums and libraries in town," Catherine reported. "He sounds like a bit of a recluse."

"Perhaps he's longing for home," Grace suggested. "I suppose he and John will prove to be good friends. Did you not say John longs for the gardens at his home in Ireland? It seems Mother has raised a horticulturist."

"I'm certain he'll prove as much an asset to them as the vineyard is to him," Alexandra said.

"I hope he'll find some time this summer for his sister in London," Grace replied. "Speaking of yearning for home, Alex, do you ever miss Old Stormy?"

"So much so that I've arranged a visit in June," Alexandra confessed.

"How I wish I could accompany you," Grace said, "but business, you know. I couldn't possibly tear away."

The ladies were greeted by the tinkling of a bell when they wandered into a shop that advertised high tea on a board out front. They were escorted to a dainty table of wicker, where a porcelain tea set and silver utensils awaited them.

"It must've been more difficult for you to leave there than anyone else, Alex," Catherine added as they settled onto the wicker chairs painted white. "Your two sisters left for the reason of marriage, but you suffered single-handedly when you left your home. Even your father had your mother back by that time."

"I've been fortunate to have had the opportunity to return there on occasion. The new caretakers are pleasant and hardworking, with the Wrights by their side. They said I'm welcome any time I like. They even promised me my old room when I come to stay."

"How I miss the Wrights," Grace lamented. "She was like a mother to us in so many ways. I hear they'll be joining us upon the completion of Muir Ceann."

"I'm in the hopes that the work will not prove as difficult at the castle with so many there to care for it. The Wrights are aging, you know," said Alexandra. "Though I don't miss the hard work at the lighthouse, I long for the cool summer evenings, standing at the railing. I so loved watching the sun setting, the breezes tossing our hair."

"Remember the three of us standing up on that tower in a little row, chins cupped in our palms, listening and learning from the sounds of the sea?"

"Those times are long past now," Alexandra said, caught up in her memories. "You know, it's strange that Papa has not expressed much desire to return to Brentwood and Old Stormy. But he's building a new tower for us, did you know?"

"Stephen and I haven't yet been to the island. Tell me about it," begged Grace.

"Already you can see it taking shape on the outer wall," Alexandra said. "One side of the island drops off in a cliff. That's where the tower is being constructed. You'll be so surprised to see it, Grace!"

A woman shaped like an apple and covered by an apron shuffled over to fill their pot with hot water.

"How excited I am for our week together," Grace said, "and how good of you to spend it with me here in town, Alex. We've all been invited to Stephen's parents' home for dinner tonight. I'm certain you'll remember his brother, Preston."

Feeling Catherine's foot tap her leg under the table, she looked over at her coy smile.

Alexandra took her seat at the dinner table and eyed the young man seated opposite her. Straight tawny hair dusted his shirt collar, and his skin tone told of a man who was fond of the outdoors.

"I've registered for the America's Cup, Father," he was saying, "which begins in August."

"Oh, Preston," his mother groaned from across the table, "I regret the day your father ever agreed to purchase that yacht. Those races are dangerous and far too competitive. I fear they will be the death of you."

"Perhaps I could move to Spain and take up bullfighting," Preston said in answer. "Would that put your mind at ease, Mother?"

Mrs. Sutton rolled her eyes.

Alexandra fought hard against her own advancing smile.

Servants arrived, one with baskets of bread. Another filled the crystal flutes with red wine.

Grace whispered in Alexandra's ear. "Don't dare tell me you think he's not handsome."

Receiving no response, Grace leaned over to Catherine next. After a session of back and forth whispering, they broke out tittering. Alexandra could just imagine what they had conspired between them.

"I believe, Preston," Stephen spoke up from the head of the table, "that Mother would find more satisfaction in seeing you gainfully employed in a more ordinary field."

"Shall I consent to confining myself to that stuffy office with you and father, poring over law books and reference manuals?" Preston answered and cast a wink at Alexandra. "However, the two of you must be much more physically fit than I. To lift some of those volumes would require arms of iron. I'm surprised, Father, that you haven't yet suffered an attack of apoplexy. *That* would be the death of *me*, Mother."

"I'm always amazed at your never-ending excuses," his brother said.

Alexandra cast a discreet glance in Preston's direction. She had had a brief opportunity to converse with him prior to dinner. He had been attentive to both her and Catherine, offering wine and a tour of the gardens. But as they strolled, it was she herself whose hand he grasped to tuck into the crook of his arm. It had not been her first time meeting him. She recalled his playful and friendly manner at the engagement ball two years prior.

"You're interested in the sciences, Preston," his brother said. "Perhaps you could resume your studies."

"Ah, the sciences," Preston said with a sigh. "Yes. Perhaps even medicine." In a mockery of his brother, he dropped his gaze and began speaking to an invisible patient lying on the dinner table before him. "Mr. Smith, after countless examinatons and much deliberation with my colleagues, and considering the severity of your present symptoms and vital signs, I have concluded that the only diagnosis to be made...now you may want to sit down for this. Oh, excuse me, you're already lying down." Alexandra smirked, quick to take note of the humor on the faces of the others. "The only diagnosis to be made for your condition," Preston continued the charade, "is rigor mortis." The guests at the table broke into laughter. "Mr. Smith? Mr. Smith! I realize it's shocking, but how can I treat you if you insist on ignoring me?"

At that, even his brother could not help but laugh. "All right, all right," Stephen said in surrender. "Preston, how are you ever going to support a family of your own?"

In an undertone, their father, William, answered the question. "I've already made those arrangements, Stephen. He'll be joining the carnival when it returns to London. Perhaps he can pair up with the bearded lady. They could produce a half-ape child, and the talent among them all will secure their employment for years to come."

Preston burst out in laughter over his father's attempt at wit.

Alexandra turned her head toward Catherine, covering her mouth with her napkin, struggling to suppress her own laughter at the whole scenario.

Whatever was Grace thinking?

Chapter Nine

Jessica and Andrew Winterfield embraced her parents and said their final farewells as the two couples prepared to go their separate ways—the Vianas northwestward to return to Scotland and the Winterfields south through Switzerland and back into Italy, where they had docked their ship. *The Emerald* would be loaded with a supply of materials for Muir Ceann.

"Mother, it's a beautiful locket," Jessica said, examining a shiny gold piece in her hand. "It will be nothing short of adored by Alex. Would you like me to deliver it to her? We'll be docking in Chatham for a time, you know."

"No thank you, Jessie. I've planned to ship it from France. I think it will be a delightful surprise for her to receive a package from the mainland."

"Very well, but it may be weeks before it arrives."

"That's what I'm hoping for. With her stay in Kent for the entire summer, this will be a fitting reminder of her parents just about the time she forgets all about us."

Jessica laughed. "I think I can include Alex when I say that you and Father are always on the minds of all your children. But you're right. It'll be a lovely surprise. I suppose then we'll be meeting you again at the island."

"Do be careful. I worry about you on that ship, Jessie."

"As Smiley McGuire once said, 'Captain Winterfield is the finest captain on the seas,'" Jessica replied in a sharp Irish brogue.

They both laughed and embraced a final time.

Upon returning to the inn for their own bags, Jessica and Andrew found a telegram awaiting them. Andrew read it to himself and smiled as he looked up at his curious wife.

"What is it?" she inquired. "Unexpected messages always give my heart a bit of a jump. They often contain bad news."

Her husband's smile broadened. "Well, I suppose this news is relative."

He handed her the telegram.

"Literally 'relative,' is it not?" she said with a note of sarcasm after reading the news.

It seemed that Andrew's brother, Roman, had had a change of plans and would be joining them aboard *The Emerald* back to Chatham.

Chapter Ten

"I can't wait to show you the winery," young John Viana said to Alexandra and Catherine. Alexandra could see the excitement in his eyes.

"It has been several years since I've been here," Catherine said. "I was a child when I last toured the facility. Andrew treated Jessica to a tour prior to their engagement. But I thought it would be a romantic day for the two of them to spend alone, so I didn't join them."

"Your idea proved profitable," Alexandra said. "They were engaged two months later!"

John rolled his eyes, and the ladies giggled. He led them to the entrance of the main building, which stood three stories in height.

Inside the vestibule, a dark-haired man of medium build met them. His clean white shirt hung outside the trousers tucked into his worn boots.

"Antoine Aramis, I'd like you to meet my sister, Alexandra, and you may already know Catherine Winterfield," John said.

"I'm pleased to meet you both." The softly accented words flowed off his tongue like a song. Reaching for the hand of first one, then the other, he kissed each in greeting. "Though I have served at a handful of your parties at the house, I have never been formally introduced to any of the Winterfields." He looked into Catherine's face.

Alexandra suppressed a smile as a pink flush rose to her friend's cheeks.

"But my brother, Andrew—he toured here two summers ago. Surely you met him then."

"I heard of the master's visit. Unfortunately, I was in town that day and had not the pleasure of meeting him. But John has told me so much about the two of *you*, I feel I already know you."

"Which he has done for you, as well," Alexandra said.

"So let us proceed with our tour. I thought we could start at the beginning—with the vines," Antoine said.

When the men led the way from the vestibule, Catherine pulled Alexandra's arm. "Now I'm sorry I haven't ventured down long before."

The whispered comment left Alexandra grinning.

"He has very kind eyes, does he not?" Catherine asked.

"Very nice, indeed," Alexandra agreed.

Antoine turned back to Alexandra. "Your brother has been of great help to me already, Miss Viana. I'm most grateful for his assistance for the summer."

"You'll find him to be an honest and hard worker, *Monsieur*," she replied. A smile of warmth for her younger brother crossed her lips.

"Enough already!" John appeared uncomfortable at being the topic of discussion.

"I'm afraid you've come at a time of year when the vines look a bit shabby," Antoine was quick to say as they stepped between two rows of dried brown stalks.

About a foot from the ground, all had been parted in two, the branches lying tied to a cord strung horizontally down the row. Six to eight spindly green sprouts shot upward and curled from each dried twig.

"Don't let their appearance fool you," Antoine said. "Trapped within these sprouts is the juice of tomorrow's harvest. By this time next month, we'll have a full canopy. Based on the warm spring, I can tell you we'll have a rich harvest indeed. This should be Mr. Winterfield's best year yet."

"What kind of grapes are these?" Alexandra asked.

"Mostly Madeleine Angevine—white grapes," Antoine answered. "Return in late August and you can eat them straight from the vine. They'll be very sweet."

"Why don't we grow red grapes?" Catherine asked.

"Mr. Winterfield has been experimenting with a few reds, but they've produced poorly. We don't seem to have the heat required to sustain them here."

"No matter," John added. "Your vineyard produces ten tons of grapes each year, Catherine."

"Good heavens, ten tons!" she exclaimed.

"Even with the birds," Antoine said, laughing.

"Are they the grapes' only enemy?" Alexandra asked as the group strolled down the row.

"In this humid environment, we also have the threat of fungus," Antoine answered, "not to mention mites."

"And what have been your duties thus far, John?" Catherine asked.

"Mostly clean up, but Antoine's teaching me to do some pruning now. With the canes growing four inches a day, I'll be spending most of my time here in the vineyard."

"He's also done some work with the barrel shipment. Shall we move inside the barrel house? We'll show you."

Holding one hand out, Antoine allowed John to lead the way back down the row, bringing up the rear.

"How many men are employed here?" Alexandra asked.

"We have one winemaker, one warehouseman, two supervisors, and four more of us who do the vine dressing, maintenance, and various other duties. Believe it or not, there is enough work here to keep us all occupied year-round."

"When do you ever have free time?" Catherine asked.

"Actually, I have two days each week for personal use. Your father is very generous."

Catherine closed her lacy parasol as the group stepped across the threshold into a cool room.

Alexandra inhaled deeply. The tangy perfume of fermenting wine, coupled by a woody smell she assumed to be new barrels seeped into her nose and lungs.

Moving farther in, she followed the others to several rows of barrels stacked two stories high on iron racks. Muted light from high dusty windows washed the spacious room.

"I stacked these myself just this week," John boasted.

"These barrels will be used for this year's harvest," said Antoine. "That scent you're smelling is the Hungarian Oak, which has been toasted on the inside of the barrels."

Alexandra sniffed. "Oh, but I smell wine."

"Ah, you have a keen nose," Antoine added. "The cellar, where the wine is stored all winter, is just below us. Before venturing down, let me tell you about the wine-making. The press vats are in the big building to the west."

"You should see them," John said. "Huge tubs with fat screws to press the lids down. They're on the third story. The grapes are carried up on belts."

"After the first stages of fermentation, gravity carries the juice to the second and finally the main floor where the final product is poured into the barrels, labeled, and stored in the tunnels below," added Antoine.

"The tunnels are connected beneath all the buildings." John added.

"Let's go down," suggested Antoine.

Goosebumps covered Alexandra's arms as they descended a stone stairwell into even cooler temperatures beneath the barrel house.

"Here the barrels remain until spring when the bottling process is done. The bottling of last year's harvest was just completed, thus the lingering scent. And then there are these few barrels of red wine produced during our experiments," Antoine said, patting a fat barrel—one of just a few that remained in the cellar—the way Alexandra patted a good horse. "We store them for years."

Leading the guests down a narrow, lone passageway, Antoine halted when they came to a padlocked iron gate.

"This tunnel was blocked by racks for nearly a century and discovered only a few years ago. When the room was finally opened, it was found to contain dozens of tightly sealed bottles of the vineyard's original product, bearing silent witness to the history of the Winterfield property."

Although obviously younger than Catherine's brothers, Antoine spoke with the voice of confidence that comes only from experience. His expressions revealed a fondness for the vines and a genuine happiness in having the privilege to be part of such a fine trade.

The party moved on to a room stacked to the ceiling with filled bottles.

"Fewer things on this earth bring a community closer together than good food," Antoine continued. "But a meal is sawdust without the complement of drink. Indeed, a fine wine enhances the flavor and mood of a meal like nothing else. I've found it unique in that it's one of the few commodities that crosses national barriers. Nearly all cultures appreciate a superior wine."

Alexandra often glanced Catherine's way with a smile of approval for the handsome young Frenchman.

Near the end of the tour, a heavy-set and gruff-appearing man interrupted them, speaking in French to Antoine. Of course, all present fully understood his words, which expressed a tone of sarcasm.

"How kind of you, Antoine, to share the winery with all your friends." The man gave a look of scorn toward the two ladies, and then looked back at their guide. "Might I remind you that Winterfield Vineyard is not equipped for public tours?"

"Allow me to put your mind at ease, *Monsieur* Beaumont," Antoine was quick to respond. "*Monsieur* Marlon authorized this tour just yesterday. Did he not mention it to you? I specifically requested that he do so."

"No, he did not." *Monsieur* Beaumont glared again at the guests, then at John and back at Antoine. "You'd better finish up," he said in English. "You have work to do." He grunted and then addressed John. "As do you."

"Our shifts begin in one hour. We'll not be late," Antoine assured him in a steady voice.

The man gave Antoine and John a hard look and left.

Antoine turned to Catherine. "I apologize, Miss Winterfield. Perhaps I should've introduced you. I'm certain he would have given a much more favorable impression had he known."

Catherine frowned. "I find it advantageous to know the true character of our employees."

"With all due respect, Miss Winterfield, please don't be too quick in your judgment." With that, Antoine led them back through the barrel house.

"I'm certainly impressed with the amount of knowledge you're gaining, John," Alexandra complimented.

"And stacking these barrels was no easy task," he said, venturing farther into the room.

Alexandra turned and waited as the others headed for the door. When John caught his foot on a metal band near the bottom of a rack of barrels, she watched helplessly. He stumbled, but steadied himself.

She looked up as the barrels above began to totter. Ducking, John jumped aside. He threw his arms over and around his head. Three barrels crashed to the floor where he had been.

Alexandra covered her ears, but was unable to muffle the deafening sound.

John uncovered his head and ran wide-eyed over to the group.

The large form of Mr. Beaumont bounded into the chamber. "What happened!" he barked, glaring at John, whose face bore an unmistakable look of guilt.

Several other workers appeared in the doorway behind the man.

"I..." John struggled to explain.

"It was my fault, sir," Antoine said, stepping between the two to face Mr. Beaumont.

"If those barrels are damaged, the cost will be garnished from your wages, Aramis. Take them to the warehouse at once!" He stormed out of the room. Muttering to one another, the other workers turned to leave the scene.

"Mr. Aramis," Catherine said, "thank you for defending my friend. I'll see to it that you are reimbursed for any garnishment. I'm ashamed to have such a man on our staff."

"No, Miss Winterfield," replied Antoine. "It was my fault. A responsible supervisor would have seen to it that the barrels were positioned in a more secure fashion. As for Mr. Beaumont, he may not be the most pleasant of fellows, but he works hard for your father. He is organized and has high expectations of all your employees. I'm certain you would be comforted knowing that he's an asset to this vineyard."

Alexandra wondered whether Catherine was thinking *her* thoughts, that Mr. Aramis was truly a humble and agreeable young man.

He escorted the ladies to the front of the building, where they took their leave. Along their stroll back to the mansion, they talked of the charming Mr. Aramis.

"Catherine, how could you harbor the most handsome gentleman in the entire county? He's a much finer catch than Mr. Westcliffe. And I saw the way he looked at you. I think he likes you!"

Catherine's face reddened. "Do you really think so?"

Chapter Eleven

The following afternoon, as the shadows drew the day to a close, Catherine Winterfield rode horseback amidst the lush forests of the Winterfield grounds. Her steed trotted down a back lane. Tiny new ferns and wild flowers dotted the gravel of the ever-narrowing path rarely used by the family. It hooked into the forest just ahead.

She glanced down at her St. Bernard plodding along beside the horse, its tongue dangling from under its dark nose. Just then the dog stopped, lifted its head, and began a low barking. Catherine slowed her pace and urged the horse around the bend, where the forest gave way to a small clearing. The sound of water trickled through the evening air—the little stream where she would stop to water her horse. Several yards beyond the stream, the forest stretched before her, covering the rolling hills into the visible distance.

The spot had been a favorite view of Catherine's over the years. Stopping to take in the scene, she discovered that it had captured the attention of another. At the edge of the forest, a man stood beside a folding stool. Propped before him rested a small easel.

"Mr. Aramis!" exclaimed Catherine, nudging the horse forward. The St. Bernard began a frenzied barking. She gave the dog a sharp command, and he fell silent. "Excuse me," she said. "I apologize for disrupting your solitude."

"Are you apologizing to me for enjoying your property? It's I who owes the apology, Miss Winterfield. Your dog is a good protector."

Catherine stopped close enough to view the painting on the easel. "So I see we favor the same spot. I had no idea you are an artist, Mr. Aramis."

"I'm surprised we haven't met here before. I've been working on this piece for some time now. The reason I'm here this evening is to capture the sunset. Then it will be complete."

"May I?" Catherine asked in permission for a closer look at his work.

"By all means."

Antoine assisted her from the horse, and she fastened the reins to a nearby branch. Pulling her riding gloves from her fingers, she stepped to the easel. As she glanced over the canvas, her breath stopped short. "It's as near real as I've ever seen in a painting. How do you do it?" Feeling his gaze upon her, she looked to find him smiling.

"Miss Winterfield, I believe you were one of the subjects of a recent work of mine. I didn't realize it until just this moment."

"Tell me, how can that be since we met only yesterday?"

He crouched down to open a wide, flat bag that lay among the ferns. From it, he pulled a canvas fastened taut over a wooden frame. Placing it on the easel, he covered the other painting.

She stared at a scene that seemed familiar, though the piece was unfinished. Rows of grapevines filled the foreground of the painting. Beyond, a narrow road twisted across the canvas. A partial forest was taking shape with various shades of greens and browns on the far side of the road. Wildflowers dotted the roadside. On the lane itself, four dark horses walked, three of which carried riders—two women and one man. One of the women, who lagged behind the others, led the fourth horse by the reins. As Catherine examined it, she recognized her own blonde hair and riding attire.

"This one's me!" she cried, pointing. "And Alex and John. This was the ride we took that first evening after returning from France. I stand in awe over the details you've captured, Mr. Aramis."

Antoine laughed out loud. "I hadn't realized it was you until just this moment when I took note of your riding gear."

"How do you do it?" she repeated. "We didn't see you there and must have been out of your view within moments. How did you remember all these details—our clothing, our hair, even the patches on Duchess. It's remarkable." She could not take her eyes from the painting. "Mr. Aramis, that was no more than seven nights ago. You painted this in just *seven days?*"

He shrugged. "It took three. It's a gift, I suppose. I spend much of my free time before a canvas."

"Do you always paint landscapes?"

"No. I also spend much time at the museums in town. I started by copying various works of other artists. Now I go to study their work—their shadowing and shading, combinations of hues. Sometimes I attempt to replicate their technique. Other times I just do charcoal sketches of interesting-looking visitors at the museums. They make fine subjects because they stand for long periods of time in the same position." He looked up at the changing sky. "I've become quite adept at remembering details."

Catherine was speechless.

"Look, Miss Winterfield," he said, pointing to the western horizon. "The sunset is perfect this evening." He continued talking as he crouched back down to the bag on the ground and pulled from it a few small metal tubes. "I came out here tonight because I expected an unusual sunset—just enough clouds."

"May I stay and observe your work in action?"

Antoine stopped to look up at her. "I would be honored." After lingering in his glance at her, he returned his attention to his paint tubes. Several brushes came next from the bag. He reached up to remove the painting of the horses from the easel, tucking it away before standing to adjust the stool and squeeze dabs of paint onto a stained wooden palette.

Catherine took a position behind him to watch the brilliant orange and pink hues in the sky begin to emerge in identical position on the canvas, above and between two misty green hills. Within minutes the colors in the sky began to fade, but not before being captured by the mind and hand of the artist. As he touched the canvas with a few final strokes of white, he sat back. "And with that, it has come to completion." He turned to look back at his spectator.

"It's amazing," she said, lost in the painting.

"Miss Winterfield," Antoine stated. "There's not much light remaining. You'd better be going."

His statement shook her from her astonished state. "Oh, yes, you're right. But your painting… You cannot pack it until it has dried. It will be ruined. Surely, you'll not make it home before darkness sets in."

"Thank you for your concern," he said with a smile. "But I'm prepared to stay after dark."

"Very well," she said and walked over to the horse to loose its reins. The dog, who had been napping in the underbrush, stood, ready to follow his mistress. With Antoine's help Catherine mounted the horse. "Thank you for allowing me to stay."

She turned the horse to leave.

"Miss Winterfield," he called out. She turned the horse back again. "John's shift ends tomorrow at two. Do you think the three of us could meet here for a picnic lunch?"

"I'll pack the lunch if you'll bring a bottle of your finest wine."

"You mean *your* finest wine."

She nodded before trotting into the forest, biting her lower lip against her advancing smile. The image of his handsome face burned into her mind. Looking up, she gave a quick wink to the moon, which had risen in the ever-darkening sky.

The following afternoon Catherine sat on a spread blanket near a small lake, staring absently at the remains of a fine meal before her. She, Antoine, and John had enjoyed dried meats, fresh fruit, oysters, and, of course, a bottle of Winterfield wine. She regretted that Alexandra had returned to the city to spend more time with her sister and could not join them.

Catherine and Antoine sat together on the edge of the blanket, talking, while John stood several yards away playing fetch with the St. Bernard.

"Mr. Aramis, this artistic ability of yours—was it inherited from one of your parents?"

When he looked down, she feared the question had been too intrusive.

"I'll never know the answer to that," he said, looking back up. "My parents worked almost every waking hour. If they possessed any talent at all, it was wasted."

"Where were you raised?"

"On a small vineyard in France, just east of Bordeaux."

"My family and I just recently returned from that very area! Had I only known—we could have paid a visit to your vineyard and perhaps even sampled some of your wine."

He did not return her smile, but instead glanced down and muttered, "If you would have stepped foot on that property, you would never have escaped."

She looked with curiosity at him.

"I apologize," he said. "I don't wish to bore you with dull and unimportant accounts."

"Not at all. I would like to hear of your early life…if I'm not intruding, that is."

"Not many children are blessed with such agreeable parents as you seem to have inherited, Miss Winterfield. There were only two children in my family—a fact that disappointed my parents. They married and purchased a vineyard in the hopes that many sons would bless the union to assist them in the vineyard."

"A trade and business that can be passed on to one's children is a noble goal," Catherine suggested.

"Yes, of course, and all would have turned out, but that their first child did not arrive for four years and was a daughter. To make matters worse, they were not blessed with another child—me—for a full nine years after that."

"What a coincidence. My twin brothers are nine years my senior, as well."

"Is that a fact?" A smile dusted his expression. "I hope to find many such coincidences as we come to know each other."

Feeling heat rise to her face, Catherine turned away just in time to see her dog bound into the water after a duck.

"Scotch, no!" she called, jumping to her feet and running to the water's edge.

Through John, word arrived the following day from Antoine requesting that Catherine join him again, this time for a stroll. John agreed to accompany them and walked with Catherine to the place they were to meet the Frenchman.

"What do you know of Mr. Aramis' family?" Catherine asked.

"He doesn't speak of them unless I ask," John answered, "and when he does, it's always in the past tense. His parents must be dead."

"What has he said about them?"

"That his father was a bitter and oppressive man who would hire seasonal vinedressers and harvesters only to refuse to pay them. He said his clearest recollections of childhood are of the workers arguing with his father. He and his sister were apparently driven like workhorses, sunup to sundown, with brief periods for schoolwork late into the night."

"How monstrous!"

"At the age of eighteen, his sister eloped with the son of a neighbor who was much older than she. They stayed in France, but moved far away. Antoine was nine years old at the time."

"Did he ever hear from her again?"

"He said she attempted to contact him several times over the years, but that his parents burned her letters right before his eyes. He believed she wanted to take him away and raise him herself. A couple of her letters reached him when his parents were out. He claims to still have them."

"Did he ever try to write her back?"

"Several times, he said. He claims all but possibly one of the letters were discovered and destroyed."

"It's a wonder he has any love at all for the vineyard."

"He's never known anything else." He shrugged. "Caring for the grapes is the only skill he has."

Catherine looked away, her heart filled with pain for this man she barely knew. Of course, his most prominent skill was his painting. But she knew, as Antoine must have as well, that even a talent as great as his would have little chance of bringing him steady pay.

"So how is it you wound up in England?" Catherine asked of Antoine as their stroll commenced.

John walked ahead, stooping to grab stones from the pathway and pitching them into the forest.

"I..." His hesitation told her that her question had caught him off guard.

"Please forgive me. It's not my intention to pry."

"No, no. As my employer, you are entitled to an answer... to any question you wish."

"Please." She stopped and touched his arm. "What I wish is that you view me as your equal."

He lowered his head. She saw a sad smile tinge his lips and disappear.

"I must be out of my mind—to have started this friendship, I mean. We are worlds apart, no matter what either of us may wish. I guess I've so enjoyed your company that I haven't given much thought to anything else."

"Thank you." She felt her cheeks redden and wanted to tell him that his grace far surpassed many men she knew in her social class—foremost Gregory Westcliffe. Mr. Aramis fascinated her. She longed to know everything about him. *How* had he endured such harsh treatment by his father? What finally made him leave France? How did he get away? But perhaps it was too soon to talk of personal matters. "Please know that I would never wish to cause you discomfort by broaching painful subjects."

"Not at all. To answer your question, at the age of eighteen I grasped an opportunity to relocate to England. I met Mr. Marlon in London, and he offered me work here on your estate. That was five years ago. I suppose you could say here is where I found my 'happily ever after.'"

She laughed aloud, and the two hurried ahead to catch up with John.

Two days later, the trio explored the third floor of a museum in town. Catherine wandered back to John and seated herself upon a hard bench beside him.

He had been watching visitors stroll among the exhibits. They would stop to admire each sculpture and read about it. Some would stay several minutes, while a brief scan satisfied others.

The most noteworthy visitor in Catherine's mind stood at some distance, sketching upon a pad. He circled around a Michelangelo, stopped to draw, and circled again.

"He's magnificent," Catherine whispered to John.

"It's just a statue." John grinned.

"*Mr. Aramis*, silly! Go take a look at what he's doing," she nudged John.

"I know what he's doing. I've seen nearly all his work back at the vineyard, remember?"

"The top sketch of the sculpture is just a guise," she said, trying to keep quiet. "The real artwork is coming to life on the page beneath. He just sketched that woman in the feathered hat. You should see it—a mirror wouldn't reflect as lifelike an image. Where's he going?"

"I don't know."

Their gazes followed Antoine as he moved toward the woman in the hat. Tearing the second sheet from his pad, he presented it to her. The woman responded with a gasp of amazement. After a few quiet words, he bowed his head and moved away. The woman ran to a man in the room and showed it to him, all the while pointing at Antoine. Catherine watched the man pull a few coins from his pocket and approach Antoine.

When offered the money, Antoine's hand rose in objection. "A gift," she heard him say as he walked away.

Catherine's jaw dropped. She turned toward John and saw his astonishment.

Antoine stopped, gazed for a moment at another patron, and began to draw again. The next portrait, she knew, had already begun taking shape.

"Miss Winterfield, I cannot go on deceiving you."

The words came from the lips of Antoine as he dropped onto the blanket beside Catherine.

He and John had been fishing at the little lake on the Winterfield property, while she sat and read.

For the fifth day in a row, the three had shared an evening meal together by the water. It had become their favorite place of meeting.

She appreciated the way John tried his best to stay at a distance while always remaining in her sight.

"Deceiving me?"

"The other day—you asked how it was I ended up here in England."

"Allow me to confess first, Mr. Aramis. John has told me a bit about your adverse childhood. But don't be alarmed. I am comfortable leaving it at that…if it's what you wish, that is."

"I enjoy your company." He put his hand out and covered one of hers. "Very much. And I want you to know the truth."

She looked at his hand over hers, desiring nothing more than to turn hers up and grasp it; but she remained still.

"My upbringing is shameful to me, as you can imagine," he continued. "However, what is more shameful is not how I lived that life, but how I left it."

She sat in silence. With the evening now well along, the descending sun blazed behind the trees across the lake.

"As John no doubt explained, I was nothing more than a prisoner in my father's vineyard. With my sister gone many years before, I began plotting my own escape when I became sixteen."

Catherine looked into his face. "How did you do it?"

"With the help of one of the servants, I hid cases of wine and sold them right under the watchful but unsuspecting eye of my father. By the time I reached eighteen, I had saved enough to sustain myself for a while—wherever I was bound."

"You hadn't planned where you would go?"

"Anywhere was better than there. One night, the opportunity to leave presented itself. Knowing I might never have another chance, I left right from the field where I had hidden the money." His hand pulled away from hers, and he looked out across the water. "My clothes were ragged and dirty. I was exhausted from the day's work. The servant helped me steal one of my father's horses. By daybreak I arrived at the loading dock in LeHavre, where I could sail from France. After inquiring, I located a ship whose destination was England. Without being detected, I boarded the ship and hid among the cargo, where I fell asleep."

"You must have been exhausted."

"When I awoke, I found the ship was docked and in the process of unloading. Making a dash for the exit, I was caught by one of the shipmates. He held me tight until the captain could be summoned. All the while I fought the restraint, and as the captain approached, I freed myself. My shirt collar and sleeve were torn in the process, but I escaped." His gaze turned downward. "I know what I did was illegal. But I remember the name of that ship and the face of her captain. That man doesn't realize the great debt I owe him. Although unwittingly so, he gave my life back to me. I vowed then to repay him."

"Perhaps someday you'll have the opportunity."

"Actually, I've been to the docks before, looking. But I have yet to find his ship. I want you to know that I have repaid my father—within my first year of working here, in fact—every frank I stole."

"Borrowed."

"What?" he asked, his eyes searching her face.

"What you took from your father was merely borrowed. But what he took from you can never be repaid."

"Yes," he said. "Happiness, security."

"Your very childhood—snatched from you," she finished. "As far as I can tell, *he's* the one carrying the debt."

"Oh, thank you." He let out his breath, a broad grin overtaking his face. "I was afraid you wouldn't understand."

"So, what of your sister? Have you seen her?"

"I've had no desire to return to France. England is my home now. We correspond by mail. In her letters she sounds happy in her marriage and has a family of her own. She is relieved to know I finally escaped the miserable existence we shared. Perhaps someday she will bring her family here on holiday."

"So you've not seen Damica since the age of nine," Catherine reasoned. Tears pooled in her eyes. She could not bear to think how she would have endured had she been denied either of her brothers in a similar manner. Grief for him poured from her heart for the loving family of which he had been deprived.

His fingertips touched her cheek. "Don't sorrow for me. What I've gained far surpasses any loss."

"How?"

"Without even realizing it, my father trained me to be a hard worker. He taught me strength—physically *and* mentally. Those are valuable possessions."

"Indeed."

"But it's much different working in a vineyard where one is valued and respected. I've learned a deep appreciation for wine-making. Now I can say that working in the vineyard is more than a love of mine; it's a strong passion."

"John says you speak of your parents in the past tense. Have they since died?"

"Five years later, I know not how they've fared. When I rode off their property that August night, I vowed never to look back. Never again would my parents dictate my life. There they stay in the past, becoming ever more distant with each passing year."

She watched his eyes and in them found the strength he had described. Looking up, she saw the moon rising over the treetops, its light setting the ripples of the lake into silvery motion that reached out to caress her senses.

The respect and admiration she felt for Antoine Aramis solidified in her heart that night.

Chapter Twelve

"I bid you a farewell, Miss Viana," stated a smiling Preston Sutton. He removed his hat and bowed low before her. "I can truly say I've enjoyed your company on our many outings. I'll be forever agonizing your departure."

"Really, Mr. Sutton." Alexandra giggled at the young man's ever-present theatrical character. "It's I who will be in want of your presence, for who will be there to guide my ventures as you have this past week?"

Indeed, she would miss the fun-loving Preston Sutton. As he was the lone soul available the majority of the time, Alexandra, though with hesitation at first, accepted his invitation to go sailing on the new yacht whilst he and his crew perfected their skills for the upcoming race. His energetic personality had quickly grown on her, and before long she was quite at ease in his company.

Most people's guard soon vanished upon experiencing his good nature, she observed. The man had not a single pretense and relentlessly teased those who did. To her knowledge, he had been the one man who could overstep the boundaries of politeness and, rather than offending, find himself with yet another new friend. He seemed to collect friends like a child collects seashells in a bucket on the beach. And he relished in the company of each and every one.

More than once, she had noticed various women attempt to flirt with the handsome and gregarious young man. She watched the attempts fail each time. Whether he ignored their advances with purposeful intent or misunderstood in simple innocence, Alexandra did not know. But he seemed to talk himself out of each one the way he talked himself out of commitment to his father and brother.

Nor had he outright flirted with *her*. Yet more than once she had noted a different look in his eyes when he glanced in her direction. But he had said nothing, and she paid no heed, preferring to enjoy their adventurous outings together. By the end of the week, she looked forward to relaxing once again at the Winterfield manor.

Her sister and nephew were also present to bid her goodbye, and she embraced and kissed them both. Within moments, seated in an open-air carriage, she felt the summer breeze on her skin. Reliving the activities with Preston Sutton that were now simple memories, she felt saddened to realize they would soon fade into the distant past. Would her new friend be at the Winterfield Ball in July, she wondered?

The thought of the upcoming dance carried her thoughts back to Catherine and the perplexing situation with Mr. Westcliffe. Her dear friend simply could not marry that man.

How could she help Catherine understand that in just four short weeks?

Chapter Thirteen

On the deck of *The Emerald*, Roman and Andrew Winterfield met in a warm embrace under the guarded eye of Jessica Winterfield. Their last meeting, over two years previous, had been pleasant enough; Roman's smile had even seemed genuine when he congratulated them on the day of their marriage.

Yet, try as she might to forget them, as she now studied his face, some of the words he had hurled at her in the more distant past flooded back into her mind as though they had been spoken yesterday: *I'm not a man to be mocked and will not tolerate ridicule from subordinates like you; your father is a coward, a liar, and a cheat! It's no wonder he has produced such a disrespectful and inconsiderate brood as you and your sisters;* and *Andrew often takes my advice, and my advice to him now is that he is not in love with you.*

Watching Roman's easy manner while conversing with her husband, she flushed in anger. No doubt Alexandra's letter would prove true. Arrogance flowed through this man like the veins in a slab of marble. And as marble was solid rock, so was the heart of Roman Winterfield.

Recalling the words of her father, she shuddered: *If he is interested in Alexandra, then we've not seen the last of him.*

He could not be in love with her sister; it simply was not possible. But why else would he be returning to Kent? Her dislike of her brother-in-law intensified the longer she glared at him.

After a few moments, Roman glanced over at her. He stepped forward and put both hands out. She reciprocated as a matter of courtesy. Taking both her hands, he leaned over to place a gentle kiss on her cheek. He glanced into her eyes.

"We need not address one another so formally now." He smiled. His eyes appeared genuine, but she refused to throw caution aside. "I'm truly pleased to see you again, Jessica," he continued. "You look very well." Still holding her hands, he glanced over at his brother. "Indeed, my brother has an exceptional eye for beauty."

"Thank you," Jessica replied, wondering whether he detected her reluctance to accept his words as truth.

"I understand congratulations are in order," Roman said, "not for the two of you alone, but for the entire Winterfield family. But I must say I'm having difficulty picturing myself as an uncle."

Jessica almost laughed at the vision. How, indeed, would Roman Winterfield appear with a baby bouncing upon one knee?

"I'm happy for you both," he added.

Would there be no end to the thoughtful words? Surely, he could not keep up the façade for much longer.

"Roman, I realize you have sailed on *The Emerald* before," Jessica said, determined not to be overtaken by flattery and the appearance of a few good manners, "but I would like to state in plainness to you that this ship is now under lease by my father." Her words were kind, yet stern. "There are no longer any free rides. We're facing a long journey and are short-handed. We'll need your assistance."

"Now there's the Jessica Vian—" Roman began, "Winterfield, I remember." He gave her an indulgent smile. "I believe I've not lost my sailing skills." Tossing a look his brother's way, he continued, "I'll follow the commands of the captain."

"Please relax for an hour or two, Roman," Andrew said. "I'll call for you when I need you."

Roman bowed his head when Jessica and Andrew excused themselves.

* * * * *

Watching the two as they turned and walked separate ways, Roman felt pleased with the way he had conducted himself—as a true gentleman would have, he thought.

A folded paper on the deck caught his eye when it fluttered in the wind. Reaching for it, he saw words written in a woman's hand. About to call out to Jessica to return the letter, he stopped short upon a glimpse of the closing sentiment on the bottom of the page. He thought only for a moment before tucking the letter into his pocket.

Though it was unscrupulous to read a private document, he had to know its contents, for the two words he saw were, *Yours, Alexandra.*

Roman returned to his stateroom, the cabin previously occupied by the first mate. A large mirrored wardrobe, bolted against one wall, separated two narrow bunks. Above one bed a small window emitted light into the simple, yet comfortable quarters, and a desk sat against the wall opposite the wardrobe.

Roman paced, folded his arms, paced again, and stopped to tap his foot on the floorboards, looking back at the letter he had placed on the desk. He ran his fingers through his dark hair and finally reached for the letter.

He smiled upon reading the first few sentences. Alexandra's face, brilliant under the French sun, returned to his memory as he read her expressions of appreciation for the places they had visited.

But as the following paragraph began, the pace of his heart quickened. He had expected to read of himself in the letter, but not like this.

Her words cut through him like a sword. *His arrogance and heartless mannerisms have returned with even greater force, I believe.*

Wincing, he closed his eyes. The words he had blurted to the girl in the restaurant clanged through his mind. Returning to the letter, he could almost hear the disappointment in her voice over his relationship with his sister. Would his treatment of Catherine have differed had he been aware of Alexandra's attention upon him? Had it ever differed?

He read on. *Roman Winterfield remains obstinate and self-centered.*

His hand dropped. He threw his head back and shook it in shame. The evaluation was fair. Although it pained him to read any more of her words, he returned to the letter. She had moved on to other topics, and he read about the Frenchman who had caught her attention. It was obvious she had spent a large portion of their last day with the young man. After all, was it not he who had escorted her to the café that evening?

Roman folded the letter and slipped it back into his pocket. It seemed her mind was made up. He pondered for a moment about the young French tour guide. Stepping to the wardrobe, he studied his reflection in the mirror. Were one to judge by appearance alone, he was fair competition. However, in social graces and the art of conversation, he could not match the suave mannerisms of the French.

The words of Alexandra's letter said all he needed to know: His obstinacy and selfishness were nothing short of repelling.

Later that evening, as Jessica prepared to retire for the night, she discovered the letter from her sister sitting on the desk in their stateroom. Strange...she seemed to recall that it had been in her pocket. Unable to account for its presence there, she shrugged and climbed into bed.

Extinguishing the candle at her bedside, she pulled the cotton sheet up under her chin. Andrew would be eager to spend some time with his brother. She was certain he would retire much later.

Though still a bit early, she was exhausted from the trip. She closed her eyes and surrendered to the downy cradle of her featherbed and pillow, happy once again to be rocked to sleep by the waves of the ocean. Because of spending much of the previous two years on the ship, she had become fully agreeable to her husband's love of life on the sea.

Twilight spread while the last glint of sunlight faded from the waters on the horizon. Andrew found Roman, one foot propped up, resting his elbows on the railing.

"So who are you and what have you done with my brother?" Andrew watched his twin turn his gaze from the sea to him.

Roman gave him a broad grin and a look of genuine brotherhood. Even though their personalities were as opposite as the sand and the sea, Andrew had long ago learned to appreciate the closeness they shared and to tolerate their differences. Like the sands of a deserted beach, he himself was quiet and composed. Roman, on the other hand, often exhibited the agitated restlessness of a churning sea. Why could his brother not be more even-tempered, content? What was it he craved about gaining admiration and glory from others?

Andrew stooped to drop an unlit lantern onto the deck before positioning himself beside Roman at the railing.

"I'm sure I don't know what you're talking about," Roman said in answer to his question.

"I'd like to state that this ship is under lease by my father," he said, repeating his wife's earlier words. "There are no longer any free rides. We're short-handed and will need your help." Andrew looked over at his brother. "Now, I *know* how my brother would have responded to that command."

"Please." Roman held a palm up. "Don't keep me in suspense."

In the fading light Andrew stood tall, placed his arms across his chest, and wrinkled his brow. "Apparently, madam, you understand little of the honor and privilege of bearing the Winterfield name. It would be an insult to my forefathers to engage in the work of a deck hand. Your manner of jesting is truly offensive. Furthermore, if you choose to mingle with the laborers of this ship, I must abolish you from my association."

Andrew finished the impersonation and relaxed against the railing. Had his brother, perhaps for the first time in his life, viewed the way he had appeared to others all these years? He hoped so, as he had never before spoken to him with such directness. But who better than his twin to mimic him? And who else could do it so accurately?

"Well, then," Roman responded, "I did society a favor by eliminating your brother. Was he really as bad as all that?"

"I fear that would have been a mild response. But then you surprised me two years ago when you stood in support of John Viana—and against your own society, no less. I've never been more proud to be your brother than I was that night. And now your obvious changes continue to astound me."

A low groan escaped Roman's throat.

Andrew ignored the confirmation of what his brother's behavior must have been over the last two years.

"Despite this transformation, I find you somewhat...troubled. Will you ever find happiness?" He hesitated. "If only there was another Jessica for you."

"No! Were I to marry a woman like her, we'd both find ourselves in the grave by year's end. She's an unusually fiery one."

"I suppose you're right, but then who, dear brother? Who would be fit to complement the infamous Roman Winterfield? Perhaps the opposite of Jessica—a timid and gentle type?"

"I don't think so. An overbearing personality such as mine would soon dominate such a woman. We would both sink into an abyss of misery and regret."

"Then perhaps you would be happy with a woman of self-confidence and pride, a woman in control of everyone and everything, a woman of the world."

"Ah, a woman in my likeness..." Roman laughed, but without humor. "When I first met your wife, she described the woman of my choice in an identical way. I had to agree with her then. But now I see things so differently. I pity the woman who has allowed herself to be conquered by such a narrow-minded and self-centered view. A woman like that would drive me to insanity, as I would see in her every day the person I have come to despise—me."

"Then what, Roman? What would make you happy?" With caution Andrew added, "Scripture insists that the only road to true happiness is found through the unselfish giving of oneself to others." He paused. Roman did not respond. "I apologize. That was harsh."

"Not at all. It seems the only gift I have given anyone is a headache."

Andrew laughed. "In the past perhaps. But I see a glimmer of hope in you, Roman."

"Did Father tell you of the conversation he and I had just three months prior to your engagement party?"

The moon had begun its ascent over the eastern horizon as a stiff breeze swept across the deck of the ship.

"He mentioned it, but didn't share the particulars."

"He said that I had elevated myself so high above the general populace that I had found myself completely 'friendless.' That was the word he used, I believe."

Andrew laughed at his father's deduction. "And how did you react?"

"I left his office in a fit of rage." With a clenched fist he turned and took a step away from the railing. "After all, was I not Roman Winterfield—a man who commanded the attention of all? Was I not surrounded by admirers, the topic of every conversation and every whispered secret? Would not women gloat over me and adorn me with compliments? And men, young and old alike—would they not hang on my every word and grope for my advice? I may not have been in politics, Andrew, but I was in *power*."

Andrew watched his twin with curiosity. Was he seeing a glimpse of the brother he knew?

"I was at the top," Roman continued. "I looked up to no one, but expected everyone to look up to me. That was my view. But I had not assessed the situation properly, for there were two men who had always stood above me, though I had refused to see it all those years. One of them was my father. In one brief moment—with a word—he brought me down like a single bolt of lightning fells a mighty tree. It was almost a full three months later—three months of agony and seething anger—before I realized what I had become. He was right! I had not one friend in this vast sea we call humanity. Not one. Those who gloated over me were not my friends. How could they be my friends, when I knew nothing about them? I was so consumed with myself that I talked of nothing else. They feared me, Andrew, but they did not befriend me."

In fascination bordering on disbelief, Andrew listened to his brother's pain unfold.

"Later it hit me like a stone in the head: my father was the most valuable person in my life. In that one conversation, he proved himself my true friend. But above all, he showed me that he had been my superior all along. What I still did not understand, however, was what I was to do with that information. How was I to change? I had been let on the loose for so long that I knew not how to reverse my course. So I stayed on that course...and I stayed away. For two years I saw little of anyone. Only in recent weeks have I begun to get a glimpse of just how to make those changes. I'm determined now, Andrew. I will find happiness."

"I believe you will, Roman. I'm proud of your effort. Tell me, how long will you be in Kent?"

"Several weeks, I hope."

"And what is the dynamic force that has brought Roman Winterfield back to his family?"

Roman hesitated before speaking. "Actually...a woman."

"*What*? You just said there is no woman for you."

"She's not for me, but one with whom I hope to become re-acquainted, if she will allow it now, and one whom I hope in all sincerity to guide in a direction other than the one she seems to be taking at present." He paused. "She's none other than our sister."

"I don't understand."

"An...acquaintance...has helped me to see that I have neglected her for the entirety of her life. It's important now to me to establish a friendship with her and thereby gain the trust she should have had in me all along. I wish to be the brother and protector I should have been from her youth."

"Your intentions are admirable, brother."

"Let us hope I'm not too late."

They talked for a few minutes more in the growing darkness. Andrew crouched to light the wick of the lantern.

"I'm sorry I must end what's been the most meaningful conversation we've ever had, Roman," Andrew said, "but my ship demands my attention. Besides, we'll both be rising early." He turned to leave, then stopped. "Roman, you said two men stood above you. Who was the other man?"

"None other than you, Andrew. I'm just sorry I required nearly three decades to discern that."

Andrew stared at him in silence until Roman turned and walked away.

"Who are you?" he called after him.

Chapter Fourteen

Winterfield Manor prepared for four special dinner guests. The house buzzed with anticipation. Olivia Winterfield, shadowing the servants who dressed the immense dining room table, barked commands. Alexandra peered into the hall with its barrel-vaulted ceiling and intricate tapestries. Although only nine would be present for the meal—ten if her two-year-old nephew were counted—Olivia insisted on her best pair of silver candelabras from Paris, an enormous fresh flower centerpiece, and crystal chalices.

"Excuse me." Three servants shuffled past Alexandra, burdened by stacks of china. On a previous visit, she had seen the basement room framed with one glass cupboard after another filled with china sets by the dozens, all adorned with unique patterns, some from as far as the Orient. She wondered which pattern suited Mrs. Winterfield's fancy for the special occasion of entertaining her son, Andrew. His presence had been a rare occurrence in recent years. Indeed, it was a special evening.

Stephen and Grace Sutton were welcomed first. Everyone gloated over the blue-eyed baby, Everett, who tagged along so that his aunt Jessica could see him.

Alexandra reveled in the gathering that took place in the entry hall. Seven happy voices resounded throughout the vestibule and sunken indoor garden.

Soon the clinking harnesses of a second carriage announced the arrival of Jessica and Andrew. At the sound, Alexandra hurried out the front door, followed by the remaining party.

She ran to where her brother-in-law had already disembarked. "Andrew!" When he turned to her, she threw her arms around his neck.

Rather than reciprocate the embrace, he barely touched her with his hand before releasing her.

Puzzled, she backed away and gasped. She stood face to face with not Andrew, but *Roman* Winterfield!

All smiles, he did not avert his gaze from hers when he reached for her hand and pulled it to his lips.

"A pleasure to be in your company once again, Miss Viana."

"Likewise," she said, her voice stunted in a whisper.

In his fleeting stare did she detect a touch of sentiment? His thumb stroked the tops of her fingers. An instant later, he released her hand and stepped away. Still feeling the dampness of his kiss on her hand, she found herself looking into the suspicious eyes of Jessica, whose glare shifted for just a moment toward Roman before focusing again on Alexandra.

"Jessie!" Alexandra melted into her sister's arms. "How I've missed you."

"And I, you," Jessica said, squeezing her close.

"It's so good to hear your voice." Alexandra eased back to study her sister's face, finding no more suspicion in her blue eyes, just the look of soft fondness which she had grown accustomed to seeing over the years.

"Alex, how I long for the times of our childhood. If only I were not away so much."

"But think, Jess, soon we'll all be together at Muir Ceann. We'll make endless new memories then."

Grace approached. The sisters embraced in laughter.

"Andrew!" Alexandra exclaimed when he stepped from the carriage and flung herself into his arms.

She glanced over to watch Roman place a kiss on the cheek of his surprised mother, followed by one for his sister.

Thereafter, he returned to slap one hand around his brother's shoulder, and the party ascended the steps to the mahogany doors of the mansion.

Jessica smiled with relief to see Roman and Alexandra seat themselves on opposite ends of the table, and she noticed no further interaction between them. During the first course of the meal, he kept himself engrossed in conversation with his sister and father.

When Alexandra's attention had been commandeered by John, Jessica leaned toward Grace, who sat beside her.

"Did you notice the manner of greeting Roman gave Alex?" she said in an undertone.

"What is he even doing here?" Grace whispered.

"He surprised us as well when he telegrammed that he'd be joining us on the ship. We hadn't the opportunity to wire the rest of you in warning."

"Well, I suppose it doesn't much matter. He hasn't caused any trouble yet. However, he's been here no more than thirty minutes. I'm certain it's just a matter of time."

"I don't know about that, Grace. I've been in his close proximity often over the past several days—though I've tried to avoid him as much as possible—but I have yet to experience any unpleasant behavior on his part."

"What do you make of it, Jessie?"

"I cannot account for his good manners. I'm in utter perplexity."

"One thing alone is certain," Grace said, "that of his being unable to keep up the pretense for much longer. What were you starting to say about Alex?"

"His greeting to her, Grace." Jessica looked about, certain they were alone in their conversation. "Try as I might, I can't forget something Father said when we were together in Germany."

Grace smiled at her husband, who looked curious as to their quiet chatter. She leaned closer to Jessica when Stephen resumed his conversation with Andrew.

L. Katherine Dailey

"Tell me, Jessie."

"Father suspects that Roman may be attracted to Alex," Jessica said.

Grace broke into a coughing fit, choking on the sip she had taken from her glass. Jessica jumped and began patting her back.

"Are you all right, Darling?" Stephen started to rise from his chair, but Grace waved him back down. The entire table sat poised to attend to her.

"I'm—" she said coughing once more, "I'm all right, I assure you...I seem to have swallowed wrong." Jessica reached for a flute of clear water, which Grace drained. "Thank you."

Convinced of her recovery, the others eased back into their conversations.

"Jessie," Grace said in the quiet tone they had assumed prior to the disruption, "Father can't be serious."

"That's what I thought...until Roman's telegram arrived. Father said we'd probably not seen the last of him if his assumption were right. But it's not Roman's sudden appearance that's disturbing. It's no surprise that any man would be attracted to Alex. She's nothing short of stunning, and grows more so by the day."

"Then what's so troubling?"

"Alex's reaction to *him*. She wrote me a letter when she was with him in France. In it she gave details about his abhorrent behavior. She was ashamed and disgusted. Yet her greeting to him this very evening was so natural, so easy, as though she were pleased to see him again."

"Yes, she embraced him, Jess!"

"She *did*?"

"I think it was an accident. She backed away quickly when she saw it was not Andrew."

"Goodness! I didn't see that, but...but she still seemed happy to see him."

"You know Alex, Jessie. She's kind to everyone she meets, even when their treatment of her is less than civil. It's just her temperament."

"Perhaps you're right. Being on guard for her, I must have sensed something that wasn't there."

"I'm sure that's the case. Besides, there are some developments I think you'll find interesting. I'll relate them to you later," she said in a whisper.

Jessica looked to the opposite end of the table at the subject himself. Roman talked with his father, a comfortable smile settling over his face. Though satisfied with the peace she had found with him for the time being, the shield covering her heart thickened as she considered the possibility of her sister's involvement.

Roman dropped his head back in laughter. Jessica was a bit startled when his eyes fixed upon her. She lifted her chin as he lifted his glass to her, a coy look of confidence settling into his eyes.

A moment later his attention returned to his father.

Just what was he up to?

Chapter Fifteen

"Alex, I'm so excited to finally have some time alone with you," Catherine said, slipping into her room later that night. "You won't believe the events of the past few days since you've been gone." Catherine plopped herself onto the feather comforter that had been folded onto the bottom of the bed.

A soothing quiet, like a blanket, had crept over the house. Alexandra sat at her dressing table pulling a comb through the ends of her chestnut hair.

"Tell me about it," she said and stepped to a set of doors leading to a modest balcony. Pushing them open, she allowed the cool breeze to ruffle her white nightgown.

"I think I'm falling in love, Alex."

"I'm glad you brought that up." Rubbing the sudden goose bumps from her arms, Alexandra sat beside her friend and tucked one knee beneath her gown. "We need to talk. There are some things you should know about Mr. Westcliffe."

"Not *him*, Alex. Mr. Aramis!"

"Whatever happened?"

"That's what I've been dying to tell you. John and I have been spending much time with him. We've had such wonderful outings."

"Where?"

"Here, on the property. At the lake. In the meadow. Strolling the grounds. He's...wonderful. Did you know he's an artist?"

"I had no idea."

"He painted a picture with us in it, Alex, before we ever met him."

"Did he?"

"You were right, Alex. He does like me."

"Oh, Catherine!" Alexandra covered her mouth at her exclamation. She ran to close the balcony doors. "How did this start? When?"

"This week. I stumbled upon him one afternoon...evening really." She fell back onto the bed, flinging her arms wide. "I've seen him every evening since, except tonight. How I wish he could have been a part of our dinner this evening. I think he would like both my brothers. Oh, but Alex," she pushed herself up on one hand and stared wide-eyed, "how will I ever break the news that I've fallen for one of father's servants? I dread the day he discovers the truth. It can't be long. Gossip will spread like wildfire through the servant body. But I can't stop that, can I? Therefore, I don't care." She giggled and jumped up to dash to the balcony doors. "What if he's out there right now, Alex? What if he's roaming the grounds outside the mansion in the hopes of meeting up with me? I'm going out!"

"Catherine, please. I must object. The darkness of midnight is no place for a woman to be strolling around alone."

"Then I'm going back to my room at once so I can fall asleep and dream of him." Stopping in the middle of the room, Catherine twirled around once and skipped to the door. "Good night, Alex." She blew her a kiss and after a giggle, disappeared into the darkened hallway.

Alexandra stared at the closed door.

"Oh, dear. How in the world will Mr. Westcliffe react to this report?" she whispered to no one.

Alexandra lay awake, moonlight cutting across her bed in a streak. It was quiet, too quiet. She longed for the sound of the sea—the lullaby that had rocked her to sleep during her childhood. Even a fog horn would be welcome this night.

Visions of Roman played through her mind. More than once she had glanced up to meet his stare. He looked away each time, but she lingered in her inspection of him. She recalled his conflicting behavior toward her at the one meal they had shared alone the night prior to their leaving France. His reason for arranging the meal remained a mystery. And what had brought him back to Kent?

She assumed his entire personality would, as well, remain a mystery.

Knowing full well her questions would go unanswered, she tried to erase him from her mind. But her thoughts of him persisted. His lips had been so gentle on her hand. And those penetrating dark eyes...had he been trying to tell her something by the look he gave her?

Despite his perplexing mannerisms and offensive past, she had to admit that his was the most handsome of faces.

The families met for breakfast the following morning. Alexandra feared everyone would note the shadows beneath her eyes. She had not fallen asleep until nearly three.

The morning was peaceful and cool, and Alexandra greeted all but Richard and Olivia in the indoor garden where a light meal awaited them.

"Where are your parents?" she asked of Catherine.

"They've gone to the warehouse for the day."

"I see."

After a quick curtsey in greeting to Roman, Alexandra avoided his eyes. She did not want anyone thinking she had a growing regard for the man—most of all not him.

To her surprise and delight, after breakfast Roman suggested that the party take the horses out for a ride. Everyone agreed save Jessica and Grace, who preferred a stroll on foot.

* * * * *

The horses kept within view of the two pedestrians, Andrew a bit closer than the others as he had insisted on taking his fair-haired nephew upon his horse.

"Andrew, take care," Jessica called out.

"Don't worry yourself, Jessie," Grace said. "Andrew's got a tight hold on him."

"He's a darling child, Grace," Jessica said.

Andrew coaxed the horse into a trot, and Jessica laughed to watch the baby's blonde curls bounce with the animal's stride.

"Andrew will be the best of fathers, Jess."

"I know he will. Mother always tells me I married a man who is much like my own father, so how could he be anything but? And he's becoming more and more accustomed to living on land. The further progress is made on the castle, the more attached he grows to it. It means so much to him to have a part in its construction. He'll teach our child the greatest aspects of both land and sea."

"You so unselfishly agreed to live at sea with him, Jessie, and look what blessings it has brought. Considering your earlier fear of the water, I am both surprised and impressed. How is it that you're so young, and yet you always make the best decisions?"

"You give me too much credit, Grace. But many of my decisions were made with the help of the best teacher—Father. I only hope Alex will live by his counsel."

"Concern yourself no longer, sister. Thus far my plans are moving in the intended direction."

"Plans?"

"The developments I told you about at dinner—she spent all last week with us, Jessie. I made myself unavailable much of the time, and her only other choice for social interaction was none other than Preston Sutton. They spent much time together. I think they like each other very much."

"Preston Sutton? I don't know much of your brother-in-law, Grace, but any choice is bound to be better than Roman Winterfield."

"I feel certain you would approve of him. He's a delightful person. I've made some further arrangements for the two to dine with us in the coming weeks. And, as you know, the Suttons have been invited to the Winterfield Ball next month." Grace closed her eyes for a moment to the warming sun. "No, Jess, you need not be concerned about Alex."

Jessica determined in her mind to learn more of Stephen's brother at the upcoming ball.

After darkness had fallen, Andrew and Jessica boarded the carriage that would deliver them to Chatham, where *The Emerald* awaited them. Alexandra joined the others in waving good-bye from the front porch. Just before the coachman flicked the reins, Alexandra ran to the coach.

"Oh, Jessie, I almost forgot to mention one thing."

Jessica stepped out to hear her sister in private.

"Jessie, the letter I sent to you through Mother—I realized later that my observations were all wrong."

"What do you mean, Alex?"

"Well, the handsome Frenchman I mentioned...I saw him again the same day after I wrote the letter."

"Oh?"

"Yes. He was not at all what I had assumed. I excused myself from him right after meeting him and did not see him again." She paused, wondering how to state what followed. "And the other man I mentioned..." She glanced toward the coach, concerned that Andrew might overhear the conversation.

"Yes, Alex?" Jessica's brows rose, acknowledging Alexandra's reference to Roman.

"I was wrong about him, too." What was she doing? Yet she felt compelled to be honest. "Although I remain puzzled about his behavior, I find that he has been very courteous since my writing the letter. I've been noticing some...well... some pleasing qualities in his mannerisms." She smiled at her sister's astonishment. "I just thought it would ease your mind to know that he's not all bad."

She kissed Jessica on the cheek and turned to run back to the house.

Chapter Sixteen

Two afternoons following, Roman approached Alexandra in the library.

"A package was just delivered. It seems it's for you." He held out a small square box. "Looks to be from France."

"France? What in the world..."

After handing the package to her, Roman left the room but stopped just outside the door. He peered around the frame to observe her as she opened it.

Tearing open the paper wrapping, she pulled a note card from inside. A wistful smile dusted across her lips when she read it. Folding the note, she tucked it into a pocket and pulled something from the box. Roman squinted. An object glimmered in her hand. Pulling both fists behind her neck, she stepped over to a mirror on one wall. When her hand moved away, he saw, dropping to dangle against her chest, what appeared to be a golden locket.

He stepped away from the doorframe and hastened across the rug in the tapestry gallery. Grabbing a pillow from a sofa along the way and hurling it hard onto a chase, Roman pictured the benefactor in his mind.

Frenchmen certainly knew how to entice a woman.

"We'll be having a special guest for dinner," Olivia Winterfield announced when Alexandra and Catherine entered the mansion. They had been out on a ride, Catherine in the hopes of meeting up with Mr. Aramis. She had been disappointed.

"Mother, won't you tell us who?" Catherine begged.

"You'll find out soon enough. Dinner is scheduled to commence in one hour. Where's Roman?"

"He left two hours ago, stating he had some business in town. He may not return before dinner."

"He'd better!" she hollered and strode from the room.

Roman did not fail his mother. Just before five, he walked through the front door and pulled his gloves finger by finger from his hands, his riding crop tucked beneath one arm.

Alexandra watched him from the indoor garden, where she had curled onto a lounge to read. He took no note of her presence. Raised in the country, she was unaccustomed to seeing men in dress shirts and waistcoats, with the rare exception of the dances. She supposed there was, indeed, something appealing about city living. And Roman Winterfield, above all men, lent such charm to his apparel, she had to admit.

"Good evening, Mr. Winterfield." A servant approached to take his gloves and hat.

"I've left the carriage out front," Roman said.

"Yes, sir. I'll summon Mr. Burton at once."

A rush of guilt surged through Alexandra to spy on him. She turned her eyes back to her book when Roman moved toward the wide column of the staircase tower.

"Roman!" Olivia appeared out of nowhere and dashed to meet him. He stopped at the foot of the staircase. "Darling, so glad you've returned. We're hosting a special guest for dinner. Hurry along and ready yourself."

"Who, Mother?"

She waved his comment aside and stepped away. "Six o'clock, Roman. Don't be late."

At six sharp the family gathered in the entryway to greet the guest. The servant who had helped Roman earlier with his hat opened the door to a lady in a keen blue jacket decorated with swirls of black braiding and satin lapels.

"Surprise!" the lady blurted, raising her hands.

Catherine shot a look at Alexandra and mouthed the words, "Oh, no."

Olivia stepped forward to greet the lady.

"It's Caroline Landly," Catherine whispered in a frenzy. "Oh, I should have suspected it. Mother has been attempting to match her with Roman for years now, but she's never been so bold as to invite her for something as intimate as dinner." Catherine put her hand over her eyes. "Poor Roman."

Alexandra's gaze darted back to Roman, who stood stunned. Had he forgotten the gentleman-like response of inviting her in?

"Well, Roman," the lady said, "are you going to force me to eat on the stoop tonight?"

"No...no. Please come in, Miss Landly."

The familiarity with which she addressed him seemed to make him uneasy, Alexandra noticed.

Richard Winterfield offered a greeting and introduced her to John and Alexandra. "And you remember our daughter," he added, holding a hand out to Catherine.

"Of course. Catrina, right?" Caroline said with an artificial smile, offering nothing else.

"My name is Catherine," she corrected.

Alexandra suspected the mistake was intentional. For a certainty, a woman so obviously enamored with Roman would know the name of his only sister.

With the discomfort of the introductions over, Alexandra followed the family into the parlor for drinks, lagging behind with Catherine and John.

"How is it she doesn't know your name?" John whispered.

"Because Caroline Landly has never before tonight uttered a single word to me."

"She's quite beautiful," Alexandra said. "And she seems so confident."

"Confident, indeed. She's mastered the attention of everyone—with the exception of Roman. It's my opinion that she sees him as a particular challenge because of his past indifference, something she's not accustomed to. But my mother can't seem to get enough of her."

"Why has she not yet married?" Alexandra asked.

"Married? Please," she answered in a whisper. "There's not a man alive who would brave the ivory staircase to *her* cloud."

John laughed at that.

Alexandra studied the stately woman from behind. Caroline Landly towered several inches above her. An elegant French roll the color of glowing sunshine twisted atop her head added to her height. Alexandra summed her up in a word: regal. It emanated in her stance, her walk, her voice, and even her smile. Her royal blue dress hugged her form down to the knee, where it flared in pleats to the ground.

"Olivia," Caroline said after admiring a carving on one of the shelves in the parlor, "it has been far too long since you've honored me as a guest in your magnificent home."

"I thought so myself and decided to change that," replied Olivia. She gave Roman a discreet nudge in the ribs.

"Miss Landly, do you prefer sherry or wine?" he offered.

"Oh, Roman, please call me Caroline. We've known each other long enough to be on a first-name basis. Do you not agree, Olivia?"

"Whatever you think best," Olivia answered.

Alexandra caught Richard Winterfield rolling his eyes.

"I would adore a glass of wine," Caroline said to Roman, "but I'll settle for nothing less than Winterfield's finest."

"Of course," Roman said. "Let us all enjoy a bottle of wine together."

Alexandra watched Roman throw a scowl his mother's way when he turned to speak with the servant. Olivia put her nose into the air, refusing to meet his glare.

Surely another test of Roman's manners loomed on the horizon. Would he fail again as he had in France?

From Alexandra's vantage point at the dinner table, she could see the faces of Roman, Olivia, and Caroline. She sat tall and folded her silk napkin across her lap.

A female servant placed bowls of steaming soup at each place.

"Olivia," piped Caroline, "I cannot tell you how pleased I was to receive your invitation. Rumors abound in the city that the Winterfield Estate boasts the finest chef in all of Kent."

"We'll let you be the judge of that." Olivia nodded, a slight smile on her lips.

"And I'll take my good report back to all my friends." She shot a glance at Roman. "I'll be the envy of London society. And how long do you intend to grace us with your presence in Kent, Roman?"

"At least through July. Catherine," he said, "that reminds me. I've a surprise for you. If you're not otherwise engaged, I'd like to take you to the racecourse tomorrow."

"Tomorrow?" Catherine beamed. "But, Roman, what will they think—a woman at the horse track?" She turned to Alexandra. "What a rift I'd cause in all of London." She crinkled her nose in a smile.

"On the contrary," Roman replied. "I've made arrangements for a trip, not to London, but to Ascot. You know it's a favorite time of year for every respectable lady. Of course, it will require a night's stay over."

Catherine bounced to the edge of her chair. "Oh, Roman, you know I've always wanted to go!"

Alexandra's heart warmed at the grin on her friend's face. Roman, too, appeared contented.

"Roman," his mother spoke up, "I'm sure Caroline would love to join you on the excursion."

Horror contorted Catherine's face. She cast a look at her brother that pleaded for mercy.

"Perhaps someday," Caroline said. "I'm sure Roman would enjoy the time with his sister much more were I not tagging along."

Perish the thought of spending an hour with "Catrina," Alexandra thought. *Much less two days.* Yes, her meaning had been clear. Catherine's expression told her the feeling was mutual.

"Besides," Caroline added, "I'm afraid I'm engaged tomorrow for the duration of the day on a shopping excursion with friends."

Alexandra could detect nothing but indifference in Roman's face. He seemed neither disappointed nor pleased. She wondered just what his feelings for Caroline would prove to be.

"Alex," Richard Winterfield implored. "I intended to tell you that I ran into Preston Sutton on the pier earlier today. He mentioned your name and raved on about your time together last week."

"Yes. I was privileged to sail with him on his new yacht."

"And how do you find Mr. Sutton's company?" he asked. "I understand you had not been much acquainted with him previously."

"That's correct," she replied. "I found him to be of a most pleasant sort, Mr. Winterfield."

"Many ladies do find pleasure in Preston Sutton," Caroline interrupted with a roll of her eyes. "However, I find his demeanor silly and his conversations, with few exceptions, an embarrassment."

"Well, then," Richard said, "I suppose it was a good thing I didn't inquire after *your* opinion on the matter."

"Miss Landly," Roman said, wiping his napkin across his lips after tasting the soup. He seemed oblivious to his father's comment. "While visiting Belgium in the fall, I believe I met someone who claims an acquaintance with you."

"That does not surprise me, Roman. You and I share a common love—traveling. In all honesty, I'm surprised we've not yet crossed paths abroad. I can't imagine who it might have been; I know so many through my travels. Do tell. I'm all ears."

"I was in attendance at a dinner and met a Hungarian Count."

"Cecil!" Caroline exclaimed. "My dear man, how is he? I had the honor of meeting him two years ago. So learned is he, a true man of the world. What did he say of me? Did he sing my praises? He's impressed with my collection of fine art, which

I was once privileged to share with him and his wife by way of a personal viewing. Did he tell you of my 'excellencies,' as he says?"

"Indeed he did."

Alexandra fidgeted with the spoon in her soup, feeling no bigger than a mouse. Imagine—*a count*. Good heavens, what their connections must be! So many balls and parties Roman must attend all over Europe—with royalty of all sorts. How she wished she could slip away from the table and hide in her room. Whatever was she doing here? Looking over at her brother, she felt her brow tense. He shrugged and dived into the soup, pulling his bread apart and shoving a morsel into his mouth.

"Oh, but I don't mean to ignore your sister, Roman," Caroline said, turning her attention to Catherine. "You needn't tell me of your singing talent, dear, for rumor has it you have the voice of an angel. I would love to hear you after dinner."

A color matching the beets on her plate washed over Catherine's face. "Perhaps you'd prefer to listen to my friend on the pianoforte. I'll hear her often, as she will be my guest here for the summer."

"For the summer?" Caroline asked, assessing Alexandra. "Is that a fact? What did you say your name is?"

"Viana. Alexandra Viana."

"Now there's a familiar name—Viana—but from where do I know it?"

As Caroline pondered the matter, Alexandra shrugged, feigning ignorance about the recent reappearance of her father in London society and the negative light that had been cast upon him.

"Tell me of your accomplishments," Caroline said, her tone taking on an edge of superiority. "Do you sing, like your friend? Are you a reader?"

"I have many interests," Alexandra answered, "and know a little about numerous topics."

"She never boasts about herself," said Catherine, "but Alexandra is a lady of many fine talents. Tell her about the languages you've studied, Alex."

"Ah, language," Caroline said, "the art of the mind and tongue. You must be a world traveler yourself, for to know language without the benefit of using it in its place of origin is to stroke a cashmere sweater with a gloved hand."

Alexandra placed her spoon on the table and laced her fingers together.

"Well, are you?" Caroline leaned forward.

"Am I what?" Alexandra asked.

"A traveler, of course."

"I've left England on occasion, as when I had the privilege of touring Germany last year and France…just last month." She took her fork, picking at the salad that had been placed before her.

"Hmm…" Caroline's wisp of a smile mocked Alexandra. She sipped soup from her spoon and turned again to Mrs. Winterfield. "Olivia, I have the most delicious report out of London."

"Yes," Catherine said, appearing happy to move the focus from Alexandra and herself, "a little gossip would be fun."

"I am not a gossip," Caroline snapped. "Gossip is for the women who chase pigs around the yard and meet at the community clothesline for the latest whispers of the town drunk. Newsy is what I am. There *is* a difference, Catrina."

Alexandra almost dropped her fork. She looked at Roman, who had not met her gaze since Caroline had stepped into the house.

"My sister meant no insult, Miss Landly," he said. "Please tell us of your news."

While she rambled on about some nobleman who had fallen for his cousin only to discover her secret affair with his brother, Alexandra's head swam. Having no interest in the salad, the potatoes, or the lamb that had been served one after the other, she tried to keep up a conversation with her brother and Mr. Winterfield.

Why was this woman still at their table? From the minute she had opened her mouth, she should have been expelled! What could she possibly contribute to this household? What were *her* accomplishments, Alexandra wondered? The sum of her worth thus far equaled one lovely head of hair and no more. Even the face that seemed pretty at first had taken on a particular revulsion in her opinion.

Most perplexing to Alexandra was the fact that Roman seemed enamored by her. With the meal now well along, he had not looked at Alexandra, a gesture she had been a recipient of—and often—at their meals of late.

"Roman, I've learned of yet another of your loves," Caroline was saying now, "and I must confess it to be one of my own."

"And what, may I ask, would that be?" he said.

"Mineral pools. I've had the delight of indulging in them myself—the last time I was in Switzerland."

"Yes, they are a pleasure of mine, something I seek out during my travels."

"Well, perhaps someday your sister and I can take a little outing to Bath together. A quick trip on the train, and we'd be home by supper," she said snapping her fingers. "What better way to become acquainted a bit more? Would you like that?" she asked Catherine as though speaking to a child. "I suppose it would be uncouth if I overlooked inviting your friend along. Miss Viana, you claim such knowledge. Tell me what you know of Bath."

"That its name originates with the stones that were hewn for the architecture found there. And nothing more."

"Nothing more?" Caroline tittered, tossing a smirk toward Mrs. Winterfield. "You mean you've never been to Bath? What on earth was your upbringing? Every person of civility, nobleman or otherwise, has availed himself at least once of the health benefits of Bath."

"You'll pardon *me* then." Richard Winterfield answered the challenge. "I've never been there myself, and yet hope I've not regressed into incivility. Nor have I ever felt healthier in my life."

"Of course *you're* excused, sir," Caroline said. "Everyone knows the Winterfield's unique privilege of abiding by their own rules. No one dare hold such a thing against *you*." She laughed with Olivia.

Alexandra's stomach felt as though it would jump from her throat, such were her tattered nerves. She was grateful when the meal was over at last. Not wanting to admit defeat to this woman, yet finding the thought of spending a minute more with her nauseating, Alexandra excused herself to the library. Her brother had already taken his leave, heading off to the vineyard for what remained of the evening.

None but Catherine seemed disappointed with the loss of their company. Roman stated no objection to her leaving and appeared not to have given her so much as a glance when she walked out. But what had she expected? Being influenced by the best of the vanities, his progress toward becoming a gentleman had taken a sudden sidestep.

Yet a sliver of hope remained, for he had not complied with Miss Landly's demand to address her by her given name.

What little consequence it was, at least she had that.

After lighting a few lamps, Alexandra fell into one of the overstuffed leather chairs in the library. Her head dropped back. From two stories above, the mural on the ceiling looked down upon her. Studying the image of the angry sea crashing onto the rocky shoreline, she realized it had been over two years since she had last experienced such a storm. Though frightening at times, such fury by nature became exciting and humbling reminders of the force that had shaped the earth, indeed, the entire universe.

Her eyes squeezed shut. How she missed her childhood at times. Oh, why did children have to grow, anyway? Why did they have to leave the comforts of their home? The world brought many more challenges than the severest storm she had endured at Brentwood. Why could she not return to the comfort of her lighthouse and stay there forever?

Who was she fooling? She jumped to her feet, stunned by a sudden and silent confession: Why did she have to work so hard to distract her thoughts away from Roman Winterfield? His glances at her had become frequent and welcome, and just to be in his presence now made her heart leap. Yet at tonight's dinner, it was as though she had never existed. Had jealousy crept into her heart to watch the interaction between him and Caroline? And if so, how? She never desired his attentions. And never before had he deserved attention from anyone other than the likes of Miss Landly.

So there it was. Caroline Landly and Roman Winterfield made a good match. Determined to leave it at that, she picked up a book with a worn leather covering from the table beside her. A dark ribbon marked her place from the previous evening.

An hour later, Alexandra returned the book to the table, and extinguished the lamps one by one on her way to the concealed door beside the fireplace. Moonlight bathed the room in white through the tall windows on the south wall. Within moments darkness engulfed her inside the hidden staircase leading to the second floor guest quarters. Darting down the hallway, she paused at the railing overlooking the entrance hall. The house was silent and dark. It was apparent Miss Landly had taken her leave.

Alexandra wondered whether the scent of the woman's perfume and the soft glow of that golden hair lingered in Roman's mind.

Moments later, Roman stepped into the still shadows of the library. He lit one of the lamps he had watched Alexandra extinguish. Easing himself into the chair where she had snuggled, he found it still retained a trace of her warmth.

Scanning the room with its twenty thousand books, he reached for the one he had seen her set on the table. The gold embossment on the front cover had gown dull with time, but was still legible. *The Holy Bible*. It had been years since he had last read from it himself. The pages he fanned with his thumb crinkled as they turned, as though ready to crumble in his hand. He stopped at the black satin marker. The page heading listed one word, a name: Job. Staring at the page, he crossed one leg over the other knee.

Her mind had just absorbed these very words. What about them had intrigued her? He read under his breath.

"Then the LORD answered Job...and said... Where wast thou when I laid the foundations of the earth? declare, if thou hast understanding. Who hath laid the measures thereof, if thou knowest?...Or who laid the corner stone thereof?...Or who shut up the sea with doors...And said, Hitherto shalt thou come, but no further: and here shall thy proud waves be stayed? Hast thou commanded the morning?...Have the gates of death been opened unto thee?...Declare if thou knowest it all."

He read the words over and over. "Declare if thou knowest it all," he mumbled. Was there not a time—even recently—when he thought he knew *all* that mattered?

His gaze locked upon the mural of the mighty sea above his head. Indeed, what mortal man could possibly restrain such power? He studied the scene for a long time before returning to the pages of the book.

"Where is the way where light dwelleth?... Hast thou entered into the treasures of the snow?... Hath the rain a father? or who hath begotten the drops of dew?...Knowest thou the ordinances of heaven?...Canst thou lift up thy voice to the clouds? Canst thou send lightnings?...Wilt thou hunt the prey for the lion?...Who provideth for the raven its food?...Hast thou given the horse strength?...Doth the hawk fly by thy wisdom?...Doth the eagle mount up at thy command?...Wilt thou condemn me, that thou mayest be righteous? Hast thou an arm like God or canst thou thunder with a voice like him?... Deck thyself now with majesty and excellency; and array thyself with glory and beauty.... Look on everyone that is proud, and bring him low.

"Then Job answered the LORD, and said, I know that thou canst do every thing and that no thought can be withholden from thee....Therefore have I uttered that I understood not; things too wonderful for me, which I knew not....Wherefore I abhor myself, and repent in dust and ashes."

Roman felt sure he had read the words before, but they sounded unfamiliar. Why? Had he considered himself above their counsel? What about now? The words pricked his heart as he read the verses once and then twice. At the stroke of midnight, he lifted his gaze and lay the book in his lap.

Threading the black ribbon between the pages where he had stopped, he returned the book to its place on the table. The words tumbled over and over in his mind.

Who did he think he was all these years?

Extinguishing the lamp, he retired to his room.

Gathering her robe around her body to ward off a chill, Alexandra blew out the flame of the candle on her bedside table. Before slipping underneath the coverlet, she noted a light pass beneath the crack of her door. A soft knock followed.

"Who is it?" she asked in a quiet voice, not wishing to awaken anyone in the household.

"Just me," Catherine said, stepping inside with candleholder in hand. "I'm sorry to bother you, Alex."

"No bother at all." Alexandra relit her candle, adding to the light of Catherine's flame. "Is something troubling you?"

"No. But perhaps it should."

"Sit down and tell me."

"I just find it odd in a very pleasing way that my brother is here—and paying me attention. You heard his invitation at the dinner table. The races of all things! He's not fond of the sport, you know. It would appear he had only me in mind when he arranged it."

"I'm happy for you, really."

Catherine leapt to her feet. "'Happy' is an understatement of how I'm feeling, Alex." She turned about the room in a manner that left Alexandra laughing. "I've never in my life experienced my brother's affection." She plunked down on the edge of the bed. "Oh, Alex, even when others doubted him, I've always known he's a wonderful man. What do you think of it all?" Her eyes almost danced in the velvet of the candlelight.

"I think, for whatever reason, his eyes have been opened to your wonderful nature. And I also think it's about time."

Could what she had said to Roman in Paris have had a bearing on his return? Alexandra wondered.

"And no one will blame me if I take advantage of whatever time I have with him," Catherine said. "Between him and Antoine...when will I ever settle down enough to get a good night's sleep?" She surprised Alexandra with a fast kiss on one cheek and the next instant was gone.

Alexandra extinguished her candle for the second time and sat in darkness.

Indeed, no one would blame her one bit.

"What will you do for the next two days, Alex?" The question was posed by Catherine at the breakfast table the following morning. Roman sat beside her, eyes fixed upon what appeared to be a news journal.

After a brisk walk in the summer morning air, Alexandra had returned to a table set in the indoor garden. Every slice of fruit, every egg cup, every glass sat in nothing less than perfect arrangement. The smell of hot tea wafted about the entire room.

The servants must have been up before daybreak. She hated to disrupt the ensemble by taking up her spoon.

"With John working at the vineyard," Catherine continued, "and Mother and Father busy at the warehouse, perhaps you should accompany us to Ascot." Her brows rose in question toward her brother. "Roman?"

"I wish you would join us, Miss Viana." But his attention remained upon the paper.

"I wouldn't dream of intruding. Your time together is so rare. Besides, my plans are to tour one of the museums in town today; and tomorrow, well, let's just say I'm sure to enjoy the solitude."

It was not a lie. Far from tiring of seeing his face, she was hoping that the activities of town would force her thoughts toward anything but Roman Winterfield.

Chapter Seventeen

"Roman, there's a matter I'd like to discuss with you," Catherine said from under the curve of her parasol.

He saw her blink against the bright sun, a little breeze flipping the ruffles of her cuffs. The roar of the crowd had died down with the end of one race. A waiter decked in white gloves placed a glass of lemonade on the table before her, a dark ale before Roman, and left.

"I know it can't be a secret for long," she added.

"I'm listening." He watched her intently. How odd that the young lady before him, the sister he had seen grow from infancy, was nothing more than a stranger to him.

"It's about a man I've met—someone for whom I have great respect and toward whom I find myself more and more drawn."

"Yes, I know about Mr. Westcl—"

"His name is Antoine Aramis," Catherine blurted.

"Aramis?"

"Yes. A Frenchman who lives here in England."

"Ah, yet another Frenchman," he mumbled. "That seems to be a trend of late."

"What do you mean?"

"Never mind. Just referring to a friend."

"I want you to meet him. I think you would like him."

Roman already liked him, for any man was better than that scoundrel, Gregory Westcliffe.

"He's a very talented artist, Roman. Although he pursues painting as nothing more than a hobby, you should see the realism he captures on canvas. And his personality...he reminds me a bit of Andrew with his mild temperament. Also, he's very handsome."

It appeared Gregory Westcliffe had been erased from her mind, at least for the time being. Perhaps his interference in her affairs was no longer required. Roman would wait to see how the situation progressed.

"Well, if it isn't Roman Winterfield."

Catherine turned to a man behind her, who, after bowing his head to them both, winked at her.

"Preston Sutton," Roman said, standing in courtesy. "I believe it's been years."

He made certain there was neither cordiality in his voice nor a welcoming invitation. He had no desire to pass any amount of time humoring Preston Sutton. The man's tone was always mocking, his behavior beyond tolerance. He recalled the discussion at the dinner table two nights previous about Alexandra's recent excursions with the man, and here was one subject on which he could agree with Caroline Landly.

"I hope I find you in good health this weekend," Preston said.

"Likewise," Roman said, crossing his arms.

Grabbing a round white chair from a neighboring table, Preston seated himself. "Ten-to-one on my last horse. How did you fare?"

"I'm an observer this trip," Roman said, finding his seat again and staring at the young man through narrowing eyes.

"Then you won't mind that I'm doing all the winning, although I admit to disappointment in not being the object of your envy."

"What a surprise to find you here, Mr. Sutton," said Catherine. "And a pleasant one, I might add."

"I'm considering the purchase of one of these magnificent creatures. Were I to find a fit jockey, I may see a new vocation in my future. My father always reminds me that I already possess more than is humanly possible to ever put to use, but he doesn't understand my passion for the many adventures of life. Speaking of adventures, Miss Winterfield, I've had the pleasure of spending some time with your companion, whom I understand will be with you for the duration of the summer."

"Oh, yes—Miss Viana. Did you enjoy your time together?"

"'Enjoy' is an understatement. She's a woman with passions equal to mine. Have you had the opportunity to become much acquainted with her, Roman?"

"Somewhat, yes."

"It was actually she who introduced me to the idea of owning a race horse," Preston said. "Indirectly, of course. She has such a fondness for the creatures. I thought I would surprise her at our next meeting, which will be sooner rather than later, as we have an upcoming dinner engagement. She's a remarkable woman, one of whose company a man could never tire." Preston stood to leave. "Well, I suppose I'd better return to the task at hand. Enjoy the races!"

Roman watched the young man depart. *So, Miss Viana, who will it be—the suave Frenchman or the frivolous Englishman?*

Alexandra hastened past the remaining exhibits and toward the way out of the museum. Had she not peered out the second-story window to see the sun sinking in the sky, the museum might have closed with her inside. A light touch on her arm startled her. A canvas was thrust before her eyes. She stopped short at a perfect image of herself on the page.

"A portrait for the pretty lady," the artist commented in a heavy French accent.

"Mr. Aramis! You sketched this portrait? When?"

"I work in silence and with discretion, Miss Viana. My subjects rarely sense my presence. Now what do you think—your true impression?"

She looked back at the charcoal drawing. "Your work should be framed and placed on one of the walls of this museum. Catherine mentioned to me that you're a talented artist, but I never would have imagined to this extent."

"A pretty subject makes my work easier," he complimented. "So where is your delightful companion?" They strolled side-by-side down the staircase.

"Catherine is spending the day with her brother."

"Ah, yes. She mentioned that he was in town. I suspect that's the reason I haven't seen her for the past two days."

The pair stepped outside onto a street bustling with pedestrians.

"Miss Viana, may I take this opportunity to express the deep respect I feel toward Miss Winterfield? She may not realize it, but in these two short weeks, she has added a dimension to my life that I never could've dreamed."

"I hope it's not too forward of me to inform you that she has expressed to me a mutual respect."

"And yet she frightens me."

"Yes, I can understand that, when one considers the position of her family—and your position with the winery."

"You must think me insane for pursuing such a romance."

"No, Mr. Aramis. In my eyes—and John's, and Catherine's—you are a man of integrity. She being such a woman herself deems the two of you equal."

"But how would I support her? Were she ever to accept me, her father no doubt would not. His disowning her could lead to her disinheritance. I could never do that to Catherine."

"Whether or not Mr. Winterfield would resort to such drastic measures, I know not; but I hardly think material considerations would undermine any feelings that may yet develop between the two of you, since that has not hindered their starting."

They arrived at the place where Alexandra had tied her horse. She pulled her gloves on, and Mr. Aramis assisted her onto the horse. "And where is your transportation, Mr. Aramis?"

He looked down. "Oh...I walked, Miss Viana. I enjoy the outdoors and the exercise."

She was cut to the heart at her thoughtless question. Of course he did not own a horse.

"Will you be telling Miss Winterfield of our meeting?" he asked.

"Yes. I believe I must."

"And will you tell her about our topic of conversation?"

"I'm sure she'll inquire."

"So be it," he said. He patted the horse on its rump and stepped back a few paces. "Oh, Miss Viana, your portrait—a gift." He pulled a roll from beneath his arm and held it out to her.

"Mr. Aramis, this is more than a gift. It's a treasure," she said, reaching for the scroll. "If you'll not allow me to buy it, then please allow me to pay for a cab for your return trip."

"Thank you, but I come here often and am familiar with all the shortcuts home. Who's to know? Perhaps I shall even beat you back to the estate." He turned and disappeared into the crowd.

Alexandra sat in contemplation for a moment. Indeed, what *would* their lives be like were they to marry? She decided that even if Catherine's father did disown her to a life of poverty, that fate would deem her happier than were she to marry Mr. Westcliffe and all his riches.

But would Mr. Aramis bow out rather than allow that to happen?

Chapter Eighteen

Outside the window of a tiny French cottage, a man watched a couple sitting down to dinner at an hour when other families would be long asleep. He glanced at the nearby bushes. His comrade, protected by the shadows and his dark skin, was all but invisible.

The weatherworn faces inside the cottage reflected no joy and likely were much younger than their appearances suggested. Even in the dull yellow light, deep crevices, downturned around their lips, spoke of years of anguish and hard work.

The man at the window stepped up to pound on the front door. When the woman answered, he offered no greeting; nor did he so much as remove his hat. "Where is your son?" he demanded in French, though his accent belied his Bedouin origin.

The woman stood wide-eyed. Her husband appeared behind her. "What do you want?"

"Tell me where your son is, *Monsieur* Aramis."

The woman's husband stared at him, his eyes dark and cold. He turned and walked toward the back of the cottage. The woman stayed at the door, glaring at him. When her husband returned, he handed over an envelope, old and yellowed. The post office address in Canterbury, England, was faded but still legible.

The visitor folded the envelope and tucked it into a pocket before quickly taking his leave into the night. His companion rushed from the bushes to join him.

Four nights following, Alexandra Viana rode in the open carriage as late afternoon breezes sent her hair fluttering in wisps like little kisses over her cheeks. Her thoughts were on Roman Winterfield, who apparently had a newly found interest in his younger sister. Since the day the two had shared at the races, they could be found strolling together or in the cozy lounge, playing chess. Catherine even challenged her brother to a game of billiards the previous evening and had won while Alexandra sat quietly, writing to her parents, fondling the golden locket that hung from the chain around her neck. She had worn it every day since its arrival and kept her parents close in mind and heart.

Catherine and her brother seemed quite relaxed in each other's company, smiling and laughing often, which inspired a similar reaction in Alexandra. For Catherine's sake, she could only hope the relationship continued to grow in a positive fashion.

She smiled as the horses carried her along, her blue eyes taking in the countryside bathed in the late afternoon sunshine.

Reaching the modest Sutton home on schedule, she was greeted at the door by Stephen, who was immediately followed by his brother, Preston. She stepped inside, and the door closed behind her.

She arrived back at the Winterfield home long after midnight. As she removed her gloves and cloak, she thought of Preston Sutton and his perpetual light-hearted mood. She had enjoyed the evening with her sister, her nephew, and the two men. They had played cards until late, long after Everett had dozed off. She was surprised that the loud talking and laughter had not awakened the youngster.

The Winterfield house still retained the lingering scents of a delectable meal. Before retiring to her bedchamber,

Alexandra walked through the great tapestry hall to its end and into the library. She lit the small lamp, sank into the familiar chair, and reached for her Bible. As she pulled on the black ribbon, which dangled from the bottom of the pages, and began reading, she realized, for the third night in a row, the marker was much further along than where she had remembered placing it. As a test, the previous evening she had folded the page corner where she had placed the ribbon. She now inspected the page corner to find no fold, and upon examining previous pages, found the folded corner three pages back. "Now I know I'm not losing my mind," she mumbled to herself. She left the ribbon where it was and began reading the folded page.

Fifteen minutes later, she closed the book, placed it on the table, and extinguished the lamp. Crossing the floor, she left the room through the door near the fireplace, but, instead of climbing the staircase, stood silently on the other side of the door in the darkness.

She listened for any noise and, upon hearing none, sat quietly on the bottom step in total darkness.

Moments later, a light appeared on the floor from underneath the door. Her heart jumped, and she stood to move toward it. Without a sound, she opened it just a crack. The room was lit up, but she saw no one. Pulling the door further toward her, she glimpsed the profile of a man. He was sitting in the same brown leather chair she had occupied and was reading from her Bible. At first glance she thought him to be her brother, John, but then realized it was Roman Winterfield! Were he still awake when she arrived home, why had he not spoken to her?

Watching him in silence for nearly an hour as he read, she grew more and more fascinated with his responses. Now and then a smile would appear at the corner of his lips; other times he would nod or sit staring in apparent contemplation at the ceiling above, but most often he sat absorbed in the words, page after page.

She smiled when he smiled, burning with curiosity, yearning to discover which thoughts had touched him so. When his lids began to droop, hers did, also. She watched him place the marker between the pages where he stopped and return the book to its place. Shaking her head in amusement, she realized he had no idea of the single action that had given him away.

After tiptoeing up the darkened staircase to her room, she fell fast asleep, an unexpected sense of happiness settling over her.

Chapter Nineteen

"Grace, are you certain we should be doing this?" Alexandra's discomfort heightened as their phaeton passed beneath a thick archway of gray brick with high rook-like towers stationed on either side. She peered up at the open spiked gate hovering above them. "This is very awkward," she added.

Their horse trotted ahead, but she looked back at the impenetrable walls locking them on all sides into grounds of sweeping lawns and trees swaying with the breeze. An eerie quiet followed them along the gravel drive.

"I'll say we're here on business," Grace said, not a hint of concern in her voice. "You wouldn't believe the access I have to places of privilege upon mention of my connection with the Suttons. It's as though a barrister were an inspector from Scotland Yard."

"That would be a lie, Grace."

When she turned back to face the castle, Alexandra sank against the seat, all her breath leaving her body. "Look at that," was all she could muster. With its battlements and bastions, the weathered gray stone forming massive walls and turrets gave the impression that the entire structure was suited in armor, decked for conflict.

"Then what?" Grace asked. "Would you have me say we were out for a drive around Surrey and ended up at the castle in want of a tour—a castle that has been uninhabited and shut off from the public for two decades? We just thought they'd open it up for us? Do you think that would prompt the steward into allowing our admittance?"

"Just why are we here, Grace?"

"Because the gate was up. How could we pass this opportunity? Besides, it was your idea."

"Oh, no you don't. You can't pin this on me."

"You said you wished you could see a portrait of Father as a young man."

"Yes, but coming here to do it was your wild imagination." Their carriage crossed a narrow bridge. Alexandra looked down at the black waters of a moat. "I don't think I need to see his portrait this badly," she said. "Oh, what he would think of us?"

"Perhaps your only flaw, Alex, is your lack of appreciation for adventure."

"That's not true. I have far greater flaws. Besides, I always enjoyed our outings as children. Recall our excursion to Ireland? And did I not spend weeks in Germany with our family? I just returned from France, for heaven's sake!"

"And you've been living on an island off of Scotland."

"See there. I think I've proven myself very adventurous."

"But think, Alex. You have never ventured anywhere without Father and Mother. Your outings have been for the sake of safe travel, not true adventure. There is a difference, you know."

"Tell me."

"Adventure is exploring the unknown, is never preconceived, and always involves—to some degree—danger, or at least the perception of it. Coming with me to this castle on a moment's spur—unannounced and unwelcome—now that's adventure."

"No. That's distasteful."

Inside, the fortress smelled of dust. A draft moved the hem of Alexandra's skirt. She clung to her sister's arm, looking at hallways and staircases leading off in every direction. Their slightest footstep echoed through the shadowy vestibule, try as they might to tread lightly.

"Do you suppose that's the family crest?" she whispered. Alexandra gazed upon a large shield of gold and red, divided into quarters. Two white lions, reared up on hind legs on the left, faced two white horses in a similar stance on the right. A long, upright sword divided them, its golden hilt crossing the shield at the top.

"It must be." Grace stepped away. "Hello?" Her voice ricocheted from every corner. No answer came in return.

The old but solid wooden slats making up the heavy front door had opened with a creak and permitted their entry. Now it stood shut behind them, closing them in a chilly dungeon-like chamber. Alexandra wanted to run for the sunshine.

"The steward must be out," she said, shivering. "I'm sure that's why the gate was up."

"But where are the groundskeepers? We saw no one, Alex."

"I think we should leave."

"Not on your life." Grace scurried up a wide staircase, pausing at the landing to throw aside the heavy drape covering a tall window. Light gushed across the stone blocks of the staircase while dust scattered everywhere. "What a view!"

"Grace, truly, I don't think we should be—"

But her sister disappeared up the remaining flight of stairs. She ran after her.

"Alex!" Grace's voice echoed from somewhere above. "Look at this."

She attempted to follow her sister's voice, but ended up in a long hallway with a dozen closed doors. She turned and dashed back toward the staircase.

"In here," Grace called.

Alexandra ran toward a splash of light on the floor at the base of three wide steps. Following them, she stepped into a room bright from a wall of windows. She stopped short. There was Grace, standing mesmerized before a thick table of mahogany.

"Have you ever seen its likes in your life?" Grace uttered.

Alexandra walked over and lifted from the table a wine glass painted with swirls of gold. Across the entire surface of the massive table, every conceivable space filled, sat glasses in like style to the one she held amidst solid gold goblets, gold cutlery, and utensils and candlestick holders of silver and pewter. Carving knives fanned to cover one corner. China bowls with plates stacked beneath sat atop pads of silk.

"Set for a king," Grace whispered.

"Who are they expecting?"

"I don't think anyone. Perhaps they put everything out to be cleaned."

Hepplewhite chairs, with their shield-shaped backs of light woodwork, sat in silence—twenty of them—tucked beneath the tabletop.

"What will we say are we to be discovered?" Alexandra asked, setting down the glass.

"If no one's home, how will anyone know we're here?"

"If they come home, they'll see the carriage out front."

"Then we shall tell them the truth. That we're the grand-daughters of Ivan Everett, that's what. This is our inheritance, Alex, can you believe it?"

"If we can't, how will anyone else? We'd better get out of here or else face arrest."

"Candlegate belongs to Father now, Alex. To us. You look enough like him to prove your relationship."

"It's a rare occasion that Papa's shadow ever enters that gate. I doubt the stewards here would even recognize him."

"Can you imagine him in this castle? I can't believe he was raised here. Alex, just imagine this room under the glow of the fire, with all the candelabras burning, the aromas of a grand feast wafting about, and a hundred dignitaries in all their splendor." Grace swirled about the room. "Yes, My Lord." She curtsied to an imaginary fellow. "And how was the hunting in France? What's that? You say you'd like my husband and me along next season? I'm afraid our schedules will not allow it." She laughed, but Alexandra failed to appreciate humor at such a moment.

"We shouldn't be here, Grace."

"Well, I am not leaving until I finish our tour," Grace said and walked from the room, Alexandra close behind. "I've imagined this place ever since Father told us of it our first stay at the Winterfield mansion. Remember that night?"

Alexandra followed her through the corridor she had been down earlier. Light from windows with iron frames set into deep bays lit their way. Every door they opened revealed rooms filled with furniture covered in dusty sheets. Velvet drapes in drab colors hung drawn and cobwebs gathered in every corner.

"Look at that ceiling, Alex." Grace said, stepping onto the ornate rug of one room.

They admired crown molding framing the room, carved into white grapevines. Swirled cornices, interspersed along each wall, supported the bulky molding.

"This must be a sitting room of some sort," Alex said, stepping in.

"Imagine curling up there before the fire nook on a blustery night, watching snow skitter by the windows and hearing the wind howl."

"Thus far, I can picture myself doing only one thing in this structure—groping for a way out. I can't imagine Papa playing in these rooms as a child or skipping about through these hallways."

"His childhood was very different than we could ever envision. But I'm sure he had happy times here. Try to imagine these being rooms being lived in. Of course they keep them cold and closed off now."

"I suppose you're right."

They opened the door at the end of the hallway to an outdoor catwalk lining the cylindrical tower of the keep.

"What battles must've been fought here," Alexandra said, growing more adventurous since they had yet to encounter anyone. She meandered out along the circumference of the tower. "Soldiers of battles long past must have shot flaming arrows from this very spot. Come look. From here one could see an army approach from any direction."

"Do you suppose there's a dungeon beneath the floorboards down there?"

"I'd rather not know."

"There's more to see. Come on." Grace grabbed her arm to pull her back inside.

Portraits of Earls and their wives of generations past lined the walls of several long galleries back down on the main level.

"Look at this, Grace," Alexandra called, standing beneath one such portrait outside the door to the library. Her sister came running. "She must've been no more than thirty when this was painted." They stared at the portrait of a woman decked with a high silk collar and long strands of pearls. The eyes held no brilliance, like the women in some of the other portraits. The lips, tiny rose petals, offered just the hint of a smile. Carved into a bronze plate on the frame the name 'Lady Margaret Everett' appeared.

"So, this is the woman who hated Father so much as to hide the truth about our mother's survival of the shipwreck." They stared at it for a long time. "And yet she looks so kind. She must've died somewhere in this castle," Grace said, looking above and around.

"Many people died here, I'm afraid. More than we care to know about. Can we get out of here now?"

"I don't understand, Alex. There's not one portrait of Father anywhere."

"She disinherited him. What portraits there were must have been destroyed."

"I have difficulty believing a mother—even a hateful one—could do that. Let's keep looking."

Alexandra followed her sister into the library.

"You look at these portraits in here while I rest up," Grace said, pulling the dusty covering from one chair and sinking into its velvet cushion.

"Have you ever seen so many books, Grace? They must be more numerous than even the Winterfield's collection."

"And it all belongs to us."

"*Hello?*" The voice of a man echoed down the gallery.

Grace jumped to her feet. "Oh, Alex, we've been discovered!"

"What's our excuse for being here, Grace? What did you conjure up?"

"I didn't." She grabbed Alexandra's arm and pulled her toward a small door in one corner. Ducking through, they found themselves in a servant's hallway, lighted by a dingy window on each end. The corridor, thickly scented with years of dust, must have been long forgotten. Grace pulled the door closed in a soft click.

"Do you think he'll find us in here?" Alexandra asked, placing an ear beside the door.

"I don't know, but look, Alex." She pointed toward the floor.

"Oh, Grace." A portrait sat on its side, propped against the wall. Grace reached out to right it. "He's so handsome," Alexandra whispered. She dropped to her knees, her fingers skimming over the sandy hair and pale skin of her father's face. "Just an adolescent, perhaps even younger than John." He stood before a cloudy charcoal backdrop, holding a pheasant by the talons in one hand and propping a hunting rifle in the other. "This must've been completed before he went off to school." The face, though recognizable, held no expression. "He looks so..."

"Vacant," Grace finished.

"There's no mistaking his face. But so much is missing."

"I wish we could take it with us."

"*Who's here?*" called the stern voice of the man, muffled from inside the library.

Alexandra sprang to her feet and ran after her sister down the long hall. A doorway at the end took them up a long flight of steps to the second story and the servant's suite of rooms, obviously lived-in. Running through to another door, they stepped into another shadowy hallway. Vaulted ceilings intersected in thick, curved archways of gray stone, just like they had seen throughout the entire house.

"There," Alexandra whispered, pointing toward a whitish light. "That must be the staircase leading to the vestibule."

Tiptoeing over, they peeked around the archway. Alexandra could see between the stone balusters of the balcony that it was, indeed, the main entryway.

"We'll sneak down the stairs and run for the door," Grace said, stepping onto the first stair.

Hearing not a sound, they managed to muffle their footsteps. Chills skittered down Alexandra's arms. She held tight to her sister's hand as they descended the cold staircase, open to the vestibule on one side. Their feet settled onto the stone floor in what seemed an eon later. Peering about again, down every connecting corridor, Alexandra grabbed the fabric of her skirts and chased after Grace toward the front door. Upon swinging it wide and bursting out into the sunlight, she heard the voice again from behind, *"You there!"*

Alexandra glimpsed back just long enough to catch sight of a man racing down the staircase they had just taken. She pulled the heavy door to a slamming close and the two ran for their carriage. Jumping in, Grace grabbed for the reins and whipped the startled horse into action.

Relieved to have made the escape and panting from the experience, Alexandra turned back to watch the servant emerge from the castle. He jogged a few steps after them, but threw his hands up in defeat.

"That was a close call," Grace said, urging the horse to keep up the pace.

"And it's not over. The gate, Grace, it's down!"

Grace veered the horse sharply. The carriage tipped, dumping the ladies onto the gravel drive. Alexandra watched the horse trot ahead as the carriage righted itself. It disappeared around a corner of bushes.

"Oh, my hip," Grace groaned. "At least you had a softer landing, Alex."

"You broke my fall," she said, struggling to her feet.

"Maybe this wasn't such a good idea after all."

"How are we going to get out of here?" Alexandra assisted Grace to her feet, swiping the dust from her cotton skirt. "I wonder why that man didn't chase after us. Are you all right?"

"I think so. I'll probably have a colorful bruise to explain to Stephen."

They went in the direction the horse had taken. Hobbling around the corner, they discovered another gateway, a smaller one, this one standing open, and the horse nowhere in sight.

"Our poor horse is in more of a panic to get out than we are," Grace said, managing a little laugh.

Outside the open gate, their horse had halted.

"We'd like some of your tomato bisque, please," Alexandra said, perusing a menu while the waiter placed two glasses of water on the table before them.

"And some bread," Grace added.

"Yes, madam," he said and walked back toward the kitchen.

They had found the little restaurant in the town not two miles from the castle gates.

"What a day," Alexandra said, sighing and melting against her chair back.

"Wait till Catherine hears about our excursion. This was more exciting than a hundred horse races."

Alex reflected for a moment. "I may regret saying so, Grace, but I'm glad we went there today."

"It was worth every harrowing moment to see that castle. Candlegate, Alex! We saw *Candlegate*, Father's homestead."

"Do you think he would've taken us through it were we to ask?"

"Possibly, but why wait? There's no telling when he and Mother would be paying it a visit again," Grace said.

"I could imagine Jessica taking a risk such as we did today, but you, Grace? You said I lacked adventure. I never knew you to be the adventurous type either. Perhaps you overstep certain boundaries from time to time, but whatever possessed you to think we could trespass upon Everett property without getting caught?"

Grace gave her a look of surprise. "In reality, Alex, we are Everetts. Therefore, we were not trespassing. I wanted to see where we came from."

"Where we came from? We were never there."

"Well, we should have been."

Alex shook her head. "I still can't believe we did this. Wherever did you find the daring to do it?"

"Helping Stephen so much in his work has given me more courage than I once possessed, I suppose."

"And that painting of Papa—how I wish we could've found it sooner."

"He must've been no more than sixteen when it was completed. And here he was to be the future Earl. Look what he gave up, Alex,"

"He's my hero. There will never be another man like him."

"Oh, dear!" Grace jumped up from the table. Alexandra watched her dash out the door. From the window, she could see her searching the waiting carriage out front, underneath the seat, and in the little hatch in the back. She came back in. "My riding cape, Alex. It's missing."

"The library, where you stopped to rest."

"I left it on the chair. What will I do now?"

"It's lost for good, I'm afraid."

"Mother made that cape for me." Grace's frown turned to sudden laughter. "Can you see us returning to ask the steward for it?"

"Did you see the look on his face?" Alexandra could not contain her own laughter. "The distress we must have caused him to come home to strangers prowling around his castle."

"He'll never leave the gate open again."

"I suspect that was the reason he didn't take up the chase after us," Alexandra said. He knew he'd left the side gate open. Otherwise, he could've overtaken us."

The waiter returned to the table with steaming bowls of soup, a basket of bread, and a little cup filled with pats of butter.

Grace spread her napkin over her lap. "Ah, how grateful we can be for people's little mistakes."

Chapter Twenty

The following morning Alexandra rose a bit later than usual, but was still awake before breakfast was served. Startled by a soft rap on her door, she opened it to Catherine.

"Good morning, Alex. When did you arrive home last evening?"

"It was after midnight, I'm afraid. Grace and I had quite the adventurous day. I hope I did not disturb anyone by returning so late."

"Were you to investigate, you would have found John and me missing at that hour."

"Oh?" Alexandra smiled. "And how is Mr. Aramis?"

Catherine smiled and sat on the edge of the bed. "Oh, Alex, he's a wonderful person. I know no other man quite so interesting or so kind. He truly appreciates the finer things—and I do not refer to material possessions. I always treasured beauty in the land, but I realize I have missed so much now that I am able to see things through his eyes. For five years he has worked on this estate. Why did I not notice him before? And John is so kind to accompany me as often as he does. Will you join us this evening as well, Alex? Mr. Aramis so enjoys your company, as do I."

"Absolutely."

"I do hope your time at the Suttons was enjoyable because last evening in this house was dreadful."

"Whatever happened?"

"Oh, of course, you didn't hear. Miss Landly joined us for dinner again."

"Miss Landly? Did she show up unannounced this time?"

"No, she had an invitation—from Roman."

"Roman?" Alexandra's heart began to race. She looked down, lest anything be revealed in her expression.

"Yes, can you believe? Oh, I cannot bear to see him give in to my mother's wishes. I so dislike Miss Landly. What is to be done, Alex?"

"Nothing, Catherine." Still looking away and feeling defeated, Alexandra added, "The decision is his to make."

The Winterfield Ball was a mere twelve days away. Alexandra could not miss the signs of distress in Olivia Winterfield.

"No, no!" The mistress of Winterfield Manor reprimanded the servant who set a plate of food before her. "These eggs are runny. I specifically said poached hard. And where's the toast? You know I eat my toast with my eggs."

Alexandra grieved for the servant, who picked the plate up. As she turned toward the door, Catherine called out, "I'll eat those eggs." The servant cast a quick glance at Mrs. Winterfield, who gave her approval by a flutter of one hand, though her eyes rolled.

Up to this point, each morning, the breakfast table had offered a time of quiet talking. Though a habitual late-arriver, even Roman had been prompt in joining the family for the morning meals since returning to Kent.

"Mother," he said, "you're allowing the anxieties of this party to get the best of you."

"It's just that there is so much that yet must be done. How will we ever ready ourselves for a ball when my house staff is floundering with the ordinary?"

"What can we do to help?"

"You know very well only I can care for these things, Roman. You can help me by being out of my way."

Alexandra's eyes grew large. She looked down so as not to let her hostess see her expression.

"Very well," Roman said. "In that case, Catherine, will you join me on an outing today?"

"Anywhere you like."

"There's a hidden meadow that Andrew and I discovered as children. It has been our secret all these years, so I don't believe you've ever seen it. I'd like to venture there again and see if it's still as I remember. We can take a picnic lunch. It's a bit of a hike but, I recall, very worthy of the effort. John, can you join us?"

"I'll be at the vineyard today."

"Surely they can manage without you in this instance," Roman argued.

"I'm certain of that. But I've promised a full day's work. I'll go along the next time."

"Very well. Miss Viana?" He turned to Alexandra.

"Oh..." She hesitated, sure that he was only inviting her out of obligation. "...Perhaps you would prefer to have Miss Landly along. I can keep myself occupied today."

"No," Roman answered at once. "I don't care to invite Miss Landly. The meadow is a secret place, and since the Winterfield's and the Viana's are as close as two families can be," Roman looked over at Catherine and back at Alexandra, "we would be honored if *you* would accompany us."

"Yes, please do come, Alex." Catherine begged. "Your presence would make the day complete."

"All right, then. I would be honored, as well."

The three cast off aboard *The Sapphire* mid-morning under a warm sun. The usually choppy waters of the Channel were calmer than they had been when Alexandra was out with Preston Sutton.

She sat beside Catherine at the bow of the ship. The wind forced their bonnets back, and she untied hers to tuck it beneath one leg. The salty scent of the water filled her nostrils. Closing her eyes, she immersed herself in memories of peering over the lighthouse railing on warm summer days not unlike this one.

After what seemed at least an hour, she walked back to take a seat near Roman, who was standing at the wheel. "Just how far were you and Andrew allowed to venture as children?" She raised her voice above the sound of the water and the wind.

He laughed. "I'm afraid what we were allowed and where we actually went were two very different distances."

"Apparently so."

"We're nearing the bay now. Just a mile or two, if I remember correctly."

Soon Roman lowered the sails of the main mast, and the parenzello slowed. It had been some time since they had seen any other ships, except far in the distance. *The Sapphire* neared the shoreline where a small cove appeared.

"Roman, is this where you intended to take us?" Catherine called out from the bow. "I don't see any meadow. In fact, I don't even see a beach or a dock. Are you certain this is the place?"

He lowered the remaining minor sails before dropping the anchor. "This is the place, all right," he said, leaping over a taut rope. "*The Sapphire* will hit bottom if we move any closer. We'll have to take the rowboat from here."

"The rowboat?" objected Catherine. "To where?"

Putting one arm about his sister's shoulder and leaning over so that his face was level with hers, he pointed. "Do you see those boulders there?"

"Yes," Catherine replied, looking toward a steep slope covered by large, white boulders that rose from the water in the middle of the cove. Alexandra followed the direction of Roman's finger. Many feet above the rocks, the slope disappeared into thick forest.

"At the top of those boulders is a pathway that cuts through the forest to the meadow," he said. "I admit it appears somewhat more intimidating now that the fearlessness of childhood has faded. I suppose this will be a bit of a test of our dexterity."

"You mean a test of your dexterity," Catherine said. "This is a savage place. I'll be content to stay right where I am and enjoy my lunch on the ship."

Roman sighed. Alexandra was pleased that he did not give in to his typical anger. He looked her way. "What do you think, Miss Viana?"

"Well, my curiosity is certainly piqued, Mr. Winterfield. I believe my shoes are sturdy enough," she stated, feeling more courageous than usual. What had her sister called her? Unadventurous? Would she have a story for her!

"Good then." He lowered a bag with two lunches and a water canteen into the rowboat. Swinging both legs over the side, he descended the ladder and dropped onto the waiting skiff. He looked up at the two ladies, who were peering down at him. "I'll steady the ladder for you, Miss Viana."

Alexandra stood tall. "Good-bye, Catherine."

"You'll never be able to climb those boulders, Alex."

"Not if I stay here." Alexandra stepped to the larboard side and dangled both legs over. With her skirt and petticoat wrapped about her upper legs and held in one hand, she descended the rope ladder one rung at a time. Within moments, her feet hit the rocking boat beside Roman. "Phase one accomplished," she said, already proud of herself.

"It may be a couple of hours before we return," Roman called up to his sister. "Don't worry yourself over us."

Alexandra took a seat on one hard bench and held tight to the sides of the rowboat. Within minutes the boat bottom scraped the rough shoreline. Roman hurdled the bow, his boots landing in soft mud. After securing the boat, he reached out to assist Alexandra ashore. Her heart raced when his hand wrapped around hers.

They began their ascent up to the forest line.

Her shoes slipped a couple of times on the smooth, round rocks. But Roman maintained a tight grip on her hand while she grasped a fistful of her skirts. Within just a few minutes, he pulled her to her feet at the top of the hill of boulders. She panted from the exertion and looked down across the blue inlet. Its waters spread into the opening of the Channel. Gulls screeched in echoes, soaring through the bowl of the bay. Before hopping off the back side of the boulder, she waved at the tiny figure of Catherine on the ship.

They sat on a fallen tree trunk just inside the cover of the forest to drink some water before resuming the hike. Alexandra peered around the dark, dense forest. The distinct scents of pine and molds filled her nostrils. Not the soft, grassy mulch to which Alexandra had grown accustomed throughout most of England, the forest floor was solid black soil. Mosses covered the trunks of the soaring pine trees. The lower branches were devoid of any needles. Jagged, broken, and bare limbs jutted from every trunk. She looked up to catch rare glimpses of the blue sky far above the treetops, but only filtered light reached the barren floor. Besides the occasional spider web, she noted little evidence of any wildlife. Sitting in silence, she listened for the scuffling of animals or the chirping of birds. Other than the wind's rustling of the treetops, an eerie stillness surrounded them. Even the breeze did not reach the forest floor.

The enticement Alexandra had experienced at the thought of embarking upon an adventure dwindled to serious doubt. Thoughts of exploring Candlegate and the panic of nearly being discovered raced through her mind. She decided she could waltz back there with ease in comparison to traversing the forest ahead. What if they became separated?

"There's only one pathway that leads to the meadow." Roman tied the lunch bag about his waist, taking another gulp from the canteen. "The trees are so dense in spots that, even as children, we could not squeeze through."

"What is the possibility of becoming lost?"

"Great, indeed. There are many ways to choose, but each leads to an eventual dead end."

"Eventual?"

"I recall following some pathways for half an hour before being forced to turn back."

This is an adventure, she kept telling herself and, according to Grace, *danger is the essence of adventure.*

He looked at her, and a smile broke out on his lips. "There's nothing to worry about, I assure you." He tied the canteen with a rope and flung it over his head to cross his chest. She wondered how his white blouse with its billowing sleeves would fare on their trek. "Ready to move on?" He rolled the sleeves to his elbows.

Nodding and tucking the golden locket behind the lace neckline of her dress, she took hold of his outstretched hand and found it hard to believe that she was undertaking an adventure alone with the villain, Roman Winterfield. Whatever would her sisters think?

They crept over roots and fallen trunks, ducked under branches, and pressed themselves between trees and limbs. The forest sloped in a steep downgrade at points. With her free hand she clutched onto tree trunks, branches, and roots, oftentimes slipping in the hard-packed soil of the hillside.

Soon the waters of the bay were long behind them. Alexandra tried not to dwell on the spindly fingers of tree branches lingering all around, awaiting a chance to catch her, to seize the fabric of her dress, to snatch more strands of her hair from its tie, or put more scratches on her fingers and cheeks. A shiver tiptoed over her bare arms when she stopped to think about the cool dank air.

Her one consolation proved to be her guide. From the black waves of his hair to his brown cotton slacks tucked into tall boots, she found comfort in his form. Choosing to concentrate on his warm and firm grasp, she found her feelings difficult to believe. Was this the same man who, just two years before, opposed, even assaulted with his words, her family? Either he had been undergoing some drastic changes of late or her own standards were diminishing. Since this was no time to ponder such depth of thought, she abandoned it for the thrill of the moment.

They waded through shallow mud that attempted to separate them from their shoes, and leapt over tiny streams. They dodged spider webs and pulled themselves free when their clothing caught on broken branches. Roman glanced back at her often.

He stopped momentarily to assess the pathway while she pondered a gaping hole in the skirt of her dress. Smudges of dirt and mud covered her. Yet she felt no desire to utter a single word of complaint, happy just to be by his side.

After thirty minutes of slow progress through the musty forest, she asked to stop. "We're not lost, are we?" She sat to rest on a fallen tree trunk.

"I wouldn't let that happen." He smiled and she nearly melted. "Do you hear that?"

She strained to detect the rushing of water in the distance. "It sounds like a river." Anxiety welled up within her. He had not mentioned a river. Would they have to cross it?

"We're not far now." He urged her ahead.

With every step, the rush of the water sounded clearer, louder.

"Do you see there?" He stopped to point ahead.

A bright wash of sunshine lay just beyond them.

They climbed over several more fallen trunks and stumbled over other large roots before finally reaching the clearing in the forest. Branches surrounded the opening. Roman stepped through and turned to help her through as well.

When her foot stepped in soft green grass and warm sunlight splashed onto her face, Alexandra stood to behold the sight before her. Her mouth and eyes opened wide as she gazed about at a sea of wildflowers in every imaginable color. Tufts of green poked through a thousand blossoms in search of the same sunlight that warmed her. A forested cliff-like wall loomed over the meadow at one end, where she discovered the source of the rushing water. Not a river, but a waterfall tumbled over the edge of the cliff. Its waters cascaded into a clear blue lake, billowing into a cloud of mist.

Alexandra burst out into the meadow and spun around, her skirt wrapping about her legs. She broke out into laughter and darted toward the falls, her skirt held up with both hands. The thick trees of the forest were but a blur as she ran alongside them.

Behind her, she heard Roman laugh at her reaction. Turning back but a moment, she saw him run after her, the water canteen flailing behind him. She glanced over her shoulder to see he had stopped to catch his breath, his hands on his knees, his gaze intent upon her.

At the water's edge, she dropped to the ground to unlace her shoes. Flinging them aside, she stepped into the water near the shore and squealed with the cold shock.

Soon he caught up to her and fell breathless into a patch of wildflowers near the water. He dropped his head back on the ground and laughed out loud.

Thirty minutes later, they sat together like civilized people on a spread blanket, enjoying the light meal he had brought along. She wiggled her toes, now back in her leather shoes, thoughts of the cool water and Roman's warm hand playing about in her mind. "I must be in the Garden of Eden. This is without doubt the most beautiful spot on all the earth. How did you ever discover it?" She watched a bumblebee visit a nearby flower, then skip and bob to several others.

"Boys are natural-born explorers, I suppose."

"How could there be such beauty so inaccessible to the very ones created to enjoy it?"

"I imagine it's enjoyed by much wildlife."

"No wonder you kept this paradise a secret. Does your memory serve you accurately this day?"

"No," Roman answered, staring across the landscape. Her gaze followed the outline of his profile. "It's even more beautiful than I remembered." He turned to meet her gaze. She dared not voice the words that came to her mind: That the dignity in his looks far surpassed the splendor of the landscape.

He stood to take a few steps and turned in a slow circle, gazing at the entire circumference of the meadow. "We're surrounded on all sides by dense forest and steep hills. Even if they knew of this place, few people would be willing to venture here. One could get lost in any direction other than the one I showed you."

"And I cannot be certain now where we exited the forest," Alexandra admitted.

Roman shrugged and looked at her. "Then I suppose you're doomed to live here forever."

She smiled, thinking it would not be such a bad place to pass eternity.

"There's something else I'd like to show you before we leave."

They packed their utensils into the bag and Roman flung it over one shoulder. Alexandra followed him as he walked along the shore, rounded the far end of the lake, and headed toward the waterfall. He assisted her over stepping stones through a wide stream flowing from the lake and continued along the opposite shoreline. Nearing the churning waters, she found the falls deafening. A cool mist hung in the air all around them, dampening their hair and clothing.

Roman turned and called out to her. "There used to be a passageway behind the falls." She could barely make out his words. "Andrew and I pulled some deadwood from the forest and made a walkway so we could pass behind it. You'll get wet; do you want to continue?"

She nodded. He grasped hold of her hand.

Ducking behind a leaning tree, she sloshed several steps through thick mud. He pulled her up onto a floor of several wet logs, laid side-by-side. A wide cave opened to their left behind a tangle of vines, water seeping from its walls and dripping into a deep pool just yards from where they stood. She looked with awe through the streaming water of the falls at the glowing meadow. Spending several minutes behind the falls, she emerged with her guide in even greater wonder over the hidden treasures of the meadow.

Within moments, they were back in the sunshine on the side of the lake where they had picnicked. She stood speechless, chilled from her damp clothing, gazing one final time at the glory of the scene, the powerful waters falling in an endless roar.

It was then she noticed that he still grasped her hand.

*　*　*　*　*

As they walked back, Roman in the lead, the roar of the water faded. They continued until reaching the jagged break in the forest wall.

"I didn't realize how far this was from the lake," Alexandra admitted.

"You ran so fast when you saw it, I venture to say you could've outrun any contestant at the racetrack."

She laughed, but became filled with sorrow when she turned to glance once more at the magnificent meadow arrayed in all its beauty.

"We'd better go if we're to be home before sunset," he urged in a gentle manner.

"Will you bring me here again someday?"

His answer was slow in coming. His gaze inspected her face and settled on her eyes. "I promise. Someday." He reached up to touch her cheek. She looked down at a smudge of mud on his fingers.

Their clothes and hair were almost dry by the time they stepped into the murky forest. The hike back, although mostly uphill, intimidated her less. They once again reached the bright sunshine and looked down upon *The Sapphire* in the bay below, awaiting the return of her captain.

Roman assisted Alexandra down the hill of boulders, which challenged her less than the ascent.

Before long, she hoisted herself over the side of the ship from the top of the ladder, followed by Roman.

They found Catherine asleep on the deck of the ship, under the shadow of one of the collapsed sails. Roman pulled up and secured the rowboat and hauled in the anchor.

From the railing of the bow, Alexandra watched Catherine awaken underneath the shadow of a full sail, taut from the wind that filled it. The ship skated at full speed toward home.

Alexandra rested against the larboard side, the image of the secret meadow engraved in her memory. She pulled the locket out from underneath her clothing and allowed it to dangle over her lace collar once again. How her mother, who was so fond of gardens, would have loved the adventure. Perhaps she could in the future have the opportunity to treat her parents to a day at the meadow.

After the boat had docked in the Chatham harbor, Roman assisted his sister from the ship. She walked to the waiting carriage in the late day sun. Shadows lengthened, muting the colors of the day.

Roman extended his hand to Alexandra. When she stepped onto the dock, he looked down upon her dress. "Look at you," he said, still holding her hand. "I'll buy you a new dress tomorrow."

"That won't be necessary. You've gifted me with a most precious day, Mr. Winterfield—one I will never forget. One far more valuable than a thousand dresses."

She watched his gaze settle upon the locket against her heart. Why, she wondered, did his smile vanish upon sight of it?

"The pleasure belongs to me." A cold edge crept into his voice. He released her hand and gestured toward the carriage, stepping aside for her to pass.

Chapter Twenty-One

Alexandra had tied her horse to a nearby tree, along with Shadow, who stood harnessed and tied, but without a saddle. She loved the late afternoon sun that brightened the meadow on the Winterfield property where John had run Sampson the full perimeter the previous month. Now Sampson grazed several yards from where she stood. Holding out some oats with one hand, she hid the harness behind her back. A bag of oats hung from her left shoulder. She spoke quiet words and sounded a series of clicks. The horse lifted its head, ears piqued forward in curiosity.

Offering to take the horses to the pasture and collect them in the afternoon while Olivia and Catherine shopped for new gowns for the ball, now just ten days away, she treasured the opportunity to spend time with the magnificent animals she so loved. Cinnamon was her favorite, and she took her riding more than the others.

Much of her thought, however, had been focused on the complex situation into which Catherine had entangled herself. Had her friend not considered the consequences of her actions or the potential confrontation that would occur upon the return of Gregory Westcliffe? She had continued meeting Antoine in the evenings, keeping their romance hidden from her parents, though Alexandra herself had become aware of whispering among the servants in the house as they glanced Catherine's way. Roman had even met the young man when in town with Catherine; but according to Catherine, he had no idea of Antoine's being an employee of theirs.

How would her parents respond upon hearing of either of her romances? How would Roman react to discover the truth about Antoine? What would Mr. Westcliffe do upon his return to find Catherine in love with another man? Fearing Catherine was treading on dangerous ground and would soon face an eruption of enormous proportions, she faced each passing day with a greater degree of anxiety. It was time to confront Catherine and force her to prepare a plan of action.

It was also time for her to demonstrate the depth of her regard for Catherine. Thinking that her friend would in all likelihood be in need of an escape, Alexandra had included her in the arrangements to spend two weeks at Brentwood Lighthouse with the Wrights following the ball. Though she had not as yet done so, she planned to ask Catherine to accompany her.

Alexandra knew she herself would also benefit from time away from the Winterfield estate. Her affection for Catherine's brother was growing by the day, and she found it increasingly difficult to keep her feelings suppressed. Reflecting as she did often on the glorious day spent alone with Roman in the enchanting meadow, she marveled at how different her feelings were than they had been two years earlier. To see him smile and laugh was no longer a rare occurrence; but each time she witnessed it, she was overcome by her attraction to him. Keeping her gaze in check while in his presence became impossible; it would focus on him despite her most valiant efforts to the contrary. When in the library, she spent large spans of time studying his face among the family portraits. She could now see through the condescending expression there to the appeal of affection and kindness she now found so often in his eyes.

While pondering these things and attempting to lure the reluctant Sampson over, she heard the soft beat of approaching hooves. She turned to find the subject of her thoughts riding up on his father's horse.

"I thought you might appreciate a bit of assistance in rounding up the horses," Roman said.

"Thank you." She squinted into the sun, holding one hand up to shadow her eyes. "Sampson has decided to ignore me this fine afternoon."

Roman swung down from the back of the horse.

Sampson looked over at him, tossed his head back, and trotted a few yards in the opposite direction.

"Yes, he can be a stubborn one," Roman said.

He took the oat bag from Alexandra's shoulder. She dumped the oats in her hand back into the bag and handed the bridle to him. Swiping her hands together to remove the dust, she watched Roman approach the horse in slow, steady steps, speaking in a deep but gentle tone. The horse lifted its head and walked to meet him. Its lips flapped over the oats in his hand.

Roman glanced back at Alexandra, who had to laugh.

"For the past thirty minutes, I've been trying that same approach, but managed only to drive him farther away." She watched Roman slide the harness over the horse's muzzle, the bit slipping between its teeth. The remainder of the harness went over the ears. Roman buckled it and led Sampson back to where the others had been tied.

"Job well done," she said.

"For some reason, a man's voice has a greater impact on this one." He patted the horse and treated it to more oats. "Miss Viana, I've been meaning to ask you about a matter."

She had grown accustomed to the dark, almost black hue of his deep eyes. However, in the sun's reflection, Alexandra found in them russet streaks.

"During our excursion in France, you mentioned that Catherine was courting Gregory Westcliffe," he said. "Was that true?"

"I reported to you what was told to me by Catherine herself, and I assumed it to be so since my sister, Grace, also played a role in their meeting. Yet, the situation now seems to be very different, would you not say, Mr. Winterfield?"

"Pleasingly so."

"I was surprised to learn then that you had not already been made aware of your sister's relationship with Mr. Westcliffe, he being a long-time associate of yours, until, that is, Catherine revealed to me that their courtship was a secret—to all her family."

"Even to my parents?"

"Your parents most of all, from what Catherine said. It seems he wanted their relationship to be a surprise."

Roman looked away, and Alexandra noted one side of his upper lip rise. She had had her own reasons to dislike Mr. Westcliffe, but what reasons did Roman harbor? He had made no attempt to hide his displeasure upon learning of his sister's attachment to the man while in the museum in France. However, it seemed Gregory Westcliffe was a man of great admiration among his society. Catherine had even expressed the opinion that her parents would be ecstatic about the union. Alexandra could not imagine why Roman had taken such opposition to him. Perhaps it was best not to intrude any further into the matter.

"Do you ever ride bareback, Miss Viana?" Roman must have concurred with her conclusion, for he changed the subject, calling attention to Shadow. The horse stood tied to the tree, sneaking a leaf here and there.

"Rarely. And never on a horse I do not know very well."

A mischievous grin appeared on his face. He stepped over to Shadow and patted her sleek, charcoal coat.

"Mr. Winterfield, I would not advise it. How well does she know you?"

"Well enough," he replied, looking into the horse's eye and rubbing his hand under her chin and across her jaw under the bridle.

"Please don't expect me to assist you onto that horse, Mr. Winterfield."

"No need." He loosened the reigns from the tree and led Shadow to stand beside a large stump. Lifting the reins over her head, he took them in his left hand and, stepping up onto the stump, thrust his weight up onto her back. Alexandra flinched when Shadow stepped to the side and tossed her head. But Roman held firm, throwing his right leg up and over. He turned the horse around to face Alexandra, a victorious smile advancing over his lips.

She offered no smile in return.

"See? She trusts me." He coaxed the horse into a trot in a wide circle around her. Alexandra watched as he rounded in front and disappeared behind her back, coming around again. A few clicks of his tongue and the horse moved into a canter, the circle widening. "She's a good horse. Very gentle."

"You've proven your point, so please stop now," Alexandra begged.

Without rancor, she admitted to herself that Roman was a skillful rider. He moved in a balanced rhythm with the stride of the horse, his strong legs gripping its flanks. Glancing over at Alexandra often, that proud smile still prominent on his face, he kept up the perfect tempo. Although impressed by his agility, she frowned when, on his way back around, he broke the horse into a gallop along the forest edge. The distance between them increased in no time.

In a swift motion and for no apparent reason, as Roman looked back at her, the horse took a sudden sharp turn. Roman's equilibrium lost, he was thrown from the horse, hitting the ground with a thud she heard even from that distance. Shadow trotted away.

"Roman!" Abandoning the formality of address, she ran toward him. It seemed an eternity before she reached where he lay in a heap in the grass. She fell to her knees. "Roman," she called, rolling him onto his back. A trickle of blood streamed over his temple. He groaned, but his eyes remained closed. "Speak to me!" When there was no response, she ran for her horse.

Roman opened his eyes in slits to an unfamiliar man sitting beside him. Beyond, he noted his mother, sister, and Alexandra staring at him. Around him the room began to sway. The familiar heavy walnut bedposts, burled bureau, and feather pillow beneath his head told him he was in his own bed chamber.

It must have been evening. His three lamps cast an orange light over the entire room, and the uncovered windows sat dark and quiet.

"Who are you?" Roman asked of the man, surprised at the weakness in his own voice.

"You've injured yourself," came his mother's voice. "This is Dr. Chambers."

"What happened?" Roman asked in a whisper, dropping his eyelids closed. Lifting one hand to touch his head, he winced as a sharp pain pulsed across his scalp. Sensing some type of band around his head, he moaned.

"You fell from the horse." The melody of Alexandra's voice drifted into his ears. So sweet was her tone, always so sweet, and the face of an angel. His last memory—that of looking into the sparkle of her eyes as he trotted past her in the field—returned to his mind. She had watched him, had not taken those eyes off him.

"You tried to warn me, but I wouldn't listen, would I?" His words came out in a slur.

"That's right," came her gentle response.

"Roman," his mother's voice boomed in his aching head, "you've suffered a severe blow to the head and have probably broken at least a few ribs."

"You'll be sore for awhile, Son, but you'll be fine," said the doctor. Roman flinched at a touch to his eye. The doctor forced open each lid, after which he stood and turned to Olivia. "He should tolerate his usual diet. Check his pupils regularly, and summon me if you notice any of the symptoms I mentioned earlier."

"Of course, Doctor," replied Roman's mother, leaving the room with him. Her voice returned to him in echoes as she walked with the doctor through the hallway and then down the staircase.

Catherine and Alexandra must have remained, but he heard no other sound besides his own patterned breaths.

He wanted to doze, but pain charged through his head and now his left side as well. He wanted to open his eyes and bask in the loveliness of their guest, but his eyelids refused to budge. Moments later, he heard light footsteps and an aggravated sigh near his bed.

"Hello, Mother," he whispered. His tongue felt like leather and his lips like the desert sand.

"Roman, you realize this situation will limit my ability to make further progress in the preparations for the ball. My attentions are forced upon your recovery. It may even be necessary to cancel this party to which we've all been looking forward."

"I can manage without your help," he said.

"You think so, do you? Show me," his mother challenged. "Show me this instant that you can get up out of that bed without assistance."

Roman fought to open his eyes, blinking several times, and raised his throbbing head. When he attempted to move his arm, he cried out in pain and fell back into the pillows.

His sister and Alexandra stepped forward, ready to help.

Olivia remained still, her arms crossed. "Of course I'm right, Roman. I hope you realize the tremendous burden you've placed on me."

"Mother," Catherine spoke up, "is there any reason Alex and I can't care for him?"

Roman smiled. Straining to open his eyes again, he managed to focus on Alexandra. Her blue eyes, now dark in the muted light, were fixed upon his mother.

"No, Catherine. You have your own responsibilities; and I will not tolerate a guest of the family to engage in work of any sort in this house. I'll see to him myself."

"But Mother," Catherine argued. "John's working at the vineyard. We can work here. Really."

"I'll not hear another word!" Olivia spun on her heel and left the room.

Roman moaned, his eyelids not responding to his weak attempt to keep them open.

"Girls!" he heard his mother holler from somewhere downstairs. "I'll not call you again for dinner."

His sister kissed his cheek, and he heard the two scamper from the room.

The following day, while her mother attended to other responsibilities, Catherine read in her brother's room. The house remained hushed so he could sleep, but at the noon hour, loud voices of two ladies echoed up from the foyer below. Catherine hastened toward the main staircase. As she descended, she found her mother giving instructions to a young lady, whose back was to Catherine.

"Dear," Olivia said upon taking notice of Catherine, "I've arranged for a caregiver for Roman."

The woman turned around, an arrogant grin on her painted lips. "Hello, Catrina."

Catherine made no attempt to hide the horror that must have overtaken her expression when she stared into the face of Caroline Landly. A movement from the balcony one story above caught her attention. She looked up to find her own horror written across the face of Alexandra Viana.

Olivia escorted the lady past Catherine and up the stairs toward Roman's room.

Chapter Twenty-Two

Five cold, stormy days followed Roman's accident. Wind hurled rain against the windowpanes like little daggers. Thunder rumbled in the distance.

Alexandra and Catherine put forth their greatest effort to occupy themselves indoors, all the while listening to the endless chatter of Caroline Landly on the second floor, her domineering voice resonating from the walls throughout the house as she read to her patient, fed him every meal, and now and then assisted him to his feet. She fluffed his pillows, tidied his room, straightened his blankets, and watched him nap. She attended his every need, fulfilled his every request.

"Who was at the door?" Alexandra asked of Catherine when she threw herself onto the sofa in the music room in exasperation, dropping a bouquet of yellow roses onto the floor.

"I don't even know her name."

"Not another one."

"When is this going to end, Alex? Trinkets and cards, candies, books, games. One even came by with a new pen and stationery with a request that he write to her during his recovery! I suppose the one thing he actually needs is more vases in which to put all these ridiculous bouquets. Roman is brought to his knees, and the women line up to assist him back to his feet."

Alexandra could not miss the note of sarcasm in his sister's tone. "Word spreads quickly in London," she whispered. Her own heart had sunk to her shoes days before with the appearance of the women, one after another. And there it had stayed. If only that fine sunny afternoon, the day of his accident, had been like this one, Alexandra mused, he would not have been hurt, Caroline Landly would not have been called, and these women would have kept their sentiments to themselves. Oh, why had she ever agreed to stay the whole summer? Her escape to Brentwood could not arrive soon enough now.

"They come all this way for nothing, you know," Catherine was mumbling. She rose from the sofa to wander about the room. "Even I can't go near him with the buzzard, Caroline Landly, on guard. She shoos me away every time I come close, no matter the reason. I can glimpse him through the open door and nothing more. 'He can't be disturbed,'" she mocked. "'He's sleeping.' 'I'm shaving him now.' Heaven help us when he recovers enough to be seen again in public. There'll be no end to the doting."

Alexandra's fingers ambled over the pianoforte keys in half-hearted tones. Any meaningful concentration on the music proved useless.

Miss Landly stayed for dinner most nights, eating with the family. Later she would serve Roman his meal in his room and watch over him until late into the evening. By the time she would take her leave, Alexandra and Catherine would have already retired. Early the next morning, she would be back on task as though she had been employed for a lifelong position.

Alexandra struggled to keep civil company with her at the dinner meal, but it proved almost unbearable. Caroline Landly seemed to be a woman of vast knowledge on every subject under the sun. Advice from her was abundant and her opinions final. Somehow all topics led back to the self-exalted Caroline. She boasted of her experiences, bragged of her intelligence, and prided herself on her many fine qualities. Often before dinner was finished, Alexandra, along with Catherine, would admit defeat and leave her to ramble on with Mrs. Winterfield, whose appreciation for the woman seemed to have escalated to adoration.

Day by day Alexandra heard her reports of the patient's returning strength. Of course, this lent favor to Caroline's own dutiful efforts, yet she always had some excuse as to why he could not leave the confines of his room or receive visitors.

Now and then Roman's voice, too, resounded through the hallways with occasional laughter from both. But Caroline continued to remind them that he still suffered extreme pain.

Alexandra locked herself in the library most days, burying her thoughts in letter writing and a variety of books. She looked at her Bible on the library table day after day, disappointed to find the marker right in the place she had left it the previous night.

One day, as she passed Roman's room, she could not help but overhear one of their conversations.

"There's a book in the library I'd like you to get for me, Caroline."

Alexandra's head dropped, her heart in agony to hear him surrender to Caroline's wishes to address her in such a familiar manner.

"Anything, Roman. You know all you need do is say the word."

"It sits on the table next to one of the leather chairs. Its cover is brown leather."

"And what is the title of this book?"

"The Holy Scriptures."

Alexandra smiled at his request. However, it was followed by a loud sigh from his caregiver. "Really, Roman, I have as much respect for the book as anyone, but it's not Sunday, you know. I'll choose a book for you. Surely among the thousands of literary masterpieces down there, we can find an interesting topic." Before he even had an opportunity to object, Alexandra heard Caroline's footsteps. She hurried behind the large grandfather clock in the hallway and remained undetected as Caroline passed by.

Unable to fight the frustration that had been mounting the previous days, she fled to her room, securing the door behind her. When Catherine inquired after her, Alexandra responded that she wished to be alone. She would keep her tears of disappointment to herself at all costs.

"I changed my mind, Caroline," Roman said when she returned from the library, book in hand. "Please summon Miss Viana. I'd like to see her—in private."

Caroline looked down her nose at him. "Very well." She left the room in a huff and returned moments later. "Your sister reports that Miss Viana has closed herself in her bedchamber and has requested that she not be disturbed."

Roman nodded and lay silent as Caroline pulled up a chair beside him and began reading. His thoughts were far away.

That very night, Alexandra tiptoed into Roman's bedchamber. The form of his bed appeared in the candle light. Sneaking over, she placed the soft leather-bound book beside the pillow where his head lay.

As he slept, she gazed upon his face in the soft yellow circle of light. The shiny dark waves of his hair appeared black against his pale skin. The auburn hints so visible in the daylight were now hidden in the shadows.

Her gaze moved to his closed eyes. How was it that the male gender always seemed to inherit such lush lashes? She gazed for a long time at his lips. Their perfect contour looked as soft as satin. Recalling the smiles his mouth had borne of late, she could almost hear his warm laughter.

She reached out to touch his cheek, but drew her hand back, realizing with suddenness that his skin, clean and shaven, was so only because of his caregiver. Agony tugged at her heart to imagine Caroline's fingers caressing his cheeks as she shaved him.

Her brow wrinkled as she felt a familiar ache in her throat. A tear fell from her eye to land upon his arm before she could stop it.

Lest he awaken, she extinguished the candle and fled from the room.

Chapter Twenty-Three

Just four days remained before the grand feast and ball. The commanding Olivia Winterfield set the entire household in an uproar, her servants polishing silver, scrubbing floors, washing windows, beating dust from the rugs, and carrying armloads of china and linens up from the basement pantry.

"Good heavens, Doris," she scolded one of the women working in the indoor garden. Alexandra cringed at the shrill tone. "I've told you a thousand times—milk! Not water. Milk is what shines these leaves, not just cleans them."

"Yes, Madam, I'm sorry," the servant said and scurried back to the kitchen.

"Does she speak English?" Olivia muttered, stepping to the table where Catherine and Alexandra were busy counting and stacking linen napkins. "Is she hard of hearing?"

"Mother, how many guests are we expecting?" asked Catherine.

"Three hundred and fifty."

"Gracious, where will they all be seated?"

"Catherine, please, I have enough anxiety over it without your remarks."

"But Mother—"

"Outside…in the yard. We've no other option but to hold it out there."

"But the rain—"

"Catherine, enough!" Her mother stormed from the room.

"Let's hope for a break in the weather," Alexandra added as Olivia's footsteps faded down the hallway. "I'm beginning to understand the wisdom of your father in keeping his distance from the house."

"And your brother's. He's been working in the mud and rain all these days."

"And yet I'm certain his environment has proved much tamer than ours."

Catherine dropped her head back in laughter. "I wish I could dismiss this household as easily as he does. I'm envious that John's been sharing his evening meals with Mr. Aramis." Her voice dropped to a whisper. "I've not seen him since this storm set in. How I long for his company again. Did I tell you— your brother has been acting as messenger between us."

"No, I was unaware of that," Alexandra said, glancing at the doorway. "Catherine, we must talk. You do realize that Mr. Westcliffe will be here in just four days."

"I do." She looked down.

"What are your intentions for him and Mr. Aramis?"

"I've informed Mr. Aramis of the situation. He knows I've a decision to make."

"A decision? Catherine, your very actions indicate you're resolved. Your feelings for Mr. Aramis can no longer be mistaken or hidden."

"As I said, I've a decision to make. Mr. Aramis knows of Mr. Westcliffe's position and wealth and his connection to my family."

"A marriage would be imprudent at best when you've feelings for another man. You must see that. Besides, you don't know your family's view one way or the other about Mr. Westcliffe." Unsure about Richard and Olivia's opinion, she remained convinced Roman harbored a certain amount of disdain for the man. "Please, tell me you'll ask for their judgment on the matter."

"Did I tell you Mr. Aramis has been scheduled to be on duty at the party?" Catherine directed a happy smile at Alexandra, nonchalance written all about her face.

"Oh, Catherine, no..." Alexandra whispered, feeling the blood rush from her face.

The eruption she had been fearing was due to occur the very night of the ball.

Three nights prior to the ball, Roman ventured from his room to dine with the family.

"Where is Miss Viana?" he asked, noting her chair sitting empty.

"She has been invited to the Suttons again," said Catherine. "Oh, Roman, how good to have you back with the family."

"What do you mean by 'again'?"

"She has been spending some time there. She so enjoys herself. I'm certain Preston Sutton will be in attendance at the ball." Catherine cast a smile of delight his way.

He looked away, heat rising to his face.

At last, the fog and rain retreated. With just two days remaining before the party, Olivia and Catherine readied themselves early in the morning for a trip to town, stating something about a last-minute purchase.

"We'll return by evening, Alex," Catherine assured. "Are you certain you won't come?"

"Yes. Thank you. I've been longing to take Cinnamon out for a ride and am compelled to do so today lest the rain returns."

"I forbid you to curse our party by such sentiments, Alex," Olivia scolded. "If you will not accompany us, then suit yourself, but there will be no more talk of rain." The woman turned on her heel and rushed Catherine out the door.

Alexandra waved to them through one of the front windows while the footman assisted them into the carriage.

After they had gone, she grabbed her riding jacket and, slipping her arms into the sleeves, stepped out onto the wide front porch.

Everything sparkled, wet with freshness. She drew clean, crisp air into her lungs and spun around one time on her toes, feeling the cool air rush in a whirl about her.

For a brief moment she wondered what Roman was up to. Earlier, when she had come down for breakfast, his door stood open, though he had not joined the family for the meal.

She shrugged and quickened her pace toward the courtyard, anticipating the view of the property. It would be spangled with dew, reflecting the light of a thousand particles of the sun. What beauty awaited her. She adored her rides through the Winterfield property.

The question she had pondered moments before found its answer when she passed through the tall iron gates of the courtyard.

There in the bright sunshine, stretched upon a long chaise relaxed Roman Winterfield—with Caroline Landly propped on a chair at his side.

Alexandra stopped short at the sight of them.

Ducking her head, she hurried past, muttering a quick good morning.

Roman's posture straightened. "Miss Viana, good morning."

From the corner of her eye, she saw his head turn with her as she whipped by him. She heaved a sigh of relief upon passing through the stable doors.

She stood in the shadows waiting for her heart to calm, listening to Caroline's voice. Whatever she was saying to him Alexandra was happy not to know.

She headed down the corridor of stall doors. An unusual—eerie even—silence filled the stable.

"Hello? Is anyone here?"

After receiving no response, she let herself into Cinnamon's stall.

"Hello, girl." She stroked the horse's muzzle and neck. "Remember me? I know it's been a few days."

The horse stood still while Alexandra slipped the bridle over her nose and ears. Pulling the saddle from one short wall, she lugged it over, and heaved it onto Cinnamon's back.

While reaching below the horse's belly for the strap, she stopped and listened again.

An odd rustling had begun somewhere nearby.

Stepping back into the corridor, she closed Cinnamon's gate behind her.

Three stalls down she peered through the slots of one gate and found Duchess pawing the straw on the ground and pacing and twisting around to glance at her side. The horse dropped to lie in the straw and began rocking to one side, then the other, her eyes wild with agitation.

Alexandra crept into the stall and crouched down. "There, there, girl," she said in a soft tone.

Duchess twisted about, impatiently rolling to her other side.

"Hello?" Alexandra called, standing again. "I need help!" she cried through the gate.

Again, no one answered her call.

Leaving the stall, she ran in a harried search of the long stable, but found herself alone with the horses. Gathering her skirts in her fists, she darted toward the large main doors and burst out into the courtyard, sprinting toward Roman.

"Excuse me, but—" she called as she approached the pair near the main gate.

"What is it?" Miss Landly responded first.

"I need your help, Mr. Winterfield. It's Duchess, your horse—it appears she's in labor and is very distressed."

Caroline jumped to her feet, putting herself in front of Roman. "Just what would you have *us* do? I've a patient of my own here as you can see, and might I remind you that he's in no condition to go traipsing around in that stable. Had it not occurred to you that Richard employs staff for that sort of thing? I suggest you find one of them." She waved Alexandra away.

"Thank you. I thought of that," Alexandra replied with all the politeness she could muster. "There's no one available.

I realize you're here because of your concern for others and know you could no longer stand to leave an animal suffering any more than you would a human, were it in your power to help."

Caroline grunted and Alexandra raised her chin higher.

"Miss Landly," Roman spoke up just as the woman was about to lash back. "Perhaps you're unaware that Duchess is not my father's horse. She's mine."

Alexandra watched with disbelief when a pleasant smile seeped across Caroline's lips. She turned to face Roman. "Of course you're concerned about your horse." Her voice dripped with sweetness. "What would you have me do?" When she turned back to Alexandra her expression reverted to the rock it had been before, her eyes solid iron.

"Go for the veterinarian," Roman said.

"Me?" Caroline planted her fists on her hips in a way that almost made Alexandra laugh.

"Of course," he said. "I'm sure Miss Viana has much more knowledge in this sort of thing. She should stay here with the horse."

Caroline uttered a low growl and stormed past Alexandra.

Unbelievable, she thought, watching the woman stomp through the gates and out of their sight.

"Mr. Winterfield, I realize it was one of these very creatures who left you in your present condition—"

"No," he interrupted, "I did that myself. Come here, please. I'll need your help to stand."

Alexandra hastened to his side and sat on the edge of the chaise. "How much do you know about foaling, Mr. Winterfield?"

"Absolutely nothing." Her heart leaped at his touch when he placed his left arm around her shoulder. With hesitation at first, she slipped her arm around his waist and grasped his hand that rested on her shoulder with the other. He studied her face for a moment before nodding. They stood, both at once. Roman winced. "Thank you. I can walk on my own, but slowly."

It seemed an eternity had passed before they crossed the patterned brick of the courtyard. They found Duchess in much the same state as Alexandra had left her, and still there was no stable hand to be found.

"From the way she's acting," Alexandra said, "I fear the foal may be stuck."

"What does that mean?"

"One of a number of possibilities. It could be breech or up-sidedown...It's misplaced somehow, I'm certain of it."

"What should we do?"

"First, get her to her feet," she said, stepping into the stall and tromping through the straw to the opposite wall where the harnesses hung. "She'll be much easier to work with in that position."

"You've done this before."

"I was raised with farm animals," she said, concentrating on placing the halter on the horse. Preferring not to see his disgrace over her upbringing, she avoided looking at him. "We had several horses." With the halter secured, she stood. "I'll need you to pull her while I push from behind." She handed the reins to him and stepped to the back of the stall. Crouching behind the horse, she gave a command and pushed with her shoulder.

Roman cried out in pain as he pulled, but with Alexandra's assistance in the rear, they managed to urge the horse to her feet.

Roman wrapped one arm around his side and doubled over. Alexandra reached for the reins and then for him, helping him to the straw on the ground. His breaths came short and shallow, and his eyes clamped shut.

"Will you be all right?" She feared almost as much for him as she did for the horse.

"Yes—" he groaned.

She led the horse out of the stall to walk her a few yards and then turned to walk back. "I'm sorry!" she said, peering in.

"You—" he winced in pain, clutching his side, "are to blame least of all." His breathing appeared to have slowed a bit but remained shallow. His head fell back to bump against the slotted wall. "What can I do?"

"Hold her. I need to take a look."

He struggled to his feet and took the reins. Alexandra moved to the rear as the horse tossed her head. Roman held her firm.

"Well, what do you see?"

"No sign of the foal yet." She stepped back around. "Which might be good. Her water hasn't broken yet. We may have a little time. Try to keep her on her feet. I'll be right back."

"Where are you going?" Fear filled his eyes.

"Just to the door at the end of the corridor. Don't worry. I'll be quick."

She ran the length of the hallway and to the pump just outside the stable in the back, grabbing a pail along the way. The pump arm resisted, requiring all her strength, but after a few pushes, a gush of water sounded from below ground. Two more thrusts of the handle coaxed a trickle and then a stream from the faucet. Water filled the bucket and overflowed.

She wondered why the stable master had neglected Duchess in such a manner. Surely, the horse had shown signs of labor long before now. Most foals were born at night; still, someone should have been assigned to her continually the past few days. However, given the nearness of the party and Mrs. Winterfield's state of hysteria, the stable hands had in all likelihood been assigned to more pressing matters. In the process, poor Duchess had been forgotten.

The full bucket proved almost too heavy to carry, even with both hands. But she managed to lumber back inside after scanning the grounds again for any sign of one of the stable servants. Just inside, she set the pail down near a supply closet, finding some clean rags, a large bar of soap, and a short, thin rope. As she grabbed for them, Roman called out, "Come quick!"

She tucked the supplies beneath one arm and took the handle of the bucket. Water splashed over the sides to the floor and down the front of her as she rushed toward the stall.

She found Duchess lying in the straw once again. Roman stood nearby hunched over, staring wide-eyed at the horse, one hand tucked around his side.

"She wouldn't stand any longer," he said, his voice frantic.

The horse rolled from side to side, the whites of its eyes growing into large crescents.

Alexandra removed her riding jacket and dipped both arms into the icy water up to her elbows. She rubbed the soap over her arms and wiped them dry with a rag before stepping to the horse and kneeling in the hay.

The expression on Roman's face matched the fear in the eyes of the horse when Alexandra slipped one hand into the tight birth canal. Deep within, through a slippery thick membrane, her fingers skimmed over a bony, rounded structure. Twisting her hand to one side, she located what felt like the foal's sharp hooves.

Withdrawing her arm, she rocked back onto her heels to reach for one of the rags. "I'm going to need your help."

"What exactly will that entail?"

"The foal's upside down. It must be turned. I can't do it alone."

His expression went from concern to utter terror. He backed away. "I cannot do this!"

"Then I'll sit with Duchess while you get me a rifle," she said, casting a serious look upon him.

"I'll do no such thing. We'll wait for the doctor."

"There's not enough time. She's suffering. Do you understand? If we put her down, the foal may still have a chance. Without your help, both of them will die. She's your horse...as is the decision."

In silence, he stepped to the bucket and looked down into the water. Rolling up his sleeves, he plunged his arms in and soaped them as he had seen her do.

Admiration for him and his terrified but willing spirit enveloped her like the warmth of a fire on a cold night. His action came as a surprise, and yet it was what she would have expected from any gentleman—and Roman Winterfield was well on his way to becoming just such a man.

He stepped over to kneel beside her in the hay. Grabbing the rope, she tied it into a slip knot on one end.

"It's going to be tight. We're working against contractions. You'll need to start by tearing open the membrane."

"The what?"

"Please, just listen. Slide your hand in as far as you can." Without hesitation he complied while she held back Duchess' tail. "That's right," she commended.

Roman's face remained serious, not at all the expression of disgust she anticipated. His hand and forearm disappeared into the birth canal.

"Good heavens, my arm," he hollered. "It's going to be crushed!"

"It will seem that way. Don't worry. We'll be done in no time. Do you feel anything?"

"I think it's the foal. Rounded in the front, then long and flat."

"That's the lower jawbone. Can you tear that membrane?"

"It's too slippery."

"You'll need to use both hands."

"You can't be serious."

"Very. With every contraction, we lose precious room in there. Quickly!"

With a grunt and this time a wince she interpreted as pain— either from his arms or ribs or possibly both—he obeyed and a moment later was drenched with a gush of fluid that soaked the front of him and spilled onto the hay.

"That's good," she said, "just the water. Now we've no time to lose. Take this rope."

A wet hand emerged to grasp it.

"I want you to slip that around one of the hooves." She wiped a strand of hair from her face. "You'll feel them." She kept hold of the other end of the rope.

"I think I found one."

"When it's around the leg, tighten the knot." She glanced down at Duchess, lying still for the most part but twitching now and again.

"Do you have it?" Alexandra asked.

"No, it's too slick, like it's inside another membrane."

"Tear that one, as well." She watched his face. His brow remained tense, and his gaze moved from her eyes to the wall.

An instant later, he moved back, pulling both arms from the horse. "I can't do this." Reaching for a rag, he wiped down his arms, massaging them. "I'm losing the sensation in my hands."

"Give me the rope," she said. "I'll snare the hoof." She slid her arm inside. "But you will have to do the rotation. Even in your injured state, you're much stronger than I am."

He grimaced. "Why is no one here in the stable to help Duchess? Who is responsible for this? I'll have his head."

"Your mother." Alexandra located one small hoof, feeling the sharp edge. Looping the knotted end around the foot, she tightened it and withdrew her arm. "But that isn't important now. We're losing time. I need you to reach in and follow the rope to the foot."

After a moment's hesitation, he hurled a look of opposition upon her and knelt once again. One arm re-entered the horse.

"I snared a leg," she said. "Can you feel it?"

"Yes. Now what? Hurry!"

She rushed around to his left side. Reaching beneath him, she grasped the loose end of the rope.

"Now locate and hold onto the other leg," she said.

Scooting closer, his free arm on the horse's rump, he said, "Yes, I feel it."

"You'll need to cup your palms over both hooves. They're sharp; we don't want to injure Duchess." He grunted in dispute but obeyed, forcing his free hand into the canal. "All right. I've got them both."

"You're going to pull the free leg down and around to the other side of the head while I pull the rope up. Ready?"

His perspiration told her of his tattered nerves. When he nodded, she pulled.

"It's not working," he complained.

"Wait for the contraction to end and try again. Tell me when."

"Now!" he said. She pulled once more. He hollered in pain. Duchess twisted around and whinnied. "Try again." She pulled when his arms flexed. "It's coming!" he cried.

Roman pulled out and threw his arms back onto the ground, panting. With the following contraction, Alexandra saw two tiny hooves emerge. Another contraction thrust the head out. A few more and the short neck, withers, and then the entire body slid onto the straw at Roman's feet.

He stared in astonishment at Duchess' miniature replica. All but the head was covered in a glistening, transparent sheath.

The mare lay still on the ground. Before long, she twisted around and began to clean the dark foal.

Alexandra settled into the straw beside Roman, winded from the strain. She gazed over at him. He exhaled as though he had forgotten to breathe.

With eyes fixated upon the foal, he did not seem to notice that his once-white shirt had been soaked through and was now covered with smudges. He pushed a lock of hair back from his face, leaving a dirty smear on his forehead.

"You did it," she said, unable to suppress her smile.

"I did that?" he asked. "You mean she's going to be all right?"

"Both of them will." Alexandra scooted over to the foal. "It looks as though you have yourself a filly, Mr. Winterfield. A healthy little girl." Alexandra reached for a clean rag, which she tossed to him. "Duchess is your horse; therefore, so is her foal." She wiped her own hands clean with another. "You know," she said, unable to pull her gaze from the new foal, "a birth is never a mundane event. Mr. Winterfield, you just participated in a miracle."

Licked clean by its mother, the newborn unfolded two spindly legs from beneath her body that seemed to stretch half the length of her mother and struggled to push herself up. She stumbled and fell against Roman. He laughed and stroked the fuzzy mane. Alexandra laughed with him.

"Mr. Winterfield, your ribs. What of your pain?"

"What pain?" He laughed again at the foal's struggles to steady herself, her gangly legs spread wide and trembling.

"Bella Piccolo," he muttered. "That will be her name."

"Bella Piccolo? What does it mean?"

He seemed lost in his thoughts, and she wondered whether she had made a mistake in asking.

"I passed the winter in Italy," he finally answered, dropping his head against the stall door and closing his eyes. "One cold night, I found myself stranded in the countryside. A young farmer and his family took me in. After a warm meal and a glass of wine by the fire, I was more than a little surprised when he handed me a blanket and showed me to the door. I—Roman Winterfield, a man accustomed to only the most luxurious of inns—was directed to their barn. I slept on a mound of hay just like this," he said, opening his eyes and nudging a piece of straw with the toe of his shoe. "Upon waking to the sun streaming through a slat in the wall, I found I was being scrutinized by a heifer helping herself to my bed for her breakfast. The farmer's wife treated me to the freshest eggs, a slab of ham, and the fluffiest biscuits I'd ever laid eyes on. Other than the sleeping arrangements, they treated me like a king. I wondered why this family had met my every need and yet withheld from me a bed? Prior to leaving, I just had to ask. Do you know how the farmer responded?"

"I can't imagine."

"His little Piccolo. Bella Piccolo. With that, he called to his wife, and she appeared, a little girl in her arms. He explained that the child's bed was the only one in the house. Even he and his wife had no mattress on which to sleep."

"His daughter was so precious that not even for a guest would he displace her," she suggested.

"To that impoverished farmer, I may have appeared a king, dressed in my cashmere coat, leather riding gloves, and top hat. But his daughter was far more important—she was an angel. And with those ringlets the color of the rich coffee and her dew-drop eyes, I could have believed it myself."

"Bella Piccolo," Alexandra repeated, "beautiful, small, or, more loosely, 'beautiful baby.'"

He patted the filly's neck. "This baby's hair is that same rich color. And just look at her eyes."

"There couldn't be a more fitting name."

"Nothing is too good for this baby, just like the other Bella Piccolo."

It was a full hour later when Caroline Landly returned with the veterinarian.

"In here," Roman called out upon hearing their voices.

Caroline stopped short at the stall door, eyeing first Roman, who had struggled to his feet, and afterward Alexandra.

"Had Miss Viana not been here, I could have lost both my horses," Roman said when the doctor stooped to examine the foal.

Alexandra followed Caroline's glare, looking down upon her own blouse and skirt just beginning to dry from the water that had doused her earlier. Covered with dirt and dust, she would have looked more presentable had she sowed the fields all day on her hands and knees. Heat rushed to her cheeks upon imagining what her face must have looked like. Several strands of hair drooped before her eyes. She tucked them behind her ears and rolled her cotton sleeves back down, buttoning them at the wrists.

It was then she noted Roman's expression as his gaze moved from Caroline in her perfect velvet jacket and white ruffles to his own filthy clothing to Alexandra's equally soiled attire. It finally rested on her face. How could she interpret his stare as anything other than shame?

"Congratulations," the doctor said to Alexandra. "Both horses are fine and healthy."

"The credit belongs to Mr. Winterfield," she said. "It was he who delivered the foal." Mortified at her appearance and desperate to flee, she put her head down and stepped around Caoline.

Outside the stables, she ran for the house.

During the dinner meal, Alexandra kept her eyes downcast. She could not bear to meet Roman's gaze.

In her usual character, Caroline Landly dominated the conversation, boasting of her heroic task in locating the veterinarian that day.

How could Roman put up with such conceit? Yet he did. Day after day, it seemed she was more pleasing to him. His sudden embarrassment to be in Alexandra's presence—much less to be discovered doing the work of a stable hand—told her all she needed to know.

She finished her meal in silence and excused herself.

Later in the evening, Alexandra accompanied her brother and Catherine to the small lake on the Winterfield property. There they found Antoine awaiting them, skipping stones across the water. The recent stretch of rainfall had left a blanket of dew, and as the sun took its leave, a chill the likes of an autumn nip lingered in the air.

The foursome stayed for several hours, until the moon appeared, sending ripples of light dancing across the lake's surface.

Conversation flowed among three of them. However, Alexandra could focus on nothing other than the events of the morning and Roman Winterfield's reactions to Duchess' grave situation. She decided that his willingness to comply had sprung from his heart, for she was discovering one new pleasing trait after another in him every day. And the expressions in his eyes—everything from apprehension to exhilaration—told her he was a man of deep compassion, and, yes, perhaps even humility.

The story about the farmer's little girl...well, it overwhelmed her with a feeling...some sort of feeling. But what exactly? What had she seen in his face as he described the child? Affection? Fondness? Warmth? Touching as they were, all those terms fell short of his expression. Was it tenderness for a child he found so adorable? Try as she might, she could not define his look.

It had been six weeks since his return to Kent. Almost bursting into laughter over her earlier fear of his ruining her summer, she could not seem to get her fill of his company.

What would her sisters say? Here was Roman Winterfield, the person who had inflicted countless blows to her family. How could she, the youngest of them, now confess love for this man?

And what did it matter anyway? His growing attachment to Caroline Landly had raised a barrier between them. What a despicable woman!

But then there was the ball, right on their heels. She wondered if he would, just once, ask her for a dance. She could picture it now; he would spy her across the room at the punch bowl, just like Stephen had with Grace. He would approach and ask for her hand. On the floor he would slip his palm around her waist. And they would waltz...

"Where are you?" Catherine asked, plopping herself down on the blanket.

"What do you mean?" Alexandra looked away even though she knew her blush could not be detected in the moonlight.

"It's like you're out there somewhere." She pointed to the black velvet of the sky. "On some distant star."

"I assure you, my feet are planted firmly on solid ground." Yes, right here on Winterfield property. Here...near him. "Never mind me." Alexandra looked up at Antoine standing beside her brother in the light of a lantern on the lake shore, two fishing lines cast into the water. "You're living what most people only dream about, Catherine."

Alexandra lay awake in the dark. Only the sound of the breeze rustling the sheers over her open balcony doors broke the silence. She recalled again the vision of the child in Italy— the one Roman had burned into her mind through his words.

"No!" She pushed herself up. "Not that. Anything but that." The expression on his face… It was not affection for the child. It was not fondness, for he had seen her but one brief instant.

It was *longing*. No other word could describe that look. Roman Winterfield longed for a child of his own, a wife and family.

A single tear dribbled down her cheek. Admitting defeat to Caroline Landly, she buried her face in her hands. Miss Landly would be the one to bear his children—a woman against whom Alexandra could not, in the remotest of possibilities, compete.

Crying herself to sleep, she grieved the loss of a man who would never know of the deep love she had cultivated for him.

Chapter Twenty-Four

With the ball scheduled for the following evening and the household frantic with preparations, Antoine Aramis fled the mania that had reached even the vineyard for the peaceful solitude of a library in town. How could he have refused John's request to accompany him when the young man begged for the means of escape?

Hours later, while John talked with the librarian, Antoine stepped out into the bright afternoon sun. It had been a long day pouring through pages of dusty archives.

He rubbed his tired eyes and opened them to a barrage of passing pedestrians. The sun, on its daily trek across the sky, paused just over the treetops to cloak the street with shadows. Clods of dirt, propelled by hooves of trotting horses with carriages behind, jumped from one place to another.

In the breaks between the moving vehicles, Antoine's gaze settled upon two men across the lane, conversing in the park. Their faces seemed familiar to him, though he could not recall specific times or places. He stepped back into the shadow of the library's entryway. Uneasiness crept through his bones as he watched them. Their olive skin and hawk-like profiles suggested they were not of English descent, though their pinstriped slacks and high collars helped them blend. How had he known them?

"Here you are!"

Antoine jumped at the voice. Thrusting one arm out, he pushed John back. "Get the horses," he commanded. "I'll meet you out back."

John retreated into the library. Antoine stayed and studied the strangers, who appeared to be scrutinizing pedestrians and riders alike.

With unexpected suddenness, the library door swung open, striking Antoine full force on the back.

"I beg your pardon," a man apologized.

But Antoine had been thrown forward into a passerby. Both fell to the ground, where the heel of another man's shoe came down on Antoine's hand. A woman let out a scream when her feet became tangled in his legs and she tumbled down beside him.

"I'm so sorry, my dear man, my dear lady," the man who had come out of the library said, trying to assist all of them up.

Antoine struggled to his feet and grasped his hand in pain. He pulled the other man upright, put his head down, and walked to the corner. Looking back, he found the attention of the two strangers focused directly upon him. They darted across the lane toward him, dodging carriages and upsetting the horses.

Antoine raced around the corner of the building where John sat on his horse and held the reins of Antoine's. They galloped down the side street and mixed into the crowd on another road.

Alexandra Viana bounced with excitement, waving at the carriage approaching Winterfield mansion. Within moments, she embraced her parents, who had arrived a day early for the party. Mr. and Mrs. Winterfield greeted the couple in a similar manner.

"Angela," Olivia said, "come with me out back. I'm in desperate need of a woman's opinion."

"Very well," Alexandra's mother said, a note of hesitation in her voice. She had not yet removed her hat or gloves. "Why not the girls?"

"No, not the girls," Olivia griped. "They're no help on the matter of décor." She tugged on Angela's arm, leading her into the mansion.

"I tried to help her," Richard said, the remaining party tagging behind. "But she refused my advice."

"This is none of your affair, Richard."

"No," he mumbled to Alexandra's father, "none of my affair at all. Just so long as I keep my pocketbook wide open."

Alexandra cupped her hand over her mouth to hide her giggle.

"I can't tell you my relief, Angela," Olivia chattered, "when days of rain finally came to their end."

The sun had begun its plunge as a signal of the close of the day when Roman descended the wide winding staircase to escort Caroline to the front entrance. Alexandra stole a look behind to watch Caroline tuck her hand into the crook of his arm. He led her out front to her own carriage.

Alexandra followed the others to the yard in back. Shading her eyes from the shards of sunrays breaking through the leafy trees, she slipped her arm around her mother's shoulders.

Soon Roman joined the party. After resting his gaze upon her for the briefest of moments, Alexandra was pleased when he walked straight to her father.

"Mr. Viana, I trust your trip was safe and comfortable."

"It was, thank you. I understand you sustained an injury during our absence."

"Yes. However, I'm now on the mend and find my energy increasing by the day." He stepped over to take Angela's hand to his lips in greeting. "You must accompany me to the stables, Mrs. Viana. I've a surprise to show you."

"Oh, no," his mother interrupted. "Not that silly foal. We've more important things to do."

"I'd love to see it," Angela said.

"Not now, Roman," his mother insisted.

"I'll look for you in half an hour," Roman said, excusing himself.

After dinner, young John Viana grasped the opportunity to escape to the billiard room with his father and Richard Winterfield.

"It appears your son has made some remarkable changes, Richard," the elder John said, assessing the triangle of balls at the other end of the table.

"He has certainly surprised us these past few weeks," Richard replied.

"So," John continued, leaning forward to aim his cue, "how long has this romance between him and my daughter been brewing?" The white ball clashed into the triangle of colored balls, sending them scattering.

"For quite some time now, John."

Young John Viana stood with both hands on the cue in front of him, wide eyes darting from his father to Richard and back again to his father.

John stepped back from the table to give Richard room for the next shot.

"Actually," Richard continued, "I believe it may have started in Paris, though I don't have the idea Alexandra was aware of it at that time." He crouched to examine the angles of the balls. Leaning over the table, he struck the cue ball with a sharp tap. It cracked against the solid yellow ball and sent it spinning into the side pocket.

"Nice shot, Richard. Upon consideration, I believe your assessment is correct."

"Your shot, Son," Richard said to young John, who stared in astonishment. "You know, it's been quite an entertaining battle. And there's been an interesting factor thrown into the equation—a young caregiver by the name of Caroline Landly."

John missed the shot for which he had aimed, wanting nothing at the moment except to escape the conversation.

"Ah, yes, Caroline Landly," his father said, "the stunning yet hollow young lady who has been stalking Roman these three years at least."

"Yes, the very one," Richard volleyed as John's father eyed the next shot.

"Just two years ago, I would've considered them a fair match," his father said, "but I can't envision that now." He circled the table and stooped to study the balls.

"No. He'll recognize that, if he hasn't already, and make his feelings known to Alexandra, I'm certain. Just a matter of time."

"So, Richard, do you think it too soon to prepare ourselves for the wedding? I've already made some minor adjustments to the southern wing of Ceann Castle."

Young John's eyebrows arched.

"Perhaps you should first prepare Jessica. She didn't take well to Roman from the beginning. I hardly think she'll be quick to change her opinion despite the improvements he's made."

"Thank you, Richard. Actually, she's the reason for the adjustments in the architecture plans. I thought it wise to allow as much distance between them as possible. Also, when traveling with Jessica in May, I did take the liberty of easing her into the idea of a serious attachment between the two. Though she'll not be pleased, I believe it won't come as a complete surprise. John," his father said, directing his attention to him. He wiped a bead of perspiration from his temple. "John, what's your assessment of the situation?"

"Well...uh...I think...there's a mutual respect between them."

"There you have it," the senior John said, extending his hand to Richard. "Let's congratulate ourselves on what will no doubt prove to be yet another uniting bond for our two families."

Richard smiled with confidence and took the hand in a firm shake.

Young John could not stop his lips from dropping open in disbelief.

Later in the evening, Alexandra opened her bedchamber door to a soft knock. The serene face of her mother greeted her.

"Please come in." The door remained ajar.

Angela led her daughter to the vanity, motioning for her to sit. Taking a brush from the table, she stroked her daughter's silky chestnut hair. "I believe there's at least one person in this house who will be cheated out of the benefit of sleep tonight," Angela commented.

"Poor Olivia," Alexandra stated. "She has worked herself and her entire staff into such frenzy. I do hope all turns out well with the party." Alexandra gazed at the reflection of her mother in the mirror. With her black hair left to cascade over her shoulders, it was hard to discern the difference between her and Jessica.

"And what of you, Alex?" Her mother looked up at her reflection. "How has your sleep been since you arrived here?"

"Is it that obvious?" Up to that point, Alexandra thought she had hid her feelings well.

"Only to one who knows you as I do."

"I've only recently come to grips with it myself." She sighed and stood to pace. Settling on the edge of the bed, she pulled her knees up to tuck them beneath her nightgown.

"What's your conclusion, Alex?"

"Mother, I've not admitted this to any other person, but... oh, what am I doing? I've not uttered it aloud to anyone."

"Alex, it was not my intention to force your thoughts, but if you'd like to talk—"

"I'm in love with my sister's brother-in-law," she blurted. "So deeply that it pains me. There. It's said. Oh, Mother, if only I could be certain of his feelings."

Their conversation fell on a hearing ear in the corridor. Roman Winterfield had escaped his own room to venture to the library. Upon noticing the stream of light from Alexandra's room on the hallway floor, he had stepped over and heard them talking.

With Alexandra's confession, he moved away from the door. Their further words became muffled, but he had heard all he needed. Closing his eyes, he lowered his head.

So, there it was. Her choice had been made. Her love had been declared for Preston Sutton.

Roman stood breathless as the pain in his side returned in all its fury. This time he knew his ribs were not to blame.

Deciding to forego the library, he returned to his room in silence.

Chapter Twenty-Five

Alexandra sighed with relief after peering out the large wall of windows that flanked the indoor garden. The day of the ball had arrived with a spectacular sunrise in a sky dotted with broken clouds. Gardens splashed with color framed the green lawn. Lush hillsides rolled into the misty distance. Bits of azure sky promised to smile upon the evening gathering. By the time of the party, the sunset's palette should provide an umbrella of golds and corals.

The servants had accomplished what appeared impossible just two days previous. Preparations for the large crowd, Mrs. Winterfield reported over breakfast, were running ahead of schedule.

By noon, a sea of tables with white linens ruffling in the breeze decked the yard. Each place setting boasted bone china painted with birds of blues and gold, tiered in three plates of descending sizes and topped with a small bowl. Silverware flashed in reflection of the sun, and crystal flutes and decanters sprayed the tables with sparkles.

Guests would come into the formal foyer, greet the Winterfields and the Vianas, and pass down the large hall to enter the back lawn through an archway covered in white flowers.

Alexandra paced her room all afternoon, under duress at the thought of facing her two sisters. Had her feelings been so clear to their mother, certainly she would fail in her attempts to hide them from the two closest friends she had had since childhood. But hide them she must, for she had heard that Caroline Landly was to be Roman's special guest for the evening, a fact which vexed his sister and convinced Alexandra that there would never be a reason for a confession to Grace and Jessica.

Instead, she would suppress her feelings throughout the evening, and two days later have her escape to Brentwood—with or without Catherine. Perhaps there she would find some comfort, some peace, where she could reason with her heart. A recent letter from the Wrights confirmed that the new caretakers would be absent during the time of her visit.

Her sisters arrived early. Gathering in Alexandra's room just like old times, they dressed and groomed for the gathering. Alexandra sat on the bed in her slip as Jessica emerged from the dressing room in a flowing dress that matched the pale yellow roses in the garden. Her black hair created a striking contrast against the buttery fabric. Try as she might, Alexandra could not fight the tears that filled her eyes at the recent changes in her sister's form. The round protrusion beneath the layers of material was now undeniable.

"Alex, are you alright?" Jessica stepped over to her. "You seem a bit emotional today."

"Yes. I'm overjoyed that you have found such happiness in your life, Jess. You bring honor to the Winterfield name." She jumped to her feet. "Excuse me..." Dashing into the dressing room, she sat on the cushioned stool behind the closed door and wept.

"She wasn't so emotional when I was expecting," she heard Grace tell Jessica.

"I don't think that's it," Jessica muttered. "Look at her eyes, Grace. That luster, the laughter that brings those blue eyes to life...it's gone."

"Do you need help with your corset?" Grace asked, just outside the door.

"No." Alexandra wiped the tears from her cheeks. "I'll be just fine."

When she emerged, her tears had dried and she was dressed in a dusty-green satin dress. The off-the-shoulder sleeves were short and puffed and the bodice hugged her torso to the waist, where the satin split to show drapes of white beneath. The skirts flared to the floor.

"Would you help me with the buttons?" she asked in a sheepish voice.

Her sisters pushed the tiny sage satin buttons through loopholes from between her shoulder blades to her waist.

"Alex, you look gorgeous," Jessica said, stepping back.

"How fortunate any man who wins your hand for a dance tonight," Grace added. "You're astonishing beyond words."

Her sisters pinned and coaxed her hair into a perfect French twist lined with tiny flowers. Thin strands framed her face.

As they talked and worked on each other's hair, Grace and Jessica charmed laughter from her as they talked of their childhood. Their mother poked her head in from time to time to check their progress.

Both families were prepared and waiting in the entrance hall when the first guests arrived. Olivia appeared unruffled on the surface but Alexandra suspected a bundle of nerves beneath the façade.

The men looked dashing in their black waistcoats and starched shirts, bowties neat under their chins. Alexandra tried not to look at Roman, but could not help herself. Her pulse quickened when he returned the glance with a soft smile.

Very soon the house began to fill with guests.

"I'll see you out back," Grace whispered to her sisters and took the arm of her husband. Alexandra watched them disappear where the corridor turned.

She stood beside her parents farther back in the entrance hall, behind the Winterfield family, offering greetings and directions to the gardens. She was detained but a few minutes talking with a young woman she had met while in town with Catherine. When she looked over again, she saw her father conversing with Caroline Landly. How thankful she was that she had not witnessed Roman's greeting of her.

As usual, the woman was stunning. Alexandra could only dream of having such a figure. Her long, slender hand settled onto one curvy hip, leaving the other free for gestures while she spoke. Even her gestures were elegant. Caroline brushed past Alexandra, ignoring her presence, when she was escorted away by a servant to the yard in back where the other guests mingled. Alexandra wanted to die when she discovered that Caroline's hair had been fashioned into a golden French twist.

William Sutton arrived, accompanied by his wife and Preston. Alexandra's parents greeted them with an embrace. Preston lingered for awhile to chat with Alexandra before following his parents through the mansion. Finding a moment, she slipped toward the staircase tower and dashed up to her bedchamber suite, pulling the flowers and pins from her hair along the way. Stationed at her dressing table, she let her cinnamon hair fall over her shoulders. Staring at the image in the mirror, she saw little more than a child caught up in a grown-up's game.

"You'll never compete," she mumbled, propping her chin in one palm. "Why even try?" Caroline had invested years learning the social graces, had lived in luxury all her life, and had been kissed by beauty itself.

With no time to create a new style for her hair, she pulled most of it up into a bun and let the remaining strands dangle down her back, thankful for the curls nature had given her. Fashionable or not, it made no difference. She dashed out the door toward the stair tower.

A full hour later, when it seemed almost all the guests had been welcomed, Alexandra and her parents joined the Winterfield family at the door as one final carriage arrived.

Alexandra's breath stopped short when Mr. Gregory Westcliffe stepped out. How had she forgotten about him? He greeted Olivia with a kiss. Catherine glanced at Alexandra. There was no mistaking the terror that froze her friend's expression.

Upon seeing him again, Alexandra understood his power over Catherine. He stood as tall as Roman and had broad shoulders to match, which dwarfed Catherine's tiny frame. And those eyes. Alexandra felt sure they could pierce the black of the darkest night sky. The sand-colored, wavy hair softened him a bit, but the round spectacles added to his intimidating look of superior intelligence and confidence. Yes, Gregory Westcliffe had become a master at using every trait and talent to his advantage.

Olivia tittered, sounding like a coy schoolgirl, as Richard offered the man his hand. "And you know the Vianas," he said.

Alexandra's father had earlier taken a position beside Richard.

"Mr. Viana," Gregory said. "It's a pleasure to see you, as always."

"How are the plans coming along for the tower?" Alexandra's father asked. "I've not seen you these past weeks."

How strange, Alexandra thought and leaned toward Catherine. "I thought his letter to you stated he would be at the island working with my father until the ball," she whispered.

Catherine returned a bewildered look, but offered no comment.

Alexandra watched with interest when Mr. Westcliffe approached Roman, whose dark eyes betrayed his disdain.

"Ah, Roman Winterfield. What a surprise to find you at home. I had expected that you'd remained abroad. It has been far too long, my friend," Gregory said, extending his hand.

"Has it, Westcliffe?" Roman said, more of a warning than a question. His mother stared in disbelief when, rather than take the extended hand in welcome, he moved both hands behind his back. "How quickly two years can pass."

"Oh, but time is a constant for us all, Roman," Gregory bantered, his voice sounding almost hostile. "Its speed changes only with our perception." He stared for a moment and added, "If you will not accept my greeting, them I am forced to offer my hand elsewhere." He bowed his head and stepped toward Catherine.

"You remember our daughter, Mr. Westcliffe," Olivia stated, shuffling past Roman, chastising him with an angry glare.

"It would be a crime to forget the charms of such a lovely young lady." He took her hand to his lips. "Hello, Miss Winterfield."

Catherine's gaze dropped to the floor at the intimidating stare.

Anger burned in the eyes of Roman Winterfield. His lip curled.

Gregory Westcliffe offered only a brief greeting to the remaining members of the welcoming party. Alexandra was content when he bowed his head to her, stepped by, and followed his host and hostess through the grand home to the grounds in the rear.

Alexandra overheard her mother whisper to her father, "It's as though he's never met Alex before. How is one to account for such inconsistencies? What do you make of him, John?"

"I'm inclined to agree with Roman Winterfield," he murmured in return.

The descending sun had warmed the air but not overheated it. Candles set into flower rings on the tables flickered with soft flames. Large oak trees shaded the gathering and added a soothing rustle when the breeze fondled their leaves high above. Many of the guests had already seated themselves. Servants offered hors d'oeuvres and wine.

Alexandra slipped over to Catherine's side.

"Will you be all right?" she asked in a whisper.

"Alex, look! There's Antoine." He was dressed in a white jacket and gloves and carried a tray of glasses. He spotted her, as well, and winked, but looked away again.

Alexandra frowned. Catherine had not answered her question.

"Miss Winterfield," a deep voice came from behind them. Alexandra's heart jumped. "I would be honored to join you at your table for the meal."

"Of course, Mr. Westcliffe."

Satisfied, he stepped away.

"Catherine..." Alexandra began.

"Don't worry yourself, Alex. I've decided to let him down as gently as possible after the ball."

"Why wait? You're only risking yourself, Catherine. His letter...you know he's thinking of proposing."

"I will not embarrass my parents, Alex. But, please, keep as close to me as possible. He'll surely be unable to propose if he fails to get me alone."

Gregory returned. "Shall we?" He led her toward the table where her family would be seated. Alexandra followed in close proximity. "Miss Winterfield," she heard him mumble, "you seem a bit out of sorts this evening. Are you not happy to see me?" Before she could give an answer he added, "I suppose the grief you sustained during my absence has lingered a bit."

Catherine rolled her eyes for Alexandra to see.

Before long all the guests had taken their seats. Roman pulled out the chair beside his own to help Caroline. Glancing at the adjacent table, he watched Preston Sutton doing the same for Alexandra. The man always seemed to be surrounded by a crowd of friends, but this evening he had been paying particular attention to her.

He looked up when Catherine approached their table on the arm of Gregory Westcliffe.

"I've been invited to join your table," he announced, seating Catherine and then himself opposite Roman and beside Olivia.

"Why...I'm..." Olivia stammered, looking from Gregory to Catherine. "...so pleased."

Roman nodded and offered his best smile. Stifling the urge to gloat, he watched the man's solicitous attentions to his sister. *You'll be singing a different song,* he thought to himself, *when she tells you her heart belongs to another.* He longed to see the arrogant Westcliffe put in his place. The moment could not come soon enough.

As the meal progressed through all its tasty courses, he purposely ignored his sister's suitor and instead attempted to focus his attention upon Caroline. His mind and gaze refused to cooperate, however, and he found himself looking beyond her to the disquieting interaction between Alexandra and Preston. The entire neighboring table, including his own brother, engaged in laughter and conversation. The merriment was almost more than he could bear.

Oh, how he wished to trade places with Preston Sutton.

"...well," Caroline was saying to Olivia, "even men will compliment my complexion." She leaned forward and whispered loud enough for all to hear, "and I don't dare reveal my secrets. Why, not even my closest friends are privy to them. You know, there are certain benefits to surrounding oneself with those, shall we say, less favored in appearance. Of course I don't mean you, Olivia."

His mother snickered, and Roman's contempt at being in Caroline's company ignited. Just then, he glanced across the sea of guests to spy a young servant pouring wine from a crystal flask. He strained his eyes, hoping they were playing tricks on him while the muscles in his torso tightened, flaring the pain in his ribs. "Excuse me," he interrupted a conversation between his parents and Westcliffe. "Catherine, may I speak with you in private, please?"

Gregory nodded with a condescending smile, allowing Catherine to leave the table.

She followed him into the house through a side door and into the parlor.

"What's the meaning of this, Catherine?"

"Of what?" she asked, her eyes large and filled with terror.

"How long did you think you could keep it from me? Did you not stop to think that I would discover the truth at this gathering tonight? You must think me a fool!"

"What do you mean?"

"Do you deny that you've started a romance with one of Father's servants? A *servant*, Catherine." He stepped away from her, throwing his arms into the air. "'He's in the wine business, Roman.' That's what you told me when we met him in town. He's in the wine business, all right. Did you think I wouldn't notice him serving the wine here tonight?"

"Antoine Aramis is a good man," his sister said. Tears filled her eyes.

"I don't challenge that point, Catherine. Upon first acquaintance, it would seem so; however a true gentleman would not allow you to hide his identity. A true gentleman would consider *your* welfare and not his alone."

"I love him, Roman." A tear slipped down her cheek.

He turned away, pounding his fist against the solid paneled wall. The pain in his ribs blazed. "Catherine," he said, looking back at her, "you will be an outcast from this society, and it's probable you will be expelled from this family. Where would *that* leave the two of you? Toiling and struggling and in oppression and poverty. Love cannot support a family. Love cannot put bread on the table. Your love will drown in despair, and then what will you have? Does *he* not see that?" Tears streamed down her cheeks. "Do *you* not see that?"

"Roman, please don't be incensed with me," she pleaded.

"If I'm incensed, it's with your protection as its object."

Catherine attempted to wipe the tears from her face to no avail. They kept coming. Her chest heaved with sobs.

"Be in love, Catherine." He cupped her shoulders in his hands. "But be sensible about with whom."

He rubbed his aching temples, turned, and left her alone in the parlor. In the tapestry gallery, he found the orchestra busy tuning their instruments and servants bustling about in final preparations of the dance. He walked to the library and pulled the door closed behind him. The solitude calmed his temper, but how could he rejoin the party and the ever-irritating company of Caroline Landly?

Nearly an hour later, Roman emerged. He had watched the sun sink behind the hillsides from the library windows. It was time he made a reappearance before someone began searching for him.

The tapestry gallery had been transformed into a grand ballroom. With the oriental rugs and furniture gone, the polished mahogany floor reflected like glass the people standing about on it.

He spied Catherine among the guests, satisfied to see that her eyes had dried. She was talking with Alexandra, who looked radiant in the soft light of the candelabras.

He had never seen her more elegant. The way her hair spilled over her ivory shoulders, like a stream of brandy from an alabaster carafe, gave her such an inviting look. He recalled the day spent in the secret meadow and smiled to himself. The vision of her running through the wildflowers with the pristine waterfall as a backdrop would be forever etched in his mind. It had been one perfect day in paradise—an experience that had come with such little effort, the first time in his life he had understood the gratification of true giving with nothing expected in return. He would relinquish all he owned to relive that one day and see the happiness he had brought to her.

"Where have you been, Roman?" Caroline's too-familiar voice tore him from his thoughts.

"Lost in a dream," he muttered, unable to take his gaze from Alexandra.

"One would hardly believe the transformation," Caroline observed. "Such an unsightly condition I found her in at the stables just two days ago. In my opinion, that's where she belongs."

"A little smudge can't mask true beauty, Caroline. It can even serve to enhance it."

"And how is that, Roman?"

"The truly beautiful person need not hide behind the façade of the outward appearance." He turned his eyes toward Caroline. "The beauty is on the inside."

"My, my, aren't we becoming philosophical? Have you saved the first dance for me, Roman?" She reached over to cup his chin in her palm.

"Yes," he stated, feeling his eyes grow cold. "Of course." After all, she was his personal guest.

The floor cleared as the musicians signaled the beginning of the dance. Couples sauntered onto the floor to stand opposite one another, two lines quickly forming. Roman led Caroline to a place on the end. He spied his sister on the opposite side far down in the long line. Her partner was Gregory Westcliffe. Also nearby, he found Andrew and Jessica, and Alexandra with, not Preston Sutton as he had expected, but her father.

He looked straight ahead at Caroline Landly. She was, indeed, a glamorous woman, a 'trophy' as Jessica had once described the woman with whom she had pictured him. Those were the first words he had ever heard from Jessica. How he had deserved the chastisement to which she had subjected him, although he did not view things her way at the time. If only he could erase the past and begin anew with her, with her family. As it was, his noble deeds had manifested themselves too late to draw the heart of Jessica's sister.

The dance began and he surrendered half way through, the pain in his side flaring once again.

After resting a few minutes, Roman approached a small group that included Alexandra and her three siblings, Stephen and Preston Sutton, and Roman's brother.

"If it isn't Roman Winterfield," remarked Preston, who stepped away from the group to meet him. Though several years Roman's junior, Preston had never appeared intimidated by him. Indeed, no man, regardless of intelligence, social position, or financial standing, intimidated Preston Sutton. It seemed his greatest pleasure in life was that of making jest of his elders and those of high station.

"Mr. Sutton." Roman nodded in greeting.

The others continued in their conversation, taking no note of him.

"Rumor has it you had a little mishap with one of your horses," Preston teased. He lifted Roman's arm, scanning him from head to toe. "It appears there's no lasting harm. Tell me, how is it that such an expert horseman surrendered control to the animal?" He laughed.

"Let it suffice to say that I was distracted."

"Please accept my apology, Roman. I don't mean to laugh at your expense." Preston wiped the smile from his face. "In all seriousness, it's not your practice to approach me in conversation, so I must assume that I owe your presence to another member of our group."

"I commend you on your astute observation. I mean no offense to you personally, but there's a certain young lady with whom I'd like to dance, one who has become a dear friend to me over these past weeks—that is, if you'll allow her absence."

"Now there's a first on both counts. First in that you, Roman Winterfield, should see the need to approach any woman and that you've found a 'dear friend' in anyone!" Preston's continued laughter was annoying, but not unexpected. "And what do you mean, if I'll allow it? I know to whom you're referring, Roman. Indeed, she has become a close friend of mine, as well." Preston took a few paces backward and raised both hands. "You would have me appear a selfish man, Roman. We can't have that, can we? She's free to make her own decisions." With a confident smile, Preston stepped away.

Roman approached Alexandra, who was conversing with her sister.

"Mrs. Sutton," he said in greeting first to Grace, "it's a pleasure to have you and your husband as guests this evening."

"Thank you. It's a rare treat to be in attendance at a Winterfield ball."

"Miss Viana." He turned his attention to Alexandra. "Might I invoke you for your hand in the next dance?"

"It would be my pleasure, sir."

He bowed and left, noting the look of perplexity on her sister's face.

When the orchestra began he returned to take Alexandra by the hand, leading her to the floor.

For the first time since his return to Kent, he knew not what he should say to her. The declaration she had made to her mother the previous evening would not be erased from his mind. This one dance would no doubt prove to be his single opportunity to take her in his arms and could be their final private conversation.

And yet perhaps it would be better if they did not talk. What could he say? That Preston Sutton could never be loyal to her love? That she was a fool to have fallen for a man of such nonsense? That, given time, she would find herself longing for better?

No. She had, from the time of their reacquaintance, shown herself to be the most dignified woman he had ever known. To injure her feelings in any small way would destroy him.

So he would enjoy her gift of the dance in silence. He would remember how it felt to have her so near and would preserve in his memory the flowery scent of her hair and the last look into the blue of her eyes.

"I'm very proud of you." It surprised him when she spoke.

"I would be honored to know the reason," he managed to respond. "There are few whose opinion I respect as highly."

"Do you mean that?"

"I wouldn't have said it otherwise."

Why did she look away as though his words had pained her?

"You were listening when we talked in the museum in Paris," she said. "I'm delighted that you have taken such an interest in Catherine."

"I'm coming to regret my past neglect and the many missed opportunities." For Alexandra herself had been present at several gatherings two years before and his brother's engagement party. Why, she had been a guest in his home a year prior to that. Yet his narrow, self-centered mind had not allowed him to take notice of her then. How different their relationship could have been. "My sister is grown now," he said. "She makes decisions on her own."

"Perhaps. But what has made a world of difference is that she's going into adulthood knowing how much both her brothers care for her."

Care, indeed! He had just chastised Catherine to the point of tears. Yet they were words she needed to hear. How he wished he could say the same to Alexandra, who was about to make a similar mistake.

Looking down at her, he saw the locket resting over her heart sparkle in a golden flash as they passed one of the candelabras. He had not noticed before that she was still wearing it. Why would she hold on to the Frenchman's gift in light of her declaration about Preston?

The nagging pain from his injury blazed again with intensity. He suppressed the signals, content to endure the few precious moments with her and grieved when the dance ended. Departing the floor, he took note of Caroline Landly glaring their way, whispering to a friend.

"Thank you," Alexandra said.

She lingered a moment as though she wanted to stay, but turned away when Caroline walked toward them.

As the evening wore on, Roman sought to find Jessica and invited her to dance. She agreed at once.

When he took her hand, she looked at him with skepticism. Yet unlike the first and only dance they had ever shared three years ago, she returned his gaze this time.

"You look beautiful this evening," he said. Indeed, who could deny it? Her black hair had been curled and pinned up. The deep blue of her eyes was identical to the hue he had come to admire so in her sister.

"Take care, Roman," she responded. "Those were the words you chose at the beginning of our last dance together, which, I might remind you, ended on a rather sour note."

"I remember." He thought back to that distant evening and decided to play a little game. "But don't think I asked for this dance for the purpose of praising you, Jessica," he responded in similar words he had used that night, though this time he said it with a smile.

"That thought had not occurred to me, so I must admit you have piqued my curiosity, Mr. Winterfield."

His pain had begun again, but he stayed, amused that she would play along. "Actually, Jessica, I had rather hoped to ask your feelings regarding a certain matter."

"Oh?"

"If you'll recall," Roman explained, "the evening of your engagement party, I presented a request to you that you felt you could not grant to me at the time."

"Ah, yes. You asked for my forgiveness."

"Then tell me, do you feel you have seen improvement in my mannerisms?"

"Yes, I do."

"And have I not shown greater respect to your father, your sisters, and to you?"

"I have observed that you have."

"And do not my present tone and choice of words display a man of marked changes?"

"I agree on all counts."

"Then I ask you once again..." He stopped the dance and led her from the floor. "...can you yet allow yourself to forgive my past behavior?"

"Mr. Winterfield...Roman...I can't quite account for the changes I've witnessed, nor do I know from where they stem, but my answer is the same tonight as it was then."

"'True sincerity is only proven over time.' Those were your words to me then."

"I'm impressed at your memory. Time is the only standard against which such behavior must be measured. Although your progress thus far is promising, I have just become reacquainted with you in recent weeks. I'm afraid it's still too soon." At least her tone was mild. "Thank you for the dance." She stepped away, leaving him with his thoughts.

Roman stood alone for but a moment before he found himself surrounded by women all too anxious to hear the details of his tragic injury, to shower him with sympathy, and to ask how he had liked their gifts. Soon, however, the presence of Caroline Landly frightened them away.

"Really, Roman," she said in an undertone, "to see you dancing with these contemptible daughters of John Viana is an embarrassment to say the least. Some of my friends helped me to recall why that name is so familiar. Don't you realize what he's done?"

"I'm well aware of the situation, Caroline."

"Despite the family connection, which I understand you cannot avoid, must you solicit the hand of each of them? You know very well they would have nothing and would be nothing were it not for the generosity of their late grandmother. John Viana did not deserve to benefit from that inheritance. He chose the life of commoners for them all, Roman. They're a humiliation to this society!"

"Come with me." He grasped her arm and escorted her through the crowd to the front entrance of the mansion.

The air was still and warm. With the closing of the door behind them the sound of the music changed to that of the hum of conversation and laughter taking place among groups of coachmen outside.

"Would not the veranda out back have been a little more romantic?" she asked in an alluring tone, a coy smile passing her lips.

"Caroline, listen to me. While in Paris I heard the story of an old man who lived on the streets of the city long ago."

"What are you talking about?" Her shoulders drooped.

"Day after day, year after year, he sat and begged for money from passersby. In the beating sun and the driving rain, he had no protection. In the darkness of night, he had no light. And throughout the years, he had no companion."

"Roman, I'm sorry that you're not well enough to enjoy the dancing. I'll be satisfied with mingling. You know how proud I am to be on your arm." She moved closer, her fingers skimming his elbow.

"Stay for just a moment and hear me out. It was obvious that the man had sustained an injury many years before, for his face was badly disfigured, but what most did not realize, was that the man had been deaf all his life."

"What is the point in all of this?" Rolling her eyes, she took a step back.

"How do you feel about this man thus far?"

"Fine. I'll play along. A beggar is a burden to society and a degradation to an otherwise respectable town. Now, may we please return to our friends?"

"One day the man was found dead on the street. Some of the people were touched by his desperate state and so endeavored to learn more about him. What they found was that, years before in his attempt to rescue a child from a burning building, he had also been rendered completely blind."

Caroline stood glaring, her hands on her hips.

"The man was blind and deaf, Caroline." He awaited a response, but received nothing more than her scowl. "Do you not see that at times people find themselves in situations for reasons that are beyond their control? Not everyone can be so fortunate to be born into wealth and prosperity, but they're still human beings, which fact alone deems them worthy of respect."

"Roman, why that man or the disgraceful Viana daughters, or any other person for that matter, wound up in such a position is not my problem."

Roman stared at her for a long moment. "It's not my problem either, Miss Landly," he said in a soft tone. "I simply desired to see whether you cared." In her eyes he read her realization of the grave mistake she had made. "I think you'd better go." He beckoned her coachman.

His last image of her was her gaping lips while he walked into the house and closed the door behind him.

Catherine Winterfield made every attempt to avoid Gregory Westcliffe's company, but somehow he was never far away. Once during the evening, she had managed to escape him and was startled by a whisper from behind. "Miss Winterfield."

"Mr. Aramis!"

"I must speak with you." She followed him to a quiet corner. "I have but a few moments. You remember the day we met your brother, Roman, in town. Do you recall that I thought he was vaguely familiar?"

"Yes. I remember you said that."

"I've discovered the reason just tonight."

Catherine glanced about to confirm the absence of Gregory Westcliffe and strained to hear Antoine's following words.

"It's your other brother."

"Andrew?"

"Yes. I recognized Roman because of their similar appearances. Catherine, Andrew was the captain of the ship when I stowed away to England five years ago."

"It can't be."

"I vowed I would never forget his face. For a certainly, he is the man. And here I've been living on his very property all these years," he whispered.

"Mr. Aramis, were he to recognize you, he could have you arrested." What dreadful news! First Roman scolded her because of Antoine's poverty, and now come to find out he had stowed away on Andrew's ship. Could the situation grow any more grim?

Antoine stiffened. His lips clamped shut, eyes focused on someone behind her.

"Miss Winterfield." She shuddered and turned to find Mr. Westcliffe, who stood glaring at Antoine. Gregory took Catherine's arm and he led her away.

"Miss Winterfield," he muttered with irritation, "why do you keep disappearing?"

All she could think about was her desperate need to locate Alexandra and John. "Mr. Westcliffe, you must excuse me." She stopped short. "I promise to rejoin you in a few moments." Though trembling inside at his glare, she lifted her chin. "I must insist."

"Very well. But I'll come searching for you in fifteen minutes."

She hurried to Alexandra, whom she found talking with John. The hour was nearing eleven. Just how long could the evening possibly go on?

"Alex! John! I must speak with you—now." She led them to the corner where she had moments before spoken with Antoine. "Roman has discovered the truth about Antoine. He's very angry with me."

"I'm sorry, Catherine," Alexandra said.

"It doesn't end there, Alex. Antoine…he…he recognizes Andrew."

"Of course he does," John said. "He works for him."

"No, John. He met Andrew five years ago, before ever gaining employment here. He stowed away on *The Emerald.*"

"What?" Alexandra blurted.

"If Andrew recognizes Antoine, I just know he'll have him arrested."

"Catherine, Andrew is not a vengeful man," Alexandra reassured her. "Don't be so quick to conclude the matter. After all, the incident was five years ago."

"No, Alex," John interrupted. "She's right to be concerned. Andrew doesn't know Antoine. He's likely to respond as any good captain would, regardless of the passage of time. Demand for justice could blind him from hearing Antoine's side. I'm surprised Andrew hasn't noticed him yet. He would be wise to leave here at once."

"But he's on duty until midnight," Catherine objected.

"How could Andrew remember his face after five years?" Alexandra asked.

"Alex," Catherine said, "Antoine recognized Roman and Andrew. Why would Andrew not recognize him?"

"We must keep them apart for one more hour," Alexandra said.

Catherine's stomach tightened as she looked across the room. "Why does any of it matter now?" she whispered.

There by the orchestra was Mr. Westcliffe conversing with her father. Broad smiles crossed the faces of both as her father extended his hand to the young man, slapping him on the back in a merry gesture. The music ended and the dance floor cleared. Catherine watched her father signal to the orchestra to remain silent and placed one arm around the shoulder of the handsome Gregory Westcliffe. He motioned to her mother to join them, and the three walked toward the empty dance floor.

Catherine's face dropped into her palms.

"Are you all right?" Alexandra's hand slipped over her shoulder.

Catherine peered over her fingers to see her father grab an empty wine glass and a fork from a nearby table.

"No!" Catherine squealed.

A wave of silence rushed through the crowd, followed by a shrill ring as her father tapped a fork on a crystal wine flute.

"Your attention, honored guests," he called out to the assembly. Catherine's mother looked a bit bewildered. "Upon first arranging for this extravagance, my dear wife and I had no motive other than to please you, our friends, with an enjoyable summer dance."

"No," Catherine repeated.

Alexandra grasped her shoulders. "What's your plan, Catherine? You saw this coming, but you refused to acknowledge it."

She offered no response.

"However," Catherine's father continued, "I seem to have discovered another purpose for our gathering—one of great surprise and pleasure. I ask that my daughter, Catherine, please join us here on the floor for a special announcement by Mr. Gregory Westcliffe."

The guests began to murmur and search the crowd.

Catherine fought the urge to hide behind John. Oh, why had she not known Gregory would pull such a stunt?

John and Alexandra's faces reflected the same dread that she herself felt. They stood speechless as the crowd parted and hands reached out to pull Catherine forward.

She looked over to see Antoine weave his way to the front of the crowd and hoped her fear could be seen in her expression.

A great applause had begun and grew louder with her every step.

She met her mother's gaze. Olivia's eyes sparkled with tears, a smile of approval on her lips.

The crowd quieted when Gregory approached to take Catherine's hand. She scanned the faces surrounding the dance floor and fixed her eyes on Antoine. His expression reflected both anxiety and strength. Her words to Alexandra just the day before rang through her head, *Antoine knows I have a decision to make.* And now he would be forced to witness it.

Catherine's heart pounded. Her knees trembled. She feared she would collapse.

"Catherine Winterfield." The smooth voice of Gregory Westcliffe floated through the room. She could not look at him. "I can no longer hide my growing attachment to you. It consumes every fiber of my being."

Her eyes flashed to Alexandra, who covered her mouth, despair and tears seeping from her eyes.

Catherine could kick herself for allowing it to come to this. Why would her father place her in such a spot? Was he so sure of her feelings? She searched the faces for Roman and found him staring, speechless.

"I stand before you a man in agony," Gregory continued, "and beg that you put my pain to rest with your acceptance of my hand in marriage." His tone sounded so genuine.

The guests stood in silence, poised to break into applause. All eyes lay upon her as she lifted her head and searched again for the eyes of Antoine. His expression offered no indication of his wishes for her, though anguish now covered his face. He stood like a statue, awaiting her reply.

She looked up at Mr. Westcliffe and found him glaring narrow-eyed at Antoine. Her heart raced. Had he not caught her just a few minutes earlier speaking with him? It was apparent now. He knew.

Catherine inhaled, focusing on her suitor. He was handsome indeed. She recalled Roman's earlier words. *Have the sense to be realistic. Have the sense to be realistic.* Was this realistic? Gregory was a stable and secure member of society. He would have no difficulty in supporting a family. Could Roman be right? Would her love for Antoine be smothered under the shroud of poverty?

"Catherine...dear," her mother said, "what is your answer?"

"Mr. Westcliffe," she said loud enough for all to hear. "I'm certain you have given such a proposal much contemplation and would think no less of me were I to request equal time to consider it. I cannot give a reply at this moment." With that she pulled her hand free and hastened back through the crowd of astonished expressions toward Alexandra and John.

"Catherine, what an opportunity to refuse him," John scolded in a whisper, taking hold of her arm and leading her away.

Alexandra trotted behind.

"I couldn't embarrass him before all these people."

"Given the circumstances," Alexandra spoke up, "it would have been perfectly fitting."

"I think I'm going to faint. John, please fetch me some water." Alexandra escorted her to a chair away from the guests as John slipped back into the crowd.

Gregory Westcliffe watched Catherine walk away from him. His nostrils flared in anger. He turned to glare at the servant with whom he had caught Catherine in private conversation. He beckoned to two of his friends and whispered a quick command to them. While they made their way to the supervising attendant, he shot his most threatening glare at the servant. It angered him further when the man, rather than cowering, crossed his arms and stared back.

When his friends returned with their report, Gregory ducked out of the room.

The quick exchange did not go unnoticed. Roman Winterfield followed in Gregory's steps, keeping a safe distance behind. Out in the entrance hall he kept to the shadows and was surprised when Gregory headed straight up the main staircase to the second floor landing.

A guest who had followed him from the ballroom clutched Roman's arm. Roman chatted but a moment before cutting the conversation short and dashed up the staircase.

He heard a scuffle and followed it down the corridor. Nearing his parents' bedchamber, he noted a faint streak of light across the hallway floor.

Ducking into the shadows, he watched Gregory step from the room and pull the door closed behind him. It was apparent that the man was familiar with the house, possibly having had toured through its rooms at some point in the past. The mind of an architect would not be quick to dismiss the floor plan.

Gregory hastened past Roman, who remained hidden. Roman followed him back down the staircase, out the main door, and into the darkness outside.

What is he up to? Roman wondered. Why had Westcliffe entered his parents' room? Where was he headed now? Roman followed him around the side of the mansion, through the gardens, and out into the grounds behind the house. It was not long before Gregory disappeared into the darkness of the Winterfield property. Losing track of him, Roman retreated to the house. The only practical way to leave the property was the main road. Gregory Westcliffe would have to return sooner or later.

Inside, Catherine's parents demanded her presence in the library.

"Why did you not tell us of your relationship with Mr. Westcliffe?" Her mother made no attempt to hide her anger.

"He asked me not to. He wanted our courtship to be a surprise."

"Well he certainly succeeded in that," Richard said, sounding no more than annoyed. "However, I'm perplexed as to the reason you didn't accept what appeared to be a pre-arranged proposal. Had I thought for a moment you had any intention of giving an answer other than acceptance, I would not have placed you in such a precarious position. I apologize, Catherine."

"Apologize!" shouted Olivia. "Apologize for what, Richard?" A pointed finger shot toward Catherine. "You have embarrassed us beyond words. And poor Mr. Westcliffe—he has left the party, you know. I'm sure he's feeling completely dejected. How could you carry on a secret romance with this man and lead him to believe that you love him only to demean him before all his society? I want an explanation, Catherine. Why did you not accept him?"

Catherine stood firm just as she had seen Mr. Aramis do in the ballroom. "What exactly did Mr. Westcliffe tell you, Father?"

"He reported that you and he have been courting in secret for several months and had recently become engaged. He said he desired the opportunity to make it official before all society."

"Gregory Westcliffe received his just due, Mother. We're not engaged."

"Yes, I can see that now," her mother responded with sarcasm. "But you will be. You'll not make that mistake again. A proposal from a member of such a prominent family may very well never be repeated. You'll accept him at the first opportunity—if tonight's events haven't caused him to retract his proposal."

"Father!" Catherine turned to him with pleading eyes. "Have I no say in this matter?"

"You realize that both your mother and I favor the Westcliffe family, but the decision is yours to make."

"Roman does not like Gregory. You saw the way he shunned him earlier," Catherine argued.

"Roman doesn't like anyone," her mother retorted.

When Gregory Westcliffe reappeared, he carried a large, flat object. With perplexity and anger mounting, Roman followed Gregory back around the house to his carriage. The coachmen, gathered in little groups, took no note as Mr. Westcliffe placed the object in his carriage and retreated back into the mansion.

Roman waited a few moments before approaching the carriage and climbing into the dark cab. Dim lamplight entered through the window. He moved the object into the lamplight. It was a painting. Three figures rode horseback, surrounded by forest, with grapevines in the foreground. Squinting, he could make out the artist's signature. It said 'Aramis.'

Leaving the painting in the carriage, Roman slipped back into the house.

It was apparent Westcliffe had not been discouraged by the earlier episode. He conversed with Roman's mother. Roman sneaked closer.

"I'm so relieved you came back," she was saying. "I apologize for any embarrassment my daughter might have caused."

"I was testing her integrity, Mrs. Winterfield. Under such pressure, a weak mind would have given way. Now I know the level of her strength. She'll make a good wife."

Anger boiled through Roman's veins. He retreated to his bedchamber, closing the door behind him.

Long after midnight the party began to dissipate. Olivia Winterfield let out a sigh of relief as the last guests waved goodbye from their carriage windows.

Alexandra almost jumped when Olivia clapped at the exhausted servants.

"This is no time to relax. I want this house cleaned up tonight."

While she barked commands, Alexandra walked Catherine to the protection of her room.

"You look as though you've not a drop of emotion left, Catherine." She sat on Catherine's bed while the petite blonde disappeared into her changing room.

"I haven't seen Antoine since that awful scene, Alex," she called out. "I fear the worst—that I've greatly disappointed him in not refusing Mr. Westcliffe. Why did I not listen to you?" She emerged in a nightgown and crawled straight into her bed. "And Roman's earlier words—had you only seen his anger."

"I'm sure he didn't mean them. Give him time to adjust to the idea of Antoine."

"The pressure is too much. Mr. Westcliffe, Roman, Mother, and Father. Even Antoine. I've been getting advice and counsel from all sides. I cannot withstand another minute."

"Get some rest, Catherine. Perhaps things will be a little clearer with the light of day."

Alexandra blew her a kiss and extinguished the lamp.

* * * * *

Downstairs, she found Jessica bidding her husband good-night as they parted ways—he to their bedchamber suite, and she to take Alexandra's arm.

"Talk with me for awhile, Alex."

"Aren't you exhausted? It's late, Jess. You and that child need your rest."

"In just a bit. As you know, we're leaving in the morning and I've seen so little of you."

Alexandra had taken notice of Roman's absence just after Catherine's embarrassing scene, though she was certain he must be somewhere in the mansion. Perhaps he had retired early. After all, his injuries were only ten days old. She had seen the pain in his expressions several times during the evening, even while he danced with her.

She had also been watching earlier when he had escorted Caroline Landly to the door. Intrigued when he had returned to the party without her, Alexandra decided the woman must have fallen ill and been forced to return home.

But what difference had her absence made anyway? Alexandra's one dream of dancing with Roman had been fulfilled. There would be little interaction between them from now on, she was certain.

The corners in the library, the room to which they had walked, hid in shadows where the light of the oil lamps failed to reach. Beside the painting just above them, much of the second story of the large room also remained in blackness.

"Oh, Alex, do you remember the first time we ever saw this room?" Jessica asked, glancing up toward the mural. Alexandra fell into one of the leather chairs and looked up. Filtered light muted the sea depicted there, making it appear even angrier. It was as though it would come alive at any moment.

"It's just as when we first discovered it," Jessica said. "Can't you just hear the waves crashing?"

"So much like home at Old Stormy. I wish you would join me there, Jessie."

"We'll be in Spain by then. They won't hold that shipment of tile for long."

Alexandra pushed herself up to stroll over to the five portraits of the Winterfield family hanging above the heavy mahogany desk. She examined the handsome face of Andrew.

"Remember first seeing these portraits? Who could've ever imagined then, Jessie, that you would actually meet the alluring Andrew Winterfield—and later capture his heart."

Jessica came to stand by her side. She reached out and pulled from the desktop a worn leather journal.

"This is where my love for Andrew began," she said, fanning the pages of one of the logs belonging to *The Emerald*.

Alexandra focused on the face of Roman Winterfield. The expression caught by the artist showed his self-centered, high-minded attitude. She almost laughed at the way he portrayed himself then.

Jessica replaced the leather-bound log book. "And who would have ever guessed that you, Alexandra Viana, would fall in love with a man like Roman Winterfield?"

Alexandra locked eyes with her sister, feeling the smile vanish from her face.

"Yes, Alex, it's quite obvious now. Grace and I saw the look in your eyes as you danced with him. And we've been watching you as you've been watching him all evening."

"He's not the same as the man in that portrait, Jessie. You'll not see that expression on his face now."

"Perhaps not tonight, Alex, but soon."

"Not that it matters in the least anyway. His heart belongs to someone else."

"Roman's heart belongs to no one but Roman. This disguise will fade, you'll see."

"Why would he have any reason to carry on a pretense with me, Jessie? I'm not a person of prominence. He would have no reason to give me a false impression."

"I've never desired to understand the mind of Roman Winterfield. I'm content in keeping a good distance between us. You would be wise to do the same. Whatever happened to your childhood dreams, Alex? What happened to the standard you set long ago? Have you forgotten? You were our 'hopeless romantic,' remember? You would settle for nothing less than a prince, you said then."

"Yes, and even you would chastise me for my unrealistic dreams. Childhood fantasies fade with maturity, Jessie. However, my standard has not changed. It's still very high. And I've found a man who has met it; I've found that prince."

"Alex, don't," she said under a heavy stare.

"I'll prove to you that Mr. Winterfield is not simply putting up a front. Follow me."

She extinguished the lamps and pulled her sister by the hand to the hidden stairwell. They pushed the door closed behind them and sat on its steps in the darkness.

"Mr. Winterfield comes here to read in the evenings."

"And you watch him from this hiding place—Alex, why would you do such a thing?"

"It's not just any book he reads, Jessie, but God's Word. He pores over those scriptures. He's changing, Jess. It's not just a façade...or my imagination. See his expressions for yourself."

They sat in silence, waiting for the light underneath the door, a light that did not come.

"So much for your proof, Alex," Jessica said nearly an hour later. "I retain my opinion. I'll see you in the morning." She climbed the staircase. A soft click echoed from one story above when Jessica closed the door behind her.

Alexandra fell asleep in the dark stairwell, still dressed in her satin ball gown.

A shadowy figure crept down the main staircase tower. It placed two sealed letters on the table near the front entrance and disappeared into the darkness outside.

Chapter Twenty-Six

Morning arrived early for the tired group within the walls of the Winterfield manor. Alexandra awoke to a sharp voice she recognized as belonging to Olivia. She was obviously complaining about some matter and cared not who she disturbed.

Stirring awake, Alexandra tried to recall returning to her room the previous night. A loud knock on her door startled her. Catherine burst into the room, blurting words too fast for Alexandra to follow.

"Catherine, calm yourself." Alexandra jumped from her cozy sheets and assisted her friend into a chair. "Now, please begin again."

"Oh, Alex, the entire house is in an uproar."

"What could possibly have arisen at this hour?"

"It's Mother. One of her most prized possessions has gone missing—an expensive jeweled necklace."

"Was she wearing it for the party?"

"No, it was in her bureau in a case. When she awoke this morning, she noticed the case on top of the bureau. It was empty, Alex. She has had the whole servant body combing the entire house ever since. Father has summoned the constable and already they've begun searching the servants' quarters. The family has gathered in the library. Perhaps you should come, too."

Alexandra nodded and hurried to her dressing room.

"Oh, Alex, during the search, Father discovered two notes left by Roman. It appears he left sometime during the night."

Alexandra stopped and looked out at Catherine.

"One of the notes was for me," Catherine said. She pulled the letter from her pocket and handed it to Alexandra.

Catherine's name had been scrolled across the outside of it. Turning it over, she found a broken wax seal.

"It's all right," Catherine urged. "Please read it."

My Dear Sister,

This letter is two-fold in purpose. First, I request that you would allow me to make a retraction of the harsh words I hurled at you earlier last evening. I could not have been more wrong in my assessment of the situation. I charged that it would be your love of a poor man that would force you into a life of destitution and regret. However, after pondering matters, I realize it is the very quality of love that will prove to be your shield, your protection. Please allow me to explain.

I did not tell you before, but two years ago Father threatened to disown me; had it not been for significant changes he later saw in my disposition, I believe he would have carried out his threat. I would have been erased from this family, stripped of my inheritance, and left to share with you nothing more than a name—an empty and meaningless name.

Yet, though angered and disappointed with the man I had become, Father stated he would not force me into financial ruin. He would have allowed me to retain my position as an employee of Winterfield Imports. It was his love for me that moved him to protect me in this way. He showed me love, Catherine, though I deserved nothing.

So I was wrong when I thoughtlessly stated that Father would oust you from this family because of your love for one of his hired hands. Unlike my past behavior, Catherine, your motive is pure, your heart true, and your love loyal. These are qualities that Father would admire. He will not abandon you to a life of poverty, for he loves you.

And if for some reason he would abandon you, your brothers would not. I feel I can speak for Andrew as well when I say that we will support you in any way required.

Of all the words I spoke to you last evening, only four merit repeating: 'Be in love, Catherine.' And might I add, marry for love. Accept nothing less.

My second purpose in writing to you is to sound a clear warning about Mr. Westcliffe. Do not accept his proposal, Catherine, tempting as his charms and the comforts he offers may sound. I will make my reasons known upon my return. I sincerely hope that it will be sooner rather than later, which is what I fear.

Your Brother, Roman

Alexandra's eyes misted at his sentiments. Yes, Roman Winterfield had changed. No one would convince her otherwise now. She handed the letter back. "He's a good man, Catherine. I can say in all sincerity that you are very fortunate in your being related to him, as well as to Andrew."

"Thank you, Alex. I believe I am, as well."

"And may I know the contents of the other note he left?" Alexandra asked.

"It was addressed to my parents and stated that he would be away for awhile due to a pressing matter that would not wait. But that is his typical way, and so none of us are surprised."

Catherine's gaze moved to the floor, and Alexandra noted an uneasy expression on her friend's typically cheery face.

"Mr. Aramis?" Alexandra asked.

She nodded.

"He doesn't know your reason for doing what you did last night. Your motive was pure. Your reaction was one of kindness toward Mr. Westcliffe."

"I've sent John to him with a note of explanation in which I've relayed that I have no intention of accepting Mr. Westcliffe. Oh, I do hope John returns soon with his reply."

While Olivia gave her report to the constable, Alexandra's father pulled her aside.

"I'd like a word with you," he said. Leading her into the room that had been transformed back into the tapestry gallery, he invited her to sit on one of the sofas.

"What is it, Papa?"

"Alexandra." He sat beside her and tapped his fingers on one knee. "I've never known you to be a person of deceit. I did not raise any of my children to live by such a degrading trait."

"Deceit? Papa!"

"Though nearly twenty-three, you're still under my charge. I'll tolerate no such attitudes."

She jumped to her feet. "What have I done?" Her one secret was her affection for Roman. And *that* she had confessed to her mother.

He stepped across the room and back to hand her a knitted cloth.

Holding it up, she let it fall open. "Grace's cape," she whispered, sinking back onto the sofa.

"The steward described you to the letter, Alexandra."

"Oh, Papa." Her gaze fell to the rug in shame.

"There are reasons I've not taken you children to Candlegate. It's a place of misery and appalling memories for me. I'll not relive them with you or any member of this family. Your mother and I stop in Surrey periodically, but solely because of my responsibility for the property."

226

Though his words should have struck her in chastisement, they were gentle, caring.

"We just wanted to—"

"The reason matters not. I know you feel you were not trespassing because it is your family's ancestral home, but the fact that you ran from the steward tells me your conscience knew your presence was, at best, questionable. Perhaps I made a mistake in not taking you there myself, but I'm not yet ready for that." He turned as though to leave, then came back to face her. "I want you to respect my request to stay away from Candlegate. Is that clear, Alexandra?"

"Yes, Papa. I'm sorry."

The pained look on his face stabbed her heart. Her head dropped in shame. Why, she wondered, had he continued to hold onto the place? Why had he not relieved himself of it long ago?

He lifted her chin and searched her eyes as though he could read her sincerity there.

"Grace must answer to her husband now, not to me anymore," he said. "I hope you'll take the respect you have for me into your own marriage. I know it won't be long."

With that, he walked back to the library, leaving her in perplexity over his last comment. What could he have meant by it?

An hour later, her parents and Andrew and Jessica were out in front of the mansion while the servants packed the carriages for their departure.

Alexandra's father put an arm out toward her, and she nestled underneath it. They walked a few paces away from the others.

"Papa, I never meant to disappoint you."

"I know that. I'm sure you were there at the instigation of your sister."

"No. I'm responsible for my own actions. What did you mean by your reference to my marrying?"

He sighed and walked a few more paces. "I promised myself two years ago that I would not neglect you at your greatest time of need as I did your sisters, though unintentional. Why is it my daughters always fall in love when I'm least prepared?"

"And what reproofs have you to offer me, Papa?" She put her head down, embarrassment rising to her cheeks. Her mother must have relayed to him her confession the night before the party. "I know if your sentiments match those of my sisters, you will, indeed, have much to say on the matter."

"I can say just one thing." His grip on her shoulder tightened. "I trust your judgment, Alexandra."

"Are you aware of the man's identity?" This was not the response she had expected.

"You know him better than your sisters do."

"You've not neglected me, Papa. It was I who chose to come here for the summer. But I have missed your advice many times these past weeks."

"And how did you fare without it?"

"The principles with which you raised me served me very well. Even I have been surprised at the level of coping skills I seem to possess. So, in essence, I suppose you did prove to be with me. I may have fallen in love during your absence, Papa, but you need not be concerned. Mr. Winterfield's attentions seem to be focused in another direction. When we all reconvene in Ireland in six weeks, this matter will no doubt have blown over just as a threatening storm and will not seem as gloomy as it now appears."

"No doubt," her father answered, leaving her wondering again, this time about the playful smile he tried to hide—without success.

"Catherine, pacing in that manner will only compound your anxiety."

Alexandra and Catherine had been watching from the library balcony for John's return.

"I just wish I knew Antoine's thoughts. How will he respond to my message?" She passed Alexandra yet again. "How long can it take him to deliver a message, Alex? It's been over an hour."

"Don't forget. John said he had a bit of work to do. He'll be home soon, I'm sure."

"There he is!" shouted Catherine. Alexandra turned to spot a horse galloping toward them in the distance. "Here comes John."

They hurried through the mansion and out the front door, running the length of the house and across the cobblestone courtyard toward the stables.

John swung down from the horse.

"He wasn't there." He handed the note back to Catherine.

"Where is he? Did he go into town?" Catherine's eyes pleaded in desperation.

"For his own sake, I hope he stays there," he said.

"What do you mean, John?" Alexandra asked, reading the concern on his face. "What have you not told us?"

"The necklace—it's been found."

"Oh, that's wonderful news," Catherine sighed.

"No, Catherine," John said, looking down. "It's dreadful news. The necklace was found in Antoine's quarters. A warrant has been issued for his arrest."

Drowned by emotion and overburdened with the continual stress of the previous days, Catherine collapsed.

John caught her small frame before she hit the ground.

Chapter Twenty-Seven

Although having retired long past midnight, Antoine Aramis had arisen and departed from the estate just after sunrise. His night had passed with little sleep despite his fatigue.

He spent much of the day at the library, buried in reading. Thoughts of Catherine ran rampant through his mind, and feelings of doubt and confusion clouded his concentration.

More and more distressed over Gregory Westcliffe's proposal, he wandered the town for awhile. Late in the afternoon he headed toward the museum in hope of diverting his thoughts through his artwork.

After a while, he glanced up at the clock, surprised at the time that had passed. He had been sketching exhibit pieces on the third floor and was relieved by the distraction it had provided for the last two hours. A number of visitors meandered about despite the nearness of closing time. He crouched to the floor to tuck his work into his case and, upon standing, recognized two faces among those milling about. They belonged to the two foreign men he had seen outside the library the previous day.

Picking up his case, he began walking in the opposite direction, chastising himself for his absent-mindedness regarding the men. How could he have forgotten about them? Why had he not been more careful in public?

When he cast a quick look over his shoulder, he realized that he had, indeed, caught the men's attention. One pointed toward him, and they both quickened their pace.

Upon first visiting the museum a few years earlier, he had grumbled about the maze-like floor plan. Now he knew it well and was grateful to its designers. Dodging around exhibits and behind walls, he headed down a long, empty corridor, which would lead to a back stairwell and the alleyway behind the building. Just before the doorway to the stairwell, the corridor wall gave way to a carved iron screen, fixed into the wall, which opened to a view of the exhibit hall. He raced down the corridor, stopping before the screen. Finding no trace of the pursuers behind him, he peered through the screen before passing it. The floor was almost empty now, except for the two men.

One saw him, and both rushed toward the iron screen. Antoine ran for the stairwell as he heard one of them slam up against the screen. It held tight to the wall.

"You can't run, Sabiir. We know who you are," one of them shouted in a foreign tongue. "You cannot hide."

Knowing mere moments remained before they discovered the entrance to the corridor, Antoine raced down the steps and burst out into the alleyway. He dashed to the front of the building and mixed into the crowd of pedestrians.

The sun began its descent below the horizon as Antoine raced through the city streets, following the shortcuts he knew well until reaching the cover of the outlying forest. Half an hour later, he dropped his case to the ground and fell down beside it.

His heart raced, not just from the exertion, but perhaps more so from the encounter.

Suddenly, he realized that the man had yelled to him in a language other than English or French, and that he, Antoine, had understood every word.

Near midnight, Catherine paced the floor of her bedroom suite. Distressed to the point of nausea, she clutched her belly. Earlier in the evening, she had sipped on a cup of warm milk at Alexandra's insistence, but it brought only temporary relief. After a short two hours of fitful sleep, she was wide awake, mulling over in her mind again and again the horrible plight of Antoine Aramis.

Where was he? What could she do to help?

An hour later, a light tapping on the glass of her balcony door startled her. After peering through the sheers she flung the door wide.

"Mr. Aramis, where have you been?" she asked in a frantic whisper. "What are you doing here?" She pulled the sheers tight over the open doorway. "If anyone were to see you, they would have you arrested." She snatched her lacy dressing gown from a chair and draped it over her night clothes.

He glanced around the dimly lit room. "Miss Winterfield, I'm in great danger. I must leave the country tonight, but I had to see you first."

She heard footsteps in the hallway. A knock sounded on her door.

Antoine tugged on the tie to the heavy brocade drape and let it fall in front of him. She checked to make sure his shoes didn't show before hastening across the room to grab a book.

"Catherine." It was her father! "Open the door."

She pushed her breath out, turned the lock, and cracked the door open.

"Father."

"I saw the light under the door." Thank heaven he had not heard their voices. "Is everything all right?"

"Fine. I...I'm having trouble reading—I mean sleeping. I thought I would try to read awhile." She held up the book.

"Catherine, you're trembling!"

"It's just that...you scared me."

"You've had a difficult time of late, I know. Can I get you anything?"

"No thank you, Father. I'll be able to sleep soon, I'm certain."

"Very well then." The look on his face implied he was not convinced. "Good night."

"Good night, Father."

She closed the door and wilted against it, listening to his retreating footsteps.

Antoine met her halfway across the room.

"You must listen to me," he whispered, taking her hands. She saw desperation in his eyes. "John found me at the lake not more than two hours ago. He gave me the message you wrote, then told me about the events here this morning. I'm not a thief, Miss Winterfield."

"I've never believed you were."

"I'll prove my innocence...somehow...when I return."

"Why must you leave? Your disappearance will solidify the charges against you."

"I realize that, but at the moment...I...I can't explain to you why I must go. I hardly understand it myself. I assure you, however, it is unrelated to this jewelry incident. I'll return as soon as I can; you have my promise." He stepped over to the door, placing his ear against it. Walking back to her, a sudden smile broke over his face. "I sold some of my paintings while in town today. The shop owner guaranteed me he could sell them. He agreed to purchase more—sight unseen."

"That's wonderful."

His smile disappeared. "Miss Winterfield, last night at the ball, I thought I was on the verge of losing you."

"Never." She reached out for his hand.

"I know that now after reading your note. Catherine, you belong to me and I to you. I may not speak with the eloquent words with which Gregory Westcliffe seems to be gifted, and it may not be in my power to offer you a home a fraction of what your father has provided, but what I have is yours, my heart most of all."

"Do you really mean it?"

"I purchased something for you with some of the money I received today." From his pocket he pulled a shiny gold band. "Am I insane to entertain this idea? Here I am, nothing more than a peasant! But I'm compelled to ask if you will consider my proposal of marriage."

Tears began to well in her eyes.

"Do you see that I can support you? I love you, Catherine. It seemed I had nothing of value to offer any person, and here, you—a woman who has everything—has found value in me. Regardless of your answer, I'll still feel privileged that you bestowed upon me the honor of your friendship."

Tears rolled in tiny streams onto her cheeks. He gently wiped them away with his finger.

"It's not my wish to pressure you in any way. You may give me your answer when I return. However, if you know now that you cannot accept me, no one need ever know that we have met here tonight." He stepped away, awaiting her reply.

"You were correct about Mr. Westcliffe," she said. "But his eloquent words are empty. His charms fade after learning his true character. You, on the other hand, though having little in the way of riches, have a heart of gold. Many women marry for comforts and luxuries, but I will exchange all that if I can marry for lasting love. I've no need to take any more time before giving you my answer. I've known for some time now that I love you, too. I accept your proposal."

He placed the gold band in her palm, closing her fingers around it and raising her hand to his lips. "Keep this during my absence, but we cannot marry until I can prove my innocence and speak to your father. I'll make everything known to you the moment I'm able to return. Whatever happens, don't waver in your confidence in me. Be strong for me—for us. Everything will be all right, I promise you." He slipped his arm about her waist and drew her close. She allowed his lips to settle upon hers in a gentle kiss. A moment later, he pulled away.

"I'll not waver," she whispered.

He disappeared through the sheers and vanished into the night.

More tears welled in her eyes and ran in torrents off her chin. Where was he going? When would she see him again? What sort of danger was he in?

She buried her face in her pillow and sobbed, clutching the dainty gold band.

Chapter Twenty-Eight

"Please, Mother, let me go with Alex," Catherine begged. "I need some time away...to think things over."

"You owe Gregory an answer, Catherine."

"And he will get his answer when I return in two weeks."

"Let her go, Olivia," her father said.

"Two days, two weeks, or two months will not change her answer, Richard. She will marry Gregory and that's final."

"That decision is not yours to make, Olivia."

"She started this romance, and she will finish it. I will neither have her muddy the Westcliffe's good name, nor bring reproach upon the Winterfields. Two weeks? That's an insult to him."

"I'll not hear another word from you on the matter. Catherine, you're free to go with Alex to Cornwall." Richard turned and left the room, Catherine following close behind.

Olivia's glare followed her husband and daughter, but neither turned back with even a hint of apology for their short-sighted attitudes. Did they not realize that this might be Catherine's only chance to marry, and into the Westcliffe family yet?

Ever since her daughter's childhood, Olivia had worried that this plain child, who came along years after her handsome brothers, would end up a spinster, growing old alone and a burden to Andrew and Roman. Catherine, alas, tended to favor her father's very ordinary mother. At least Olivia's sons had had the good fortune to take after *her* family.

Well, she would have to put her mind to correcting the horrible mistake Catherine seemed determined to make. Meanwhile, she would see to it that the ungrateful Mr. Aramis never worked for another family of substance.

While the search for him continued, she would make sure all her servants knew exactly where they stood. She had already locked away her jewelry and begun an inventory of every object in the mansion. At least in her presence the rest of her servant body showed the good sense not to voice any support for the criminal. And they were about to learn firsthand the consequences of stealing from the Winterfields.

During the train ride to Penzance, Alexandra tried to read a book she had borrowed from the Winterfield library, but found her efforts in vain. Instead, she worried over Antoine and Catherine's future. Were his name not cleared of the charges, he could be ousted from the country or imprisoned. Despite the evidence, in her heart she could not believe that Antoine was a thief.

On the contrary, he had proved himself an honorable man, a trustworthy and hard-working employee. Her thoughts flashed back to the day John had damaged the barrels at the winery. Antoine was willing to have his wages garnished for the error that was no fault of his own. Indeed, he was a man of great integrity.

But how did the necklace come to be among his belongings? And where was he now? Was his life in danger as he had described to Catherine? If so, why?

Perhaps it would have been better had she and Catherine never agreed to the tour of the vineyard. But then Catherine would have become engaged to the despicable Gregory Westcliffe. There seemed to be no good answer.

And to where had Roman disappeared? For a certainty, he was in no condition to travel. But at least he was not home under the watchful eye of Miss Landly.

Her conscience shamed her. Caroline Landly had no doubt won the heart of Roman Winterfield. She was, after all, a beautiful woman who would likely favor him with handsome sons and lovely daughters. Even the thought of that woman's bearing his children sickened her. She forced her mind in a different direction. Had not she herself succeeded in gaining his admiration and friendship? Had he not taken her—not Miss Landly—to his secret meadow? Had they not shared privately that remarkable place? Sighing, she tried to content herself with that.

For a moment, she watched Catherine stare out the window and fondle the little gold band hanging on a chain around her neck. What stress her friend had endured since returning from France. And it was bound to worsen. How would Catherine's parents respond to the engagement of their only daughter to an employee, one who now appeared a criminal? Her brothers might not be so willing to support her now. Whatever was to become of her?

The journey on the train seemed endless, and Alexandra fell asleep shortly before they arrived at the Penzance station in the late afternoon.

"How will we get to Brentwood?" Catherine asked as they disembarked.

"We'll hire a carriage," she responded, trying to shake off the fuzziness that came from being awakened before she had finished her nap.

The carriage had barely stopped when the Wrights rushed out to welcome the girls. Alexandra allowed herself a nostalgic moment as she hugged the woman who had been a mother figure during most of her childhood, and then she introduced Catherine. Within minutes, the girls hurried along the path into the forest that led to the rocky beach, the rowboat, and Brentwood Lighthouse.

"Supper will be ready in an hour," Mrs. Wright called after them.

"We'll be back." Alexandra turned around, walking backward and allowing the wind to carry her words.

A few minutes later, they stood atop the crown of the great lighthouse, looking out over the sea. Its waves rolled over the island's rocky edges; a stiff breeze ruffled their hair.

"Oh, Alex, if only the wind could take my troubles away on its gales." Catherine sighed. "What a magnificent place to be raised. It's no wonder you miss Brentwood so."

"My life now is much more comfortable, but my fondest memories are of this being my home." Stretching her arms out, she let the breeze surround her. "It's sad to think this could be my final visit here. The Wrights will soon join us at Muir Ceann, and never again will any of us receive an invitation to Brentwood." She turned to Catherine. "I'm so glad you came with me. I was sure you would love this place almost as much as I do."

They stayed to watch the setting of the sun.

"I wish Antoine were here to see this, Alex. I doubt that even his surpassing talent could capture such glory."

"I'm sure he wants nothing more than to be with you, too, wherever he is."

Catherine's wistful look touched Alexandra's heart. "I can't look to the past anymore, Alex. I'm dismissing all thoughts of Gregory Westcliffe, my parents, and Antoine's troubles. Instead, I'll think of nothing other than our future together. We deserve happiness, and we will have it."

Night had fallen by the time Antoine reached the small French château. No drapes covered the windows; oil lamps illuminated the room. Standing in the shadows, he watched the activities of the people inside. The cramped structure with its modest furniture implied a family of meager income, yet the smiling faces within appeared content.

Joy rose in his heart at the sight of the beautiful olive-skinned woman, whose long black locks had been pulled back in a tie. She directed three children in preparing the table for the evening meal. An infant sat in a homemade chair, pounding a spoon on the table.

His sister's features and slender form were just as he remembered. Recollections of her kind demeanor and soft smile flooded his mind. Early in his childhood, she had earned his admiration. Try as he might, he could not recall a single time she had voiced a word of reproof.

A tall, husky man stepped into view, seated himself at the head of the table, and nodded. The family bowed their heads before their meal.

He had not seen his sister since he was nine years old. He prepared himself for disappointment were she not to recognize him. He wanted to think she would, but it had been so long. Still, she was certain to have the information he was so desperate to unearth, the key to his safety and his foreseeable future. He approached the door and knocked.

After some shuffling inside and the sudden hush of voices, the door opened. *"Oui, Monsieur?"* The warm gaze of his sister greeted him. "May we be of assistance to you?"

Antoine smiled to hear her graceful words in French, a language he had abandoned five years prior.

"Is there a place at your table for a weary and hungry traveler?"

"We do not dine with strangers here. So allow me the courtesy of your name, and you may dine with us as a friend."

"Ah, but I'm much more than a friend to you, though I'm not surprised you don't remember my face, Damica. I was but a child when last our eyes met."

Damica examined him from underneath a furrowed brow. After searching the features of his face, her gaze settled on his dark eyes. Sudden recognition forced her lips to part. "It can't be!" she shouted. "It can't be!"

"Damica, who's there?" the deep voice of her husband called out.

"Antoine," she said in answer and rushed onto the porch to grab hold of him. Covering his face with kisses, she smeared tears onto his cheeks.

"What?" The man inside hastened to the door, trailed by the three young ones.

"It is Antoine. Children, it's your uncle of whom I've told you so much."

All three children rushed him at once, the youngest jumping up to wrap her arms and legs around him. He stumbled backward, laughing.

The meal was warm and tasty, and the family reveled in Antoine's presence. He told them of his life, his art, and his beloved fiancée. The children bombarded him with questions, but the subject of their grandparents was broached by none.

Damica's eldest child, a daughter fourteen years of age, reflected her mother's gentleness and beauty. She stationed herself in the chair beside him.

"Tell me everything about your fiancée, Uncle. Don't hold back a single detail."

"Ah, but a picture can tell you so much more than all my words. Do you have a pencil?"

The two middle children scampered from the table and returned with a pencil and tablet. They stared in wonder as a beautiful face began to form on the tablet before their eyes.

"There is kindness and understanding in her face," noted the eldest daughter.

The nose was petite and the soft lines of the mouth turned up in a slight smile. Antoine's fingertip touched the drawing. For a moment, he became lost in the one and only kiss he had ever shared with the dainty lips.

"She likes to laugh," blurted out one of the younger children, which sent them all to giggling.

Antoine sketched her hair as it was the last time he had seen her—hanging loose, its silky strands brushed to the side of her face and flowing over her shoulders.

"She's rich," stated the second oldest. "Look at her hair, so smooth and neat, and her skin doesn't have any wrinkles like she's been outside working in the sun. See the lace collar?"

"Well," Antoine chuckled. "She *was* wealthy. Or will be... until she weds me."

* * * * *

Later, Antoine and his brother-in-law left Damica inside to bathe the children and tuck them in while they conversed under a perfect starry sky. Sitting on a wooden bench beneath the window, Antoine heard their mother assure them that their uncle would still be there in the morning. Then he heard her footsteps on the creaky staircase as she descended from the sleeping loft.

She came out to sit beside her brother.

"How are you at painting night skies, Antoine? Can you capture the array of all those tiny diamonds?" she asked.

"I've never tried."

They sat in silence for several moments.

"What sort of trouble are you in, *mon frère*?" He looked over to find her staring at him. "France holds nothing but bad memories for you. More than once I've read in your letters your vow never to come back. It must be a serious matter, indeed, that would force your return."

"I'm not certain myself. But I do know I am at the mercy of your memory...of my childhood. I'm not your natural brother, am I, Damica?"

"No, Antoine." She looked down at the ground. "You were four years old when you came to live with our family. You called yourself by the name of—"

"Sabiir," he interrupted.

She nodded. "Mother and Father forbade you to use that name and scolded you severely each time you defied them. It wasn't long before it escaped your memory...or did it?"

"Two men have been trailing me." Antoine pushed himself to his feet and took a few paces onto the narrow stone pathway before their little cottage. He reached down to pluck a long blade of grass and twisted it in his fingers. "They caught up with me three days ago." He dropped the grass to the ground. "I escaped their grasp, but I recognized them, Damica. What is more...I understood their language. 'You can't run, Sabiir,' they said. 'We know who you are. You can't hide,' they called out to me. But I did run, and I was able to hide from them."

Damica rose and walked up beside him. "I'm not surprised you understood their words. Do you not remember when we were children that you taught me many words in your native tongue? We played games and recited nursery rhymes in your language, but you never spoke the words in front of our parents. I doubt you've said a single one since I left when you were nine. Oh, Antoine, I have always feared for your safety. What did you do when they found you?"

He looked off into the distance, aware that she was standing beside him, but her words registered slowly. "I'd forgotten about the games and rhymes, but I remember now. That must be why I understood the words that were shouted at me." He paused and took a deep breath. "A few days ago I sought shelter on my employer's vast property. I watched the sunset while the men's strange words rang over and over in my mind, and I remembered a rainy day in a large city." He looked back into his sister's face. "I must've been very young. I was with a man who was not my father...at least I don't think so. It took some time to recall, but I believe his name was Rios."

She put her hand on his arm.

"I loved Rios," he continued. "He protected me. But that day he could not protect me. There were few people on the streets, probably because of the rain. Rios and I walked hand-in-hand. I skipped to keep up with his long stride. I remember splashing in the puddles that had collected from the rain." He laughed at the memory; then his smile faded. "Out of nowhere, several men appeared and grabbed hold of Rios. They reached for me, but I escaped. Rios called out to me in my native tongue as he struggled under the grip of the men. He said, 'Run, Sabiir! They know who you are. Hide, Sabiir!' The final words I heard from Rios ring clear in my mind this day, though they had been buried all those years. He called out to me, 'Remember who you are, Sabiir.'"

Antoine turned to pace a few steps. Damica tucked her hand into his and walked with him. He looked down at her.

"I recall nothing after that, and I did forget who I was. How did I come to live on your family's vineyard, Damica?" He clenched his fists in frustration. "Who am I? What do those men want from me? Who was that child Sabiir? And does this marking have some significance?"

He loosened the top few buttons on his shirt and pulled it aside to expose a dark blue tattoo on the back of his right shoulder, the diameter of a small plum.

Damica glanced at the mark. "When you were a boy, this tattoo appeared much like the face of a large cat, but I cannot see it clearly, even in the light of the full moon. No doubt, the years of growth have distorted it." She shook her head. "None of this matters, Antoine. You're safe now. Bring your fiancée here, and leave the past where it is. You can build your future and your family with us."

He skimmed his fingertips across her cheek. "I can't stay here, Damica. How is it you think those men located me in Canterbury? Father must have given them my post office address. There's no other way they would've known. No one saw me slip onto the ship that night, and if they had, they had no way of finding me in England. They'll be here next, I guarantee you. He would also have given them your address. Where else would I have gone when I fled from them? They could be here tomorrow."

The two walked back to the bench. Damica scooted to snuggle beside her husband. "The men you describe, Antoine—they may be the same ones who often appeared on our property when we were children. At times I would see one of them standing in the distance, just staring, as if...as if to confirm you were still there. When Father would see me look up from my work, he would scold me and warn me to ignore the stranger. When I again looked up, the man would be gone. Several months later I would see another one in the same manner, just watching. They never approached us, never seemed aggressive. But to see them there, just watching..." Damica's eyes looked away as though she were observing a man there in the distance. She shivered.

"What did it all mean? Who are those men?" He, too, looked into the blackness and spoke as though to himself. "So,

I must rely on Father for the information about my identity." He looked down in sadness. "It might as well be sealed in a cast iron tomb for which there is no key."

"Perhaps not, Antoine. I remember something else. The first night you came to us, I discovered a document of some sort sewn into the lining of your coat. I couldn't read the strange writing, and Mother and Father didn't notice it. For some reason, I knew not to show it to them."

"What did you do with it, Damica? Where is it?"

"I sealed it in an empty wine bottle and hid it behind some loose bricks in the wall of the barn."

"You must go, both of you," her husband said. "You must retrieve that document. I'll go with you if you like. My mother can care for the children."

Antoine's gaze did not move from his sister's eyes. "We'll be more discreet if we're only two. There are many buildings on that property, and many more bricks. Our chances of finding that bottle undisturbed are slim. It's a long journey. You'll be away from your family for some days, and neither of us knows what consequences we face should we be discovered on Father's property. What do you think, Damica? Will you go?"

"I'll pack a few things, and we can leave in the morning."

The blazing sun crossed the lazy afternoon sky and sat near the horizon when Antoine Aramis and his sister reached their destination, the outskirts of a miniscule village at the base of the Pyrenees. Antoine twisted in the seat that had grown increasingly uncomfortable during the long journey on the train. Perhaps the intense heat of the day would pass with the setting of the sun.

Though glad to have completed the trip, he felt no joy. The familiar landmarks brought forth unpleasant memories of years of oppression and neglect. If only he could have found another way to obtain the information he needed.

"Why can I not look upon those mountains and see only their splendor?" he mumbled as their carriage drew them ever nearer.

"Long ago, I vowed to return for one reason alone," she said, "to rescue you. I'm sorry I was unsuccessful in my attempts. By the time I was able to try again, you had gotten yourself out."

"And I, on the other hand, vowed never to return again, for any reason."

"Yet here we are," she said, "with all our cruel recollections intact."

They rented a room at a small inn near the center of town, relieved not to have recognized the owners. After consuming a light meal, they retired.

"Don't sleep too soundly," he reminded her. "I'll wake you at midnight."

"I can't move a muscle," she said, falling onto the simple bed. "Nor may I be able to sleep."

He pulled a blanket from the wardrobe and draped it over the small sofa.

"Remember how you used to revel in angering Father, Antoine?"

"I don't know that 'revel' is the right word," he said, going back to the wardrobe for the spare pillow. "All I recall is the hatred building in my heart. I would suffer any punishment just to avenge myself."

"Do you remember the time when you were nine, just before I left, when you collected a huge jar of spiders and worms?"

"How could I forget that day?"

"I can see Father now, chasing you to the vineyard. But you were too fast for him. He caught up with you just as you dumped the entire collection into the vat!"

"And spoiled months of his hard work." He lay back onto the pillow, kicking his feet over the arm of the sofa. "With Father's temper, I'm surprised he didn't break my neck then and there."

"And the time you broke into the money box and distributed all the funds among the workers?"

"He was a hard taskmaster. No worker ever came back for a second harvest, don't you remember? They had to fight for their pay!"

Damica laughed at the memories. "You constantly tried Father and Mother to the greatest degree."

"And, indeed, the entire household suffered many times at my expense. But I was merely expressing my frustrations."

"And you felt justified in your actions."

"I'm sorry," he said, laughing.

"Actually, you showed great ingenuity, I thought."

"Oh, yes," Antoine replied with a hint of sarcasm. "And extreme lack of concern for others."

"I, for one, enjoyed your little antics. You never attempted to conceal them, always admitting your guilt. And you faced your punishment with a snicker, which only added to Father's fury. You know, had you not become a member of our family, life wouldn't have been worth living."

"Life is not always fair, is it?"

"You shouldn't have been forced to live on that wretched farm, but perhaps there was some good in it," she said. "You saved a life that would have otherwise suffocated under the oppression. Mine."

He awakened Damica to a dark room, save for a stream of moonlight that had discovered a gap in the shutters covering the small window.

"We must go," he whispered.

Damica rose and peered out the window. "At least we'll have the benefit of the moonlight."

"Yes, but we'll need the lantern once inside the barn."

They stepped out into a cool breeze.

On the road near the Aramis property, Antoine tied the horses to a cluster of bushes where they would not be seen.

After passing under the fence at the property line, he grabbed Damica's hand and darted over the tilled soil. Carrying a shovel and lantern in his free hand, he guided her through rows of vines, staying low as they crept along in the shadows cast by the moonlight. Twenty minutes later, a series of small buildings came into view. They stopped at the last row of vines, crouching in the shadows.

"Which building, do you think?" he asked.

"I'm almost certain it was in that one," she whispered, pointing to a large barn. "Yes, I know that's the one. I hid the bottle behind the bottom bricks of the first stall."

He took hold of her hand again, and they stepped out of the shadows into the full light of the moon. Running as fast as his sister would go, he thought his pounding heart would leap from his chest. When they reached the barn, he remembered the dogs. He hoped his father had kept them indoors that night.

They stood panting, backs pressed against the wall, once again in the cover of shadows. He looked around the corner, ready for any sign of their being detected. Only after he was certain of their safety did he beckon for her to follow him around to the barn door. Damica's eyes, as wide as those of a spooked horse, glowed white with the reflection of the moon.

They slipped inside, and he pulled the door closed. The musty odor of hay and animals invaded his nostrils. Several of the horses began to stir. Lighting the lantern, he gazed about the familiar structure.

"The bottle was in that corner stall," Damica whispered, pointing.

Creeping over to the unoccupied stall, she pushed the squeaky door open. They froze. Moving ahead after all remained quiet, they pulled back fistfuls of hay to expose the brickwork behind it.

"Oh, Antoine," Damica whispered. "The bricks have been repaired." He watched her inspect them. "No. No, this wasn't the spot. It was farther down."

They moved brick by brick across the floor of the stall, pulling away the hay as they went. Finally, his fingers settled on a loose one.

247

A loud whinny from a horse resounded throughout the barn. They stopped. Damica looked as though she would cry. When the horse fell silent, her expression eased. They resumed the task, wiggling the loose brick from the wall. The one beside it came out with ease.

Antoine set the lantern near the opening to peer into the dark hole. Reaching in to clear away a cobweb, he slid his hand inside. With a sudden jolt, he jumped to his feet. He swept a large spider from his arm and almost overturned the lantern. Damica steadied the lamp. Her eyes were wide with fear. In the dim light the spider scampered away over the straw.

He thrust his hand back into the hole, his sister's watchful eye upon him.

His fingers touched something. He flinched. Pressing forward he felt a layer of fine dust. Brushing it aside, he felt his fingers skim a smooth, rounded object. He pulled his arm back and nearly hollered with relief when he saw in his hand the base of a brown wine bottle.

"That's it, Antoine," Damica said in a harried whisper. "That's it."

When he pulled it out, they found the cork still intact.

Damica bounced with excitement. Antoine crouched by the lantern and worked the cork from the neck of the bottle. Dropping it in the hay, he turned the bottle on its side. A small paper scroll, bound by a thin piece of twine, slid silently onto his palm. Slipping the twine over one edge, he unrolled the parchment, holding it in the light.

"That's the document," Damica said, her fingers covering her mouth.

Antoine scanned the strange writing. It looked ancient, as though a record from a past civilization, another era. Its letters had been scrolled with strict care on a page now wrinkled and yellowed. Differing colors of ink had been used, and large block-style letters started new sentences and paragraphs. The script denoted excellence, the penmanship artistic. Parts had faded, but none was illegible.

He rolled the document up again and slid the twine back around it. Handing it to his sister, he replaced the bricks and the straw.

One of the horses again whinnied, and he heard it pacing in its stall. Before they could stand, a deep voice broke the silence.

"So you're back to take more." The two jumped to their feet and came face to face with their father. "Did you not take enough from me over the years?" he accused in a sharp French tone.

The man glared at them through mere slits, his seething anger palpable. From one hand a rifle hung, its barrel toward the floor of the barn.

Antoine stepped in front of his sister, his arms behind him as he took both her hands and pulled her close. He stared back into the angry eyes but stood silent.

"You never appreciated anything, Antoine. I saved your life. You ate my bread, you slept under my roof, I taught you a valuable trade, and all you could do was take. You never gave anything back. You were a miserable burden from the start, a thankless, inconsiderate, selfish burden. And here you are, under the cover of darkness, to take from me again. What is so important that you're sneaking back to get?"

Antoine remained silent.

The old man huffed like a raging bull. "You'll not leave this estate with one single piece of my property."

"You preserved my life, *Monsieur*, and for that I am grateful," he said. "And, yes, I stole from you. But I repaid every franc at my first opportunity. And by any standards other than your own, the truth reveals that it was you who stole from me."

"How dare you call me a thief!"

Antoine swallowed the fury rising in his throat. "How about my identity? You ripped that from me. Then you stole something even more valuable, something that can never be replaced—you pulled my childhood right out from under me."

His father sneered. "Return whatever you've stolen and get out. Now!"

Antoine's jaw tightened. "I'm not finished. You may have deceived me by calling yourself my father, but you did not give me life. You all but crushed the very life from me with your hateful yoke. You are a heartless man, *Monsieur* Aramis. I will never again call you my father, for a father cherishes and protects his children. If your life has been one of misery, blame yourself. You built this estate on the tears and the blood of others. I can never reclaim my childhood, but I will reclaim my identity, and you will not stand in my way."

The man glowered at Antoine and then looked beyond him to the face of his daughter. "What of you, Damica?" he said in the same angry tone. "Will you continue to deny me the satisfaction of knowing my own grandchildren?"

Antoine spoke before she could respond. "You have no right to consider yourself a grandfather. Now stand aside. We are no longer your property."

He glanced down at the rifle. The old man's finger tightened around the trigger.

Without warning, a large dark hand appeared from the shadows behind their father. It grabbed the man across his chest. Startled at the touch, he jumped. The rifle fell from his hand, thudding onto the dirt floor. He tried to reach for it, but was held in place by the strong, tall man behind him.

Antoine grabbed for the lantern and held it up. Matthias, the servant who had helped him in his escape five years before, stared at him.

"It's safe for you to go, Antoine, Damica," his voice boomed.

Mr. Aramis struggled to pull free, but the grip only tightened.

"I'm still indebted to you, Matthias," Antoine said. "I've not forgotten your kindness to me, and I will find a way to repay you."

"Just go. It's repayment enough." The tall black man followed the couple with his eyes as they slipped past him and out into the moonlight.

They sped across the vineyard and never looked back.

* * * * *

Antoine guided the horses along the road. Neither he nor Damica spoke for a long while.

"Antoine," his sister at last said, "of what advantage is the scroll if you can't read it?"

"I know a linguist employed at the cultural museum in London. He'll be able to tell me more about it."

The answer seemed to satisfy Damica, but offered him no comfort. Upon his return to London, he would have to reach the museum before his two pursuers reached him—not to mention the authorities because of the theft at Winterfield Manor. How could he prove his innocence?

And when would he ever again see his beloved Catherine?

Chapter Twenty-Nine

Roman Winterfield returned to his father's estate more than a week after Alexandra and Catherine had departed for Brentwood. He rushed through the front door at the dinner hour and found his parents alone, dining at a table set for two in the indoor garden.

Olivia Winterfield snapped her fingers at the servants and ordered another place setting. While the servants hustled about to accommodate the new arrival, Roman seated himself.

"Father, Mother, I must speak with you. It will not wait."

"And you won't believe the events that have occurred during your absence," Olivia said between commands to the servants.

"Where has everyone gone?" Roman asked, glancing around the otherwise empty table.

"Catherine has accompanied Alexandra to Brentwood," his father replied. "They are due to return at the end of the week, and—"

"And, Roman, that event is in itself another subject of which I must inform you," Olivia interrupted.

"And..." Richard glared at his wife for the interruption and looked back at Roman. "John is working at the vineyard this evening."

"Ah," Roman acknowledged.

"Now, what is it?" his father inquired.

"First I must know—Catherine did not accept Gregory Westcliffe's proposal, did she?"

"Not exactly," replied his mother. "That's the subject I wished to tell you about."

"What do you mean, 'not exactly'?" Roman leaned forward.

"Well, she hasn't given him an answer either way, but she will accept him. I'll see to that."

"Only if you'd like to see your daughter married to a felon, Mother—a man who will be imprisoned for what remains of his natural life."

"A Westcliffe a felon? Preposterous."

"What are you saying, Roman?" His father stopped eating.

"As you're well aware," Roman started, sitting back in his chair as a plate of warm food was placed before him, "the Westcliffes and the Winterfields have been allies for many generations, and Gregory and I have been well acquainted since childhood. I had respect for Gregory and his chosen profession."

"Yes, yes, go on," his mother said impatiently.

"However, I was shocked and disappointed when, a couple of years ago, he approached me at a social gathering and offered me a very lucrative business proposition, a 'rewarding opportunity,' he called it. He offered a very generous sum of money in exchange for the transportation and temporary storage at the Winterfield Imports warehouse of a modest shipment of overseas merchandise."

Richard's brow furrowed as he listened further to his son.

"Undoubtedly, my expression matched yours at this moment, Father. When I began questioning him, he became enraged at my inquiries. Straight away, I suspected something was amiss. He left the party infuriated. Any further contact between us was terminated, and I did not hear his name again until recently when I heard he had been hired as one of John Viana's architects."

"Please get to the point." Olivia shifted in her chair.

"At that time, I hoped he had abandoned any activities that could put him and others at risk. However, I became concerned again when Alexandra Viana mentioned his name to me while in France as the man with whom my own sister was then involved! As I thought on the matter, I became concerned and decided to return home to investigate the matter further. Just prior to my injury on the horse, I discovered the courtship had remained a secret from you, her own parents." Without touching the food before him, Roman stood and began to pace the floor. "Do you see? The only reason Westcliffe would have desired that the courtship remain confidential is because he feared I would hear of it."

"Perhaps he was afraid you still felt ill toward him," his mother reasoned. "That is hardly a reason to reject such an advantageous marriage proposal. You don't realize the relief your poor, doting mother experienced upon hearing that Gregory Westcliffe was interested in Catherine. Young men aren't exactly knocking down the door to keep company with her. She can hardly be called a beauty, and her shy nature doesn't lend itself to assisting her to the altar, if you understand my meaning. Most of the less attractive girls at least have personality to recommend them."

"Mother, can you have lived more than fifty years and yet be so blind?"

"I beg your pardon."

"Catherine's quiet spirit is what enhances her beauty, yes, her beauty. Any man of consequence will have appreciated that as well." His anger at its pinnacle, Roman forced his mind back to the real matter at hand. "And as for Westcliffe and his dealings, a man need feel no shame were he participating in no wrongdoing, especially since it had been some time since the incident. So I suspected he was still involved in questionable activities. Upon Mr. Westcliffe's return to London—the night of the ball—were we not all surprised when your friend, Mr. Viana, stated that he had not seen Mr. Westcliffe in several weeks? Many in this society seem to be aware that he is working with Mr. Viana's team of architects. However, if he was not with the Vianas and he was not in London, just where was Mr. Westcliffe those six weeks?"

"What are you saying, Roman?" his father demanded.

"Please, Father, allow me to finish." Roman walked back to place both hands on the tabletop. "Now, consider the manner in which he behaved at the party. Do you recall his surprise at my presence? Sensing my continued suspicion of him, he arranged a setting in which to propose to Catherine whereby she would be so pressured that she would not be able to refuse him. I know not what he said to you, Father, but somehow he manipulated you into creating the situation for him."

"Indeed, he did." Richard nodded, anger in his eyes.

"How shocked he must have been when Catherine postponed her answer. Had she accepted him, they could have married without delay. I have no doubt he would have persuaded her to do so; he has such cunning mannerisms. I would not have had the opportunity to contest the marriage and would have been unable to convince Catherine otherwise anyway, and he would then have had direct access to Winterfield Imports. He had already gained your favor despite my obvious dislike of him. Any objections I would have voiced would have been minimized, and he would have eventually convinced you to hand him control of the warehouse."

"Roman," his father said, "without proof of his intentions, an accusation such as this against a man of respect, and, might I remind you, a man of your own society, could actually be considered slander."

"I realize that, Father." He stood upright. "I intend to proceed with caution. May I?"

His father nodded.

"After the proposal at the ball, I watched Gregory Westcliffe as he obtained some information about one of your employees. He then left the party for awhile, but he was not alone, for I followed him. Did you note his brief absence?"

"Yes," his father stated. "After his disappearance, we called Catherine into the library for an explanation."

"I trailed Gregory from the ballroom," Roman continued. "He first went upstairs to your bedroom suite, and for what reason, I cannot seem to account." He noted his parents glance at each other, but neither interrupted him. "He was in your suite but minutes before exiting the house and disappearing into the darkness out back. Some thirty minutes later, he returned with an object in his hands, which he placed in his carriage and then rejoined to the party." Roman paced a few steps. "I boarded his carriage and found the object he had deposited there. It was an oil painting. The name of the artist was clear. It said 'Aramis.' Antoine Aramis is one of your employees. He works at the vineyard and was serving the night of the party."

"The poor man was framed!" exclaimed Olivia. "You mean to tell me it was Gregory Westcliffe all this time and not Antoine Aramis at all?"

"What do you mean?" Roman asked, returning to stand beside his mother. "Of what has Mr. Aramis been accused?"

"My sapphire and diamond necklace. It was stolen the night of the party and located in Antoine Aramis' quarters out at the vineyard."

"The man will stop at nothing." Roman tossed his head aside. "And had he not been trailed, he would have succeeded in his plot. An innocent man would have been jailed."

"The poor young man," Richard grieved. "And here he's a fugitive for a crime he didn't commit."

"He's gone?" Roman asked.

"Yes, he has not been seen by a single soul since his shift ended at the ball at midnight," Roman's father related.

"I see." Roman thought of his sister and how she must be agonizing over the situation. "And the plot thickens still more. I stayed in London the night of the ball. The following morning, I did something unscrupulous myself."

His mother's hand flew to her throat. "What did you do?"

"I entered Mr. Westcliffe's flat after he left. I was in search of something, anything, any evidence at all of wrongdoing."

Richard Winterfield's voice rose. "What did you find, son?"

"More evidence than I ever expected or desired. The entire flat was stocked with imported goods—crates to the ceiling.

Artwork, crystal, silver, pottery, rugs. Much of it was strewn over the entire apartment as though the sale of the merchandise had been in progress for some time. And, of course, Mr. Aramis' painting was there. He must have stumbled upon the piece in the servant's quarters when he planted the necklace the night of the ball. Then I discovered the most incriminating evidence of all—invoices without proper documentation, logs, and journals. Father, can you believe? The man has already begun to schedule shipments to the Winterfield Imports warehouse."

"What!" his father exclaimed.

Roman stepped back to the table and pounded one fist hard on its top. The crystal wine glasses and silver jumped. "The ink has not yet been set on the marriage license, and his illegal activity has already begun without regard for its consequence to you or Catherine or the Winterfield business." He closed his eyes and sank into his chair. "I left his flat with a few items and documents I believed would not be missed. I've spent the past week at loading docks and warehouses. Gregory Westcliffe is now and has been for some time engaged in the illegal import and sale of stolen goods."

"Why in the world would a talented architect resort to such a crime?" Olivia appeared baffled.

"I've asked myself that very question time and again, Mother. Who really knows? Perhaps he's bored in his line of work. Or maybe old-fashioned greed is the motive. It's quick money and very hard to trace. I think what surprised me the most was the sloppiness of it all. One would never imagine a meticulous architect sinking into such slovenly disorder."

"We'll call on William Sutton at once, Roman," his father declared.

"I am ahead of you, Father. I've already turned over to him all the evidence I collected." Roman sat at the table and looked at Olivia. "No, Mother, Catherine will not marry Gregory Westcliffe, and how grateful we can all be that she did not accept his proposal and is now out of harm's way."

"Oh, dear." Olivia covered her lips with her fingers.

"What is it, Olivia?" Richard stared at his wife.

"Gregory Westcliffe called here just this morning. He was grieved that he had not yet received a response from Catherine. He was very eager, and..." she paused.

"And what?" Richard pressed.

"I gave way to sympathy for the man. He's so persuasive, Richard!"

"What did you do?" Richard's tone demanded an answer.

"I...I revealed to him Catherine's location. He said he would go to her immediately."

Roman threw his chair aside. It hit the tile floor in a crash. "How could you, Mother?" He stepped back and slammed both palms on the table in front of her.

She jumped back.

"Why must you always trespass into the private matters of others?" Roman's face flushed with anger.

Olivia sat wide-eyed. She offered no excuse as she glanced from one to the other.

"I hope I'm not too late." Roman blurted, dashing from the room.

Chapter Thirty

Jessica Winterfield sat at the desk in the stateroom of *The Emerald*, examining the invoice of the cargo that had been loaded earlier in the afternoon. The ship swayed and pitched on the waves, a sensation to which she had grown quite accustomed, perhaps even to the point of fondness.

Setting the ink pen on the desktop, she stood and stretched her arms above her head. The ship rocked again, and she staggered, nearly tumbling to the floor. The changes in her shape had occurred so fast that, at times, she felt like a stranger in her own skin. And now, gazing at her reflection in the full-length mirror on the opposite end of the small stateroom, she hardly recognized the figure that appeared there. She turned to the side and smoothed the fabric of her dress over her protruding belly. More than three months remained until the birth of the baby, yet were she to grow any larger, she feared she would burst! How much more could a body stretch?

She thought of Grace, whose frame was much more slender, yet she had carried and delivered Everett with no trouble at all. Would her own confinement be as uncomplicated? She hoped so.

She caressed her belly, pondering the life snuggled inside. Who would this child prove to be? Would it be a son, a strong, dark-haired, and handsome lad who resembled his father? Or a daughter, bold and forthright like her mother or gentle and soft-spoken like her aunts? Would the child inherit the brilliant sapphire eyes that ran through her mother's bloodline, or the deep, reflective ones of his father? Perhaps of greatest importance was whether she and Andrew would succeed in inculcating in their child the most precious of traits—the wisdom and integrity that had been bestowed upon them by both their own fathers.

Contemplating all the possibilities, she stepped to the small window and peered out at the few remaining rays of the golden sunset. As the glowing streaks surrendered to shades of gray, she thought of her home at Brentwood Lighthouse. There she had stood atop the lighthouse crown many a night while she and her sisters watched the sun sink into the ocean. So many views of the sea reminded her of her childhood home.

Her thoughts turned to her younger sister, who was there at this very moment. Although she had seen Alexandra just two weeks before, she was grateful that Andrew had agreed to a small detour; they would stop in Chatham en route back to Scotland. Concern for her sister awakened her some nights. The worry when their father had first warned her of Roman's attraction to her sister had only increased, for now she knew of the mutual affection between them.

As the first twinkling stars appeared, she wondered at the irony of it all. Recalling the few conversations she and Alexandra had shared about the man after first meeting him, she chuckled when remembering the nickname they had invented for the overbearing Roman Winterfield—The Ogre. And a fitting title it had been.

Now, it seemed, Alexandra had been able to crack the hard shell. Even more unbelievable, she had discovered something likable beneath it.

She was anxious to return to Kent to speak with Grace. Surely, something could be done. In mere hours, the ship would sail into port there.

The second mate checked the ship's hull one final time before retiring. Examining the heavy straps securing the cargo, he carried out his responsibilities with the utmost dedication.

The Emerald carried a full load—even some cargo up on deck—with crates and lumber destined for Scotland, the Viana construction site.

At the sound of a faint noise, the sailor paused. He heard the noise again. When it occurred a third time, he walked quietly in its direction. The glow of a dim light passed over the floorboards in front of him, cast from behind a column of crates.

Peering around the crates, he saw a strange dark-haired man crouching on the floor. An iron bar in one hand, the man was attempting to loosen one of the floorboards.

"Stop where you are!" the second mate ordered.

The stranger jumped up.

Leaping forward, the sailor cornered the man. The stranger ducked and tried to flee, but the mate wrestled him to the floor. The man twisted, pulled himself free, and leapt to his feet. Still watching the sailor over his shoulder, he ran headlong into a column of crates.

The sailor watched the dark-haired man crumple to the floor, unconscious.

"I think you'd better come, Captain." Andrew's first mate had found him on the top deck. "It appears we have a stowaway."

Within moments, Andrew and two more sailors reached the quarters of the first mate and stepped into the cabin. A young man lay unconscious on the bunk.

"Discovered him in the hull pulling up some of the floorboards, Captain," reported the second mate.

Grasping him by the shoulder, Andrew turned the man onto his back. "I can't believe this!" he exclaimed.

"What is it, sir?" asked the second mate.

"This very man stowed away on my ship some years back. And both times to Chatham from France. Just how many times am I to transport him free of charge?"

The crew members stood in silence as Andrew's anger turned to concern. "Why is he unconscious? Is he all right?"

"He had a blow to the head, sir, his own doing," explained the first mate. "He'll prob'ly wake up with a nasty headache."

"Keep this room locked, and don't leave him alone." Andrew moved toward the door. "I want to be informed the moment he stirs."

"Yes, sir."

Andrew looked back at the unconscious man who was dressed in similar ragged clothing as the first time. He stepped back over to the bunk and placed his fingers against the man's throat. The pulse felt strong. Lifting one limp arm, he found small scars, scratches, and bruises scattered about on his dark skin. The hands were dirty and calloused. The stranger appeared thinner than he had at first glance.

"Have Mr. McGuire warm some stew," he commanded. "This one will be hungry when he awakens."

"Yes, sir."

An hour later, Andrew once more stood in the cabin beside the stowaway. The stranger had devoured the stew and bread and held the bowl out for more. The captain studied the wary glimpses shot his direction between bites.

"What are you doing aboard my ship?" he asked when the man finally put down the bowl.

Clenching his jaw, the stranger gave him a sullen stare.

"Perhaps had you offered to work aboard my ship, I would have granted your passage," Andrew persisted, his voice taking on an edge.

The man's expression remained unchanged.

"Do you understand what I'm saying?" The captain walked closer to the stranger, locking the man's gaze with his own.

Incomprehension glared back at him.

"Keep him under guard until we reach Chatham," he commanded, turning to leave. "We'll turn him over to the constable there."

Before sunrise Andrew arose to relieve the first mate.

"We should dock within the hour, sir."

"And how is our 'guest' doing?"

"Sleeping soundly."

"I don't doubt that. He probably has a full stomach for the first time in what appears weeks."

Jessica joined her husband on deck. When he explained the events of the previous evening and that the stowaway had been on their ship before, she recalled reading about the incident in an entry in the ship's logs recorded a few years earlier. A frown creased her forehead. Why would the same man stow away twice on the same ship...unless he chose *The Emerald* for a special reason?

Excusing heself, she descended the creaky staircase into the hull, lantern in hand. She located the place where the man had been discovered. The iron rod remained on the floor beside a dark hole, where one of the boards had been splintered in two.

What brought him aboard *The Emerald*? Was he hiding something on the ship? Or might he have been trying to retrieve something that had been placed there before?

Andrew had said he would examine the spot after they docked, but her insatiable curiosity got the best of her. She could not allow so much as a minute more to pass without knowing what the stowaway had been doing...or seeking.

She stepped to the hole and knelt with difficulty.

Patting her expansive belly, she whispered, "We won't be down here long, I promise."

Her slender hand slipped easily between the planks, and her fingers glided over the boards of the framework below. *What is this?* Her fingers passed over a small box-like object. It shifted with her touch. Wrapping her fingers around one edge, she turned it on its side and retrieved it from its hiding place.

Dust covered the rectangular container, which eliminated the explanation that the man had placed the object beneath the floorboards the night before. And based on the amount of dust, she doubted it had been placed even five years before when the man was on the ship the first time. No, this box had been in its place on *The Emerald* for many years longer.

How did it get there? And if it had been there for so many years, how did the young stowaway know of its location? She had peeked in on the man before going to the hull. This box looked older than he did.

She wiped the dust from its lid and examined it in the light of the lantern. No exterior markings or labels identified its owner or origin, and it had been sealed tightly with nails. Tucking it under one arm, she returned to the top deck to locate her husband.

Jessica followed Andrew to their stateroom, where he, too, examined the wooden box.

"Whatever the contents, its owner ensured that it was securely sealed," Andrew stated as he turned it round, shaking it.

"Will you open it or leave it to the authorities?" Jessica asked, attempting to mask her curiosity. Andrew would make the right decision regarding the mysterious item, she knew. Still...

"As I see it, this box is the property of *The Emerald*," he said, searching the room and locating a small tool. He pried the lid from its place. Underneath a layer of thick straw, they found two ornate leaded-crystal perfume bottles, each sealed with a gold cap.

Jessica lifted one from the box to cradle it in her palm. She admired its delicate carved patterns and gold lip, as Andrew examined its mate.

"Indeed, they're beautiful, but hardly worthy of stowing away and risking capture to retrieve them," he said, a puzzled expression on his face. "Even with the gold caps, they would yield only a fair price at best. Why is the man so desperate to recover them?"

"Perhaps they're family heirlooms or hold some other sentimental value."

"So much that he would risk arrest to get them? Why not just ask for them if they were only trinkets? And why hide them here? Why hide them at all? And when were they hidden? How did he know about them? There must be a greater significance to this."

"How will we ever know? You said the man refused to speak to you. But if he tells the authorities, we will have to relinquish them."

"Oh, no. These items will not be handed over to the authorities until they've been examined by the expert."

"Who?"

"Roman."

With *The Emerald* docked, Andrew escorted the stowaway, hands tied behind his back, through the Winterfield Imports warehouse and into his father's office. He sent an employee to summon his father. As they waited, the young man sat on a wooden chair, head down, his dark hair dangling in dirty strands to cover his face.

Andrew sat opposite him. "Who are you?" he asked. "From where have you come? Where have you been these past five years? What's the significance of the crystal bottles?"

He expected no reply and received none. The young man did not so much as lift his head in response.

The office door opened; Richard Winterfield entered the room. He stopped upon sight of the ragged young man and glanced at his son.

"Turns out we got more than we bargained for, Father. This man was found in the cargo hold last evening."

"I see," replied Richard.

"It seems he speaks no English, he suffered a head injury, he appears a bit malnourished, and..." Andrew paused, "...he has stowed away on *The Emerald* before—five years ago. You may recall I filed a report about the man after he escaped the grip of my crew, but this time he was not so fortunate. This is that man. I'm certain of it. I shall never forget that face. Shall I notify the authorities?"

Richard Winterfield stepped over to the young man and cupped his palm under his chin. Lifting the man's chin upward, he brushed the hair from his face. As the dark eyes looked upward, Richard dropped his hand and stepped back. "Antoine! Where have you been? You've been cleared of the charges of thievery, yet must I now have you arrested for stowing away on my ship?"

"Father, you know this man?"

"He's an employee at the vineyard. Though I didn't hire him personally, I've met him several times. He looks a bit thinner, but I suppose that's because he has been without a home for the last two weeks."

"I don't understand."

"He disappeared after a charge was brought against him for an apparent stolen necklace from your mother's dressing table. The necklace was discovered in his quarters, but we have since discovered the true thief and have cleared his name."

The young man remained silent, his gaze fixed upon the opposite wall. He had no observable reaction to Richard's words.

"You mean to tell me he speaks English?" Andrew exclaimed.

"Of course." Richard addressed the disheveled man again, a softer tone in his voice. "Antoine...son...I know not where you've been, but I would very much like to see you restored to your position at the vineyard. Simply state that you agree, and I'll make the arrangements."

The man sat in silence.

"Antoine, do you understand?" Richard asked.

No response.

"Apparently you do not realize your situation here, son. I have the power to release you or to have you arrested. Which will it be?"

The man finally did respond, but in a tongue unfamiliar to either of them. He spoke several sentences and then fell silent again.

Richard shook his head and looked at Andrew. "I know not why he insists on playing this game and trying my patience."

Richard tried speaking to Antoine in French, but was ignored.

"His eyes show no sign of recognition of you, Father. What shall we do?"

"He leaves us with no other alternative. Notify the authorities, Andrew."

Chapter Thirty-One

Roman Winterfield stared into unrelenting rain in the misty light of the early morning. The train had been moving westward the entire night, its progress unaffected by the intensifying summer storm.

As the train drew closer to the coast, his anxiety level increased. What would he find upon reaching Brentwood? Could his sister be swayed into marrying Gregory Westcliffe despite her love for Antoine Aramis? Yet, he would put nothing past the conniving and convincing Westcliffe, who would resort to any and all means of deceit to attain his own selfish goals. He hoped his sister had taken his letter of warning in all seriousness and that she would stand in firm defense against the man.

Of course, Alexandra Viana was with her. He smiled at the thought. She would prove a strong support for Catherine, especially if she had read his letter.

Still staring at the driving rain, he became lost in his thoughts of her. He missed being in her presence, for he had seen her almost every day the six weeks prior to the party. In all his life, he could not recall such a yearning for any other person. Oh, perhaps when he was a young child and found himself away from his parents. But no one since—until now.

The storm took him back to the rainy days prior to the morning she had interrupted him and Caroline and the gentle but firm manner in which she had expressed her concern for his horse. How she had slipped her arm around his waist to assist him to his feet. He could still feel her touch, and he longed to take her hand again in his, to see her smile as she had after the birth of the foal. The loveliness in her face beneath the smudges lingered in his mind. It was the same day that, in his eyes, Caroline's good looks had melted, revealing features of the most distorted and hideous kind. She would never—could never—compare with Alexandra's calm nature and modest eloquence.

Then there was the time she had stood up to him at the café in France when he had scolded the young girl who had spilled the tray of food on him; and the earlier incident that same day when she had unexpectedly appeared at the pottery shop and concluded the shrewd business transaction with the Frenchman. Indeed, she had been right, for Roman's father later reported that the vases had sold in no time for the equivalent of thirty francs apiece, even more than the amount she had estimated. Where had she, a product of the working class, learned such skills in commerce? Pondering the thought but a moment, he settled on her father's influence, her recent climb into the aristocracy, and, perhaps most noteworthy of all, her impeccable sense of what would please the female gender.

Looking back, he knew that single event had inched him closer to a turning point in his life. He had never before glanced her way, but that day in the potter's shop, he had discovered her exceptional beauty. As he grew to know her, that beauty was eclipsed by her admirable integrity, her respectful and delightful way with others, her quest for greater wisdom, and her general zest for life.

Recalling his return to Winterfield Estates in June, he had to laugh at the alarm in her expression when she had thrown her arms about him, only to find he was not Andrew. Caught unaware himself, he had not realized her mistake until the incident was over. He envisioned it again and in his mind took her into his arms.

Yes, he admitted to himself, he was, indeed, very much in love with the youngest daughter of John Viana, a man he had also grown to respect.

But would he, Roman, be able to show the strength he had come to esteem in Alexandra? Would he exhibit the courage to confess his feelings to her?

He could no longer keep his regard for her concealed. Although he acknowledged her love for another man, Roman would make certain that she knew of the impact she had made on his life. He must do it soon, for once she married, she could allow no opportunity for such a confession.

The downpour persisted as the train pulled into the station at Penzance. Upon stepping into the building, Roman inquired about any sign of Gregory Westcliffe, but no one recognized the name or description he gave.

Tired from the long journey and eager to reach his destination before the unthinkable occurred, he attempted to attain transportation to the lighthouse.

"Sir, it's an hour's ride north to Brentwood, and that's on a good day. I'm certain the road has been washed out by the storm. Not a carriage in this town could offer a safe passage," one man argued. "A friend of mine runs the Rosewood Inn just outside of town. Give him my name, and he'll rent you a room at a reasonable price."

Roman thanked him and asked another man for directions to the town's livery. Tightening his overcoat about his torso and throat, he pulled the brim of his hat down and stepped out into the driving rain.

More than an hour later, Roman fought to make his way down a muddy road against the howling wind on the back of a horse he had purchased at the livery. Though the pain in his ribs had subsided in previous days, it now nagged at him again. Ignoring it, he pressed on.

The animal slipped often on the muck the road had become. Roman questioned his decision to venture on and even thought himself lost more than once. He knew not whether the roaring in his ears was the wind or the sea; he must be somewhere near the shore, but he could not see it through the mist and rain.

It seemed like hours before he reached Bristlecone, a little town near the lighthouse, and only then did he find comfort in the fact that he was not lost. The main street sat vacant, save a few burning lamps, the flames enduring the storm encased in glass high atop their posts. Flowers potted in baskets hanging from the lampposts swung in the wind. The fragile blossoms bowed in defeat, many thrown to the ground to meet their demise in dirty puddles. Baskets blown from their posts tumbled with the gusts down the lane. Flowers once secure in window boxes had been beaten into the soggy mud that housed them.

Cold and soaked through, Roman caught sight of an orange glow from a nearby window. He stopped at the pub to warm himself and inquire for further directions. Here, too, he found no one who had seen any sign of Westcliffe, and he hoped the fury of the storm had forced him back to London.

The owner of the pub shook his head in disbelief when, after just one brandy, Roman stated his intent to once again brave the storm. Mounting the horse out front, he noted several faces collected at the window to watch him, the stranger in the storm, disappear into the mist.

Roman saw a dim white flash in the distance. A weaker scarlet one followed. At the low moan of a distant foghorn, he knew he had found Brentwood. Nudging the horse on, he lost sight of the beacon amidst the thick forest. Dusk had crept upon him when he spotted a house in the clearing ahead.

Warm light flickered in the windows, and plush billows of smoke rose from the stone chimney, only to be chased away by the wind. He paused for a moment, looking upon the childhood home of the Viana daughters. "Who would ever want to leave such a place?" he wondered aloud, admiring the house and the green misty forests that surrounded the clearing. Somehow, it reminded him of the secret meadow where he had taken Alexandra.

As he neared the cottage, the crown of the lighthouse in the distance with its life-saving beams came into view again, penetrating the rain and fog.

He could not remember ever being more relieved to reach his destination. Hoping to encounter Westcliffe, he reveled at the thought of forcing the man out into the storm to fend for his own way back to town. But upon finding no other horses tied to the post, he felt certain the man had not bothered to fight the storm.

Roman stepped up to the porch and pounded on the door.

Greeted by the astonished face of an older woman, he entered the welcoming warmth inside. Because the woman looked familiar, he assumed they had met at Andrew's wedding.

"Give me your coat," she said. "Catherine!"

Shivering, he handed her his hat as well. The delicious smell of the upcoming meal filled his nostrils. His stomach reacted at once.

Catherine came running from what appeared to be the kitchen. "Roman!" She leaped into his arms despite his wet clothing. "What are you doing here? How did you find us through this storm?"

"Have you seen Mr. Westcliffe?"

"No. Why? Does he know where I am?"

"I'm afraid he obtained that information, but perhaps the storm has kept him at bay. I've made some startling discoveries about the man, Catherine, and must inform you at once." He looked about into the one room that was visible from the entrance hall. "Where's Miss Viana?"

"She and Mr. Wright are at the lighthouse. Mr. Wright will be staying the night there, but Alex should be returning soon for dinner."

"That lighthouse is out in the ocean. How will she get back?"

"Don't worry. She grew up here. You should hear her stories. She helped rescue an entire crew once during a storm out in that sea. This little storm is no threat to her, I'm sure."

Roman accepted the explanation with considerable reservation. This was no little storm, and he had heard reports from the men in the pub that it had been strengthening.

The woman he assumed to be Mrs. Wright excused herself after retrieving a blanket for the soaked traveler, leaving him to talk with his sister in the parlor in front of the fire.

Moments later Mrs. Wright called down from the second story landing. "Come quick!"

Following Catherine, Roman rushed up the stairs toward the frightened voice. Mrs. Wright summoned them into an upstairs bedchamber that afforded a direct view of the lighthouse.

"Look!" she cried. "The rowboat has been smashed to pieces!" She handed a telescope to Roman. "The waves have overtaken the dock!"

He peered through the spyglass at the angry sea crashing in violent waves against the rocks of the lighthouse island. Wooden planks lay scattered about on the tiny island and in the waves. He discovered the frame of the rowboat tied to the lighthouse base, the waves thrashing it to and fro.

At the base of the lighthouse, a door opened. The face of a man appeared, only to withdraw at once behind the door pulled closed against the rushing water.

"Is there another rowboat, Mrs. Wright?" Roman demanded.

"On the beach, if it, too, hasn't been washed away."

He bolted from the room and down the stairs, once more ignoring the intense prodding of his injured ribs.

"Roman!" Catherine shouted.

Hearing her footsteps behind him, he refused to be deterred and was outside in seconds. Sloshing along the muddy pathway, he crossed the clearing and disappeared into the forest. The waning twilight reflected off and matched the gray ocean, barely illuminating the short pathway through the trees.

The waves had reached the edge of the forest, and he found the rowboat tied to a dock now mostly submerged. The boat appeared to be intact. Fighting the powerful waves, he waded to the skiff and loosed it. Rain pelted his face, its fury soaking him to the skin.

He crawled into the boat and unlatched the oars. Soon the water between him and the forest widened. Despite the fiery pain in his side, he clenched his jaw and rowed with all his might against the hammering waves. Stroke after stroke sent torturous lashes pounding throughout his entire body. His own shouting drowned in the wailing of the wind.

Looking back often, he kept adjusting the direction of the little boat toward the lighthouse.

What seemed an eternity later, the boat neared the island. The door at the base of the beacon opened, and Mr. Wright stepped out. Roman threw a rope toward him, trying with desperation to steady the small boat. Thrown against a rock, the boat lurched forward and settled between the waves. Surprised the tiny craft remained seaworthy, he tossed the rope again. This time, Mr. Wright grabbed hold of it. The waves crashed into the open doorway while Mr. Wright wound the rope about one arm and pulled the boat toward him, grasping the frame of the door with his other hand.

Roman maneuvered the craft toward the entrance. He climbed out of the boat. As Mr. Wright held tightly to it, he secured the rope, then fought the waves to the doorway.

"Alex!" he called against the wind into the dark tower.

An expression of terror on her face, she emerged. He grabbed her hand. Wrapping his arm about her, he clutched the frame of the door as a massive wave broke the island. It threw them against the outside wall and receded. Taking advantage of the lull, he guided her to the rowboat where Mr. Wright had climbed aboard, holding the battered vessel close to the pillar. The water rose by the minute. After lifting Alexandra into the boat, he loosened the rope and jumped in himself.

While Mr. Wright held Alexandra, Roman manned the oars. At least the waves helped rather than hindered on the return, pushing them back toward shore.

At last, the trio arrived safely at Brentwood House. Met with kisses and hugs from the two ladies who, too, became soaked with rain and sea water, they shut the storm out behind the strong door of the cottage.

In the kitchen, Roman shivered fiercely, fumbling with the buttons on his shirt, his fingers stiff from cold. At the insistence of Mrs. Wright, he peeled the wet clothes from his body, leaving them in a heap on the floor. Wrapping himself in a wool blanket, he joined his sister in the parlor.

"Here." She wrapped another blanket around him. "Lie down until dinner. You're exhausted."

With his hair dripping, he lay back on the lounge and closed his eyes. Pain pulsed through every muscle. The warmth of the fire reached his face, and soon his shivering waned.

He still could not believe he was in Alexandra's home. Somewhere between fatigue and the sleep his body demanded, he recalled her huddled against Mr. Wright in the little boat. At first, she had seemed so afraid. But through the driving rain, she had lifted her face. In her eyes he found no fear. They remained fixed on him until the boat reached the shore. What was it he detected in them?

Upon opening his eyes, he saw the hands of the clock read an hour later. At the sound of soft voices and the clinking of silverware, he heard his stomach growl in complaint.

Roman savored the pork stew placed before him. He complimented the ladies on the warm bread that melted in his mouth and listened with interest to the ongoing conversation.

"Never have I seen the sea overtake the island to reach the door of Old Stormy," Mr. Wright declared. "I've grown accustomed to being stranded out there during storms," he said between bites, "but this is different."

"It would almost be believable in the winter," his wife added, "but in summer?"

"How long will that lamp burn?" asked Roman.

"You read my mind," Mr. Wright answered. "We had just refilled the well before you came for us. It'll only last a couple more hours."

"What of the ships out there?" asked Catherine, frowning.

"Its dangerous water," said Mr. Wright. "We'll just have to hope there'll be none."

Following Viana tradition on stormy nights, the ladies gathered clean bedding for makeshift beds on the couches and floor of the parlor so that all five could sleep together before the crackling fire.

Upstairs, Mr. Wright peered through the scope from a second-story bedroom window. He watched as the last dim flash from Old Stormy passed over Brentwood House, and then died in the pitch of the unrelenting storm. For the first time in its long history, Brentwood Lighthouse stood lifeless and dark. The ships were now at the mercy of the angry sea until the passing of the storm and the lighting of the beacon once again.

A flash of lightning lit up the sky. He saw the bone-white pillar and then it was gone again, swallowed up by the darkness. Placing the scope on the bureau, he descended the stairs to join the others in the parlor.

Before the warmth of the fire, the five drifted to sleep one by one. Alexandra nestled into the down comforter that had been laid out on the chaise, and Roman on a pile of blankets on the rug before the hearth. Never in his life could he remember sleeping on the floor in any house for any reason. Even in the barn in the Italian countryside, he had at least a pile of hay on which to sleep. And yet, despite his recent injury, never could he remember being so comfortable, so content. He was grateful to be safe and in the presence of the two women who mattered most in his life.

For a long while he and Alexandra again gazed into each others' eyes. What was she thinking? What was she feeling? No matter how he wished otherwise, he knew in his heart it was nothing more than gratitude.

After several minutes, she drifted into a silent slumber. He watched her blankets rise and fall in even rhythm with her breathing. Her peaceful beauty was the last image he saw before succumbing himself.

The fire burned low as the winds howled outside the cottage. Rain pelted the windowpanes, lightning shot zigzags across the sky, and thunder bellowed its fury overhead. Alexandra thrashed in her sleep, her head tossing to and fro.

The rain battered the tiny island. Standing in the dimness of a small lantern inside the base of the lighthouse, she heard someone call her name. She pulled on the door, but it would not budge.

Again she heard her name.

"I'm here!" she cried out. "The door...I can't get out!" Her words faded into the thunder.

"Where are you, Alex?" the voice called more urgently.

"I'm trapped!" She tugged on the stubborn handle.

Water seeped beneath the door and soaked her shoes. Taking a step back, she screamed.

Someone pounded on the other side of the door. Water surged into the entryway when it burst open. A man reached in and grabbed her by the hand, pulling her out into the storm. She looked up into the face of Roman as the beacon's light faltered and died.

"You're safe now," he said, holding her close.

A sudden wave yanked her from his grip. It clawed at her legs and dragged her beneath the surface. She held her breath. Every ounce of her strength fought against its force. He called out for her. She tried to answer, but water gushed into her lungs.

Drenched with perspiration, she bolted upright. There before the dying embers of the hearth he lay, peacefully slumbering. She collapsed into her blankets.

The nightmare had faded, but the storm continued unabated. Would it ever stop?

Chapter Thirty-Two

The hazy light of sunrise barely penetrated the windows of Brentwood House. The winds had died, but the rain continued in a soft drizzle.

Aware of someone whispering her name, Alexandra stirred awake to a gentle shaking of her shoulder. She opened her eyes to the wet face of Roman. His hair dripped onto her blankets.

"Come with me," he whispered.

Alexandra rolled out from beneath her blankets and followed him to the front door while the others slept on. He assisted her with her boots and cloak. Pulling the hood up, she followed him out into the misty drizzle. Guiding her along the muddy footpath through the forest, he led her onto the beach.

She looked in disbelief over the ocean, still and empty. The lighthouse pillar was nowhere in sight. Tearing her gaze from the shocking scene, she stared in desperation at Roman.

"It's gone," he said, shaking his head. "A part of the wall remains on the island, but everything else—the rest of the pillar, lens, staircase, all the internal gears and ironwork—gone to the bottom of the sea."

Tears filled her eyes. She was too stunned to speak.

"May I take you to the island?" he asked.

She nodded.

He helped her onto the rowboat and, with his back to the island, maneuvered the boat across the rippling water. She stared straight ahead, beyond him, as they neared the island.

When they reached the shore, he pulled the small boat from the water and held his hand out to her.

She climbed over the side of the boat and walked past him, staring at the devastation. A curved section of the pillar, perhaps twenty feet in height, was the only remnant of the structure that had stood as her protection not twelve hours before, the haven of her childhood, her family's very reason for being.

With vague awareness of his presence behind her, she looked out at the sea she thought she had known well.

"So powerful, so untamable," she said to its vastness. "How can you be so graceful at times and...and yet so angry?" The volume of her voice rose. "A giver to a whole world of mankind," she wailed, "but a thief to me?"

Her lips quivered. Tears coursed down her cheeks.

"I'm sorry," Roman said in a soft voice. "Would you like to be alone? I can wait for you in the boat."

Alexandra's face dropped into her hands. Hearing his footsteps draw near, she turned into his arms and collapsed against his chest. She wept, his cheek resting on her head.

Several minutes later, she stepped away from him. Waves lapped like tongues against the rocks. Planks and debris littered the surface of the sea.

She turned to stare at the crescent of stones. Here stood the only evidence that an important landmark for weary seafarers had once existed on this spot. Sadness washed over her like waves crashing against the shore. How many would die because the warning light had been stilled?

Walking past the ruins, she paused to pick up a stone fragment. White paint covered one side, paint her father had applied with his own hands. Dropping it into her skirt pocket, she treaded around a patch of high grass that had somehow withstood the storm's fury and walked over to Roman. She looked up into his dark eyes. "My life has been spared because of your kindness. I owe you a great debt."

"There was a time when your sister saved the life of my brother," he said in a quiet voice. "The Winterfields were indebted to the Vianas. I believe that debt has now been paid."

They rowed back in silence. Upon returning to the house, they found the others had also discovered the destruction of the lighthouse.

"I'll ride to town and send notification to the Committee," said Mr. Wright, pressing his hat upon his head.

The drizzling rain continued, and Alexandra's mood fit the dreary day. Droplets trickled down the windowpanes like the tears that streaked her cheeks, mourning the loss of the beacon.

While stacking linens in the wardrobe at the end of the upstairs hallway, she spied Roman outside down below. Tromping through the mud with Mrs. Wright, he scattered hay about with a pitchfork for the horses.

Watching this stately man of the gentry participating in the most meager of tasks of a hired hand seemed almost too much to bear. And yet to see him participating in the humble activity lent such appeal to him. She wanted to cry and laugh for the same reason, for the exertion he had put forth in altering his personality, indeed his very being.

Never would she have thought that the unexpected presence of the man she had grown to love would put her under such strain. If only she could tell him of her feelings, perhaps then her mind would be put at ease. Yes, that was it. She would go down to him and tell him; she would just blurt it out, right there for the horses and pigs to hear...

She marched to the top of the stairs.

...and Mrs. Wright.

No. Not in front of Mrs. Wright. They must be alone.

Who was she fooling? She could only come to regret any such attempt. He had proved himself her friend, yes; but his true regard was for Caroline Landly.

The chimes of the clock by the staircase reminded her that the time was drawing near to pack her cases for the trip home.

Chapter Thirty-Three

An hour later, Roman shook the rain from his overcoat, hanging it on a hook in the entryway, along with his hat. Stepping into the parlor, he found his sister and Alexandra sitting down for tea.

"There's no sign of the weather's letting up," he said. "We'll have to leave within the hour if we expect to catch that train in Penzance."

"We're already packed and prepared to go," his sister reported.

"Catherine," he said, stepping to the sideboard to pour himself a cup of tea, "though I came here anticipating Westcliffe's tactics, I also bear some wonderful news. I'm sorry I haven't had the opportunity to tell you sooner." He turned to face them, cup in hand. "Mr. Aramis has been cleared of the charges against him."

Catherine jumped up to embrace him. "Is it really true?"

"As I started to tell you last evening, it turns out the real culprit was Westcliffe himself."

"That scoundrel. I can't believe he would frame Mr. Aramis," Catherine said.

"Then for certain you wouldn't believe what I discovered in his flat," he said, dropping a lump of sugar into his cup. "Sit down and I'll tell you everything."

He explained to her and Alexandra the details of his investigation and his findings, including Antoine Aramis' artwork.

"The painting he describes is the one of us, Alex. Do you remember?" Catherine asked.

"Oh, yes."

"So Mr. Westcliffe had planned all along to use our family business for his illegal transactions," Catherine said. "I'm so ashamed that I ever let him near our family."

"How were you to know?" asked Roman, leaning against the sideboard.

"Alex knew, didn't you?" Catherine said. "You tried to talk me out of him more than once. How is it you possess such wisdom?"

"His letter to you was void of any affection," she answered, "and he treated other people in such a peculiar manner, me included. It wasn't wisdom on my part, just observation."

"Roman," his sister said, turning her attention to him, "thank you for taking the time to show your concern. I think this would be the appropriate time to notify you of something."

"Go on," he said, watching her glance with doubt toward Alexandra.

Catherine bit her lower lip. "I'm engaged to Antoine."

"What?...When?"

"The night following the ball he came to me. He knew of the charges against him, but proclaimed his innocence. I believed him. He proposed to me that night, and I accepted. I was encouraged by the letter you left me the following morning, but even now I fear your response."

Roman nodded, considering her words. Leaving his cup, he stepped over and extended his hands, pulling her to her feet. "I can't tell you how Mother and Father will react to this news, but I'm proud you stood by him, Catherine. I couldn't be happier with your decision." He kissed her cheek. "It seems you yourself are coming into wisdom of your own."

Catherine wiped a tear from her cheek. "Roman, I'm overwhelmed that you went to such lengths to protect me and to tell me of Antoine. Were those your only reasons in coming all this way?"

"Well..." This was not the time to confess his feelings for Alexandra. He hoped the opportunity would soon present itself, but not in the presence of his sister. Certain that Catherine knew of Alexandra's feelings for Preston Sutton, he feared embarrassment to them all were he to make such a declaration. Yet Alexandra's eyes were fixed upon him. Her posture stiffened, as though anticipating his response. His mind raced. "Concern over you and the news of Mr. Aramis—those were my reasons."

He was surprised when Alexandra jumped to her feet. "Excuse me," she whispered and ran toward the front door. With no head covering or cloak, she dashed into the rain outside.

"Stay here," Roman ordered his sister and ran after Alexandra.

She was several paces down a stone pathway leading toward the back of the house.

"Alex!" She stopped with her back to him, her head down.

When he reached her, he took hold of her arm and turned her toward him. He was met by a look of intense irritation emanating from red-rimmed eyes.

"Why did you arrange for us to dine alone in Paris?" she demanded.

What had prompted such a question? Why did she even care? Dropping her arm, he stepped back. "The reason was inconsequential then and remains so to this day."

"Inconsequential?" she lashed out. He was unaccustomed to hearing such frustration from her. "A man goes to great lengths to rearrange the dining plans of eight people for reasons that were at the time inconsequential?"

His voice took on a sharp edge when he saw the ever-present golden locket dangling around her neck. "Perhaps you could accept the faults of others more easily were you to look in the mirror. It would appear, Miss Viana, you're a woman suffering from a divided heart. Can you deny your affection for the benefactor of that locket to which you seem so attached?" Even Preston Sutton deserved loyalty.

Her expression contorted into one of confusion. "Of course I have affection for the giver. Mr. Winterfield, I know not of what you're accusing me, but I would be a heartless person, indeed, were I to have no affection for my own mother."

"Your—the locket is from your *mother*?" Oh, what a mistake he had made.

"Who did you believe it to be from?"

He dropped his head. "The package arrived from France," he said, his voice quieting. "Who else would it be from but the Frenchman?" His hand clenched into a fist. How could he have been so presumptuous? Here was yet another incident to add to his growing list of failures.

"What Frenchman?" she asked.

"The one from the palace," he said with a sigh, not looking at her. "The man who escorted you to the restaurant the evening of our meal together."

"That man happened upon me as I strolled through the park. I wasn't with him ten minutes when he became embarrassingly forward with me. I tried to excuse myself, but he insisted that I have an escort to the café. I never saw him again. I don't even know his name. Why did you not ask about it at the time?"

"It wasn't my business," he mumbled.

"And that was the reason for concluding that our dinner together was of no consequence?"

"That was but a small portion." Roman gazed at the forest, still unable to look her in the eye. What a disappointment he had always been to her. "I never should've attempted it in the first place. I knew better than to think a woman of your caliber could have any interest in a man like me." Finding the courage to look back, he saw perplexity in her expression. "You don't see it, do you?" he asked.

"See what?"

"You know the sort of man I was. Three years ago your sister tried to warn me of the self-destructive course I was following. But her harshness only challenged me. Later, my father tried to force me—with threats—to change my ways. While I succeeded for a time, I eventually succumbed to deeper anger and was driven farther away than ever before. It wasn't until I met you again that I was able to understand how to change. Without even realizing it, you showed me what it is to care. You taught me restraint by your own example. You helped me to at last know the greatest happiness in giving. You allowed me to experience for myself what it is to share. And it was you who made me see that there may still be time to establish a relationship with my sister. I would've remained blinded to that fact had it not been for your words of concern, and I thank you for that."

Stepping closer, he took her shoulders in his hands. She remained still.

"I may regret it for the rest of my life," he continued, "but I want you to know that it was you who allowed me to find, if even for a moment, real love. I want you to know that I love you. I fell in love with you in Mr. LaRon's shop in France, though I didn't know it at the time." He wanted to think those were tears dropping from her eyes, yet was unsure due to the rain wetting her cheeks. "But I was well aware of it by the time I arranged for that dinner in Paris. I...I had to be alone with you." He turned away from her again, his fingers running through his soaked hair. "But I also realized by then that we are not equals, nor could we ever be. You are my superior in every possible way. That was the reason such an evening was of no consequence. You could never love me. I knew that for certain when, en route back to England on *The Emerald*, I found the letter you wrote to your sister from France."

"The letter..." he heard her mumble. "Please let me—"

"That confirmed what I had suspected all along—I was a failure. I knew then you were beyond my reach, and later I saw your attentions toward Preston Sutton. I concluded that my mother must have been right: Caroline Landly was the woman for me. I tried to like her. I honestly tried. And I found that my mother was right. Miss Landly was a good match for the man I had been. But since coming to know you, I'm not that man any longer. Because of you I will never be that man again. I dismissed Miss Landly the night of the ball."

Alexandra looked as though she wanted to speak. He did not give her a chance, wanting her to know everything before he lost his courage.

"I overheard you confess to your mother your love for your 'sister's brother-in-law,' and I knew at that moment Mr. Sutton had captured your heart." He looked up into the bleary sky at nothing in particular. "And yet, even knowing all these things, there was another reason for my trip here. I wanted to see you. Just being in your presence brings me peace and the greatest joy. One last thing I've learned along this journey is that true love is selfless. My love for you causes me to desire your happiness above all else." He closed his eyes, his chest filling with pain. "I accept that you have given your heart to Mr. Sutton."

With a shake of her head, Alexandra stepped forward. Before she could speak, a voice interrupted them.

"Excuse me." They turned to find a young man standing in the rain, his horse a few paces behind. "Are you Alexandra Viana?"

She nodded, shaking from the cold.

"I bring a letter from London," he said.

The two stood and stared at the young man. Roman wondered how much of the conversation he had overheard. Surely, he could not have been there long.

"The rain will destroy the letter if I deliver it here," the courier said. "May we step into the house?"

"Of course," Roman replied. He did not look again at Alexandra, though he held an arm out to show the two into the house.

Once inside the vestibule, Roman tipped the courier, and when offered a warm cup of tea, the man agreed to stay.

Mrs. Wright led them to the kitchen, where Catherine brought blankets for the three.

"Can you please read the letter for me?" Alexandra asked of Catherine. The courier handed it to her.

"It's from John!" Catherine announced and began reading aloud.

"My Dear Sister,

Please return at once with Catherine. Antoine has come back to Kent. However, the news is not good. He is in custody, arrested under charge of stowing away on *The Emerald*, and has been uncooperative with all, myself included. I feel that Catherine is the key to his release.

Yours, John."

Catherine's hands dropped. "The night he came to me when we were engaged, he was very excited because he had sold several of his paintings." She looked up in desperation at her brother and Alexandra. "He had no need of stowing away on any ship. He had the money to buy a ticket." Bursting into tears, she rushed into Alexandra's arms.

"We'll leave at once," Alexandra said, looking up at Roman.

Though the train was filled to capacity, the journey back to London was quiet for Roman Winterfield. Catherine and Alexandra had found room to sit together on one hard bench. He sat several rows away by the window.

Eyes downcast, Roman stared at the passing vegetation, paying little attention to the beads of water trickling over the pane. From the corner of one eye, he could detect Alexandra and sensed the weight of her stare.

But he sat lost in thought. The words he had long desired her to hear had been spoken. He felt certain they would share very few words in the future.

A gloomy horizon awaited him—his work abroad, a life of isolation. The pain of his broken ribs, unbearable as it had seemed at the time, surrendered to the agony that now gripped his heart. The weight of his loss all but crushed him. It seemed as though he were dying inside.

The sooner he could escape her presence, the sooner his pain would subside. Oh, he would see her again sometime. After all, she was a close relation to Andrew. What would happen then? What would he say? Would his pain return each time his gaze fell upon her? How could he ever again look into those eyes?

And yet, he did not regret falling in love with her, nor any of the feelings he had confessed.

His heart sank even lower when he thought of her pending marriage to the undeserving Preston Sutton. Despite what she must think, that man could not make her happy. Alexandra was defined by great depth of character. The essence of life breathed from her every word, her every movement. And what was Preston Sutton but a one-dimensional wretch on a never-ending quest for pleasure? And what was she to him? Some toy to fulfill his momentary needs? A thing he would squeeze the life from then cast aside in exchange for some new pursuit?

His stomach turned at the thought of them together.

For a brief span of time he had known what it was to be alive in its fullest sense. Now, in his despair, he felt himself slipping back into the hard shell he once had been. Desperate to cling to the man she had helped him to become, he repeated the vow he had made to her: he would never revert to his former self. Despite his great effort, however, the anger crept in, the jealousy of and hatred for Preston Sutton.

To keep his resolve, he made yet another. Only in leaving England permanently would he have any chance to retain the values she had taught him. To show gratitude for all she had done for him, he found no option other than to put a great distance between himself and the rival who had won her heart.

Her face had not moved. There she sat, just a few short yards away. He wanted nothing more than to look at her, to move closer, to hear her voice.

He would take her anger, he would accept her counsel, he would cherish her reproach. He could accept anything her lips had to speak...anything but her sympathy. And that was what he would find in her eyes were he to glance at her now.

Unable to bear her expression of pity upon him, Roman did not look up.

Chapter Thirty-Four

"Five years ago, the man stows away on my ship," Andrew murmured, pacing. "Then he secures a decent wage as my father's employee. Later he steals from my mother and goes into hiding, though he's cleared of that charge. He proceeds to stow away on my ship again, attempting to recover some worthless crystal that had been hidden beneath the floorboards years before. Upon being discovered and captured, he refuses to explain his actions or to speak to anyone, instead choosing to use a foreign tongue even though he speaks English." He stopped in front of Roman, "And now this very man is engaged to be married to my sister?"

Roman, Catherine, and Alexandra had reported to the courthouse upon their arrival in London. There they had met Andrew, Jessica, and young John Viana. Five of them waited in the hallway of the courthouse while the jailer escorted Catherine alone to Antoine's cell.

Alexandra had never seen Andrew in such a state. Looking at Jessica, she found similar bewilderment.

"Calm yourself, Andrew," Roman urged. "What's done is done. There's an explanation for all of this. Catherine will be able to coax him to talk. Now what's this about some crystal aboard the ship?"

Andrew pulled the wooden box from his coat pocket and turned it over to Roman for his inspection.

"What is it?" John asked, stepping closer.

Alexandra wanted nothing more than to approach Roman. As he had done on the train, however, he had been careful to keep his gaze from her. No matter. There would be time to speak with him in private later in the evening at the Winterfield Estate. For the time being, she would allow him to set the distance between them.

Roman removed the lid and, even several yards away, Alexandra could see two crystal bottles. Removing the bottles, he turned the box back to his brother. With a wrinkled brow, he stepped over to the window to hold the bottles up to the light, studying them one by one.

"What do you think?" his brother asked, composed once again.

"Give me the box." He exchanged the bottles for the box and inspected it inside and out, repeating the procedure with its lid. He pushed aside the remaining straw that had cradled the bottles and pulled from it a yellowed page. "It appears you missed something, Andrew," he said. Upon opening the folded page, he held it flat so they could all see it.

Alexandra strained her eyes. The meticulous calligraphy on the sheet appeared to be an official document of some sort. In a few sections, the blue ink had faded, but others remained dark and clear. The language was unfamiliar. At the top of the page was the faint face of a leopard.

"John, do you know Mr. Etrea of the cultural museum a few streets down?" Roman asked.

"He's an archaeologist, isn't he? I met him when in town with Antoine once."

"More important, he's a linguist and a man I trust will be able to discern the origin of this document. Will you summon him? Give him my name, and tell him we have an urgent matter."

John nodded and ran from the courthouse.

As soon as John left, Roman took the two crystal bottles from Andrew's hand. One after the other, he hurled them against the brick of the interior wall. The crystal shattered into pieces.

"Roman!" Andrew shouted.

Alexandra stood stunned as Roman hastened to the corner and sifted through the crystal fragments.

"Just what I thought," he called, stepping back to the group.

Alexandra gasped at two items sitting on his palm. One was a thick gold ring, and the other appeared to be a diamond the size of a walnut.

"Upon closer inspection, I could see the bottles each contained some type of object," Roman explained. "I recognize some of the letters in the document and have heard tales over the years of a missing diamond from a small nation near Arabia. It's known as the Desert Ice. I've always believed it to be a legend."

Desert Ice? Why did that term sound so familiar to Alexandra? Of course. Roman and his father had spoken of it while their families had toured in France. Would not Richard be surprised to hear it had been on the *The Emerald*—his own ship—all this time?

Roman held up the ring. Alexandra could see it had an emblem of some sort etched onto a raised flat surface. They passed the objects among themselves and returned them to Roman, who placed them in his pocket.

"I suspect," he said, looking at the three, including Alexandra, "that we're about to learn some deep and very old secrets. So for the time being, please do not to mention these objects to any other person. Do I have your word?"

All nodded their agreement.

Just then Catherine emerged from the jailhouse, tears streaming down her face. "That man is not Antoine," she said between sobs. Alexandra hastened to her and led her to a wooden bench. "I don't know who he is."

Andrew knelt before her. "What makes you say that, Catherine?"

"He doesn't recognize me. He looks like Antoine, but he's different. And I don't understand his language." Catherine dropped her face into her hands, crying all the more.

"Did you not say that the man suffered a head injury, Andrew?" Alexandra asked. "Perhaps that's the reason he doesn't recognize her."

"But how does one account for his language?" Roman answered instead. His gaze lingered upon her for a moment before shifting away.

"Of course," Andrew blurted. "Why didn't I think of this before? May I see the prisoner one more time?" he asked of the jailer. "Come with me, Roman." The three men disappeared behind the door while Jessica and Alexandra tried to comfort Catherine.

The two brothers followed the jailer to the cell of the stowaway. The man had been fed, bathed, and supplied with fresh clothing. Roman almost called out Antoine's name upon seeing him. After the jailer had unlocked the cell, Andrew stepped in. Grasping the man's shirt collar, he yanked the sleeve from the shirt, and spun the man around.

"Roman, Catherine's right. This isn't the same man. The man who stowed away on my ship five years ago was Antoine Aramis. He admitted it to Catherine—and he had a strange tattoo marking on the back of his right shoulder. This is not that man, Roman. There's no tattoo."

They returned to the group to report the new finding.

"So Antoine is still missing," Catherine wailed.

Roman took his sister into his arms. "Mr. Etrea will explain it all in no time," he said, hushing her.

As the courthouse window blackened with the falling night, the guard lit the lamps in the room.

Just then the front door opened. A gray-haired man with olive skin entered the room with Alexandra's brother lagging behind.

"Mr. Winterfield," he said, stepping at once to Roman, "a pleasure to make your acquaintance once again." The man's smile exposed crooked and discolored teeth. Deep crevices sprawled from the corners of both eyes. His attire looked clean but wrinkled, his shirt rolled at the sleeves.

"We became acquainted several years ago while I was re-searching the origin of some old pottery I had purchased over-seas," Roman explained to the group after introducing each of them. "Mr. Etrea, this small party you see has stumbled upon a puzzling discovery, and I asked you here to assist us in sort-ing the pieces. I understand you are acquainted with a man by the name of Aramis."

"Yes, the young artist. He has consulted me on various works he's found in the museums."

"My sister has recently become engaged to him, and we believe Mr. Aramis has a direct link with this." Roman handed him the document.

Mr. Etrea stepped toward a lamp burning on the wall by the window. A crunch came from beneath his foot; he looked down at the shards of crystal on the floor. When he looked up, Roman folded his arms across his chest and offered no explanation.

Alexandra watched the interaction between the two and wondered about the heritage of the dark-toned man now stand-ing under the light. In a strange way, he reminded her of An-toine.

Scanning the paragraphs, he nodded. "Hmm...you say An-toine is linked with this document?"

"That would appear to be the case," Roman replied.

"Who else knows of it?" he asked, stepping back to the group.

Roman shook his head to acknowledge that no person out-side the room had any knowledge of it. "What is it? What does it say?"

"First, I would very much like to speak with Antoine. Where can he be reached?"

"We would all like to know the answer to that question," Roman said. "However, there's an intriguing young man in custody in this very facility that I think will provide some an-swers—if we can locate someone able to speak his language."

"And might I perhaps be that person?"

"That, Mr. Etrea, is my precise assumption." Roman held one hand toward the door to the cells. He summoned the jailer who escorted Mr. Etrea from the room. The door closed be-hind them.

"Do you think he understood the document?" John asked of Roman.

"Oh, yes."

"And do you suspect he knows of the ring and the dia-mond?" Andrew posed.

"I don't doubt it for a moment."

Twenty minutes later, Mr. Etrea reappeared in the door-way. "You had better come with me—all of you."

The party followed him back to the cell. Mr. Etrea spoke to the prisoner in his language, pointing and explaining the iden-tity of each of them.

"You failed to prepare me, Mr. Winterfield, to discover Antoine's identical twin in this cell. Antoine is apparently un-aware of his brother's existence. His name is Behren Asonti, and Antoine's birth name was Sabiir. They are sons of the late king of a small country on the Arabian Sea called Palmeria."

"Excuse me, Mr. Etrea," Catherine said, "but do you mean to tell me that Antoine is not French at all, but a prince of this country, Palmeria?"

"Not a prince," he stated after a short burst of laughter. Then the smile disappeared from his face. "Antoine is their king."

"Pardon me," the guard interrupted, "but there's a man out front who said he was told he could find Mr. Etrea here. His name is Aramis."

All eyes fell upon Catherine, whose heart began to race at the mention of Antoine's name. She looked at Mr. Etrea.

"Go greet your fiancé, Miss Winterfield. Take your time, but please explain the discovery of his brother. We don't wish to shock the man."

Catherine nodded and hurried to the courtroom. The door opened with a creak. She ran to the arms of Antoine.

"Catherine, what are you doing here? I was told to meet Mr. Etrea in this building."

"Antoine, wait until you hear the news."

"I've made some startling discoveries myself."

Not long afterward, they joined the group in the jail. Antoine felt a bit out of place, especially when his eyes fixed upon Roman. Alexandra stepped over to embrace Antoine, and John offered a welcoming shake of his hand. He tried to hide his surprise when Roman stepped over and extended his hand as well.

"It's a pleasure to see you again," Roman said in greeting.

"Thank you," he replied with hesitation.

And then he saw Andrew. Yes, this was the man, the ship captain who had given him his freedom.

"Ah, I finally have the pleasure of meeting the stowaway that escaped my crew five years ago," Andrew said, stepping forward. "I'm Andrew Winterfield, captain of *The Emerald*."

"Yes, I know." Antoine clasped Andrew's extended hand. "Captain, I have long desired to locate the man who unknowingly gave my life back to me in a new land and thank him with all sincerity. And, of course, pay for my passage. Finally, that opportunity presents itself. Until recently I was unaware that I've been working for your family."

"And soon will belong to this family, I hear. Please meet my wife, Jessica."

He bowed his head in greeting. "Yes, I recognize you from the party, Mrs. Winterfield."

"Antoine," Mr. Etrea said, stepping forward. "Allow me to introduce your brother, Behren Asonti."

One by one, the group moved out of the cell. With caution, Antoine approached what appeared to him a mirror image. His double grabbed him in a rough embrace, laughing and slapping him on the back, speaking in his foreign tongue.

Antoine began to laugh, as well.

"Do you understand his words, Antoine?" Catherine asked.

"Some…yes. He says something about finding me and people rejoicing." He turned to Mr. Etrea. "Tell me what he's saying."

Instead Mr. Etrea stepped over to Andrew and pulled him away from the group. Andrew nodded and left.

Mr. Etrea returned to the others. "Captain Winterfield will have the charges dropped," he said, "and pay the fines to have Mr. Asonti released."

Chapter Thirty-Five

A sigh the weight of an elephant seeped from Richard Winterfield's lungs. Slowly, he rose to his feet and stepped around the chair where Antoine Aramis sat.

"If I may say so, sir," Antoine said, turning to watch him cross the room to stand before one of the library's many bookcases, "I would share your concerns were she my daughter. I realize I would be the last man were you to make the choice yourself—"

"Please don't misunderstand me, son," Richard said, "but don't you think this issue of your ancestry should take precedence at the moment?"

"Mr. Winterfield...sir." At once on his feet, Antoine strode to Richard's side. "Come what may with whatever Mr. Etrea has to say about my past, my priority is your daughter. Before leaving, I made a vow to her that I intend to keep. I will give her happiness and will provide for her needs."

"Can you, Antoine? Can you provide for her? For a child, for two children, for three?" His tone began to heat up.

"Not on my current wages. That's why I'm also giving you my resignation."

"Now I've heard it all." Richard threw his hands in the air and stepped away. "Please tell me how it is you plan to support my daughter on no income."

"I'm a painter, a craftsman, a master in my trade. I sold several pieces two weeks ago. Mr. Winterfield, I can support a family. I know I can."

"And I have every confidence in your work. You are, indeed, a man of extraordinary talent. But selling a few paintings one time hardly assures a continuing income. No matter how great your talent, your name is unknown. It could take years for the public to seek out your work and to pay a suitable price for it. Just how do you intend on surviving in the meantime?"

"Mr. Winterfield," Antoine said, his voice turning to stone, "several things I will never ask of you. First, I'll never ask to be placed among the ranks of your sons. Now that I've resigned, I'll never ask you for work. And I'll never ask for a place in this home nor any part of an inheritance. And I am not asking for the hand of your daughter—that she has already promised me. The only thing I request of you is your blessing." He walked toward the door. "It would ease your daughter's mind were you to give that to us. You may be assured I'll be a good provider for her and a good father to your grandchildren."

Catherine's father stood with his arms crossed, eyes fixed upon a high shelf of books. Antoine waited but a moment before turning the knob and stepping over the threshold. He pulled the door closed behind him in a soft click, leaving the man to his thoughts.

He found most of the others gathered in the salon with its oriental screens and draping brocade ceiling. Andrew sat, staring at Behren, who was in an animated discussion with Mr. Etrea. The ladies and John whispered amongst themselves in a corner. The only one missing appeared to be Roman.

"Antoine!" Mr. Etrea jumped from the sofa. "There's much to discuss, if you please."

"Give me one minute with my fiancée." He pulled Catherine into the corridor with its massive archways linking it to other rooms and the indoor garden.

"What did he say?" she whispered.

"He needs some time."

"Oh, Antoine, I was dreading this." Tears welled in her clear brown eyes.

"He'll come to the right conclusion. Of that I have no doubt." He took her by the hand. They stepped back to the

298

group, where he escorted her to a velvet-cushioned sofa. After all the others had settled into their seats, Antoine pulled a chair between her and Mr. Etrea, fixing his eyes on the man who looked so like himself, save the dark shadows beneath his eyes and the sunken cheeks.

The tall figure of Roman entered the room. He seated himself quietly. Catherine's father followed behind him. Without a word, a gesture, or even a glance at either Antoine or Catherine, he pulled up a chair beside Roman.

"This young man here has quite a story," Mr. Etrea began, standing to pace the room. "Listen carefully, Antoine. Your life will never be the same. As I explained before, you and your brother are the sons—the only two sons—of Sabiir Asonti, the last king of Palmeria. Soon after your birth, your father died of an illness from which he had been suffering for several months. Suspecting that the throne would be overtaken by his generals after his death, he devised a plan through which the kingly line could be reestablished."

Behren interrupted with what sounded like a question. Mr. Etrea interpreted. "Your brother has asked to see your right shoulder."

Looking about at the faces in the room, Antoine saw bewilderment in his fiancée's expression, curiosity in young John's, nodding from Andrew. He stood and loosened his collar and the buttons of his shirt. Turning aside to his brother, he dropped the shirt back. Behren jumped to his feet, talking rapidly.

"He says the tattoo was in the likeness of a leopard," Mr. Etrea reported.

"What tattoo?" Catherine asked.

Those in the room gathered around Antoine.

"A marking that has plagued my curiosity since I can remember," Antoine answered. "A leopard," he mused. His sister had been right—the image of a large cat.

"Why, of course," Andrew said, leaning in for a closer look.

"It's badly disfigured, but I believe he's right," said Catherine.

"Remember the document from the box?" Roman asked. "It had a similar image sketched at the top."

"But why was I tattooed, and why a leopard?" asked Antoine, adjusting the collar of his shirt.

The others settled back into their seats, all eyes on the Bedouin linguist.

Antoine strained to understand his brother's response when asked the question by Mr. Etrea, but he managed to grasp only a few words of Behren's answer.

"Antoine," Mr. Etrea said, "your brother relates facts described to him by your mother. Your father led a swift though small army that could ambush and overtake offenses three times its size when necessary. Yet, he was more of a hunter than a warrior and fought only when threatened. He had no interest in conquering other lands, just in protecting his own, and was called The Leopard by surrounding nations. He was a generous king, sharing plunder with all his people. From the greatest to the smallest, he held banquets for them all and beautified their cities. It was neither unusual to see him strolling through the streets alongside the common people, nor a rarity to find him tilling the fields among the farmers."

Behren interrupted with one more detail.

"It also seems your father was a great artist," he announced. "His talent remains preserved in tile work and murals all around his capital city."

"A precious gift, indeed, to hand down to one's son," Catherine said, reaching for the hand of Antoine.

Behren continued to talk.

"Your father felt the greatest work he ever accomplished was also his smallest, as well as his last—that of the image he tattooed onto the back of his newborn son, which would later identify the true king." Mr. Etrea paused to listen to more. "He sent the infant away the night after his birth, under the care of a trusted steward."

"Rios," Antoine interrupted. "His name was Rios. I remember him."

He stood and walked to the window, staring out but seeing nothing. What did this mean? How could he be king of a country of which he knew nothing? He looked down at his work-hardened hands. How could he be a king at all?

Behren started speaking in a fury. With more reluctance than curiosity, Antoine turned to face him, his glance darting to Catherine's ashen face and back to his brother.

"You were to be guarded," Mr. Etrea translated, "and trained in the way of the king until you could return and recapture the throne from your father's generals. Rios had trained your father. He was his tutor and mentor. Before Rios' departure with the infant, the king wrote two identical statements, declarations if you will. One he ordered to be distributed among the people after his death and the other he sent with Rios. Behren suspects the original still exists somewhere in his home city." He turned to Roman. "The copy sent with Rios is the document you showed me earlier, Roman. You should have seen Behren's reaction when I showed it to him an hour ago."

"What's in the document?" young John asked.

"It advises the people that the throne would be overtaken, but for only a brief period. In time, the king's heir would stand and regain his rule over the land. Sabiir urged the people to exercise patience and created anticipation among them. It also states his hope that his son would lead the people as he had—with fairness and justice. Your father also sent two objects with Rios, disguised by the town's glazier, who hid them in two small crystal bottles."

Antoine saw Roman cross his arms over his chest and lean against the back of his chair. He cast a cold glare upon Behren. At that moment Antoine realized that Behren's gaze had been jumping from one to another in the room while he spoke—except Roman.

"One of the objects was your father's signet ring," Mr. Etrea continued, "and the other the diamond from the king's scepter, a jewel that had been handed down five generations. By the time of your father's rule, it had become a showpiece in the palace."

"So the child would have in his possession the ring and the diamond," Antoine said.

"Disguised inside carved crystal, they would be unrecognizable to outsiders," Andrew added.

"The king also created a certificate of birth for each of his sons," Mr. Etrea continued. "Your certificate was sent with Rios as well, Antoine."

"While away those two weeks," Antoine explained, "I was in France with my sister. She recalled a document sewn into the lining of my coat, one she hid from our parents years ago. With her assistance, I returned to my parents' vineyard and retrieved this." From his pocket Antoine pulled the small scroll that had been recovered from the Aramis property.

"So that's where you had to go." Catherine's words were barely audible.

"Yes. It corresponded with a very unpleasant event here at the Winterfield manor, I realize. But now you see why I had to leave."

Antoine handed the scroll to Behren. After examining the certificate, his twin grew very excited.

Behren spoke, and Mr. Etrea translated. "My father's generals, once trusted and loyal friends, had become greedy and hungry for power. Father knew that after his death, one of them—he suspected one called Pashur—would imprison the queen and take the throne. However, Rios would have already escaped with the heir and the objects that would later identify him and prove his royalty. The new king would be trained in a distant land, and in time would return to claim the throne."

Behren's eyes narrowed. He looked straight at his brother.

"The night of our birth, the king learned that he had fathered two sons. His plan, he thought, was further solidified. He made adjustments and presented the younger twin, me, as his heir. He tattooed the older child, and the following night Rios and a servant escaped with the infant. One week later, my father died in the arms of the queen. His last words expressed confidence in his plan and in the proclamation he had prepared to be distributed in secret to the people.

"Pashur moved at once to take control of the palace with the support of the other generals and soldiers loyal to him.

True to Father's prediction, he had the queen and her child imprisoned. But the outworking of the plan was well underway."

The intense look in Behren's eyes sent shivers skittering through Antoine's entire body.

"Unfortunately," Behren continued, "our father's hastily conceived plan had snags. Pashur noted Rios' absence and suspected a threat to his power. He sent soldiers out among the people to search for him and interrogated the palace servants. The midwife who had delivered the babies soon confessed that there were two sons born to the king that night. In a fit of rage, the self-appointed ruler sent forth troops to track down Rios.

"Mother, imprisoned within the castle walls, kept abreast of the situation through various servants. For some time it appeared that the heir was safe. But four years after the disappearance of her firstborn son, the queen received a visitor under the cover of darkness. It was the servant who had escaped with Rios and the child. He carried a message from Rios.

"He had been living with Sabiir in France but feared Pashur's men had caught up with him. So he made provisions to carry out the king's instructions. The servant reported that the certificate of birth had been sewn into the child's clothing, and Rios had taken the declaration, along with the two bottles, and hidden them in a cargo vessel he had noted often in the harbor in Marseilles. Rios' message contained one sentence, 'The diamond is on *The Emerald*.' The servant gave the queen a diagram of the location of the box and spelled out for her in English the name of the ship, then disappeared.

"Several weeks later, my mother learned that the servant and Rios had been captured. There was no mention of her young son."

Antoine heard a gasp echo throughout the room, but he could not tear his gaze from his brother's face.

"For years my mother grieved for you, Sabiir. Fearing the worst, she believed Pashur had you executed at age four out of sheer spite."

When Antoine's head dropped, the room fell silent. He stood to move away from the group, trying to absorb the impact of his brother's words. Long ago he had thrown to the wind all hope that he would ever know the truth about the strange marking on his body and his loveless upbringing. Why had *Monsieur et Madam* Aramis treated him with such severity? What had he done to incur the wrath of his assumed father? How could his sister have left him, never to look back?

Like a seamless silken garment, one measured to fit his arms, his torso and back, the story cloaked him. Not a snag, not a missed stitch. He stood draped in the truth and the anguish of it all. The firstborn son of a king—heir to a throne—and yet he was nothing. His whole life had been a fraud.

"They weren't my flesh," he mumbled.

"Antoine," came Catherine's soft voice, a shadow from some corner in his mind.

"I didn't belong to them," he whispered. Yes, his sister had admitted that fact, but locating the document on the Aramis vineyard had created ever more holes, countless unanswered questions. "Is any of this true?" he pleaded of Mr. Etrea. "Can this be real?"

He turned his hands over and back, studying his knuckles, nails, and palms. Glancing over at the strange man in their midst, he saw an identical pair of hands. Antoine's fingers settled on his temples. *You can't run from us, Sabiir. You can't hide.*

"It is true, isn't it?" He shook his head, trying to dislodge that which could not be denied. The Leopard, the diamond, *The Emerald*, the birth certificate, the men in the museum…it all made too much sense.

Feeling his legs weaken, without looking at a face in the room, he walked back and dropped onto the cushioned chaise beside Mr. Etrea.

Behren's voice began again, and all Antoine could do was drop his head into his palms and squeeze his eyes closed. In the span of a few brief weeks, he had been made complete. It was not a history he welcomed, but it was truth. His answers had finally come. He listened intently as his brother's story continued.

"All the while, Pashur permitted me to live with our mother. When I grew old enough, I was allowed to tend the castle gardens. My hard physical labor made me strong. Under guard, I worked alongside the wall, where I could hear the bustle of the marketplace just outside. I longed to be among the people. Now and again I heard them curse the name of Pashur and his heavy taxes. And they would speak of their expected king.

"Our mother told me everything she knew of my father, everything about his personality and his techniques. He was still a young man when he died, just thirty-nine years of age, and our mother respected him deeply. And because she feared the execution of the rightful heir, she began to train me to become the king. In the far reaches of her mind, she fostered the hope that you still lived, Sabiir, but with the passage of time that hope faded."

Beginning to despise his real name, Antoine refused to look up at the mention of it.

"Then word reached her of Pashur's dread of your return. He would have no reason to fear had you been executed, so her hope sprang back to life. When I was twenty years of age— three years ago—more news reached our ears by means of a young man whom my mother presumed to be a guard. Rios was alive! He had been imprisoned all that time under heavy guard. The servant passed on a single sentence uttered by Rios, 'The diamond is on *The Emerald.*'

"Mother knew what Rios had intended by sending the same message again. Without delay, she began preparing me for an escape. The townspeople knew not who I was, and so would be suspicious were I to escape and declare myself king. Had not the declaration stated that their king would possess the signet ring and the diamond from the scepter? He should also have in his possession a copy of the declaration and a certificate of his birth. And he would carry the indelible mark of the king. I had not even one of those things. I had to reach France and locate *The Emerald.* With three of the five objects, the people would be sure to accept me. We knew not whether the ship was still in service, but it was our only hope."

"Hmm," said Andrew, "it seems Antoine chose *The Emerald* by accident, but his brother chose it by design."

"I knew nothing of the scepter diamond or the signet ring," Antoine said, looking up. "I did not board your ship for the purpose of finding them. So, yes, Captain, I stowed away on your ship only because it was about to sail." Antoine turned to his brother. The muscles in his jaw twitched. "Please continue, Behren." He lowered his head again.

"Our suite was under greater scrutiny than in previous years, and the servants devised clever means of smuggling coins into us, one by one. Mother helped me to escape the castle for brief periods. I switched roles with a servant who was of similar appearance to me. I stepped right past the guards. Walking the streets, I conversed with the people, made purchases, and began to learn the life of the average man. When my mother felt we had enough to pay my way to France, I bid a farewell to her and left the servant in my place one last time, escaping into the shadows of a moonless night.

"Pashur had not seen me in years. I would have passed undetected had I encountered him, but I did not. I slipped by the guards and escaped the city before daybreak.

"That was fourteen weeks ago. I'm tired, for most nights I have no place to sleep. I'm hungry, for I cannot adjust to the food that I've been able to acquire. I'm ill and frightened every waking moment."

Antoine lifted his face. How had this inexperienced young man survived such an ordeal? The only possible explanation was the valuable training he had received from his mother—their mother—and sheer determination.

"My only desire now," Behren continued, "is to gain passage back to my land after collecting what rightly belongs to me." He slumped back against the chaise, his eyes intense upon Andrew, the captain of *The Emerald*.

To Antoine's surprise, it was Roman who pushed himself slowly from his chair. With an expression tantamount to rivalry, one slow step at a time brought him to stand before Behren. With the grace of a gentleman, but the glare of an enemy,

306

Roman leaned over to place one hand on the arm of the chaise. "Indeed," he said, "The diamond was on *The Emerald.*"

Mr. Etrea translated the words to Behren. Roman extended his open palm. Upon it rested a huge round stone and a ring of gold. Behren hesitated for a brief moment before sitting aright and scooping the objects from Roman's hand.

The exhilaration Antoine expected from his brother never came. Not a smile, not a sigh, not a trace of relief moved his brother's expression. The dark shadows under his eyes had deepened since their sitting down with him. He muttered words Antoine recognized as 'thank you.'

With no response, and no softening of his own stone expression, Roman backed away to return to the chair beside his father.

"I wish I could now return to my people in peace," Behren continued, "but it cannot be so simple." He looked at Antoine. "For along the journey I stumbled upon you, Sabiir. You are our true king, our rightful leader. I cannot claim the throne of our father while knowing our rightful king is alive and well.

"You must return with me, Sabiir. With Pashur removed, you will be quick to learn our father's techniques. The people are ready. They await your return. You have the mark. Pashur lives in fear of you. He is weak and superstitious in his old age and is certain to collapse under the strain. It will be an easy task for you to overtake him. However, you must act while the conditions are ripe, while the people still hope in you." Now an emotion did cross Behren's face, one of desperation that he cast upon Antoine. "You must come with me, Sabiir. Our people need you."

Antoine glared at Mr. Etrea. "I can't return to his country. I'm a laborer, a common worker! I know nothing of these people—their culture, their beliefs. Why, I barely understand their language. How could I possibly rule them?"

"Those things matter not to this man, or his people," Mr. Etrea said in response. "Bloodline is everything. You should understand that based on your own upbringing. You're the rightful heir, Antoine. You've inherited many of your father's

307

qualities, handed to you through your blood. What natural abilities you do not possess can be learned, as he said."

"I'm a commoner, Etrea, not a ruler!"

"You are not a commoner, but a king, and you will become a ruler with the best of all things. The palaces are magnificent! Riches and glory would be yours; a great military force would back you; you would have servants too numerous to count; you would enjoy food, drink, musicians, gardens, the highest of education. Your every need, every desire, would be met. Your word would be law. There's no limit to the heights you could attain. Palmeria is a country rich in tradition and culture, a highly respected nation. It would be a disgrace, indeed, to decline such an honor, Antoine."

"But what of Catherine?" He looked over at his fiancée. Terror filled her eyes, but she said nothing. "How could she adjust to that culture? Is she even willing to leave her family, her home, everything she knows and loves?"

"No." A cold edge tinged Mr. Etrea's voice. "Catherine cannot go. Those people would never accept a European woman as your wife. To live among them perhaps, but not as their queen. Her very life would be endangered were you to attempt it."

Antoine stared in bewilderment at Mr. Etrea. Stepping over to Catherine, he took her hands into his. Her eyes began to fill with tears. Stroking her silky skin, his gaze moved to her father. Mr. Winterfield's expression stiffened along with his posture. Dropping her hands, Antoine walked back to his brother. "I'm willing to act in any means possible to restore my father's line to the throne."

"No!" Catherine jumped up as Mr. Etrea translated his words to Antoine's brother. "Antoine..." A tear tumbled over her cheek.

Roman was on his feet in an instant, taking Catherine into his arms.

"However," Antoine continued, "I consider myself an Englishman now. I will not move from this land, and I will not leave the woman who is about to become my wife. My children will not be raised in any castle. They may descend from a line of warriors, but I'll teach them peace. They may dream of riches, Behren, but they'll find greater wealth in here," he said, pointing to his own chest. "Perhaps they'll labor for the food on their table, but they'll be satisfied in the work of their own hands."

Behren glared at his brother as his words reached his ears through the voice of the translator.

"I'm proud of who I am at this moment, Behren," Antoine continued. "I am Antoine Aramis, not King Sabiir of Palmeria. I carry no shame for any decision I have yet made. Honesty and integrity are what make any man a king, even if over nothing more than his own household. I'll help your people if I can. I'll help to put you on that throne, but do not ask me again to take it for myself, for to leave the woman I love and our future together, for me that would bring the ultimate disgrace."

He stepped over to take Roman's place beside Catherine.

When Behren heard the final words in his own language, he pushed himself from the chaise, mumbling in anger.

"What's he saying?" Andrew asked.

"Oh, he calls him foolish. 'How could he choose a woman over a kingdom?' he asks. However, he says he'll accept his help."

Antoine turned at a movement in the corner. Richard walked toward them.

"Catherine," her father asked, "were you engaged to this man—my employee—at the time of the party?"

"Almost, Father."

"I recall whisperings among the servant body that night of a talented young man on my staff who would soon be more gainfully employed as an artist. I've seen his paintings, Catherine, and the integrity of the work is matched by that of its owner. I'll have my daughter belong to no less of a man."

"Oh, Father, thank you!" She rushed into his arms. "When will Mother return? I must share our news."

"Any time now," he said, laughing, extending his hand to Antoine. "I believe you're the expert in the household when it comes to champagne, son. I trust you'll choose the finest from my cabinet while I call for the crystal."

Chapter Thirty-Six

A heavy gloom hovered about the room somewhere between midair and the thick brocade of the draped ceiling above. Desperate to speak with Roman, Alexandra kept her eyes fixed upon him. But, as he had done on the train, he avoided her gaze.

Andrew Winterfield had left the parlor and now returned with a large scroll, clearing a table to roll out an extensive map. The men gathered around. The women backed away to give them more room.

When would she have opportunity to speak with Roman alone? Perhaps she should have approached him while en route to London. But how? The train had been filled to capacity. She would have appeared a fool, pressing between people, stepping on toes, possibly losing her balance to land in the lap of a stranger. No, that would have been most inappropriate. Yet she would have endured the humiliation had she foreseen that he would later make every attempt to evade her.

At the courthouse, she had managed to meet his gaze one fleeting moment. With it had come the crushing of her heart—to see in his eyes utter dejection and emotional exhaustion, as though spending every last ounce of spirit to suppress his pain. In a flash, he had looked away, and life again returned to his expression.

In the hopes of having occasion to talk once they had returned to Winterfield Manor, she mustered what patience remained and had kept silent all the way back.

Leaving Andrew to help her from the carriage, Roman had disappeared into the manor. She retreated to her room, grieved to find his door closed, shutting him away from the world—and from her. She did not see him again until an hour or so later when he appeared in the parlor after they had all reconvened.

Her patience began to unravel. A force of emotion threatened to break through like a flash flood against the wall of a weakened dam.

"Are you all right?" Jessica whispered in her ear.

"I'm fine," she said, feeling her hard pulse throughout every limb.

"What general area are we talking about?" Andrew asked, scanning the great map.

Alexandra forced her gaze to Andrew's face, concentrating on the matter at hand.

"The Arabian Sea," Mr. Etrea replied.

Andrew responded with a deep, slow whistle.

"The obvious route is the Suez," Roman said, his finger sliding over the map.

"Will it allow a ship the size of *The Emerald*?" Antoine pondered aloud.

"Oh, yes," Roman answered.

"She's well-equipped for such a voyage." Andrew pushed himself back. "Sturdy and swift, and the crew is familiar with the Mediterranean."

"Your confidence is noble," Mr. Etrea said, "and I've no doubt of the seaworthiness of your vessel, but the situation demands honesty. You're quite young, Andrew."

"Don't allow his youth to deter you," Roman said. "His experience speaks loudly."

"Let us not forget that beyond the Suez lie waters and territory unfamiliar to you all," Mr. Etrea stated. "It's not my intent to dissuade you, but serious questions arise. Who will embark on this voyage? What must you know of the people, the lands? What are the current political conditions? What is to be done once you arrive?"

"Perhaps more important, what are our odds of seizing that throne if we do undertake this journey?" Antoine mused.

Intent on the others, Richard Winterfield spoke up. "And most disturbing is a question that seems to have evaded every one of you. Do you really trust this man—Behren Asonti? His relation to Antoine is obvious, yet he remains a stranger to us all. How can you be assured of the accuracy of his account?"

"Now listen to me," Mr. Etrea insisted. "Pakistan was my home. I was a lad when Antoine's grandfather ruled Palmeria. Though I left there a young man, I've kept communications with my family. The story Behren has presented is true, every word."

"You're a band of rebels against an army," Richard retorted. "Don't fool yourselves. You're facing a world of danger."

"Might I remind you that there's someone in much greater danger," Antoine spoke up. "We may be two thousand miles away, but we're alone in our knowledge of one woman in dire need of our assistance at this very moment. The queen—my mother."

"He's right," Mr. Etrea said. "The discovery of Behren's disappearance is not a matter of if, but when. She faces execution for treason. We can only hope it's not already too late."

"We have no choice," Antoine said. "I have no choice. Andrew, I know I'm indebted to you as it is, but can I count on your assistance?"

"He'll go nowhere without me," Roman said.

"What do you say, Father?" Andrew appealed. "If not *The Emerald*, may I have another vessel?"

"You're determined, I can see that. *The Emerald* will suit your purpose, but I'll not approve of its use until you've answered to my satisfaction the questions posed by Mr. Etrea."

"We'll research each one, but first I must know—who's in?" Andrew took a step away from the map, glancing about at the men.

When young John Viana stepped forward, Richard Winterfield slapped one palm against the young man's chest. "Get the thought out of your head now, son."

"Men younger than me serve in the military. I can decide for myself."

"Not while you're in my charge."

"He's right, John," Antoine agreed. "Your willingness is appreciated, but I'll not hear of it."

Alexandra sighed with relief when her brother backed away from the table—red-faced and his eyes blazing with anger. Because of his being the youngest of John Viana's children, she feared he would always be viewed as a juvenile. But in this instance, she was thankful.

As the men debated the details of the journey, Alexandra's gaze moved to her sister's bulging belly. Always the brave one of the three sisters, Jessica closed her eyes and spoke not a single objection while her husband discussed the risks of the trip he was resolute in taking.

Would they accomplish their aim? Would Andrew's child be born during his absence? Would he even return to see his child?

She glanced at Behren Asonti. While the rest of the men spoke, he had sunk into a chair behind them, looking utterly spent. How he kept alive the previous weeks—all alone with little knowledge of the world—was unfathomable. Even after recuperation, his safe return without the help of the men was in all probability impossible.

"You'd better notify your father-in-law of a delay in his shipments." Richard Winterfield looked at Andrew and sighed.

Alexandra reached out and took hold of Jessica's hand. The men would have to go—all of them, Mr. Etrea included. An interpreter would be vital to their success, and they needed to go now. Alexandra's mind accepted that; her heart did not. A lump rose in her throat and nearly cut off her breath. The reality was that none of them might return. She bit her lower lip to force back the tears that threatened to erupt. Staring at the floor, she could no longer gaze upon Roman. The thought of his being hurt—or worse—tore through her heart like a knife.

"If we can port in Barcelona and Marseilles on the return, it's possible he'll never discern any delay." Andrew's voice pulled her back from her fearful thoughts. He pointed to the map. "We've a more detailed atlas in the library."

The last of the group to depart the room, Roman hesitated at the threshold. Alexandra tried to hide her surprise when he turned back to her, his eyes making a quick search of her hair, her lips, and even her eyes. Was he seeking a reason to stay; or was it his final look in an effort to remember her face?

When she took a step forward and opened her mouth to speak, he disappeared from the doorway.

Alexandra fixed her eyes upon the red bricks behind the arch of the fireplace of the sitting room. She had followed Jessica at her insistence that the ladies stroll about the mansion. Their stroll had reached its end in the next room when they had all surrendered, each to her own mounting anxiety over the conversation taking place in the library.

The gilt-bronze clock on the mantle pinged a lengthy announcement of midnight's arrival. The day had proved itself the most emotionally taxing in Alexandra's memory, more so even than the day when her father returned home with the mother they had all presumed lost at sea. And still it refused to end.

"What do you think of it all, Jessie?" Catherine asked, stopping to light more candles.

"Where is my father when I need him most?"

The fear in her sister's voice struck Alexandra. Jessica had every right, and every reason, to protest the journey. What she knew of Andrew, Alexandra could sum up in one word—confident. But of what value was confidence in the face of such risk?

"You need to speak to your husband," she urged.

"He has made his decision." Jessica, strewn across a long chaise, massaged her sides and protruding belly.

"Don't worry over him," Catherine said. "For the time he's devoted to traversing those waters, he might as well have sailed the world."

"It's not the voyage there or back that is of most concern to me."

"Of course," Catherine mumbled in a sorrowful tone. Moving to crouch beside the chaise she put one palm on Jessica's arm. "It's the baby. How could I be so selfish, so oblivious to your worries?"

"We both have our fears, Catherine. They're nothing short of unbearable."

Alexandra bowed her head. Neither had so much as an inkling about the sting of her anxiety.

"What do you think of that story?" Catherine asked, eyeing them both.

"Astonishing," Jessica answered. "How long do you think they'll be gone?"

"Weeks," Alexandra answered, "if not months." She would speak with Roman at their next meeting regardless of whom or how many were present.

"Tell me, Jessie," Catherine said with a tone of anxiety rather than curiosity, "what do you know of Arabia and the surrounding countries? Shall I insist on going along?"

"You heard what Mr. Etrea said. There'll be no welcoming committee for you. I'm afraid your presence would only add to the danger."

"Then I'm convinced of one thing," Catherine said. Alexandra pulled her stare from the cold, blackened logs of the fire nook to her friend's eyes, now hardened like stone. Never before had she seen such resolve in them. "Antoine is not going to that land an unmarried man."

Alexandra slipped into the crisp linens of her bed and thought of Roman's declaration to her. All that time he had loved her. If only she had not been so accomplished in the art of controlling her feelings. Yet, they had arisen so gradually. How strange, this thing called love. How much more convenient to have had a moment of realization, a single flash of recognition—*he's the man for you. Don't you see how he's drawn to you?*

But it did not happen that way. "Nor could it have…" she mumbled, perplexed by her confusing thoughts.

The dinner in Paris. His reaction to her, his responses to her attempts at conversation, so cold, so unfeeling. Why had he made it so difficult? Why had he allowed doubt to creep into his mind, doubt that she could love him? How she wished now that he would have moved ahead in his affections then and there. She clapped her hand across her mouth when she broke into a giggle.

"No," she laughed. "That never would have worked. Thank heavens things took place the way they did." She did not love him then. After spending several days in his presence, she had been more repulsed by him than ever before, even more than when her family had first met him. Had he given her the slightest idea of his interest in her then, she might have cancelled her summer in Kent. It would have been several years—if ever—before she discovered the goodness lurking beneath his crusty exterior. But years would have been too late because he would never have identified the pitiable traits of Caroline Landly. He would have married her.

And the birth of the foal. Duchess would have suffered alone, most likely even died, unassisted by her oblivious owner. He would never have been part of it, never would have come to know such appreciation for new life.

Of course, she might still have accompanied her family to the ball. What would she have discovered there? The eldest Winterfield son clad in his usual armor-like pride—that was what.

Yes, how relieved she could be that he had acted with discernment and given her time to see the changes in him.

But with the sunrise would come her glorious day, the day her heart had been longing for all these difficult weeks. She caught her breath. Exactly, what would she say to him in the morning?

"'You were wrong. It's you I love, not Preston,'" she said aloud, testing her words. "Good heavens, how dull. How about, 'I've known…' Oh dear, I've known what? 'I've known I love you for some time now...' No, no. Maybe something like, 'You were right. I didn't love you in the restaurant...' Goodness no. That's all wrong. I know...'You were right. Caroline Landly is not the woman for you. I am.'" She crinkled her nose. Well, she would just have to speak from the heart while she looked into his eyes. Then her words would come, the right words.

And how would he react to her confession? Would he whisk her from her feet as in all the fairy stories? Would he stare at her, dumbfounded, speechless? Would he shed a tear of joy and relief while she bawled an ocean of her own? Would he ask for her hand then and there?

With a smile of anticipation on her lips, she rolled to her side and slipped off into a dreamy slumber.

Hazy light and a chill woke Alexandra several hours later. A cool breeze drifting through the veranda doors she had left open sent a strand of hair fluttering across her cheek. The room filled with the scent of Mrs. Winterfield's gardens below.

Rubbing her eyes, she forced herself from the warmth of her bed. A yawn and a stretch overtook her, and she stepped out onto the veranda for a quick view. Whatever kind of day it was, it would be a marvelous one. She stroked a shiver from her arms.

Mist covered the landscape in a cottony gray. The blush of a new bud in the garden of rosebushes smiled up at her. Winding brown pathways converged, creating a utopian pattern between mounds of fresh greenery and giving her mystery laced in beauty. Indeed, it was the perfect kind of day on which to be engaged...or one step closer to it anyway.

She retreated to her changing room and emerged to splash water over her face. Her chestnut hair fell into a smooth, simple tail held in place by a white ribbon.

Not a sound reached her ears when she cracked open her door. Tiptoes brought her down the hall far enough to see a water color of light splashed across the dark wood floor before Roman's room. He was awake, already breakfasting, no doubt.

She descended the steps of the wide, winding marble staircase. A clock somewhere in one of the elaborate rooms downstairs echoed six bongs throughout the massive stair tower. Stopping to test the air for the cook's famous griddle cakes with soft-boiled eggs, she found the only detectable scent coming from the ferns in the indoor garden.

Heading toward the tapestry gallery, she passed the intricate patterns without so much as a glance and crossed the threshold into the library. There she stopped short.

Alone before the large map, a pencil and compass in hand, she found a man looking down, head covered with familiar near-black waves.

"Andrew." He lifted his tired gaze. "Have you been up all night?" She stepped forward.

He laid down his utensils to fall against the chair back, rubbing his red eyes. "A captain must be prepared. The route must be established and supplies gathered and loaded." His hands dropped to his sides. He rolled his head to one side, then the other. "Also, *The Emerald* may leave here empty, but she'll be returning with a full load. The port stops must be calculated."

"What good will an exhausted captain be to his crew? Go get some sleep, Andrew."

He nodded.

"Where is your brother?" she inquired.

"Roman's gone," he said and leaned forward, looking somewhat concerned.

"So early? Where could he have gone off to at this hour?"

"He went ahead of us...to take care of some business on the mainland. We'll port in Marseilles, where he'll join us."

"What?"

"His ship left before daybreak. He asked me to tell you goodbye, Alex."

"No!" Her breaths came fast and furious. Her vision began to haze like the fog outdoors. Her hands began trembling like a leaf in the wind.

"What in the world—" Andrew jumped to his feet and hurried toward her, but she pushed him away and stepped a few paces from him.

"When will you return?" she managed between breaths, trying in desperation to slow them.

"If all goes well, late October, but Roman shan't be with us. He asked that I drop him in France on the return trip."

"When will he be back, Andrew?"

"I'm afraid only Roman can tell you that. The last time he left, I didn't see him for two years."

Alexandra's hand rushed to cover her mouth as a gush of tears rolled over her lashes. Unable to stop them, she turned back. "Andrew, there's been a dreadful mistake. I must speak with him." Breaking into sobs, she allowed him to slip an arm about her shoulders. He leaned close to look into her face.

"Can I take a message to him for you?"

"When are you leaving?" She wiped the tears from her cheeks, but more trailed behind.

"Four days."

She nodded in haste and swallowed hard. "Yes," was all she could muster.

His eyes, so much like Roman's, brimmed with concern for her.

"Alex, what happened between the two of you?"

"Nothing. Nothing at all!" Turning, she fled from the room.

Chapter Thirty-Seven

"Oh, Richard, do you not find this exciting?" Olivia Winter-field flitted about the room, crying orders to her female attendant in the most pleasant of tones. The servant assisted Olivia with her gown and then her hair.

Richard sat and stared in amazement at his wife.

"Just think, Richard—a king! Our daughter is marrying a king."

"Olivia, would you have been so thrilled to learn of Catherine's betrothal to a vinedresser? Besides, the man is not a king. He has declined the position. The result, therefore, is that our daughter is marrying, not a king, but a common man. Do you understand that?"

"Why must you always be so negative?" She tilted her head, peering at her reflection as the servant fussed over her hair. "My son-in-law is a king, of royal blood, and Catherine's sons will be princes, and that is that. I'll learn to ignore your murmurings."

Dropping his palm onto her dressing table, he leaned very close. "What you don't understand, my dear, is that I like Antoine. But I like him for who he is right now, not for the birthright he's relinquishing. And I'm proud of Catherine, not because she's marrying someone of royalty, but because she loves him and kept her integrity to him even when everyone else—including you and me—thought him a thief. At times I find myself wondering if she is, in actuality, one of the Viana daughters. Tell me if you can, Olivia, from whom has she learned such strength of character?"

As he drew nearer, Olivia leaned so far to the side she had to grasp the chair to keep her balance. "How am I to know such a thing?"

"You'd better find out," Richard hissed, "and learn it for yourself."

He backed away. The attendant, who had stepped aside while the little battle ensued, resumed her work.

Olivia stared at her husband in bewilderment. "But why must they marry so hastily? I've been denied the privilege of planning my only daughter's wedding. And here our son-in-law is leaving tomorrow, not to return for months. Why can't Catherine go along? She'll make herself ill with worry otherwise."

"Then she's destined to be ill one way or the other. If she accompanies Antoine on this journey, she'll be physically ill. Catherine is not accustomed to the difficult life aboard a ship, not to mention the risks to her life. She must stay home."

Alexandra and Catherine had a few moments alone.

"Do you think I'm ready for this, Alex?"

"I do." They both burst out in laughter at Alexandra's unintended pun. "And I think the setting will be unmatched."

"I thought it only appropriate that Antoine should be married in his favorite meadow. Alex," she said, taking her friend's hand, "I can't thank you enough for supporting me this summer, urging me in the right direction."

"You would've made the correct decision with or without me," she said, sliding one last cornflower-blue forget-me-not into Catherine's pale locks. "You're a magnificent bride, Catherine." Determined to remain composed for her friend, she stuffed away the pain in her own heart. Catherine and Antoine had only a few precious hours as husband and wife before he would embark on his dangerous mission.

Refusing to dwell on Roman's absence, she attempted to find contentment in the fact that Andrew would be in contact with him again soon. A letter on ivory stationery sat propped between her perfume bottle and mirror on her dressing table. Were she like most women, she would dust it with wisps of her favorite scent so it would be irresistible to the senses of the man who by now would associate the scent with her figure, her face, her voice. But it was his heart she wanted to touch, not mere senses.

Later in the evening she would bring it to Andrew, and he would tuck it in safety on his person, pledged by his own promise of its sure delivery. Early tomorrow morning, he would depart and rendezvous with his brother in a few short days. Oh, how she longed to stow away! If only she could glimpse Roman's expression for herself upon reading her letter. Instead, she would exercise the patience her father had always displayed.

"Catherine, I'm so happy for you."

"Oh, Alex, do you think I am acting rashly? Although Antoine agreed to marry prior to his leaving, I think he would have been content to wait until his return."

"I think you made a wise decision. Behren insisted that Antoine's—Sabiir's—existence should not be made known to the people of Palmeria. Knowing he's alive could make them less willing to accept Behren as their ruler. But should they discover Sabiir in the process of their reclaiming the throne, he can explain that he's married to an Englishwoman and will not consider staying in Palmeria. So, yes, I believe you are perfectly right in marrying now." She looked at Catherine's pretty face and smiled at the joy in her eyes. "You look so calm."

"If I do, it's a façade. And I regret that both my brothers will not be present when we exchange our vows. I believe Roman really does like Antoine."

"I know you're right, Catherine. He would've stayed had he known of your plans. It was he who acted in haste."

"Oh, Alex, I'm so happy to have become finally acquainted with Roman. I feel closer to him than ever before in my life. To at last know that he truly does love and care for me—what a gift I've received! And I owe that to…well, I really don't know to whom. He mentioned someone in his letter, but did not reveal her name."

"His letter? Did Roman write you a letter, Catherine?" Her heart burned with curiosity.

"Yes, but I'm afraid with all my distractions, I failed to share it with you!" She reached into the drawer of her dressing table to produce a single folded sheet. "While you finish my hair I'll read it to you."

"My Dearest Catherine,

I am deeply saddened that I am unable to bid you a farewell in person. With the upcoming trip I have some unfinished business that will not wait. Therefore, I am forced to leave you with this written expression of my sentiments and request your forgiveness in so doing.

I returned to England for the purpose of establishing with you the relationship we should have shared long ago. For years, I took for granted that you should have known of my affection for you. Yet, how could you know what I had never expressed or showed?

Were it not for a very dear, very intimate friend who helped me to see beyond my former blindness, I might never have recognized the truth. I am certain she does not fully realize the extent to which she has affected my life in every other aspect, as well. I will be forever in her debt.

And so I leave you now, Catherine, content with the outcome of my stay and overjoyed that I was not too late, for I know that shortly you will embark on a new life that will not allow room for the guidance of an older brother who has arrived 'fashionably late' one time too often. Although I know we have much building yet ahead, I feel we now have a solid foundation upon which to do that building.

I am also confident in your future husband and entrust you to his care.

I know not when I will be returning to Kent. Please look after Piccolo during my absence.

Your Brother, Roman"

She put the letter back on the dressing table and wrinkled her brow. "I wonder who the wonderful friend is that he mentions. It can't possibly be Caroline Landly." Receiving no response, she looked into the mirror to find Alexandra in tears. "Alex?" She twisted around. "Alex, are you all right? Why are you crying? Good heavens, it's you! Am I right?"

Reaching for a handkerchief, Alexandra blotted the tears from her eyes and stepped the few paces to sit at the foot of the bed.

Catherine rushed to her side. "You're the one, Alex. It's you who's responsible for the changes in my brother!" Alexandra's head dropped down, one tear after another falling from her eyes. "You love him...don't you?" Alexandra gave a quick nod. "I can sense his love for you by the words in his letter, but does he know you love him?"

Alexandra could do nothing but wag her head while the tears intensified.

"Oh, Alex, I was so consumed with my own matters that I never took note of yours. I'm so ashamed. And now he's gone. How you must be hurting inside."

Alexandra lifted her head and squeezed her friend's hand. "Catherine," she said, taking a deep breath, "this is your special day. Let's not spoil it, hmm?" She did her best to dry her eyes. "I'm confident that I, too..." Sniffles and a trembling sigh cut short her words. "...I, too, have established a firm foundation with your brother, and there will be building work yet ahead."

"Alex, tell me, did he confirm his love for you?"

"Yes, he did."

"It's not possible for a person to be happier than I am at this moment!" She jumped to her feet and the cheer in her eyes made Alexandra laugh through her tears. "To have two of my dearest friends as my sisters as well. This is more than a person could ever ask!"

Late afternoon smiled with perfection upon the meadow where Catherine had happened upon the handsome young artist earlier in the summer. The air was warm, and the sky hosted an array of billowy white clouds.

Antoine stood, studying what remained of the robin-egg blue expanse, his eye drawn to a brown falcon cutting across the sky with a screech. The sinking sun and clouds settling along the horizon promised a magnificent sunset for the small party soon to gather for the ceremony. Standing beside him, his brother watched with matching intensity the movement of the clouds.

Wishing at first they could communicate, Antoine thought better of it. No, to have stayed and known his own people would have meant not knowing the vineyard, the rich English culture, and foremost, his fiancée. He would willingly relive every minute of the abuse he suffered in France to end up right where he stood. Yes, his reward had proved great, indeed.

Mr. Etrea had emphatically informed him that his brother disagreed with his decision to marry, instead hoping that he would have a change of mind once he saw Palmeria, met the people, and looked into the eyes of his mother. Then he could make a retraction and accept the crown. But now? He would be married and his roots would forevermore reside in England.

Yet, despite his objections, here Behren stood, shoulder to shoulder with his brother, to witness and support his vow. Although Mr. Etrea would not be in attendance, instead making last-minute arrangements to embark on the trip, Behren would understand the universal procedure of sacred matrimony.

Interrupting the solitude, the patterned thud of a galloping horse drew the attention of both men.

"John," Antoine called out, jogging over to meet him. Brushing a bit of dust from his black pants, he looked up as a carriage arrived, bringing Catherine's mother, Andrew, Jessica, Grace, and Stephen.

"What a magnificent place for a wedding," Jessica decared, glancing across the meadow, where an occasional wildflower peeked up. A breeze skimmed the top of the long grasses, creating waves like the sea. "I remember this meadow."

"You've been here before?" Antoine asked.

"Several times. It was covered in frost the first time I saw it."

"Yes, I've painted it in its winter coat."

Andrew walked up behind his wife and extended a hand to Antoine.

"I'm sure you never thought that stowaway would show up to steal your sister's heart," Antoine said with a laugh.

"Ah, yes, you fought—and escaped—the crew only to land yourself in the captain's family."

"A finer family in the world, I'm convinced, does not exist."

Before long a second carriage pulled around the bend and the little party hushed and took their places.

Alexandra Viana appeared first, stepping onto the footpath, a bouquet of white roses wrapped in ribbons in her hands. Stopping beside Catherine's mother, she turned to face the black carriage. The others followed her gaze. Richard Winterfield emerged, reaching in to assist the bride.

For the first time in his memory, Antoine felt absolute peace. Though finding his natural brother and the answers to countless mysterious questions, *this* was the family—the Winterfields—to which in truth he belonged. Her parents would be his parents, her brothers his. Whatever happiness, sorrow, pleasure, or pain encountered this family would meet him, too.

Contentment was not an emotion he normally experienced. But when Richard neared and placed Catherine's hand in his, he sensed this was just the start of the goodness that would fill his life from this evening forward.

Chapter Thirty-Eight

The day chased the sun over the horizon, leaving in its wake a pale blue glow. Andrew Winterfield stood beneath taut sails, watching the first star appear in the dusky sky. *The Emerald* sailed smoothly through the warm waters of the Mediterranean.

Taking advantage of a brief lull in his duties, he propped one foot upon the lower railing. His jaw muscles tightened. Had he been wrong to leave his wife at this crucial time? Two months would pass before he would see her again—eight excruciating weeks.

His thoughts took him back to her tearful goodbye. Never before had he seen such fear in her face. Thinking he could encourage her, he had tried to show her the map: the route they would be following, the ports where they would stop, and the dates they would reach each one. But she had turned aside, giving way to more tears. She had allowed him to pull her close and to stand in a silent embrace while he tried to comfort her.

And not once had she asked him to reconsider. Behind the tears, he could see her strength.

November the fifteenth. He would focus his hope on the day his child was due to arrive—several weeks after his own scheduled return—and direct his attention to the task at hand. But the ship felt all wrong without her, like a home in want of its mistress. Funny how his wife had improved the entire atmosphere of the vessel. Lighter moods, punctuated by whistling and even occasional bursts of song, had become commonplace. All ten crew members had polished their language while in her presence, with only the rare slip. They mopped the decks more often, tidied their cabins, and touched up the paint. He even noted that they tipped their sailors' caps now and then when she passed. Who would have suspected he had a crew of gentlemen beneath all their calloused hides?

Sorry for his crew, he knew it would be some time before she would see them again. A working cargo ship was no place for a child. Still, it seemed she had belonged there even more than he at times. Together they had sailed thousands of miles on dozens of voyages, hauling materials for the construction of Muir Ceann. Indeed, she would be missed.

And how he had changed since his marriage. Prior to meeting Jessica, never would he have imagined such a yearning for a place as he had for that island. The sea had beckoned to him since his childhood, but of late he had discovered within himself a longing to return to Everett Island and the emerging castle. Already, he felt the connection. Every single stone, every timber and tile had arrived on the island by means of *The Emerald* under the careful eye of her captain.

Jessica's father had played a significant role in his growing attachment to the island. John's ploy to involve him in the building of Muir Ceann had been obvious from the start. And, indeed, it had succeeded. Within Andrew's chest beat a heart tied inextricably to the family's new estate.

His head dropped. The soft sea breezes that had consoled him in years past brought no comfort this evening. Nothing could replace the craving to have his wife in his arms and to feel his child moving beneath his palms. He told himself the journey would pass quickly. His heart took exception to the thought. A heavy sigh seeped through his clenched teeth.

When the last of the silvery sunlight slipped from the surface of the rippling sea, Andrew was startled by a voice from behind him. "Isn't the same without 'er, is it, sir?"

Nothing short of death would keep Smiley McGuire from sailing alongside him. The old sailor, his wiry rusted hair now fading to ash, propped his arms on the railing.

"What will you do, Smiley, when Muir Ceann is complete and I set my feet on solid ground once and for all?"

The man shrugged and looked down. "Don' be knowin' 'bout that, yet, Cap'n."

"You realize you're partly to blame," Andrew said. Trying to get a smile from the sailor, he nudged him with an elbow. "You're the one who coaxed me to find a good wife. And remember cooking all those meals for us while she was aboard? You were so angry with me when I returned to the ship instead of staying with her in England. Or have you forgotten?"

"I r'member."

"You helped win her over. And I'm soon to become what you thought I should be all along—a family man. So what are you going to do about it?"

"Don't worry 'bout me, Cap'n. Every ship needs a good hand, and I'll be findin' somethin'. You can testify to my hard work."

Yes, indeed, Smiley McGuire, even in his fifties, was stronger than most men at any age. But his stubby fingers were becoming crooked and stiff and his back a bit more hunched.

Andrew gazed out over the sea and spoke almost as though talking to himself. "If I thought you would accept the position, I would invite you to live on the island with us." A sidelong glance revealed Smiley's eyes fixed on the horizon. "Now I know Mr. Viana has a cook. But with the family growing the way it is, he'll have to hire another." He took it as a good sign that the sailor had not objected. "After all, the island is much like a ship. She's surrounded by water...and the sun will still set over the ocean. Instead of sails, you'd have high towers and an unobstructed view of the stars. The winds and the storms you love so much would continue to strike, but the fortress would promise greater protection." Andrew turned and raised his eyebrows at his friend, who still did not object.

"I s'pose," Smiley said in a gruff undertone, "with you keepin' yerself so busy on the island, somebody would need to teach the little ones how to sail."

"Absolutely." Andrew laughed. "Very well then. I'll speak with Mr. Viana the minute we return."

With a smile beaming from his heart, Andrew hooked an arm about the sailor's stubby neck.

Roman Winterfield sat under the flickering glow of a lamp on the wall above his bunk. Legs outstretched, he scanned a newspaper page, perusing a report on the heat wave in France that threatened crops nationwide. After reading the same report three times, he realized his thoughts had wandered far from the subject.

He moved ahead to the exchange rates and then an advertisement enticing visitors to the Riviera. Promises of enchanting days and romantic nights filled the page.

Flipping quickly to the back of the paper before dropping it onto his lap, he considered unpacking. The light in his small round window had blackened some time earlier, so it had to be nearing ten. Almost against his will, he found his thoughts wandering again to England, as they had many times since the morning he left for France. Perhaps he should start looking to purchase some property for himself—somewhere other than his homeland.

The time had come to put the summer with all its events behind him. It was August, the month of closure, when the tourists packed for home and children settled down in preparation for another busy school year. Flowers, trees, and even birds agreed that a farewell was imminent. Soon they would submit to the impending winter without argument or delay.

And so would he.

Letting out a long sigh, he allowed envy of the natural elements to overwhelm him. For all of them, reunion hovered as a hope on the horizon. With the warming of the spring would come a glorious regathering—the matching of foliage with its palette of colors, the filling of the riverbeds with replenishing waters, the sweet scent of the breeze bringing the songs of the larks. These elements could bow to the winter because spring would bring them together again.

So where was *his* horizon? Where was his spring? The frigid winter ahead in Germany would well mimic his life, a fitting place to pass the dismal remains of the year.

April would find him in Austria with the unmatched majesty of the Alps and the smattering of alpine villages and medieval towns like sparkling jewels carved from the rough landscape. It was a country he had visited a dozen times, a region he, in the past, had savored.

Why then did it seem such a bleak prospect this time? Austria itself and his love of it had not changed. And spring would arrive as it had for millenniums past, swathed in beauty and vigor.

The same quaint shops would open their doors. On its western tip, the same touring boats would be readied to shuffle visitors to the garden islands, the castles, and other day stops along the Bodensee shores. Ancient woodlands and forests would awaken to the sun's returning warmth.

So why did he dread the thought of going back? What had changed?

He had. His outlook, hopes, and goals had all taken a new direction when he had seen *her* again.

If only he could go back to that fateful day in May and change his plans. He would not have gone to France. He would not have made the appointment with *Monsieur* LaRon. He would never have looked her way.

Could he erase that day like chalk markings from a blackboard? Of course, shadows of it—of her—might linger, but he could force them to the background.

But could she be dismissed in such a swift and final way? Should she be? To do such a thing would be to regret, not just that one day, but the entire summer and, most importantly, the lessons he had learned through her.

No. It was the pain he wished he could erase, not her. Never her.

A tap on his cabin door forced his thoughts to a close.

"Come in."

His brother's face appeared from around the door.

"I have something for you," Andrew announced and stepped in, holding a white folded page.

Roman stared in silence at the letter. Tucking the newspaper into its original tri-fold, he set it aside.

"I apologize for not delivering it sooner. This is the first opportunity I've had since you boarded in Marseille."

Roman nodded.

"Well…" Andrew hesitated. "See you in the morning." Roman looked down at the piece of paper, and Andrew turned to leave. "Oh, I nearly forgot." He turned back and pulled from his jacket a shallow, rectangular, brown paper-wrapped package bound in twine. "I was asked to deliver this with the letter."

"Thank you," Roman said, accepting the package.

"Have a good night, Roman."

"Good night."

Andrew left the room, pulling the door closed behind him.

Roman turned the letter over and read his name on the opposite side. It was penned in a woman's hand. He placed the brown package atop the newspaper on the bunk and closed his eyes. Could it be from Catherine? Surely not from Caroline Landly. More likely, it came from his mother, but it did not look like her penmanship.

Or maybe…could it be from Alexandra?

Loud thumping in his ears settled into a steady beat. He broke the wax seal on the back. His breath stopped at the first three words, "Dear Mr. Winterfield."

Alexandra! Any of the others would have addressed him by his given name.

What could she possibly say to him after what he had confessed?

Since his departure a week before, he could concentrate on nothing else. That last look he had taken of her recurred in his mind time and again as though she were standing right before him. How long would it be before he was freed of her? Months? Years? Or would those sapphire eyes haunt him forever? At nearly thirty years of age, he had never met anyone who had touched his life the way she had. Were he to live a hundred more, he knew in his heart no other would ever leave such an impression.

Dated the day after his departure from England, the letter would be the goodbye he had not allowed her to speak. It would tell of her sorrow for him and her plea to forgive her for the rejection she was about to give.

Not ready to read her words, to split open the wound he had been nurturing, he set the letter aside and stepped to the basin. Cool water rushed over his fingers from the pitcher. He leaned forward and splashed it over his face, rubbing some onto the back of his neck. After blotting himself dry and loosening the buttons of his shirt, he stretched his interlaced fingers above his head, inverting his palms, knuckles cracking. His hands came to rest atop his head and he looked again at the silent page resting atop the bunk.

After all she had done for him, would he now deny her one last opportunity to voice her expressions? His leaving her in the manner he did had been harsh, he admitted. He knew that the minute he chose to do it.

He had to laugh. "Oh, such a woman." She in her own kind and proper manner would not allow him the final say. He may have deprived her of a verbal response, but she had made sure he would receive her words.

He would not refuse her. Reaching for it, he skimmed his fingertips over the ink as he read.

Dear Mr. Winterfield,

I find myself quite perplexed after our conversation at Brentwood, at which time you so openly expressed your sentiments. I know you must have been struggling a great deal, and I would like to thank you for your candor.

"Let me down easy, Miss Viana. Yes, that would be your wonderful way."

However, I request equal opportunity to express to you my honest feelings. To say that
my first reaction upon hearing of your departure yesterday was one of great disappointment
would be an understatement. In all honesty I
was overtaken by anger. You confessed love for
me, but you will forgive me when I state that
true love should allow the other the courtesy of
a response. You had to have sensed my agitation
and desire to speak with you, yet you ignored
me. I would like to make known the injury that
such an insensitive action has caused. This is
the reason for my anger, which continues to
smolder within me this day.

The words should not have surprised Roman, for he had
always found Alexandra to be a direct yet respectful person.
What he found shocking was that she had yielded to an emotion that he thought impossible for the mild-mannered young
lady—anger. Yes, he had seen her clearly frustrated during
their conversation at Brentwood. But angry?

Her words stabbed him to the heart. He had been thinking only of his own pain when he chose to leave. How could
he have been so numb to hers? She had always drawn out the
best of qualities in him, and here he was responsible for bringing out her worst. He had pained a woman who had shown him
nothing but kindness. Would he ever learn?

Yet, he also felt a strange sense of relief—relief in the fact
that she was not perfect as he had begun to believe. Even Miss
Alexandra Viana could be consumed by a negative emotion.
While not taking pleasure in her suffering, perhaps the vast
chasm that he felt had divided them was now a bit narrower.

He returned to her letter.

I am also puzzled over your self-perception.
You said it was I who set the example for you in

caring, giving, and sharing, and while I would like to thank you for such great credit, I cannot accept it. Had those qualities not existed within you, they could not have been drawn forth. I may have helped you to recognize your capabilities, but the potential was there all along. The credit belongs to you, sir, for you had the strength and integrity to test that potential.

Also, qualities such as these would deem us equals. I am not your superior, as you stated, and I have never believed that to be the case.

Roman reread that sentence. It was no wonder he had fallen in love with Alexandra. Her immense beauty had been surpassed only by her unequaled modesty.

Please next allow me to broach the topic of the letter I wrote to my sister from France. The observations I reported to her then were a reflection of my feelings at the time of my writing them. However, it was not long thereafter that I began to recognize in you signs of the admirable qualities previously mentioned. I had every intention of destroying that letter and send to my sister a much more favorable report. However, I neglected to do so and later felt I could make a retraction of my misjudgment to her in person, which I was able to do when she arrived in Kent in June. I apologize profusely for the sting my letter inflicted and am once again impressed by another fine quality in you—that of forgiveness. For not only were you able to show continued kindness to me after reading such spiteful words, but you actually allowed yourself to fall in love with me and even to confess that love later. If anyone is undeserving, it is I, and I request your pardon in this matter.

How could she be so merciful when it was he who had intruded and read a personal letter? She should have scolded him for such an unethical action, and yet here she was asking for his forgiveness. Alexandra Viana was nothing short of remarkable.

> Last of all, I would like to correct a dreadful assumption on your part. You accused me of cultivating a divided heart. I would like to explain that my heart is, and has been for quite some time, firm in the love of one man. While having great respect for Preston Sutton and a high value of his friendship, I was not referring to Grace's brother-in-law in the conversation with my mother, but to Jessica's.

His hand holding the letter dropped to his side. He stared in disbelief at the dark round window. "Me? She loves me?" He swallowed hard and held his breath, unable to believe the words he had just read. Allowing the letter to fall to the bunk, he covered his eyes with one trembling hand. For the first time in his entire adult life, a tear seeped from one eye.

Walking the short length of the room and back, he glanced at the letter on the bed. Had it not been in her own writing? Jessica's brother-in-law!

How could he have been so blind? He thought of her soiled cheeks after their hike through the forest, her smile and soft laughter at his astonishment following Piccolo's birth, her blue eyes as they locked with his while he led her in the dance at the ball, her gaze upon him as the two lay in the light of the fire at Brentwood House the night of the storm, and the way she had run from the house—run from him—in the rain the following day.

Of course. Why had he not recognized it before?

Roman dropped his head back, a wide smile parting his lips. Emotion mounting, he inhaled and hollered out loud, his breath ending in laughter.

Rushing to the door, he swung it wide. "Andrew!" He ran headlong into his brother, who had propped himself against the door. "She loves me!" he yelled loud and long, grabbing fistfuls of his brother's overcoat at the shoulders. "She loves me, Andrew. Not Preston Sutton. Me."

"Preston Sutton? What ever gave you that idea?"

"Inconsequential, Andrew," he said with a laugh, recalling the word he had used with Alexandra in the rain at Brentwood. "It's inconsequential."

"Now I'm very sorry I didn't deliver that letter to you sooner."

"The letter. Andrew, I haven't even finished reading it." Shaking him by the shoulders, Roman pressed a kiss onto his brother's forehead and pushed away.

"I know exactly how you feel at this moment, Roman," he heard Andrew call out before he pushed the door closed. He scooped up the letter, and paced as he resumed reading, his fingers running through his hair.

You see, Mr. Winterfield, when I reflect on the past, I believe I began to love you while aboard the ship from France. Later, your concern for your sister, and our unique experiences together solidified my appreciation for the man you had allowed yourself to become.

I admit I feared losing you to Miss Landly. How relieved I was to discover your true feelings for her and the integrity you displayed in releasing her. I am confident that you did so in a kind manner.

You have proven time and again that the changes you have made are lasting and a reflection of the new man you have become. You have touched my heart and impacted my life like no other person.

While I may struggle with anger for the time being, it is anger of the best kind, for had I not cared so deeply for you, surely my heart would not have been so affected.

I also realize it may well be months before you return. However, it is my desire that we speak personally of these matters, for which time I anxiously await.

May you consider me each time you employ the accompanying gift.

With All My Love,
Alexandra

Roman grabbed the package and ripped the twine from it. Unfolding the paper wrapping and wiping away another tear poised on the rim of his lashes, he discovered the black leather binding of Alexandra's Bible. He opened the book where the satin ribbon was tucked and found it between the pages he had left several weeks before. He smiled to recall the morning he had awakened to find it beside his pillow. It was then he realized that she had discovered his secret readings, though she never spoke a word of it. And he thought he had been so discreet.

The lamp burned late into the night as he read and reread her letter many times over.

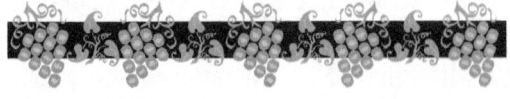

"Miserable!" Roman heard one of the sailors shout while stuffing an arm into an oilskin coat.

Rain pelted his own hood like angled daggers as he dashed by and ducked through a doorway taking him below deck.

"Ah, the stench of mold and wet timber," Andrew said in the gruff inflection of a pirate when his brother entered the galley. "Nothin' quite like sailin' through a summer storm. Gets ya' here every time," he said, thumping his chest. He filled his lungs with the musty air. His voice returned to his usual tone. "Have some breakfast, Roman." He pushed a tin plate piled high with yellow steaming fluff across the warped tabletop. "Scrambled them myself."

"Don't mind if I do." He grabbed the pepper grinder.

"You look like the cat that finally caught up with the mouse," Andrew said, leaning closer to put his elbows on the table.

"Probably because I am," Roman said, shoveling a forkful of eggs into his mouth. "Any coffee made?"

"Not before an explanation."

Roman felt his brother's heavy stare upon him, but, with the eggs half consumed, he concentrated on the sausage. He had smelled a trailing of coffee before ever stepping a foot in the door, but thought his brother's curiosity should fester a bit longer.

"Come on with it," Andrew said, drumming his fingertips on the tabletop.

Roman could not suppress the smirk slipping over his lips. "What would you like to know?"

"All of it. Everything." Andrew was on his feet. "How did you do it?"

"It was quite accidental, I assure you."

"Accidental? She's the reason you went back to Kent."

"No, remember? I went back for Catherine."

"Rubbish. You went back for Alex. No sense in lying to me. I know you better than I know myself."

"All right, all right." Roman pushed the plate away. "I did return for Catherine, that's true. But I knew Alex would be there. I was hoping to be in her presence as well."

"Hoping to be in her presence...How droll. You were hoping for more than that, and you know it."

"In all honesty, I never expected anything to come of us. I never imagined she could like me."

"You're not the same man, Roman. Surely you can see that."

"Yes, but could she? I didn't think she was paying attention."

"You are shrewd, aren't you?"

"I don't know what I did, Andrew." He swiped a napkin over his lips and crossed his arms in contemplation. "All I know is that I was almost toppled when she stepped into that pottery shop in France. The way she handled herself—all grown and...and poised. Beautiful beyond measure. I'm glad I haven't had to describe her appearance to anyone because there's nothing on this earth to which I might compare her. A gem? Gold? Porcelain? There's nothing so fresh, so stunning. Yet her charms run far deeper. Her grace is so subtle. Most of the upper class would brush it aside as meekness, but in my opinion she's the strongest of women." Lost in the vision of her face when he had last seen her, his thoughts became washed with the times they had spent alone. "Remember the meadow we found as children? Early in the summer I took her there."

"So that's where it began." Andrew pulled his chair beneath him again and leaned forward.

"For her, you mean? She claims in her letter it was long before then, though I can't imagine it."

"What happened in the meadow?"

"Secret meadow. Secret day. I prefer it remain between the two of us. But I will tell you that I held her hand often that day. It was like holding a dove in my palm."

"You've always been surrounded by women. You've taken their hands before."

"But she's different. Others may have been close by, but none has ever been inside before, wrapped around my heart, filling my mind at every moment. I've learned lessons from her I can't begin to explain. She can chastise me in her own polite way that leaves me feeling like I've fallen into a pit of fire, so great is my guilt."

"You, Roman? A man totally indifferent to the opinions of others?"

"I'm affected by her, spellbound even."

"I wouldn't have believed it had I not heard it from your own lips."

"Thrice I've had the privilege of taking her into my arms."

"I recall the two of you dancing together at the ball, but..."

"Then at Brentwood. I saved her life, Andrew." He blew his breath from his chest recalling his timely arrival at the house. "The storm the night of my arrival would've taken her had I not arrived when I did. In my frantic state to pull her from that island, I stopped and reflected only later that I had held her so close. The following morning, however, when we rowed back to see the devastation, she turned to me, willingly, Andrew. I shall never forget how she laid her head against me, just like a frightened lamb. And I savored every moment. But on the train home, I thought I'd leaped over the cliffs of Dover and was headed toward my death."

"Why? Did she reject you in some way?"

"I never gave her the chance. I confessed my feelings to her, but not wanting to hear her contempt or pity for me, I never allowed her response." He pushed himself away from the table and to his feet. "Cruel, was it not?"

"But the way she had turned to you—didn't you consider the slightest possibility of affection on her part?"

"Not then, no. She was in need of comfort. I was the only one there. At that time, I still couldn't believe it was out of affection."

"So you denied her."

"And look how she rewards me—by loving me in return. I suppose there is something I might compare her to."

"And what's that?"

"The silk of a spider's web, for its strength is equaled only by its beauty."

"I think we both know who's to be credited for such strength."

His gaze met his brother's and they blurted in unison, "John Viana!"

"How can I ever repay that man?" Roman said, feeling a twinge of anguish for the struggles he must have endured in raising three children alone.

"How?" Andrew asked. "By taking good care of his daughter. Roman, we can return to Marseille. You'd be only a few short days from home. I'm sure any man aboard this ship would do just that were he in your shoes."

Roman dropped his head and turned his back to his brother, his fists clenching into hard balls. Six days...or eight weeks. Which would it be? Pushing thoughts of Behren Asonti and Antoine Aramis aside, all he could see was Alexandra's face. She waited for him and he agonized for her.

It mattered not to him whether this crumb of a nation called Palmeria were to drop off the map. Whether governed by a savage or a saint, what possible difference could it make to him?

He had embarked on this mission to protect Catherine's new husband and his own brother. And he was certain Behren was aware of that. For even Behren, with all his suspicious glares, was no idiot. The silent communication between them had solidified into nothing short of ire in Roman, a mutual sentiment, he was sure. It would be a relief to drop the man in his own country.

But could it be done without Roman's assistance? As it was, they were a tiny band. How would his brother and new brother-in-law fare in his absence? Had his concern for their well-being been unfounded? Perhaps his presence was not necessary after all—

But the woman...

No. This journey entailed more than Behren, than Antoine, than even the protection of Andrew. At the heart of their mission was a woman. A woman whose very life must at this moment hang in the balance. A woman who had been hurled into the throes of prison more than twenty years before. And for what? For bearing a child, for playing with courage the hand she had been dealt, for caring for her progeny, for caring about her people...

Yet, she was a stranger. Even were they to reach her, was it realistic to think they could free her? And would he ever see her again? There must be a million such damsels! Could he continue to suspend his own life for every woman in need? The one and only woman he had ever cared for now needed him, did she not?

And what of the other woman back home, Andrew's wife, heavy with child? If anyone, Andrew was the one agonizing. It was he who should return. And yet he forged ahead.

Six days or eight weeks...

"What'll it be, Roman?"

Roman stepped back to his brother, throwing his palms upon the tabletop. "See me to Palmeria, Andrew," he said; "then get me back to England."

Andrew reached for a pot and poured a cup of hot black coffee. Setting the cup before his brother, he extended his right hand. "Consider it done."

Chapter Thirty-Nine

Three candles sitting mid-table smoldered to stubs while the flame of the fourth sizzled in a pool of wax. Slouched against his hard chair back, Roman focused, lids half closed, on the curl of black smoke dancing into the air and dissipating.

An hour before, he had loosened the top buttons of his shirt in an effort to expel the heat, but to no avail. The cotton fabric clung to his underarms in wet rings. Only with the setting of the sun had the scorch of their fifth Mediterranean day waned to a sticky vapor.

Behren Asonti's voice droned on. The translation from Mr. Etrea floated past him at this late hour after a day of exhausting work in the sun.

"And why is it he believes Rios not to be in the prison beneath the city?" Andrew asked in a dull voice. Roman perked up and looked at his brother, who sat pushed back, one cupped hand hiding his eyes, one heel resting upon the other foot.

"Because the servant who delivered Rios' most recent message," Mr. Etrea explained, "worked in the palace twenty miles from the city and not in the castle—"

"Which the city was built around," interrupted Roman.

"How do we know Rios hasn't been relocated with the discovery of Behren's disappearance?" Antoine, who had been leaning against one darkened wall in the corner, dropped his head to knead the back of his neck.

"We don't," Mr. Etrea answered. "We'll begin outside the city in the catacombs by the palace and work our way in. See... here." His finger ran the length of a crude map sketched by Behren earlier in the trip.

"Behren's never seen those catacombs," argued Roman. "What makes him think we can find them in that desert?"

"His mother gave him explicit directions."

"And he said earlier today that he noted the palace during his escape," Antoine added. "He has no doubt as to the location of the entrance to the catacombs."

"So we need Rios to close in on Pashur," Andrew surmised.

"Yes. Rios lived decades in the castle," Mr. Etrea answered. "He'll know just where to find Pashur."

"And if we're discovered?" Roman asked. His gaze shifted to Behren, who sat directly across the table. Immediately, he felt his brow tense.

Something about Behren Asonti had disturbed him from their first encounter in the jail. Here was a man hostile in an inert sort of way, whose presence, though appearing tranquil to the casual eye, invaded the room with a watchful and impenetrable air. His features, identical to Antoine's—faint brow, rounded chin, and fleshy mouth—clashed in an almost disruptive manner with the hard glare in his eyes that seemed to narrow each time they met Roman's.

"When Behren is identified," Antoine added, "the guards are likely to shift their loyalty."

"It's imperative, however," Mr. Etrea explained, "that Antoine keep from sight to everyone but Pashur. When he sees the twins alive and well—"

"And in his castle," Antoine added.

"He'll have no choice but to surrender."

"'The twentieth of Tishri'—September on our calendar—'will be a crucial night,' he said," reported Mr. Etrea. "As he wandered among the people prior to leaving, he overheard murmurings about a festival marking a large celebration in the city. Prominent households had already received a formal invitation to the castle for an elaborate feast, arranged by Pashur for the supposed purpose of honoring 'his' people. Most recognized it as a ploy to bribe them for their support—a veil to honor no one but himself."

"Tell me more about Pashur." Roman pinched his shirt front, peeling it from his skin. Upon its release, it settled once again against his clammy chest.

"Paranoid." The word came back from Behren through Mr. Etrea after translating the request. "His primary enemy—Sabiir—has reached maturity. Pashur must wonder whether this heir remains ignorant to his father's plans. He is also reported to be a very superstitious man, not allowing the servants to so much as mention the existence of the queen or either of her sons in his presence. He has preferred to live a pretense in which none of them exist."

"That's not superstition," Roman said. "That's stupidity."

"How surprised he'll be to discover that the ruler honored at his celebration on the twentieth of September will be, not him, but Behren," Antoine said.

"Who will pose as Sabiir from then on," Mr. Etrea added.

"But if Pashur's falseness is so transparent to the people," Andrew asked, "will the majority even make an appearance at the festival?"

Mr. Etrea posed the question to Behren. "He believes many will. What better way to ridicule Pashur, who knows of the peoples' loyalty to their hope in their returning monarch? Even his own armies support him for no other reason than their own protection. What greater mockery than to take from the man's own table while anticipating the arrival of his subjugator?"

"Pashur must have some loyal supporters," Roman disputed.

"It seems they are few," Antoine said.

Roman shot a glance at Antoine. "How much of this language are you recognizing?"

"More and more."

"And with what protection are we to face Pashur's sentries?" Roman asked of Mr. Etrea. "Or worse yet, his armies?"

Mr. Etrea again turned to Behren, whose words came back in a soft reply.

"He says shields and weapons would only prove a burden."

Roman sprang to his feet in a fury, his glare hot upon the young prince. "And what of our safety?" Wanting to shake him by the collar, he paused only briefly for Mr. Etrea to translate and pressed the matter further. "Pashur's armies will see us as invaders. As captain of this ship, my brother is responsible for the lives of every man aboard." He huffed like an angry bull before Behren, unable to wipe the scowl from his lips while the translator explained his dispute. Behren's stoic expression enraged him all the more. "I don't like you, Behren," Roman said, without awaiting a reply. "And I'll not allow you to risk the life of one of these men for the sake of your rule."

Mr. Etrea remained silent, a look of distress crossing his brow.

"Tell him," Roman said, settling back into his chair, "every word."

Before the translation could be made, Behren leaned forward and cast the same challenging look upon Roman that he had presented at their first meeting. He said a few short words that caused one of Mr. Etrea's brows to arch.

"What does he say?" Antoine asked.

"He says Roman is his *shevarrel*."

"What does that mean?" Andrew asked.

"It is difficult to explain in English—something that originates with their ancient folklore. A parallel, if you will. It is like a man who stands before a mirror, but rather than beholding a physical image of any kind, the persona, character, and behavior of another is reflected back. It is a sobering encounter because the two personalities are identical. But because of their similarities, they are rivals."

"A nemesis," Andrew mumbled.

"No. Much more intense," Mr. Etrea said. "In their fables, the two are at odds until one destroys the other."

"So you don't like me either," Roman said to Behren, his own eyes narrowing. "I can live with that."

Behren spoke again. Mr. Etrea hesitated.

"Say it," Roman said, his glare hot upon the young man.

"He says the two of you are different in just one aspect. You have no control over your spirit. He claims because of this, he is your superior."

Roman's glare shot away from Behren, his back and fists tightening. On his feet once again, he emptied his lungs in a fume while Behren said more.

"He says to think of the girl back home," Mr. Etrea said. "Your attraction to her was obvious. He believes it to be her calm manner that appeals to you and says you should imitate her composure."

Roman let out an irritated laugh that accompanied a nervous pacing about the room. Who did this man think he was? Was he trying—in his own manipulative way—to say that he, too, was attracted to Alexandra? After all, were they so much alike...

"By mentioning the woman," Mr. Etrea added, "he proves his point and states he does not wish to be your enemy. He feels your skills in world travel will prove invaluable in his cause. But you must choose now if you will be at his beck or be his enemy, for once we leave this ship, he will be your commander."

Rage erupted from the depths of Roman's core. He pounded his fist upon the table before Behren. "No man," he said, his jaw absorbing the brunt of his fury, "is my commander. Now answer me about the sentries, and I'll tell you if we're to be allies." Roman glared down upon Behren, who had sat unruffled throughout the discussion.

A brief moment later, Mr. Etrea translated, "The sentries will not see us as invaders because they will not see us at all. Remember, my father was The Leopard—a hunter, not a fighter. The hunter does not contend with an entire herd, but isolates one out of the pack. He is camouflaged, moving swiftly and infiltrating the territory without detection. He employs the element of surprise."

"Go on," Roman said through a clenched jaw.

"I have acquired the skills of my father. How is it you think I managed to escape the palace and return several times unobserved? How is it you think I traversed land and sea and was able to travel as far as France, invisible to the authorities?"

"You were caught, Behren." Roman raised an accusing finger. "Trapped by this very crew."

"I was trapped not by any man, but by exhaustion. I am healthy again. You are all strong men. Pashur will be overthrown without a single weapon. Not a drop of blood will be shed, and not one man captured. You have my word."

"I believe my brother, Roman," he heard Antoine say from behind. "Mr. Etrea is from that region. He, too, trusts Behren. *The Emerald* will cast off at daybreak on the twenty-first of September with the entire crew intact. He has promised us."

Roman twisted about to glare at Antoine and then his own brother, who remained silent. He thought about Andrew's wife, heavy with child. What if...

No, he could not allow his thoughts to visit that place. "Show me the exact locations of the castle entrances," he demanded of Behren.

"How kind of Grace and Stephen to invite me to your farewell dinner, Miss Viana." Preston Sutton strolled beside Alexandra along a quiet road near the outskirts of London. September had barely started, and yet the crisp evenings announced the approaching autumn. Green leaves showed faces dusted with hints of gold. Shadows lengthened across the dirt road even though the sun still felt warm upon Alexandra's face.

"It was an honor to have you," she said. "Thank you for asking me out on a stroll. A lovely evening, is it not?"

Alexandra considered the reason her sister had invited the young man. Perhaps she should notify Grace of her true feelings about Mr. Sutton. But what would it matter? Grace was not one to allow any situation to exist beyond what she herself created, real or imagined. To speak one's feelings to her old-est sister was to be brushed aside, persuaded down a different path.

No, Alexandra knew better. When the time arrived, she would show Grace where her intentions and feelings resided.

She smiled in Preston's direction. Not minding his presence at all, she rather enjoyed his company.

"I heard about the outcome of the race," she said. "You finished remarkably well."

But his head wagged. "Not even a contender for the prize."

"Preston Sutton, I'm ashamed of you. Is the top ten—among the world's finest, might I add—not good enough for you? It was your first race. Will you not try again?"

"Sailing is grueling. Yet it brings such a rush of exhilaration. I suppose I would be denying myself to surrender without another go of it."

"That's better." Though believing his words, they were expressed with such lack of the usual zeal she was accustomed to hearing from this animated friend.

"When will you return to London?" he asked.

"I can't say. My parents were gracious to allow my stay here this summer. It has been a wonderful experience, and I'm grateful. However, they desire my presence in Ireland for the winter. I must admit to being anxious for them and my home again. Daybreak can't come too soon."

"When your train departs, I assume."

"Yes."

An uneasy silence settled between them, nestling itself in, the way a pesky dog curls around his master's feet, unwilling to budge. Though falling fast into conversation with him at various other gatherings, she now found herself groping for words.

Perhaps her inability to converse freely resulted from her thoughts that insisted upon dwelling with Mr. Winterfield. How had he responded to her letter? Her imagination carried her in all directions. What would happen when he returned? When would he return? What commitments had he already made to his father's business? After the trip to Palmeria, his work could keep him away for the entire winter. And how would she know of his return, since she would be in Ireland?

Her heart grieved to think it could be springtime, or even the following summer, before she would see him again. Yet, she was willing to wait.

For the sake of her sanity, she forced Roman Winterfield out of her mind. But before long, his deep eyes pierced her thoughts. She remembered the time she had helped him to his feet in the courtyard before the birth of the foal and when he had unexpectedly appeared on the lighthouse island during the storm. Then her mind wandered back to the following day when he had comforted her after the storm's devastation. At times it seemed she could still feel his arms around her.

Lost in thought and the splendor of the dusk, she almost forgot that she was not alone. Preston's words caught her by surprise.

"You would not marry me were I to ask, would you, Miss Viana?"

Her shoulders drooped in disappointment. Was this to be her first proposal? It was all wrong. It was supposed to come from Mr. Winterfield. She gathered her shawl around her arms against the chill of the shadow into which they had stepped.

"I don't believe you would pose that question to any woman at this point in your life, Mr. Sutton."

"I never thought I would ever...until I met you. I may seem to you to be purposefully ignorant in matters such as romance, but you may be surprised to find even I recognize that a man would be out of his mind to walk away from a woman like you." She refused to meet his gaze, keeping her eyes on the road. "Yet it's my perception that you would not have accepted an offer from me two months ago any sooner than you would this very night, would you have?"

Lifting her face, she smiled at him and shook her head.

"No. You're distracted," he said. "You were in such a state when first we met. I knew it then. You're in love. I can see that. But might I add that I have a suspicion as to the fortunate wretch's identity. Please allow me to state with frankness that he's wholly undeserving."

"You feel that way because you don't understand him." Her feet came to a halt.

"You're wrong. Him I understand completely. It's you who has escaped my perception of sensibleness. How it is you ever came to love such a man is beyond my comprehension; yet only a woman of your courage could have sought out any admirable qualities in a man like Roman Winterfield. I'm happy for him. And envious of him." His head dropped back in outright laughter. "Envious of Roman Winterfield! I've never been envious of any man for any reason, and here Roman Winterfield, of all men, has succeeded in this impossible task. I can imagine his reaction when you tell him of our conversation."

"You wouldn't be happy as a married man, Mr. Sutton. Growing together with one special person just doesn't seem to fit your image. And leaving behind a broken heart would destroy you, I believe; I don't think you capable of carrying such a weight."

"Perhaps you're right." He stiffened his shoulders and resumed the stroll. "But I'll always remember you as the first— and perhaps only—woman who ever tempted me."

Chapter Forty

Sunlight washed through a crevice high above the gray head of the tall, thin man. The light of the new day, although a welcome sight, reached his eyes through a murky film. Dust filled the air, kicked up from the dirt floor beneath feet shod in worn leather straps. Rough walls of rock had held him captive for nineteen long years. His captors had been generous, however. Generous in the size of the underground cavern. Every sound echoed back around him from jagged and angled ceilings. The cave abounded with shallow fractures and wider clefts retreating into the shadows.

Had his echoes ever reached the ears of another human? He laughed off the thought, for what man could ignore his repeated cries for help? No, his was a chamber well-hidden from human ears. Yet, somewhere in the vicinity, a city flourished, its residents unaware of his deplorable existence far beneath the surface of the earth.

A large, heavy wooden door barricaded his cell. Once, years before, when the guard beyond the door had left behind a burning lantern, he had peered out from the small barred window upon several shallow niches carved into the rock wall of the long tunnel outside his door.

Each niche contained what appeared to be human remains—perhaps those of prominence from decades past, or even centuries. It had been a solemn day when he recognized himself as the only life amidst dozens dead in the dreary cata-combs. He wondered whether his king had been placed among them. After a long gaze upon the corpses, he had resolved never to become one of their number, yet concluded that this bleak cave would continue to be his residence for some time to come.

He felt no need of ever gazing out into the tunnel again.

Guards arrived every third day to deliver food and water and take away his bucket of waste. To ration the provisions had been a lesson he learned early. The guards rarely entered the den, but simply passed the sustenance through the trap in the door.

Often, he would overhear conversation between them. Now and then it would be scraps of news pertinent to his keen ears. He had on occasion succeeded in engaging one in con-versation. Several years prior, he had managed to befriend one of the young guards, gaining valuable information about the condition of the governor, the people, and also the queen and her son. Sympathetic for his state, the young sentry had even smuggled several carving tools into the cave. The final request to the young sentry was a verbal message for the queen. But the young guard had never returned to the catacombs. Had the message been transmitted? What had been his fate? Each day, each passing year, the man's conscience weighed just a bit more with the burden of the young man's probable execution.

Determined to protect his sanity, the prisoner devoted a portion of each day to plotting a possible escape. He had at-tempted every avenue, some several times over, but the solid rock walls resisted all attempts to facilitate his release. The small tools the young guard had smuggled to him were no match for the cave walls or the solid door. They seemed con-tent to hold their resident for now, but he told himself—and the walls—they could not entrap him forever.

The crevice above peered down at him from a height of at least forty feet. It allowed light, wind, and the infrequent rain to enter, but would allow nothing save the occasional bat to de-part. Without ropes, escape by that means proved impossible.

Nevertheless, he persevered in his hope to once again see the mountainous region surrounding his beloved city. He recorded each passing day, each month, each year as a mark on the wall.

He had also begun a project while in the bowels of the earth. After moving away the soft dust from a large section of the floor, through precise measurements with the tools, he had created a carving in the hard earth layer below—the image of every room, every corridor, and every entryway of the castle. He had determined where the queen must be imprisoned, where the governor's suites were likely located, and the probable position of each sentry.

Most all the city's residents over thirty years of age knew of him, and upon his escape, he would rescue the queen and her son and reestablish the proper rule over the district. Determination and the passage of nineteen years only solidified that pursuit, for the rightful king had now reached manhood.

The young sentry who had never returned was not the only life weighing upon the man's conscience. He was also laden with the life of his king's firstborn son, Sabiir. The boy's frightened four-year-old face—the last he had ever seen of him—plagued his dreams at night and his conscious mind during the light of day. He had never heard talk of the child's survival or even of his existence. Indeed, all Pashur's men were silent on that subject.

Therefore, he could only conclude that the boy had not returned alive and had resolved long ago to avenge the boy the only way he knew how—to carry out the plans of the young king's father by seeing to it that the boy's brother received the throne.

His incarceration inhibited the completion of his quest. Determination, however, drove him forward with each new day.

This day had proved to be like any other day for him—or so he thought until mid-afternoon. Over the years, he had become keen to the sound of footsteps, and this day he heard a faint scuffle in the tunnel. He crouched near the door and tuned his ear now to silence beyond.

Yes! The noise occurred again. Subdued voices followed. How odd. This was not the day for his rations to be delivered. Perhaps one of Pashur's men had died and would be delivered to a cold, empty hollow, where he would lie for all eternity. Perhaps it was Pashur himself. His knees creaked as he stood.

Or perhaps it was the queen, or her son…

His shoulders drooped. In nineteen long years, not one brief minute had he given thought to the possibility. How could he have been so idealistic, so imprudent in his expectations? In all honesty, had he imagined that the queen could survive all these years, imprisoned and swathed in discouragement and isolation?

His ears piqued when the soft voices grew louder. Sharp commands issued from one of the men. It sounded as though there were at least three.

He backed away from the door as the sounds drew closer. At once, the iron latch of the door clicked as the key turned inside the lock. It had been several months since anyone had entered the den. His shoulders and spine strengthened.

The heavy door moaned on its dusty hinges, swinging outward with agonizing slowness. The first man to enter the den wore a guard's uniform. He stumbled into the dusty cavern and fell at the feet of the prisoner. The guard's wrists had been bound, a rag stuffed in his mouth.

Astonished, he looked up at the doorway to find a young dark-haired man of a modest build standing at the threshold. "Are you Rios?" the stranger asked in the prisoner's tongue. When he nodded, the man stepped forward. "I am Behren Asonti."

With that, a second man of identical appearance stepped through the dark doorway to stand beside Behren. His voice was softer, yet equally confident, when he stated with a French accent but also in the man's tongue, "I am Sabiir Asonti—Sabiir V."

Rios' lips dropped open. "Forgive me, gentlemen, while I recover from this shock." The one who claimed the identity of Sabiir extended a hand. Rios at once took hold of it and pulled him into an embrace. "I feared you dead," he admitted, his eyes moistening. He pulled back to grasp him firmly. "Let me look upon you. The tattoo—let me see the tattoo!"

The young man—apparently understanding the request—loosened the buttons of his black shirt and dropped it to expose his back. The mangled face of a leopard, which he had last seen upon the shoulder of the four-year-old, had transformed to a deep blue, contorted smear.

Hearing a whimper, Rios looked down at the guard who lay on the floor of the cavern. His eyes had widened, staring in disbelief upon the shoulder of the young man.

Sabiir pulled the cotton shirt back over his shoulders and buttoned the collar as he turned to Rios. He wondered if the young man had retained any memories of him, for time and neglect had altered his appearance. His body was draped in a soiled gauze robe tied at the waist with a tattered piece of twine. His dirty feet matched the dust of the floor.

Sabiir looked deep into his eyes.

"Do you remember me?" Rios asked. "Our lessons together?" Days of sunshine in the parks of France returned to his memory with every vivid detail. He could hear the laughter of the boy and the glint in his eyes, black as ebony. And then thirty years prior when the boy's father was the child. And now standing before him were two men, identical in appearance to their father. "Do you remember?" Rios asked again of Sabiir.

"Some things, yes."

Rios rejoiced that a measure of the language had been retained, somehow, in the depths of the child's memory.

"Where did they take you? Where have you been all these years? There is so much to learn about you, yet now is not the time."

Sabiir's brow wrinkled and his head shook in a quick thrust, making it apparent that he had not understood.

"What have I been thinking?" Rios said, abruptly dropping to one knee before Sabiir. Bowing his head, he muttered, "I thought this day would never come, my king."

"Sabiir is not your king, Rios," the brother said and stepped from behind him.

Rios looked up.

"The honor has been bestowed—with graciousness—upon me," Behren announced. "I need Sabiir to assist in restoring the kingship, but it is his wish to return to England, where his wife awaits him."

Rios struggled to his feet, his gaze meeting Sabiir's.

"My name is Antoine Aramis. That is the name I will retain." His sentences were broken, but Rios understood their meaning.

"Your father was a man of great integrity. I expect nothing less of his sons. You display great strength and courage in coming all this way. And possibly even more in declining the throne. You may return to England a proud man."

It was Behren who then caught sight of the large carving in the cave floor. He stepped over to it. Rios followed him across the cavern.

"Magnificent!" Behren shouted.

"I believe your mother to be held in this chamber of rooms," Rios explained, pointing with a stick.

"Your deduction is correct. That is where we've been, together, since your disappearance."

"It will be a simple task to free her."

Behren stepped back to hover over the guard, who had not moved from his position on the ground and stared in astonishment at the two men. Behren lowered himself to pull the rag from his mouth.

"Do you remember Rios?" Behren asked, but the man did not respond. "No. I'm sure your loyalty is for the only ruler you have ever known. Pashur." Still crouched before the guard, Behren's eyes fell into a squint. "I am your ruler now. You have worked in opposition to my rule, and you will be punished accordingly. However, I am not an unreasonable man, as is Pashur. Tell me what I ask, and I shall be lenient with you."

The guard's head bobbed in quick nods.

"Tell me what you know of the upcoming celebration," Behren demanded.

"All these years, I thought Sabiir simply a legend..." the guard said nervously.

"About the celebration," Behren prompted.

"It is to begin at sunset tomorrow evening. The people will gather in the North Courtyard, where Pashur will appear on the large balcony to address them."

Behren nodded, rising again to his feet.

"Excuse me," interrupted the guard. "Forgive my eaves-dropping, but you will not find the queen where you expect."

"Tell me what you know of the queen!" Behren command-ed.

"Pashur learned of your disappearance several weeks ago. He relocated her and revealed her position to only a few select men."

"What is your name?" Behren asked, stepping closer.

"Teman."

"And are you one of those 'few select men,' Teman?"

"I read the king's declaration several years ago," the guard said. His eyes cooled. "I did not believe it." He paused, his jaw muscles tightening. "I watched Pashur destroy it, along with the entire household that had concealed it."

Behren motioned for his brother. "Had you read it care-fully, you would have noted the statement that the heir would possess several items, one of which would be a replica of that declaration." Behren's glare grew hot. "Would you recognize an identical copy of that declaration, Teman? It also mentioned that the true king would prove his identity with a certificate of his birth." He extended one hand toward his brother, who pro-duced the two documents. Behren held them before the eyes of the guard. "And would you recognize a diamond were you to see one? And what of the king's signet ring? If you have entered the castle, you have also seen the portraits of former kings, all whose left hand don this very ring." Behren pulled the large sparkling gem and the gold signet ring from a bag tied at his waist. "Sabiir is no legend. Look closely at me, Teman. Do I resemble the portrait of my father? And you saw the marking on my brother. A man may believe only what he wishes, but eventually it is the evidence that will prove the truth. You will not stop me, Teman. Nor a hundred like you."

The guard stared into the eyes of the young king for several long moments and then nodded. "I am one of the few select men, My Lord."

The sun, tinged orange, hovered over the western horizon. Short, tangled bushes and rough rocks dotted the dusty landscape, casting long shadows over the rolling hills of brown sand. A warm breeze grazed the surface of the land. Bits of sand twirled and settled around the tips of dried branches resting upon the hot ground.

Rios and the ten men with him crouched in the shadows of the bushes, peering down from a hillside.

In a shallow valley rested a small structure of adobe, a single-story house with a red roof of clay tile. There it stood, alone and far from the city.

Two figures paced in slow steps before its two entrances—one in front and one behind.

They took no notice of Rios and the others, who watched in silence. All were draped in black, even their heads wrapped in light-weight black gauze. Veils hid all but their eyes.

Waves of heat rippled the air between them and the house, just as when a stone breaks the surface of a quiet pond.

Rios studied the movements of the guards. He was quick to note the long, narrow silhouette of a rifle strapped onto the shoulder of each.

His eyes shifted to confirm the position of the men alongside him. They crouched in groups of two or three.

Behren Asonti looked at Rios, who nodded once in signal.

From shadow to shadow, the young man scampered down the hillside. When he had reached a point near the structure, Rios turned to the one called Roman and gave a nod toward him as well.

Roman—though taller and broader—followed in the footprints of Behren and arrived undetected at a position several feet behind him.

At the top of the hill the captain of the ship received the signal from Rios, and followed the steps of the other two.

Three additional men, other sailors, followed shortly thereafter. Rios watched the six black figures descend upon the structure.

He thought of Behren's twin, Sabiir, whom he had ordered, for his safety, to the confines of the caves near the city. He would not risk his life again.

Focused on the men as well as on each guard, he sat poised and ready to send additional forces if necessary.

The five remaining men watched as the guards were soundlessly overtaken, each by three black forms and dragged into the doorways of the structure. In quick motion, the guards were replaced by two black figures, one of whom turned toward the hillside and raised an arm in confirmation of the successful mission.

It had gone easier than he had imagined.

Rios looked again at the men who had remained on the hillside. Had the situation not been so serious, he could have laughed at the irony of the forces that Behren Asonti had chosen. Here crouched several burly sailors, who, just the day prior, had been hard at work on the open sea, as free as the wind itself, now hiding behind dried bushes in the middle of a lifeless desert. They could not see the smile that cracked open his mouth underneath the veil.

Rios studied the house for any sign of distress. Teman had insisted that the house was secured by only two guards outside, and reported that no guards occupied the inside of the structure. Had Teman been truthful, or had the men just stepped into a trap?

Several minutes passed. The men inside the house knew that their remaining forces would rush upon the structure if they failed to reappear within ten minutes. However, the two allies now guarding the house remained calm and quiet.

There was no time to lose. The ceremony in the castle courtyard was scheduled to begin in just over two hours.

Relief came moments later when several dark figures emerged from the structure to stand upon the porch. One among them gave instructions to the others.

Rios counted seven. The height of the men dwarfed the addition to the small group below.

A sudden breeze grasped of the black cloak draping the new figure. Enwrapping the small frame, the distinct contour of a woman took shape. Her black hood billowed in the wind, sweeping back to expose waves of coal hair, lifted by the breeze to flow behind her.

Rios stood upright and pulled the veil from his face. His lips parted as he gazed with astonishment upon the figure of his queen. With the wind and sun upon his own face, Rios found himself breathless to at long last witness the release of the woman whose face had haunted his days for nineteen excruciating years.

This would, indeed, be the day of his king's vindication.

With his brother ahead of him, holding the queen by the arm, Roman looked behind before ascending the hillside, slippery from the shifting sand. Behren and the sailors who had assisted in the rescue readied themselves to follow, the last of the guards being bound with rope.

Exhausted from the continual hot wind, from which there had been no relief since disembarking from the ship, Roman grabbed for a canteen upon reaching the others on the hilltop.

Wiping his lips with his black sleeve, he handed the water off to the sailor trudging up the hill behind him.

Pleasure filled him as the queen circled the group, placing a light kiss on both cheeks of each rescuer. She talked on and on in her foreign tongue, dabbing her dark eyes with the veil she now held in her hand.

Stopping short before Rios, she examined his face. When he dropped to his knee before her, she placed her palm against his cheek and uttered several words.

The sailors all stared in silence, caught up in the moment of the reunion.

Roman looked about. "Where's Behren?" he asked one of them.

"He..." The sailor beside him began looking around, as well. "He was right behind me."

"*Behind* you?" Roman's words lashed out. At once, he dashed back down the hillside, sliding at times, ankle-deep in sand.

Within moments, he reached the adobe structure and pressed his back against the outside wall. From inside, he could hear muffled moaning and noted the boots of one felled guard in the doorway, bound at the ankles and rolling to and fro.

Peering around the doorframe, he caught a movement inside that caused him to draw back. A gunshot split the air. The bullet grazed the wood frame above his head. He dropped to a crouch. Glancing at the hillside, he saw several sailors descending toward the back of the house.

Behren hollered out from inside. Thankfully, Roman could not understand the command—with which he would likely have disagreed. At least the man was alive.

The commotion from inside increased, followed by another gunshot. Roman dashed through the open doorway, hurdling the legs of the bound guard. He slipped behind a wide marble column.

Colorful silk curtains hung everywhere, sectioning off the room and crisscrossed to create the most elegant of atmospheres. Fat pillows trimmed in tassels sat atop elaborate rugs, undisturbed amidst clear running fountains and crystal bowls brimming with succulent fruits.

Having been one of the two to stand guard earlier, Roman had not enjoyed the opportunity to behold the interior of the little structure. *Pashur certainly knows how to treat a prisoner right*, he thought, unable to justify the irony in it all.

Another unintelligible shout from Behren told Roman he was being held near the back corner. Twisting around, he dived behind a solid wooden trunk, keeping his movements soundless. Peering from behind it, he caught sight of one of the sailors dart in through the rear door and wondered how many were now inside. Sliding along the floor to the solid outside wall, he ducked behind a large copper urn and silently cursed Behren for the promise he had made that all would turn out well.

Reaching out from behind the urn, he gathered a fistful of yellow tassels framing a purple curtain and eased it aside. There, in the corner, he saw the side and back of the other Bedouin guard. The man stood, holding a rifle propped between one elbow and his side, his forefinger on the trigger. The other fist clenched a braided silken cord wrapped around the neck of Behren Asonti, who was on his knees, his wrists bound behind his back.

His head bobbed as though he were nearing unconsciousness. Letting out another garbled cry, Behren collapsed against his captor's side.

With a noise from another corner, the rifle fired again.

Knowing the guard had no chance of reloading this time, Roman sprang from behind the curtain.

But the guard was too quick. He released the cord, letting Behren fall to the carpeted floor. In an instant, he had Roman pinned against the wall, the rifle lodged lengthwise against his throat. Roman grasped the rifle, pushing with all his might, but found he had the strength of a mouse compared with the trained fighter.

It was but a moment later when the guard was engulfed by a sailor in black and Roman was freed, coughing and dizzy from the choking, rage now boiling through every vein.

Regaining his breath and his balance, he wrested the rifle from the struggling guard who, now restrained and brought to the floor by two sailors, shielded his face with one hand.

Ready to pound the man's head into the ground for nearly taking his life, Roman raised the rifle high overhead, butt-down, poised to launch his fury upon the stranger.

But with sudden recollection, Behren Asonti's words rang through his mind. *You have no control over your spirit. Think of the girl back home. It must be her calm manner that appeals to you so.*

His anger blazed, an inferno now against Behren, but for the reason that he had been right. All his life, Roman had surrendered to the power of rage, welcoming hatred and scorn as his rulers, thinking himself strong all along. What falseness. What self-deceit.

The truth crashed as a tempest through his thoughts—*strong only the man who can restrain his own passion.*

How can I ever repay John Viana? he had asked Andrew.

By taking good care of his daughter, his brother had replied.

Good care! Would his anger someday rise even against her?

Roman's arms lowered and relaxed. No longer driven by rage, but by shame, he looked toward Behren. One of the sailors hunched over him. After removing the wrist binding, he helped the panting Behren to his feet. In slow succession, Behren grasped his throat, clung to the sailor, pulled himself aright, and lifted his gaze to Roman. A broken red ring marked where the cord had been tightened around his neck. Even so, not a slip of rage could be found in his eyes.

Turning his attention to the sailors pinning the guard to the floor before him, Roman said, "Bind him and leave him." He flung the rifle by its strap over one shoulder. "Let his new commander deal with him later."

He stepped over the man to Behren and extended his hand.

"Thank you...Friend."

Chapter Forty-One

Pashur stood alone in his dressing room, his royal apparel nearly complete, save the final piece—an ivory silk scarf, which his servant, Jair, had gone to retrieve.

He prided himself on his physical attributes, his height being one of them. Even in the tall mirrors, his reflection was cut short at the forehead. And his icy green eyes—unlike those of his fellow Palmerians—had a profound effect on his subjects. *An eerie gaze*, he had heard many times over the years. Capitalizing on this natural characteristic, he used his glare to fire bolts of intimidation through subordinates. To this end, his mirror became his ally, reflecting practiced expressions he used to great advantage.

His ability to influence others had served him well. How grateful he was that he had learned to use it early on. The vitality he had possessed as a younger man had begun to wane. As he gazed at his reflection, he found not the face of a strong leader, but an ordinary, wrinkled, and aging man. The pigment had gone from nearly every hair, and he now stood slightly hunched.

His gaze jumped to each of the three mirrors before him as though in hope of finding the vigorous young man who once peered back into his eyes. Disappointed to find all the reflections in agreement, he pondered the aging image. Where had his strength gone? When had it taken its leave? The changes had been so gradual. Could it be recaptured somehow?

Perhaps. Yes, perhaps through the strength of the people.

This night would be a turning point in his reign. He balled one veined fist. Tonight they would hail him. Their ovations would invigorate him; their praise empower him. Like never before, he would feel and know their loyalty.

The name of Sabiir surfaced in his mind. A dark scowl over-shadowed the faces in the mirrors. What a wretched people they were to believe in such a myth—a mere tale. Fools. They would have been better off to believe that Hercules would come to their rescue.

"Sabiir," he growled. Such a fable. For years he had taken the word of a disloyal midwife that there had been a second child born to the queen that dreary night so many years ago. Oh, yes, there was the boy who had been found with Rios, and had not he, Pashur himself, kept track of the boy from time to time, through the reports of his men? But he had long ago withdrawn his men from France. It had been seven years since a report of any kind had reached his ears. Now it mattered not whether the boy had been of royal birth. The only reason he had sent two men back to France in recent months was to make certain the boy, now a man, had indeed forgotten.

The existence of a twin son who had escaped the kingdom had been a ploy of the late king, a tactic invented to create fear in his own mind. Even the king's own edict had not mentioned the twin. But what better way for the king to avenge himself, even years after his death, than to fill the hearts of the people with the hope of a returning ruler—a hope that would undermine the rule of any other? Yes, indeed, the king had been a clever man.

He was also a dead man.

After years of torment, Pashur had finally decided that the true heir of the king had been there all along, in the palace, right under his nose.

Yet, the queen's son had recently escaped. Did it even matter? The people would not recognize the son even if he did declare his identity. They would not accept him as the son of their king. Besides, the young man had been missing for weeks now. It was apparent that he had simply escaped, never to return again. The city had undergone a thorough search. The lad was gone. Refusing to be intimidated by an inexperienced, untrained, and ill-educated youth, he would no more be daunted by a legend.

Tonight he—Pashur—would rouse the people in support of himself by dashing their hopes of the return of any such king. What nonsense. What absurdity he had tolerated all these years. No such fable would ever come to life for them. They had no other choice than to support him.

Awaiting the return of his servant, he gazed with intensity into the reflection in the center mirror.

A movement in the shadows that lay behind distracted him. He thought he had seen a figure pass before the doorway to his bed chamber. He examined the reflection of the room, his gaze jumping from mirror to mirror. But he caught no further movement.

Turning his face to the left, he decided this was his best side. He would remember to present it often at the celebration.

Again, a shadow moved in the background. This time, he twisted around to look, but saw no one. "Jair?" he called out in a slow, even tone.

No response.

He turned back to the mirrors, but kept his focus on the shadows of the room. More movement. This time when he spun, he came face to face with a young man whose body was draped in a black cape, the hood of which had been gathered at the base of his neck.

"Hello, Pashur," the stranger stated coolly.

"Jair!" Pashur called out toward the door through which the servant had disappeared too long ago.

The intruder stepped closer. "Ah, Jair—your loyal servant. Unfortunately, he cannot hear your calls, Pashur. He has been...shall we say...detained for awhile."

"Who are you?" Pashur asked in a low tone, throwing one of his glares upon him.

A low laugh skipped from the young man's throat. "Don't tell me you've forgotten my face, Pashur. It hasn't been that long, has it? Perhaps age has filched your memory."

Yes, Pashur had recognized the face of the young man, though it had been several years. "You may be younger and stronger than I, but you do not intimidate me, Behren. This people may be in expectation of the return of their king, but they know not the identity of him." He twisted his lips into what he knew to be a hideous smile. He began to laugh. "They would never recognize you." He shook his head and scowled. "You are a nobody, Behren. Now back to your chamber or face execution in the morning along with your mother. Guard!"

Behren smiled in return.

With that, a taller man stepped into the room from the shadows. He, too, came clothed in a cape, but his face was shrouded by a dark hood. "Will they recognize *me*, Pashur?" He reached up to push the hood back. The light fell upon an older, yet familiar face.

Pashur gave way to a slight gasp and took a step backward.

"Do you remember the face of the king's instructor, Pashur?" Behren asked. "Yes, the king's mentor and most trusted servant. Surely you recognize Rios. And the majority of the people will be sure to recognize him, as well."

"Let them recognize you, Rios," Pashur said. "However, the majority in my army will not recognize you, for it is the young who typically constitute an army, and not the old who may know you. What are the two of you but escapees, powerless prisoners? Do you know the penalty for breaking free of your confinements? You've made yourselves known to the wrong man." He forced confidence to the fore. This young upstart would not be his undoing. Yet, where had Behren been these past weeks? How had he been surviving? How had he overpowered Pashur's guards to free Rios, and how had they reentered the castle? A hint of fear sparked in the heart of the governor, but he forbade it to register on his face. He glared at the younger of the two. "Behren, the son of the king. The anonymous, faceless, unknown son of the king. Do you also believe the fable, Behren? Has your mother convinced you that you have a twin out there somewhere—a brother who will come to rescue you from the evil, oppressive Pashur? I hate to disappoint you, but any brother you may have is..." He held a palm up, softly blowing across its surface "...a mist...a mirage...a vicious lie fabricated by a desperate and dying king." Pashur's volume increased. His hand balled into a tight fist. "Tonight the people will be convinced of that, as well. I've had enough of this pitiful charade. Their loyalty belongs to *me*."

A third figure materialized from the shadows and stepped between the other two. Hands reached up to push back the dark hood. The man stepped closer to Pashur, his face an exact replica of Behren's.

"Sabiir," Pashur whispered.

"Am I not real, Pashur?" Sabiir asked in a strange accent, but in Pashur's language. "Am I a lie? Are you calling my father, the king, a liar?" Two steps before reaching Pashur, he stopped and threw the cape back to expose his bare muscular torso. He turned his right shoulder to the frightened man. "The mark, Pashur. You know about it."

Staring at the blurred marking, Pashur stumbled over the dressing stool behind him. He steadied himself, his gaze fixed on the dark image.

"You are right, Pashur," Behren said. "Our father was indeed desperate. In fact, he was so desperate to save this people from your oppression that he tattooed a masterpiece on the back of his newborn son—'The mark of The Leopard,' as was declared in his document. He then sent him far away. But how quickly the years passed, Pashur. And now, on this very day, your rule has come to its miserable end. Fitting, is it not, that our father was known as The Leopard? Twenty-three years later his cunning, his ingenuity, and his wisdom have claimed the mastery over you. From his grave he has defeated you. Yes, Sabiir is very real—a name and a face you will not soon forget."

Within moments, a flood of black capes entered the room. It was over.

Chapter Forty-Two

On the morning of the twenty-first of September, Antoine Aramis stood at the railing of *The Emerald*, overlooking the glistening surface of the Arabian Sea as the ship cut the waves at full speed. Sunlight sparkled and danced across the waters. A warm wind whipped his dark hair, twisting his linen trousers about his legs.

He gazed down at the heavy gold signet ring upon his right hand. His brother's words rang in his ears.

I want you to have this as a reminder of your true identity and as a sign that I, too, will never forget that it is you who is the rightful heir, Sabiir. Because of your courage, our father's plan succeeded. You were the true hope of these people. I will remember that always.

The events of the momentous night in the Palmerian city—his homeland though a foreign place—had, indeed, been a spectacle. Once Pashur and the few guards who supported him had been subdued, Antoine and the crew of *The Emerald* looked down from the shadows upon a large crowd that had gathered in the castle courtyard below. They availed themselves of the delicacies provided and by nine o'clock began an anxious murmuring. Pashur had not appeared, and their concerns carried up to the balcony. Had they been deceived, trapped? Were they in danger of some kind? Why had their ruler gathered them together?

At that moment, a tall man dressed in blue and ivory silk attire appeared to them on the large balcony. He stood in silence as one person after another mumbled astonishment, recognizing him as, not Pashur, but Rios. Their whisperings grew until the sound of their voices had become one unified roar. Finally, Rios raised his arms. At once, they quieted.

In a loud voice, Rios explained his imprisonment and recent release. "However," he said, as interpreted to the Englishmen by Mr. Etrea, "it is my purpose tonight not to bring praise to myself, but to read to you the words of a man who was once held in great esteem in this city." He pulled a scroll from his pocket. The people remained silent, intent on his every word.

"To my honored people, the people of Palmeria:"

The crowd must have recognized the opening sentiments of the king's declaration written over two decades before. A prolonged and thunderous cheer rose among them. Again Rios raised his arms to calm their excitement. But their cheering only increased as though they knew the words that were to follow. Rios looked back at Antoine and the others, who waited in the shadows behind him. When, unable to any longer contain his own excitement, he turned back to the people, they cheered ever louder.

Looking down again at the scroll, he began reading the words of the king. The people at once quieted.

"Since the commencement of my training as a child, I have seen that man's long history of domination over his fellow humans has resulted in cruelty and injustice on an unprecedented scale. Greed, hatred, and prejudice have come to be the rulers of this world.

Hence, it was my desire not to rule you, but to serve you; not to oppress, but to guide; not to encumber, but to encourage."

Antoine had been examining the faces in the crowd below. Hope beamed from their expressions. When Rios looked up from the document, once more a thunderous applause arose and died again as he continued.

"But it will not last. At this time, it is my duty to sound a warning. I proclaim in solemnity this day that a dark shadow will be cast upon you, my cherished people. You will soon learn that a new and distressing era has begun for the whole of Palmeria.

I, Sabiir IV, as your king, have served this people in faith. But now my reign has come to its end."

At this point, Rios had given pause. From behind him, Antoine watched with the others as Rios' head bowed. Caught up in the passion of the crowd and the words of his father for a moment—for the briefest, most unreasonable moment—Antoine thought he would step out to stand beside Rios, to infuse him with courage and strength. How thankful he had been when Rios crushed the temptation by lifting his head. The reading continued.

"For a time, you will be ruled by another. While it is my desire that this ruler will deal justly with you, I do not foresee that. Rather, I fear his harshness upon you. For a time, you will be oppressed and heavily taxed.

But do not be discouraged, for neither will it last. My declaration to you is two-fold. You must be warned; you must be prepared for endurance. However, I declare to you that a son has been born to me this very night. He will be guarded and protected until such a time when he can reclaim the throne.

How will you recognize him? He will have in his possession several items belonging to the king. First, he will have a replica of this very document."

Rios turned the document from which he had been reading to the crowd, holding it high. Antoine looked upon more people flooding through the large gates and across the vast courtyard, pushing their way into the burgeoning crowd, joining the rest in another deafening cheer lasting several minutes.

"Your king will also have with him the diamond from my scepter and my signet ring. He will possess a certificate of his birth. But his greatest identification will be the unmistakable mark of The Leopard.

"Keep your hope alive, my honored people. Let that hope live and thrive in your hearts. In your darkest hour, remember your true king. It is my greatest confidence that he, too, will lead you as I have, for that is how he will be taught."

"The document has the original signature of King Sabiir Asonti IV," Rios had called out, again parading the document over the heads of the people. "I now present to you a most honored person who has been in confinement for many long years." Rios stood aside and held one arm out behind him. "Her Highness, Queen Simone Asonti."

As the queen slipped out from the shadows, the crowd cheered wildly. She stepped up to the banister. Antoine felt her grace as she looked down upon them.

He stood in admiration of the woman he now knew as his mother. Because of the risk involved, he had not accompanied the crew on her rescue. Instead, he had waited with one of the sailors in a dark cave near the city.

His reunion with his mother had taken place later, at the castle, after Pashur had been apprehended. It had been brief, accompanied only by Mr. Etrea as an interpreter. Standing in a long embrace, neither had been able to speak more than a few words for the tears. After too many long years of wonder, Antoine finally discovered his true heritage. The beauty in his mother's face was something he would never forget. However, their reunion was bittersweet, as she soon learned that he would not, indeed, could not, reside in Palmeria, but would live out his life thousands of miles from her.

They had talked for a short while about his upbringing and about his English wife. She had spoken softly and slowly, and the words, only weeks before strange to his ears, had come with understanding. Soon, too soon, Behren summoned her. Their parting words were the queen's.

"You are as much like your father as I knew you would be, Sabiir, and I respect your decision." She kissed his cheek. "We will meet again, Your Majesty." Turning, she hurried from the room.

He wondered then, as now, when that time would come.

The crew of *The Emerald* remained just long enough to see the introduction of the new king to his people. They watched as Behren raised his hand high above his head to present the signet ring, followed by the scepter, the Desert Ice diamond again fitted into its proper place. It glistened in the light of the many bright lamps.

Several minutes later, he stepped back toward the shadows behind him. It was then he pulled the ring from his finger and handed it to his brother. After those few words, he returned to the railing.

As the crowd cheered, Antoine, Roman, Andrew, Mr. Etrea, and all their crew crept quietly out of the city. Under black hoods they walked against the crowd of people who flocked in droves to the castle gates. In all the excitement, no one took note of the strangers. The last words heard by Antoine were those of Rios, explaining that the mark of The Leopard was the training 'Sabiir' had received by the king's closest companion—his queen. It was this instruction that would allow him to guide the people of Palmeria as his father had.

After traversing the desert on horseback, the crew abandoned the animals at the shoreline, where Rios would later collect them. The ship cast off under the fading stars when morning spread its first light over the Arabian Sea.

Antoine stood at the railing. Exhausted by the unrelenting anxiety carried the previous weeks, he gazed upon the peaceful waters in wonder over the mission now completed. Had it all been just a dream? He looked again at the signet ring and smiled. No, it had been an unexpected experience that Antoine Aramis wished never to repeat.

He recalled the portraits of the previous kings he had viewed in the castle. The face of his father he at once recognized, a visage of strength and honor. Never would the vision of that countenance leave his memory, the face of the man who, in his forethought and wisdom, sent his newborn son to a faraway land.

Pondering a long while about the events that had led him to England, he thought of his wife. In silence, he thanked his mother and father for the courage they had displayed. How different his life would have been had his father not died a young man. He would have been raised in that land, in that castle, and would have been trained as a defender and a king.

His life in France had not been an easy one, but it had molded him into the man he was today. His love for the vineyard, something he would never have come to know had he been a citizen of Palmeria, and his love of art remained intact, embedded forever in his being.

How glad he was that his father's plan had been fulfilled without him. What tales he would tell his children someday.

His eyes focused on Catherine's two brothers hard at work on the ship. Though an Asonti by birth, he was now an Englishman, a Winterfield.

He stepped away from the railing to assist Roman with the head sail, happy to be going home.

Chapter Forty-Three

The afternoon sun burned through a blanket of haze to warm the Emerald Isle. The small Viana cottage, nestled into a green hillside near a high cliff, overlooked the rolling waves of St. George's Channel. Surrounding the cottage, gardens had been carefully pruned for the approaching winter. Autumn's unmistakable chill moved through the trees, now mostly bare.

The Englishman, unfamiliar with the island as a whole, located the cottage after obtaining the directions from a neighbor, and found it just as his brother had described. Looking around the grounds for any sign of life, he found none.

He tied his horse out front and approached the porch. The first rap on the door brought no sound, save his heartbeat pulsating in his ears.

He knocked again, louder, and stepped from the porch. Walking to the corner of the house, he peered up a wide stone staircase, which he assumed led to the gardens he had seen from the road. With his foot on the first step, he heard a click from the latch on the front door.

The unsteady figure of a woman appeared. One hand grasped the doorframe; the other clutched her abdomen. She wore a dusty blue dress, her coal hair hanging in a thick braid over one shoulder. Barely lifting her head, she stared at him through dull eyes, quick breaths drying her open lips.

"Jessica?" He stepped up to the doorway.

What had happened to the once-spirited, enthusiastic young woman?

"Roman," she responded in a loud whisper. "Is Andrew with you?"

"*The Emerald* is but a few hours behind me. I expect him here by morning."

Slumping forward, she burst into tears.

He grabbed her by the arm.

"The baby's coming," she said, her voice weak, "and I'm here alone."

He lifted her into his arms, and she directed him to a small bedchamber at the back of the cottage. When he eased her onto the thick mattress, she winced in pain. He watched her eyes squeeze tight, her breaths coming quick and shallow.

Roman crouched beside her, holding onto her hand, staring in silence into her face. With his free hand, he clutched his own belly.

A minute later, she took a deep breath and opened her eyes, her brow furrowed from distress.

"When did this begin? And where's your family?"

"Mother and Father have been at the island. They're due back this evening. Alex left for town this morning. I had some discomfort before sunrise, but I didn't mention it to anyone. I've felt that way before, and it has always subsided. But this time it has only grown stronger. The last few hours have been exhausting."

Roman pulled his pocket watch out and read the time. Just past one o'clock. He set it, open-faced, on the night stand and looked back at Jessica. She appeared to be resting, breathing easy. A single tear slipped from beneath her closed lashes. He retained a loose grip on her limp hand.

Within minutes she became agitated again. Her eyes flashed open and searched for Roman's. Powerless to conceal the strain that must have shown on his expression, he sought words to console her. None came. Her grip on his hand tightened. She cried out in pain.

All he could do was to stare into her face, waiting for some sign of relief. He caressed her arm in silence.

It seemed an eternity before it ended.

"Jessica, I'll go for the doctor."

"No!" she cried out. "Please don't leave me. Promise you won't leave me alone."

"At least allow me to find your sister."

"No, she'll be home soon." Her eyes, wide with terror, pleaded with him.

He looked away and released her hand to push himself to his feet. His fingers instinctively ran through his hair. "Then let me go to the neighbor. I spoke with a woman behind the hill in back, not a mile from here."

"I'm afraid!" she cried, pressing her head back against the pillow. Her tears dribbled across her temple and disappeared into her hairline. "I'm so afraid, Roman. Don't leave me even for a minute. Promise."

"Very well," he sighed. "What can I do to help?"

"Please prop a pillow under my knees."

He had seen many emotions in her blue eyes in past years—anger, frustration, even mocking humor looking out at him. But never had he witnessed unbridled panic in them.

No, he would not leave her.

He moved to the opposite side of the wide, four-posted bed and wrapped a feather pillow into a tight roll to tuck it beneath her knees. "Jessica, don't be afraid. All will turn out fine, you'll see."

Her eyes closed again. She seemed not to hear him. "Please tell Andrew I would like the baby to be named after my mother if it's a girl."

"You'll be able to tell him when he arrives," he said, walking back around to crouch beside her.

"No, Roman, I don't think so." Her eyes, now stained scarlet, sent more tears rolling over their rims. Another contraction gripped her. She squeezed her eyes tighter and cramped into a ball. "I know I'm not going to survive this. I can't go on."

"Jess, open your eyes," he commanded. She obeyed. The once-lustrous eyes stared at him, bleak and hopeless. "You are strong," he continued, "one of the strongest women I know. More so than even your mother, and she survived this four times over. Everything will be alright. I promise you."

"Something's wrong, Roman." Between short bursts of breath she repeated, "Something's wrong." A minute later the contraction eased and she relaxed, not moving from the position on her back. "It's only October. I should have another month. Why is this happening so soon?"

"Babies come at their own time, Jess. No one can predict the exact day." He took her hand into his. "You'll both be fine." He smiled with what he hoped would convey reassurance. "Let me get a wet cloth for you."

She nodded, and he left the room. By the time he returned, another contraction had started. She squeezed her eyes shut and cried out.

Rushing to her side, he took her hands. "Open your eyes, Jess. Look at me." She complied. "Squeeze my hands. That's right. That's right. Breathe. Let it out now."

Jessica exhaled, but sharply inhaled again and panted in shallow breaths.

"You're fine," he consoled, gently massaging her hands. "Listen to me. This one's nearly over. Keep your eyes on me." He patted the damp cloth over her cheeks. "Does that feel better?"

"Yes, better."

He sat with her through one contraction after another. Each time, he counseled and guided her with firm yet consoling words, fighting hard to hide his own rising apprehension.

What if her sister did not return soon? What if it was as Jessica feared, that something was terribly wrong? Why was the baby coming so early? What would he do when the time for delivery arrived? He tried to convince himself of the very probability of it. Yet, were there any complications, he would feel the brunt of responsibility.

Of all days, why did she have to be left alone today?

The contractions thrust ahead unrelentingly. Roman's pulse increased with each one while Jessica clutched his hands tightly and looked to him for support.

He wished the contractions would just go away.

Roman glanced at the pocket watch on the night stand. Two hours had passed. He stood to pace, his anxiety mounting. The contractions came more frequently now. What would he do? Where was Alexandra? Surely she must be on her way home.

Eyes closed, Jessica rolled to her side. She moaned and rolled back. She had been up several times to walk and change position in search of a degree of comfort, but with little success. Once, while up, a contraction immobilized her. She braced her palm against the wall, leaning forward. When it was over, she crumpled into a heap on the floor, exhausted and teary.

He decided she had better keep to the bed.

"Roman." Her soft voice reached his ears. "Alex told me of a beautiful meadow you once showed her. She spoke of it as though it were a dream. Please describe it to me so I can be there this very moment."

Roman stepped over to seat himself on the chair he had earlier pulled up beside the bed. He began with a description of the cove and the rocky hillside rising from the water. Before he could finish describing the looming forest, another contraction struck. He guided her through it and continued his narrative of the Eden-like meadow and its tumbling waterfall. Jessica's eyes remained closed, but she looked more peaceful the longer he talked of it.

"A rainbow is always above the pool," he said. "Andrew and I will take you there so you can see it for yourself."

"Tell me about your journey to Palmeria."

Between contractions, he described to her the splendor of the castle and the excitement when Antoine was reunited with his tutor and his mother. He told her of the seaports where they had stopped on the voyage home and the magnificent wonders found in the Mediterranean.

Another hour later, he walked to the front room and peered out the large window as he had done throughout the afternoon.

This time his heart leaped to find a horse and carriage approaching. He hastened to Jessica and found her resting. "Alex is here, Jess!"

Throwing open the front door, he ran to where Alexandra had just climbed from the buggy, her back to him. When she turned, she stopped short, her lips dropping open. "Mr. Winterfield!"

He held his hand out. "There's no time to talk, Alex. Your sister is in a dire condition. I happened upon her around noon. She said her labor began before sunrise."

When they reached the back room, she ran to her sister's side. "Oh, Jess, I'm so sorry. How could I have left you?"

"It is not your fault," Roman reassured. "She made no indication to you."

"It is my own fault," Jessica whispered, her eyes closed.

"Here I supposed you would appreciate a quiet day alone. I never should have been gone so long. Will you ever forgive me?"

Thirty minutes elapsed as the two assisted Jessica through several more contractions. Roman talked her through them and held tightly to her hands. Alexandra rubbed her back, speaking soothing words from behind.

As the sun began its descent over the Irish countryside, Alexandra stood and headed toward the door.

"Where are you going?" Roman jumped to his feet.

"To heat some water. Hot compresses may ease the pain a bit."

"Oh, no you don't," Roman objected and followed her out into the hallway. "I recall the last time you left me alone with a laboring mother to fetch some water. I thought Duchess would deliver that foal then and there. Now that you're here, you're not to leave me alone with her, Alex."

When she burst into a short laugh, he felt color rise to his cheeks.

"You mock me," he said, but supposed he could see the humor in it. Yet again, he was coming to know another aspect of the word strength. And once again, it was he who failed to show it. Oh, would the lessons for him ever see their end?

"No, I apologize," she said.

He allowed his gaze to wander over her features. "I should go for the doctor."

Alexandra shook her head. "My father knows his house. He'll go for him when he and my mother return. I need you here. It may be several more hours, maybe well into the night."

Roman pulled Jessica's door shut. "Several more hours?" he whispered loudly. "She weakens by the minute. How much can a body withstand?"

"I'm afraid she has no other choice. Your concern is appreciated, but first babies are often the most difficult. We must do what we can to help her through it."

Roman dropped his head to massage his neck, determined to get the mastery over his fear. "Of course you're right. Please forgive me." He then allowed himself a small smile. "But I will get the water started. You need to be with her."

How he longed to talk with her about the letter she had written. But other matters took precedence.

She ducked around him and returned to her sister's room.

Roman lit the stove, topped it with a pan of water, and started a fire in the front room fireplace. He lit the wicks of several oil lamps and stepped to the window.

His vision rested upon a neighboring cottage in the distance. Yellow light spilled from the windows, illuminating the front lawn. Soft billows of smoke rose from its stone chimney to dissipate in the violet sky dotted with the first dim stars of night.

Finally, Jessica's parents arrived. Caught by surprise at the situation, Angela quickly evaluated that the baby's birth would not occur for some hours yet. Jessica had become ever more aggravated as the contractions came still harder. Nothing comforted her. Roman feared she was near hysteria. He retreated to the front room, feeling any further assistance on his part would thereafter prove intrusive.

Jessica's father left the house soon after his arrival to summon the doctor.

Alone in the front room, Roman paced. Then he tended the fire, his own endurance at the cries of pain from the other room at its breaking point.

Despite their stormy past, he wanted nothing more than to gain Jessica's trust and for the first time believed he might have succeeded in that long quest. A powerful bond had formed between them during the afternoon, and her desperate distress continued to torment him with every cry.

Confronted by a wave of emotions foreign and inexplicable, he sank into a chair and dropped his face into his hands. Several tears fell into his palms.

Jessica's mother and sister had not left her side in over an hour. Though hearing their muffled voices through the wall, Roman had not heard Jessica speak for quite some time. Only her wailing reached his ears.

The front door opened. Jessica's father stepped through, followed by two men, one of whom Roman did not recognize. He jumped to his feet and took the hand of the other.

"Thank heaven you're here," he said.

"No, thank heaven *you're* here from what I've heard," Andrew responded.

Roman followed the three to the back room.

He stayed a few feet from the doorway as John peered in. "The doctor's here, Jessica," John announced, "but first there's someone who would like to see you." He motioned for his wife and Alexandra to leave the room.

At the door, Alexandra stopped to glance back at her sister and then stepped out, a smile of both concern and relief on her lips as she passed Andrew in the hallway.

Roman watched Andrew disappear into the room and a moment later heard Jessica's weeping, but softer than it had been. With the others in the front room, Roman just had to glimpse in to ease his concern. She had wrapped her arms about Andrew's neck. He sat on the side of the bed, hushing her.

"I'm sorry," Roman heard his brother say when he stepped back out. "Everything will be all right. I'm here now." And Roman had never been so relieved.

Roman paced the length of the front porch. The night air had cooled, but the front room of the cottage had grown too warm from the heat of the smoldering fire. He peered though the open doorway at Jessica's father just inside. John sat in silence in a high-backed chair, staring blankly across the room. All the others were in the room with Jessica.

"How can you sit there?" Roman demanded of John. "How can any man endure while a woman suffers so?"

John shifted his stare to Roman. "I've experienced this three times with my wife. But this night I'm numb, Roman. To hear my daughter in such agony is unbearable. I protected her from pain her entire life, but tonight I'm powerless." He clenched his fist. "It's…it's…maddening."

"I'm sorry, John. I didn't mean to criticize. You're suffering must match hers."

Moments later, they heard a baby's cry from the other side of the bedroom door. The two froze, staring at each other with wide eyes. A sudden smile of relief replaced the grimace of concern on John Viana's face. The door cracked open and Alexandra called out, "They have a son! A healthy, strong baby boy." She closed the door again.

John leaped from the chair and the two men embraced.

"Congratulations, John." Roman followed John down the hallway, staying back while John put an ear to the door.

Roman felt his shoulders relax at the sound of laughter amidst the baby's bawls.

Again the door opened. Angela's face appeared.

"She's asking for you, John." John disappeared into the room and the door closed with a click.

Roman was left alone in the hallway. He lingered, listening to the little celebration on the other side. The infant had quieted.

Once more the door opened. Alexandra emerged with a bundle. She shoved it into his arms. "Hold the baby, Roman."

And spinning back toward the room, she called out, "There's another one coming!" The door closed behind her.

Standing with a rolled blanket draping his arms, Roman found himself sure of only one thing—he was an uncle now.

Feeling no weightier than a pile of feathers, the little body moved, snuggling against him.

When no one returned for the infant, he turned and walked as though on glass back into the front room. He eased into the crook of the sofa before the hearth. Once settled, he pulled his right arm from under the bundle and lifted a corner of the blanket to expose the baby's face. Little black eyes blinked open as he examined the perfect round cheeks and nose. Fuzzy black hair covered the small head.

"Well, I would call you Piccolo," he said, "but that name has already been spoken for."

The miniature rosebud mouth opened in a silent 'o' to yawn. The infant blinked again. Roman pulled more of the blanket down to expose the tiniest hand he had ever seen. His fingertip skimmed across skin so soft, he could not even feel it. At once, the spindly fingers wrapped around Roman's the way an ivy shoot reaches around a lamppost. He let out a gentle laugh, all but oblivious to the commotion in the small room in the back of the cottage.

"You know, you gave your mother quite a scare today." He looked into the shiny diminutive eyes. "I know what you're thinking—that you frightened me to an even greater degree. Well, you're right." He could not hold back the smile that advanced across his face. "You'll grow to be a good man, just like your father. And if not, you'll have the wrath of your uncle with which to contend."

The baby yawned, closed his eyes, and drifted off to sleep. Roman could not pull his gaze from the perfect face.

Within a few minutes he, too, felt himself begin to doze. He closed his eyes and laid his head back on the large comfortable sofa before the fire.

Somewhere in his exhausted state, he heard excited voices call out that Jessica had delivered a second baby boy.

Roman's next awareness was that of someone shaking his shoulder. He opened his eyes to his brother, who held another bundle in his arms. "What's the time?" Roman asked.

"After midnight."

"I must have dozed off." He looked down at the baby still snoozing in his arms. The fire had burned low, sending out a crackle now and then, its embers still warming the small room. "Congratulations, Andrew. I can hardly believe it—twins, like you and me." The day's events whisked through his mind. "She thought there was something wrong. Little did she know there were *two* babies. She just knew something was peculiar."

Andrew smiled and crouched down so his brother could see the other baby with its identical puffy cheeks and thick black hair.

"Jessica said she would not have survived had it not been for your care, Roman. She'd like to name the older twin after you. He is to be called Romeo."

"I don't deserve such an honor, Andrew. If anything, he ought to be called Alexander. His aunt arrived at a time when I was near mad from anxiety."

Andrew peered down at the baby in his own arms. "This is Michael, after Jess's mother."

"Michael?"

"Angela means 'angel.' Michael is the archangel in the scriptures."

"Yes," Roman said, "I recall that now."

"Jessica would like to see you. Take Romeo to her."

Roman maneuvered himself to the edge of the sofa and gently rose to his feet. Andrew, too, stood. Before Roman could walk past, Andrew embraced him with one arm, the babies between the two men. "Thank you, Roman. Thank you for caring for my wife and sons."

"I'd like to say it was nothing, but I've never been so frightened in all my life. Whatever small assistance I gave was an honor, one I shall never forget."

Jessica sat alone in the cozy back room, dim in the light of one low-burning lamp. She rested now, propped up by several pillows. Still pale, her eyes opened in slits when his footstep creaked the floorboard. A weak smile passed her lips. She held a hand out to him.

"Does this mean I finally have your forgiveness?" he asked. His request for it, posed at the summer ball, now seemed so long ago.

"Roman Winterfield cuddling a baby in his arms," she said in a whisper. "Who in this wide world could have ever imagined it?"

She reached out for the baby and snuggled him while Roman seated himself beside her on the wooden chair he had occupied most all the afternoon. He sat with his feet spread, and leaned forward to rest his elbows on his knees.

"She loves you, you know," Jessica said weakly.

"Yes."

"Do you love her, Roman?"

With a long sigh, his head dropped. "I wish I knew a word that would describe my feelings. I ache for her, Jess. Yes, I love her, and yet the word is such an understatement. I never knew I could be overtaken by such an impelling, unrelenting force. She has changed my entire life course. Even if she did not love me, I'm still changed forever because of knowing her."

"Alex is probably the most wonderful woman of my acquaintance. Her kindness and integrity are unmatched. I care deeply for her and am very concerned for her well-being."

"It sounds as though your feelings for your sister parallel those I have for my brother. Jessica, I once wrongly accused him of mistaking love for gratitude because you had saved his life." He looked down in shame. "I saved Alexandra's life at Brentwood. You could now accuse her of the same mistake."

"Yes, I could. But I will not because I don't believe that to be true."

"I fiercely opposed your relationship with Andrew because at the time I felt you unworthy. You could take that stand now against me."

"Roman, I've been guilty of those very same acts. I've tried to discourage my sister in her affections for you. On the night of the ball, when I watched the two of you dance, there could be no denying the deep affection present between you. I was concerned. But later I recalled what you had said to me on my wedding day. 'May nothing ever come between you.' Then you embraced me and welcomed me as your sister." She gifted him with a faint smile. "That is what I wish to imitate now. May nothing ever come between you, Roman."

He searched her eyes for any sign of retraction of her words.

"I've seen the marked changes in you," she continued. "And I believe you will not return to your former course. In my mind the past is just that—past. The present is what speaks the truth about you. And what is more, you have my forgiveness."

He had waited almost three years to hear those words from her lips. Now that he had, he almost regretted her saying them. Had she only known about his struggles inside—a fight so new to him. Not wanting her—or Alexandra—to be deceived, he said, "Please know, Jessica, that a battle still rages within me."

"A battle you'll win," she said. "Now go to her. She needs you."

Roman leaned over to kiss her cheek. "Thank you," he whispered and turned to leave the room.

"Roman," she called out. He looked back at her from the doorway. "I meant what I said earlier. I would not have survived had I remained alone; but because of your presence and your courage, I did. You were right that everything would be just fine. I'll always be grateful for what you did for me today... and for my sons."

Roman nodded and slipped into the hallway. He entered the front room where John and Angela Viana sat together in quiet conversation. His brother, opposite them before the fire, cuddled the younger of the twins.

"There's a footpath that will take you past the stables," John said to Roman. "It leads to an overlook on the cliff."

"Yes?" Roman said, stepping toward the front door.

"It's her favorite place."

"Thank you, John," Roman replied, pulling the door closed behind him.

Chapter Forty-Four

He found her bathed in moonlight, her back to him, standing at a railing overlooking the sea. Her yellow dress appeared almost white in the pale glow, and her silken brown hair fell over her shoulders.

Roman stepped up to the edge of the pathway, allowing his gaze to wander over the soft curves of her figure. He would lock the vision forever in his memory.

Starting to step forward, he hesitated.

Doubt—a relentless uncertainty—clouded his thoughts, a doubt that had reared its hateful head on the voyage home. It had seeped into every corner of his mind, plaguing his nights, infecting his days. His silent war against it had raged for weeks now.

At first he had suppressed it, but it would not be ignored. He had tried talk himself out of it, and at last to drown it with drink. Yet it persisted the following morning, strong and clear even in his hazy state.

Try as he might, he could not rid himself of it.

And here she was, so near now, waiting for him. For no one else, just him.

Jessica had forgiven him after several long years for his transgressions against her. Would she forgive him for what he was about to do now?

He took just one step. But it was enough to catch Alexandra's attention. She twirled to face him. After a startled glance, she ran toward him.

In five steps, then six, she was upon him. Powerless to resist, he opened his arms and welcomed her in a rocking embrace. Her arms flung around his neck. Pressing his face into the crook of her shoulder, he skimmed his cheek and lips over her butter-soft skin, filling his senses with her sweet fragrance.

A low groan seeped from his throat.

"How I've longed for this moment," he said, his voice barely breaking the sound of the surf below. He thought he could feel her heartbeat, steady and strong. If only they could stay as they were, cradled in each other's arms, the remainder of the night. "There's so much to tell you," he said, "so much to say. But most of all, I must say I'm sorry. I'm so sorry for what I did to you."

"Please don't be," she said, her voice drifting around him like a gentle breeze.

"But I hurt you."

"It's all forgotten."

He drew back, his hands sliding down to grasp hers. "How do you do it? How do you forgive with such finality? How do you forget so completely?" Moonlight sparkled in her happy sapphire eyes, now dark with the night.

"I think you know how."

"Alex, I stand before you a man riddled with error, like gaping fractures throughout my entire being, most of which I fear are beyond repair."

"And the more evident my own flaws will become the more time we spend together."

"Together..." He dropped her hands and stepped back, unable to continue to look upon her.

"Roman?" Sudden distress filled her voice. "Did you not understand my letter?"

"Yes, every word."

"Did you not believe me when I said I love you?"

"I do believe you and can't imagine another day without you. But I fear for you, Alex." When he lifted his gaze, he saw the agony he had heard in her words and felt as though a dagger had slid through his heart, slow and deliberate.

"Tell me why," she said, making no attempt to approach him again. "Why should you fear for me?"

"I can't describe how I felt when I read that letter. As though I'd been lifted from the deepest, darkest pit, as though I had been given life again. And all the weeks of sailing toward the Arabian Sea, thoughts of you consumed me—how it would be, what it would be like to see you again." He reached out for her hand, looking at it, pale in the moonlight, and stroking it. "From my waking moment every day, you were there. Your face enlivened my hours, your voice whispering in my mind, 'I love you' over and over. I imagined the moment our eyes would meet again and planned our future together."

"I've done the same, so why are you afraid for me?"

"Because my thoughts on the return trip were not the same."

"What had changed?"

"I...I can't speak it," he said, dropping her hand. How could he say it? How could he admit such disgrace to one so innocent? And yet, to see her there, agony and confusion written on her face, on her pure and delicate features, was too much to bear. "I almost killed a man in Palmeria," he blurted. Scrunching his face in shame, he turned away. "I had his life in my hands, and I wanted nothing more than to crush him, to see him in pain, and relish in his last breath. I felt as though I could crack his skull with my bare hands." He grasped his head, clawing his scalp. "It came from nowhere, Alex! The most intense rage I've ever experienced. I wanted that man dead—a complete stranger."

"Oh, Roman." Her hand flew to her mouth.

"Do you see? I would never forgive myself were that rage to ever lash out at you. But even worse, my shortcomings could taint you over time. I couldn't bear to see my flaws corrupt you. I can stand here and give you a hundred promises— in sincerity even—that it would never happen, but who's to predict such a temper?"

"Why didn't you kill him?" she asked. "What made you stop?"

"Behren Asonti. Something he said."

"Behren?"

"And you. On the ship he had warned me about my angry spirit and told me to think of you. And I did. In that one heated moment, it was your face that came to my mind. And I knew had I struck a single blow, I could never look upon you again. And for that moment, I had it conquered. It was a victory. But one that didn't last. On the return trip, it came back, just like rust through fresh paint. I thought I had it covered. But when I again lost control on the ship, I knew then I was no victor. It was something that couldn't be masked." He gathered her into his arms again, feeling suddenly weak. "Oh, Alex, talk to me..."

"There has been more than one opportunity for you to vent your fury upon me. Remember my interruption in the potter's shop? Or when I reprimanded you for your harsh words to the girl who spilled the food on you? Recall my lashing you with my own angry words in the rain at Brentwood? You swallowed it all. We had our first argument that very day. You were angry and even accused me of having a divided heart. Don't you remember? Though clearly frustrated, you never acted on that anger."

But he knew full well that with time and familiarity, one lets down his guard.

"Don't forget your accomplishments since then," she added.

"They are nothing in comparison."

She pulled away to look into his face. A smile flitted across her lips. "Nothing? You returned to Kent to aid your sister in her studies, take her riding, entertaining her with chess and billiards. You even gave several days of your time to escort her to the races—the one event you knew she would love, though not your preference. And don't forget the day you took both of us sailing. Recall hiking through that murky forest? It was you who comforted me so I wouldn't be afraid. Recall running through the meadow?"

"I'll never forget that day." He smiled then, too, and laughed a bit.

"You even tried to impress me by riding bareback a few days later. Remember?"

"Don't remind me of that."

"Even in terrible pain from broken ribs, do you remember what you did next?"

"I played the fool by befriending Caroline Landly, a woman whose company I always despised."

"Forget that. Consider what you did for Duchess. You delivered her foal."

"Only with your help."

"But I didn't help you expose Gregory Westcliffe's illegal dealings."

"Yes, but my family was involved."

"Was your family involved when you fought your way across the open ocean in a rowboat during that storm at Brentwood? You rescued two people that night...one a stranger. And I'll never forget how you comforted me the following day after Old Stormy was destroyed. Did you know I watched from the window upstairs later that morning while you trudged around in the mud behind Mrs. Wright, helping her—without complaint might I add—to feed the animals?"

"You were watching?"

"I was. With pride for this man who had risked everything—his reputation and lifestyle—to become someone he thought would be better."

"I wish I had known your feelings then."

"But it doesn't stop there," she continued. "You volunteered and sacrificed weeks of your life to escort a man back to his country."

"Mostly to protect my brother..."

"What were your duties on that ship, Roman?"

"Deckhand during the day. And studying maps, diagrams, plans, and a foreign language during the night hours."

"Look at the comforts you forfeited. And what of the return trip?"

"We loaded cargo at several ports for your family's home."

"And consider what you stumbled across upon returning—my sister alone and in need. You could have left her to find more suitable help, but you didn't. Your heart told you to stay. What would she have done without you?"

"I don't know."

"Allow me to ask you, have your ribs healed yet?"

"I still have pain. But it's my own doing."

"Because you were even willing to sacrifice your health and recovery for the needs of others. Had you sat back and tended your wounds, you would have healed by now. But reflect on what you've earned through your pain."

"And my greatest anguish of all was the inability to be with you again," he said.

"Yet another sacrifice you made in completing that journey after receiving my letter. I stand in awe over a man wholly changed, a man whose flaws—fractures as you say—are closing one by one. And this last blemish, this temper, yes, it may flare from time to time, but I'm confident you will close even that."

"But it was only because of you that I was moved to do any of those things. What have I ever done for you?"

"Besides saving my life, you mean? Important as that was, you've saved me in a far grander way because you've proven to me there exists a man my father's equal, someone I hadn't thought existed."

Roman allowed his head to drop, wagging in disagreement. Her father's equal? In his opinion there would never be a man like John Viana. "So you have no doubts about me...about us?"

"What I have are hopes and dreams...and anticipation of how it will be."

"Then marry me, Alex." Having had convinced himself for weeks that she would never understand—much less accept—him, he reveled over the joy in her eyes. "I didn't intend on asking. I thought certain I would lose you tonight. But if you'll be my wife, then it's my life that has been saved. Teach me, Alex. Teach me your wonderful ways. Show me how to conquer this final enemy."

"You weren't listening to my letter," she said, slipping into a smile. "It's your potential, not mine. You will defeat it, I have no doubt. And I...well, I'll delight in seeing you do it since I'll be by your side every step."

He reached out to interlace her hair between his fingers. "I'll try my best not disappoint you," he whispered. "You'll see." Pulling her closer, he brushed his lips down the bridge of her fine nose, sweeping them across her mouth, soft as silk. And there his lips settled, cherishing the sweet taste of her.

Long past two, John Viana looked up as the handle of the door of the cottage turned and his daughter stepped over the threshold—alone.

Andrew had retired to the back room with his wife and infants, and Angela had long before retreated to their bedchamber upstairs.

Alexandra closed the door behind her in a quiet click. He rose from the chair before the hearth, setting aside the paper he had been reading. In silence they stood, their eyes locked.

Roman Winterfield paced in a square of orange light before the small cottage. He heard a noise and turned to see John step out. Roman stared as John took his time crossing the boards of the porch and down the two steps to stand before him. Their eyes met at an equal height.

"So why the delay, Roman?"

"Sir?"

"You had me a bit nervous when I heard news of your return to the mainland so hastily in August. I feared the agreement between your father and I had crumbled."

"Agreement?"

"The night prior to the ball, he and I concluded that you would soon be joining the Viana family at Muir Ceann. I had already begun the construction of your wing by that time."

Roman could do nothing but stare.

"I suspected your attraction to my daughter while vacationing in France," John added. "The following week while in Germany, I took the liberty of warning Jessica of the probability of the union."

"Alex had no idea of my feelings for her and certainly did not reciprocate them to me at that time. And yet you knew? How?"

"Have you never noticed that Alexandra is the only one of my children who calls me 'Papa'? She lost her mother at the age of three. Do you know how she responded to hear the news? I had lined up my three girls on the sofa and settled onto the floor before them. When I told them what had happened, Alexandra hopped down and wrapped her little arms around my neck. 'Don't worry, Papa,' she said, 'I'll take care of you.'" John looked up at the stars, a long sigh seeping from his chest. "To this day I've not seen such courage in any person. I know she's grown, Roman, but at times I look at her and can still see that three-year-old, my little girl. I'm close with all my daughters, but often I feel as though I know Alexandra's very thoughts. And to answer your question, I immediately noted the changes in you while in France and realized that she, too, would recognize the truth in time. A father's not blind to a man's interest in his daughter. Perhaps someday you, too, will understand that. I realized then she would be seeing you again."

"But why is it that I remained blinded to her feelings for me?"

"A simple lack of experience. You'll come to know her even better than I."

"John, I don't deserve the hand of your daughter. I've committed great atrocities against your family."

"No, Roman. My recollection is of one February night when you stood tall before your own society in support of me, the lowly keeper of a lighthouse. You are deserving." He extended his right hand. "And I stand before you now, proud to consider you my son."

Roman looked down at the hand before reaching out to tightly grip it. He met the gaze of one of the few men he had truly come to admire. "I vow to you today to do my best to raise my own children with such integrity."

John laughed and pulled him into a firm embrace.

Chapter Forty-Five

"Yes, that is lovely," Angela Viana confirmed when her daughter presented a bolt of delicate white lace. "That will overlay the satin bodice nicely, Alex."

"And perhaps we could bring the lace up into a high collar," Alexandra suggested.

"Beautiful," she said with a nod, envisioning the winter wedding.

Olivia Winterfield, standing nearby, rolled her eyes. "Really, Angela," she said with a profuse sigh. "There's no need for you to go to such trouble. The most elegant of dresses can be purchased. I saw some gorgeous choices in the Keswick catalog. No doubt, for me it would be shipped at once. We could have it in two week's time," she said with a snap of her fingers. "A nip here and a tuck there...perfection."

"Olivia," Angela said in a firm but respectful tone, "I'm here to see to it that my youngest daughter's wedding will be as she desires. And she expressed her hope that we could design the dress together. I'll not withhold that one request from her."

Olivia rolled her eyes and looked away.

"Mrs. Winterfield," Alexandra said, placing one hand on her arm. "You are too good to me. Here you have opened up Winterfield Manor for the wedding, have cordially invited my parents and me to stay here in Kent until then, and are going to such great lengths to prepare the celebration. Yet your concern is that we not overextend ourselves. Your suggestion is very good, but let me reassure you that this project with my mother will be among the most joyful of my life. Any effort is minimal when compared with the lasting memories."

Olivia's expression softened a bit at Alexandra's words. "Very well, Alex. After all, we can't have a disheartened bride, can we?"

Alexandra kissed her cheek in gratitude and turned her attention back to the fabric.

Angela smiled in amusement. She could not help but think that Alexandra's way with Olivia was certainly different from Jessica's. No wonder it had been Alexandra who had softened the stone heart of Olivia's eldest son—a task that had eluded every other woman prior to her.

The trio stepped out onto a busy London street. People bustled by on foot, on horseback, and in carriages, their cheeks flushed from the chilly air.

Olivia received greetings from well-wishers passing by, some mere acquaintances, others strangers, no doubt desirous to know her better.

They strolled past a display window, and Alexandra stopped abruptly. "Mother, look. Is that not a most handsome ring? How I would love for Roman to have that as a wedding gift. It reminds me a bit of your ring. See the etchings in the gold? The only thing lacking is a ruby in its center." She implored the two women with her glance. "Oh, may we go in and inquire of its cost?"

"Money is no object, my dear," Olivia stated. "If that's the band you wish for Roman, then it will be his. I have an account with this store."

"Oh, but I wish to purchase it myself. It will be a gift from me and no one else."

Half an hour later, Alexandra bounced from the store with her mother and mother-in-law-to-be trailing behind. She smiled to herself as they passed the storefront window, the velvet display empty where the ring had once sat.

* * * * *

With most all the afternoon to spare, they rode back toward Winterfield Manor in the carriage that had brought them, talking of the wedding the entire way home.

Alexandra peered out the window of the carriage from underneath the rim of her bonnet and smiled. Her family's first visit to Canterbury and the Winterfield estate had been four years before, in January—the same month that her wedding would take place.

This day proved identical to that one, the forest dusted in frost, shimmering in the sunlight filtering through a light fog.

The misty air had given Winterfield Manor such mystique when she and her sisters had first laid eyes upon the mansion. She recalled counting the large windows and chimneys when their carriage approached. They had stared speechless—indeed breathless—upon the looming structure.

How had she ever secured a position with such a distinguished family? No one could have convinced her four years ago that she would one day capture the heart of the infamous Roman Winterfield and carry the Winterfield name. She sat back and thought about the irony of it—Alexandra Winterfield. Yes, just like a chime, such a respectable name. Yet, it was not the name, the estate, or the family's notoriety which had impressed her so, but the man himself.

"What is the meaning behind that smile, Alex?" Roman's mother asked.

"I suppose it's because I am so gratified, so happy."

"Then I believe I'm not wrong in admitting that I favored you above your two sisters from the start. As much as I love Jessica now, I can foresee that you and I will get along famously."

"But be honest…it took some time for you to adjust to my engagement to your son."

"The announcement did prove somewhat of a surprise. But," Olivia said, leaning forward to pat Alexandra's knee, "I couldn't be happier in his choice."

* * * * *

They entered the mansion as two servants arrived to deal with the purchases piled in the carriage.

"Those are precious packages," Olivia called to them. "I want them delivered to the parlor—carefully."

Alexandra and Angela accompanied her into the parlor behind the servants, where mounds of parcels were beginning to accumulate, from fabrics to decorations to gifts by the dozens.

"Mother, you look peaked. Why not take a rest until tea?"

"Thank you," Angela replied. "I think I shall."

Once the new packages had been settled, Alexandra and Olivia escorted Angela back to the entryway, which gave way on one side to the large indoor garden. Already a transformation had begun. Where tropical plants and wicker furnishings once sat, evergreens of differing varieties and sizes were now perched, and space provided for over one hundred white chairs.

"No, no," barked Olivia, scrutinizing the new arrangements. "This simply will not do."

Alexandra and her mother exchanged smiles, Angela making a quick exit up the wide winding staircase after kissing her daughter's cheek.

The man in the middle of the floor, who was supervising the work, halted and looked up. "Is this not what you requested, madam?"

"Of course. But it's obvious it will not work." Olivia descended the five steps to the marble floor, strutting to the center of the room. "You see there," she pointed to the side. "The bride is to emerge from the parlor at that corner." She turned to face the opposite corner. "The groom will emerge from the billiard room on that end. He will advance along the banister, and wait for the bride at that corner there." She pointed to the steps she had just descended near the entryway. "Once the groom is in his place, then the bride will walk out to meet him. There is where they will exchange their vows before all the guests. Now, seat yourself in one of the chairs."

The servant complied.

"You see? The evergreens near the right corner are too tall. The guests will never see the bride. Move them to the back corner."

"Yes, madam."

"Really, Charles, I'm disappointed that you had not noted it."

"But to place them anywhere else would have contradicted your order, madam."

"So contradict."

Alexandra sorrowed for the man, who must have long ago grown accustomed to displeasing his mistress, whatever his attempts.

"And where are the candelabras that were to be delivered today?" Olivia snapped.

"They've not arrived to my knowledge, madam."

"Four weeks to the wedding and still they delay. Do they not realize this will be an evening ceremony? Or have they ordered a full moon that night?"

Of course, her questions were rhetorical to the servant, who gazed up at the dome of the glass ceiling high above.

"Move those trees, Charles." Olivia commanded and strode toward the steps she had descended moments before. After taking Alexandra's arm, she bustled into the ballroom, where servants in the large hall scooted on hands and knees, buffing the wooden floor. "More wax! More wax!" she commanded, throwing one arm into the air. "I want to see my reflection. More than a hundred will be waltzing on that floor." She strode into the library. "And how are my portraits coming along?"

Alexandra paused at the threshold behind Olivia, who gazed upon her son, Andrew. He was poised upon a stool before a black velvet backdrop. Before him stood Antoine Aramis, a palette and paint brush in hand, working at a large canvas. Alexandra admired the likeness of Andrew that had appeared on the canvas.

"Mother, don't disturb him," Andrew said, still as a statue. "He needs quiet. But do tell, what do you think? I've been given the permission to view it only upon the unveiling at the reception. Is it a good likeness?"

"I think she's speechless," Alexandra spoke up, stepping into the room.

"You spoiled my surprise," Antoine said to Olivia, setting down his tools and shifting the heavy curtain on the window to allow more light upon the subject.

"I'll be surprised at all the others," she said. "This is the first I've seen of any of them. I couldn't stand it a minute longer. I just had to see one."

Antoine had already completed portraits of the other Winterfields, including Catherine, with the exception of the groom, whose portrait would be completed the week prior to the wedding.

"Since you insisted, you might as well offer an opinion."

"Antoine…I am…awestruck by your talent. What a priceless gift the king of Palmeria has bestowed upon you."

"Now that is an accurate representation of my husband." A voice broke into the gathering from the doorway. Alexandra smiled to find Jessica standing there. She stepped over to the painting and evaluated it against the portrait that had donned the library wall for so many years. "There is no comparison," she said. "That old painting has never portrayed Andrew honestly. Antoine, you are truly the greatest artist England has ever known, and quite possibly all of Europe."

"You give me too much credit," Antoine said. He stood back and studied his work. "That'll be all today, Andrew. The light is past its prime. Tomorrow, noon, say?" He moved the unfinished portrait into a corner, facing it toward the wall. "To avoid any further 'accidental' viewings," he explained.

"I apologize," stated Jessica, "but I was asked to report to the library."

"Yes, please take Andrew's place on the stool," Antoine instructed. "I'd just like to decide how best to present you. Tomorrow I'll be finished with Andrew and we can start on you straight away. After that, Roman will be the finale. When is he due back in the country, Alex?"

"Three more weeks," she said, her voice dragging. "I'm afraid you'll be allowed just one week to complete his portrait—frame and all. Will it be finished for the reception?"

"I will work night and day," Antoine assured her with a sigh. "It will be done on time."

"I expect perfection," Olivia said. "Eight completed works will be displayed above the marble mantle in the ballroom for all to see."

Andrew stood to stretch and placed a kiss on his wife's cheek.

"But who's to paint you, Antoine?" Alexandra inquired.

"It's already done, and much in the likeness of the others."

"A fellow artist has done the honors," Jessica explained, settling onto the high stool before the black backdrop.

"Where are my babies?" Olivia asked in her blaring tone. "I must see them this instant."

"Upstairs in the nursery. With Catherine," Jessica answered.

Alexandra entered the nursery where Catherine sat, rocking a baby near the fire.

"I thought I'd better warn you," said Alexandra, "that your mother will be headed straight for the nursery after checking the progress of the afternoon tea."

Catherine laughed and turned her gaze back down upon the face of the sleeping infant. "Isn't he perfect?" she said. "I want a family of my own so much. Do you think Antoine and I will produce such beautiful babies?"

"I've no doubt," Alexandra said, stooping to gather the other sleeping twin from the cradle beside her future sister-in-law.

"And you and Roman will perhaps have the most handsome of all."

"Please, allow me the time to adjust to the idea of being a wife first."

"Oh, but once married, one should expect parenthood at any time."

"I suppose it was kind of our Creator to give us nine months of preparation." Alexandra glanced down at the peaceful infant in her arms. She twirled a soft strand of his dark hair around one finger, catching glimpses of dark auburn streaks here and there throughout the blackness. How fitting that this twin had been named for his uncle; the other twin's hair was black as coal, in the image of his father. "Catherine, I've been so busy with wedding plans, you and I haven't had the chance to sit and visit. Please tell me some more about your holiday in France."

"It was nothing short of wonderful. When I met Antoine's sister, I felt we'd known each other for years. Although disheartened last summer to discover that Damica was not his flesh and blood, Antoine nevertheless considers her his closest relation," Catherine reported. "And to see the two together, one would hardly suspect they are anything but blood relatives. Of course, Antoine bears more resemblance to the French than to his own people. It's no wonder a French heritage was never questioned."

"And how did you find Damica's manner?" Alexandra queried.

"She welcomed me with open arms, as did her entire family. They are all so very dear. Her eldest daughter treasures a sketch Antoine made of me when he was there in July. She said she'll keep it always. It's a good likeness of me. I shouldn't have been surprised, but somehow I'm always astonished at his talent. Which is, of course, surpassed by his kindness. I'm fortunate, indeed, to have such a man as my husband."

"And how do you like bearing the Aramis name now?"

"Winterfield was without doubt a difficult name to abandon. Antoine is not proud of his adoptive father, but he did not feel that to change to his birth name, Asonti, would be appropriate. We both admire the name Aramis. For me, it symbolizes Antoine and the integrity he carries, and Antoine feels that it will come to represent an honorable family line in time."

Olivia Winterfield stepped into the cozy room, stopping their conversation. She approached Alexandra. "This just arrived for you, Alex...from Germany." She held out a letter of sorts, raising her eyebrows and smiling. "You may have it if you'll allow Romeo's grandmother the opportunity to cuddle him."

"Of course you may have him." She handed the tiny bundle to Olivia in exchange for the letter.

"Before you go," Olivia added, settling onto a cushioned bench with the infant, "be a dear and stir the fire. There's a dreadful draft in this room."

In her bedchamber, Alexandra fell onto her plush mattress and propped herself up on her elbows, holding the letter before her. It was the third, and probably last, to arrive from her fiancé before the man himself would return.

She ran her fingers across the ink on the front, which spelled out her name in his masculine, yet eloquent hand. Turning the letter over, she broke the seal. As she read it, she tried to imagine the glint in his deep eyes and the smile on his tender lips.

> My Dearest Alex,
>
> I am in Frankfurt now. I arrived two days ago. This part of the country is experiencing a bitter December, which is typical, I suppose. The chill in the wind cuts to the bone. Even before the hearth I find little relief.
>
> Oh, yes, I have traveled the whole of Europe during the severest of winters and had in previous years acclimated rather easily.
>
> However, this year is different. Not the cold, mind you, but me. You see, thoughts of you will not leave my mind. To know your warmth is awaiting me in Kent makes each day here, each hour, unbearably frigid. I long for the time when I will again hold you in my arms.
>
> I will arrive in England the fifth of January. My mother informs me that I will be imprisoned by my brother-in-law the entire week following

for the making of the portrait. I understand you will be staying at the Sutton's that week. Though the thought of not seeing you tortures me, I feel it will be easier for both of us if we refrain from being together that final week.

Alexandra read the sentence again. Here she had been preparing her heart to be without him for just three more weeks and now it would be four. How could she survive, knowing he would be so near?

To see you for a few fleeting moments each day only to have to part ways again would be difficult beyond endurance. When I next see you, I must know that we will never be forced to part again.

Yes, she had to agree, although fearing the final week would prove the most difficult in all her life.

I have received correspondence from my father, as well as yours. As you and I discussed, they have both approved of your joining me in my travels for Winterfield Imports until such a time when Muir Ceann is completed. In the meantime we will also assume the responsibility for the majority of the purchasing for the castle. In that way your parents may concentrate their efforts more fully on the construction at the island, and we will have the opportunity to contribute to the project, as well.

I have also made arrangements for our honeymoon in Italy, followed by a brief visit to Paris this spring.

Once again, I find sleep scarce these past weeks, as eagerness over the upcoming events fills my mind. Anticipation burns in my heart for the evening of the twelfth of January when I will secure the honor to call you my wife from that day forward.

Please be assured of my love for you during my absence, which love grows stronger by the day.

I will be forever thankful for the moment you stepped into that shop in France—that instant when this tremendous love we share was first sparked.

Yours, Roman

Chapter Forty-Six

The large shop smelled delectably of a mixture of coffees and teas. Olivia Winterfield strolled through, pulling a porcelain tea pot from a shelf to admire the hand-painted flowers around its center. The shop, known to offer the largest selection of tea sets in all of London, was one of her favorites. And, indeed, their tea services were the finest she had ever seen—from china, to copper, to silver.

In addition, the shop carried every culinary tool known to man, not to mention beautiful table settings, from the exquisite to the common, complete with runners and place settings made from the finest lace, delicate embroidered patterns, and dyed cottons. Indeed, the shop brimmed with the finest of European wares.

Several employees scampered about, preparing tiny round tables for high tea, which was scheduled to begin within the hour according to the large grandfather clock standing amidst the glass shelving.

Olivia enjoyed playing the part of a valued customer and thrived on the fact that the owner of the shop always paid particular attention to her. She wielded great influence in all of Kent because of being the wife of one of the largest suppliers to shops like his. Richard had always been a fair businessman to all his clients, and the merchandise purchased through their import warehouse was of the finest anywhere.

The man approached her. "Ah, Mrs. Winterfield, do you approve of the manner in which I have displayed your merchandise?"

"Indeed, Mr. Anderson. Why, I believe only a blind man could pass the large windows of your shop and not glance twice." She cast a lingering look at the collection of faces gathered at the shop's front window. Even on this bitter December day, despite the frost misting the corners of the window, passersby slowed their harried paces to eye the fancy displays.

Olivia looked at a tag tied to the handle of a porcelain teapot. "I often tell Mr. Winterfield we should have opened a retail store. There certainly is money to be made, is there not, Mr. Anderson?" The mark-ups on the imported items always surprised her.

"Ah, yes, but where I may sell one or two of any single item, Winterfield Imports has sold dozens," Mr. Anderson pointed out. "I believe neither of us is hurting for profit, Mrs. Winterfield."

"Perhaps we're both right where we belong." Olivia offered a formal smile to the client.

A soft jingle announced the entry of yet another customer.

"If you will excuse me, Mrs. Winterfield." He bobbed his head and stepped away, but called back to her, "I do hope you'll be staying for tea...on me, of course."

Olivia gave a slight nod and turned her attention back to the tea sets.

"Why, Olivia, I thought that might be you."

She turned on her heel, surprised by a familiar voice. "Oh, Caroline," she stated, offering a practiced smile. "You look lovely, as usual."

"Thank you. It's been far too long, Olivia. Why, I believe it was nearly six months ago that I last saw you when I was the guest of your son at the exquisite summer ball."

"I believe you are correct, Caroline."

"And how is Roman? I trust his health has improved. I believe the greatest of all medicines is the tender care of a compassionate woman."

"And we are grateful for your care of him after the accident," Olivia said.

"So when will I have the honor of another invitation to your magnificent home? I heard your son was in town in October. I waited and waited for word from you and received none."

Olivia ignored her dramatic pout, and Caroline moved closer to take her by the arm and direct her away from the tea sets to stroll through the spacious aisles.

"Now," Caroline said in a quiet tone as though to share some tantalizing secret. "I will not pretend to be unaware of the misfortune recently befalling your family, Olivia." She patted her arm patronizingly. "Oh, how you must grieve. The shame of it all. I know this is the reason for your seclusion of late and no doubt your reason in avoiding me." Caroline placed her fingertips against her heart. "Please understand that I grieve with you, but be assured that I think none the less of you and your fine husband. You need not be embarrassed in my presence, for I realize, as some may not, that a parent can only govern their children to a certain extent, and some children will rebel regardless of a fine upbringing."

Olivia's ire began to simmer.

"But for a young woman to act so independently of her family," Caroline continued. "Oh, Olivia, first Andrew to marry a daughter of that contemptible John Everett, and now this—a servant of all people, a common employee. How disappointed you must be in Catherine. How I do pity you. But do not feel your family beyond redemption. Roman now has the opportunity to pull you from the mire into which your other children have so selfishly dumped the lot of you."

Olivia smiled, awaiting a pause.

"You need not fret," Caroline droned on. "I humbly rise to the occasion. I am a condescending woman, and one who, rather than becoming tarnished by their shame, will instead restore your family to the honorable position it once held; for if Roman were to marry into a fine bloodline, the respect the Winterfield name once carried is certain to be reestablished."

Olivia waited while, with every word, the noose tightened a bit more around Caroline's slender throat. Finally, the young woman paused for a breath.

"Caroline, I believe what you say is true," Olivia said in her kindest tone. "Roman will, indeed, bring honor to his family."

"Of course he will."

"Perhaps news doesn't spread as quickly as it should," Olivia said. "Have you not heard?"

Caroline's eyebrows perked upward. She tilted her ear toward Olivia.

"Roman is to be married," Olivia said, smiling cynically.

"Excuse me?" Her eyebrows remained up, but her smile faded.

"Yes, Caroline. And I believe you've had the pleasure of meeting his delightful fiancée."

"I have?"

"Why, yes. And his father and I couldn't be happier with his selection. Her true feminine qualities of kindness and goodness will add greatly to the dignity which the entire Winterfield family presently enjoys. I believe only the high-minded are blind to the qualities that in fact define honor, of which integrity, loyalty, and decency are just a small part. Can you guess, Caroline, the identity of his betrothed?"

Caroline's face remained raised, but her gaze dropped to the floor. She offered no answer.

"She is none other than John Everett's youngest daughter." Olivia smiled and sighed. "Yes, Caroline, Roman has selected a truly admirable woman, one who has earned great respect and who has set a fine example for all of society. I believe most will come to love her as I have. She is indeed unique, and stands far above the self-exalted." Her smile widened as she held up her forefinger. "And we need not pretend that we are ignorant to the identity of such ones, need we, Caroline? Oh, look at the time. How it does slip by." Olivia escorted her toward the front entrance as they talked.

"I don't understand—"

"And about our dear Catherine," Olivia interrupted, "you did hear, did you not, that she married into the royal family of Palmeria? Her husband is, by birthright, the king of that fine country. But for love of our daughter and wishing not to take her from her family, he gave up his throne to his younger brother in order to marry her and live right here in Kent. That hardly qualifies His Royal Highness as a servant, now does it?"

Caroline gasped. Her gloved hand flew to her open mouth.

"I do wish you a pleasant afternoon, Caroline." Olivia opened the door and showed the speechless woman out of the shop.

She pushed the door closed behind her, swiping her palms together in a gesture of final closure. Standing there but a moment, she stepped away and settled onto a dainty chair at one of the tables set for tea.

Chapter Forty-Seven

Winterfield Manor bustled with frenzied preparations for the upcoming wedding.

Alexandra busied herself with the seemingly endless tasks that kept her mind occupied. The work on her dress allowed her many precious hours with her mother. As the youngest of the sisters, she had no childhood recollection of the woman who had suffered shipwreck and fifteen years separated from her husband and daughters. She gave thanks daily for this opportunity.

The week prior to the wedding, she and Grace, along with their mother, spent much time in town. Any brief moments of solitude were at once filled with thoughts of Roman, and she did her utmost to avoid them. It had been three long months since she had last seen him, and it was nearly unbearable to think that he was now there in Kent at Winterfield Manor, and she could not see him, touch him, or hold him. Word had arrived through her brother that he had, indeed, arrived safely, and they sent messages back and forth through family members. But it proved a poor substitute.

She could bear the temporary separation during the waking hours, but at night, when she found herself alone, her longing for him tormented her. Thankfully, the events of the day left her exhausted, and sleep soon overtook her most nights. She dreamed often of sailing to exotic ports and faraway places beside her husband at the helm of the ship.

* * * * *

The night before the wedding, Alexandra paced her bed-chamber floor. Unable to settle down by the hour of eleven, she changed into her riding attire and sneaked out by way of the veranda outside her door. A ride in the crisp night air would surely calm her.

Pulling the door softly shut behind her, she waited a moment for her eyes to grow accustomed to the dimness. The moonlit path wound through the bushes toward the stable, randomly casting deep shadows across the walkway.

Without warning, a figure stepped from the dimness of the bushes onto the path ahead. She gasped. Her heart jumped. The figure stopped.

"Roman!" she whispered loudly. "What are you doing here?"

He stepped closer, enfolding her in his arms and pressing his lips against the top of her head. "I knew it would be difficult to part tonight, but I had to see you," he said in a hushed tone. "I could stay away no longer."

"How I've missed you." Alexandra thought surely she must be dreaming, her ear pressed against his chest, the beat of his heart dancing in her ear.

"I hope you won't be angry that I've broken my own rule."

"How could I be angry? It's been pure agony to know you were so close, yet I couldn't see you. Promise me we'll never be apart again."

"Never again after tomorrow, I promise."

"How did you find me?" she asked.

"Your brother told me the location of your room." He drew back and looked at her clothing. "Are you going somewhere?"

"This week has been unbearable. I couldn't sleep. I thought I would take a ride."

"My fiancée ride off into a dark night alone? I'll not hear of it."

"Perhaps you'd like to join me, Mr. Winterfield."

"Perhaps." Roman stood with his hands encircling her waist. "I could ride bareback."

Alexandra laughed at the memory of his being thrown from the horse while trying to impress her.

"I must be dreaming," he said.

"Why?"

"Eight months ago, I stood at the railing of *The Emerald*. My brother asked me if I thought I would ever find happiness. He quoted scripture to me, insisting that true happiness can only be gained through the giving of oneself to others. I have since learned that is, indeed, true, so you, my dear Alex, must be a very happy woman." He reached out to take a strand of her hair into his fingers.

"You give me too much credit."

"Not at all. At that moment—the first serious discussion I ever had with my brother—I thought about the selfless gifts you had given to me and to many others. And at that moment, because of your example, I began giving of myself to others, too. At first it was most difficult and required constant diligence on my part. But the rewards of perseverance have been great. In fulfillment of my own happiness, I can now give my life...myself...my entire being...to you. Not only that, but you also gave to me the gift of a love far beyond that of any human. It's a gift I would like to give you in return." He reached into his coat pocket and pulled from it a small object.

Alexandra took the package. It was wrapped in a silk cloth and tied with a ribbon of lace. Tugging on the ribbon, she lifted the silk wrapping, and found a leather-bound book in her hands. She tilted it toward the moonlight and read in gold embossed letters, 'The Holy Scriptures.' Near the bottom edge on the cover was also engraved her name, Alexandra Winterfield. She could not take her eyes from the letters, for though she had said it in her mind many times over, this was the first time she had ever seen her new name in print.

"I hope you don't mind if I keep your old one. I've had it with me since the night my brother delivered it to me on the ship and, with the exception of this busy week, I've read it almost every night. I like to read your notes in the margins. During my travels I've read your thoughts as though you had written them to me. I believe I have come to know you better still because of it."

Alexandra opened the front cover of the book. An inscription had been written inside in his hand. Dated January 12, the following day, the day of their wedding, it read:

For My Beautiful Bride,

I make a vow to you this day, not simply to take you, but to embrace you; not simply to have you, but to cherish you; not simply to hold you, but to protect you; to lead you and to guide you by the counsel of this book. I realize that my mistakes will be many and my faults without number, but I vow to you this day that my goal is our happiness and my effort will be without end.

May my devotion and my love stand as witnesses to these words from this day forward.

Your Husband, Roman

"That is my wedding gift to you," he said quietly.

She wrapped her arms about him. "Thank you. And I have a gift for you, as well." She turned and Roman followed her to the veranda. He waited as she disappeared behind the door to her bedchamber, returning moments later with a package of like size to the one he had given to her.

Roman loosened the string and paper around it and smiled to find an identical book in his hands, his name embossed on the leather cover. "We think alike, you and I," he responded, but in his voice she detected a bit of sadness.

"You're disappointed."

"Only because none will ever replace the one you've already gifted to me."

"What's your favorite verse, Roman?"

He smiled and looked up into the night sky. "I believe it is an entire chapter—the one I read upon first discovering your Bible in the library. The thirty-eighth chapter of Job."

"Would you look it up for me?"

Stepping to the bedchamber door to catch the light from the lamp burning inside, he fanned the pages in search of the chapter. As the pages flipped, he stopped to look closer. "Your notes..."

"I had it recovered and rebound this week as a gift for you."

"But how? It has always been in my possession."

"Catherine searched for it at my request and brought it to me."

For a moment he seemed speechless. "I'll treasure it always."

She reached up and brushed his cheek with her hand. "I received a visit this week from an old friend of yours." A playful smile crossed her face.

"Not Miss Landly."

"The very one."

"Dare I suppose she came bearing warm wishes for our health and happiness?"

"Not exactly. It was her desire that I know of her suspicions about me—that my father deceived your father and manipulated him into this 'disgraceful alliance.' She wanted to make sure I know it is actually she that you love. Oh, yes, and you, out of supposed obligation and possible bribery, have consented—under duress, of course—to this union."

He did not return the smile that played at the corners of her mouth, but instead looked down. "Heavy charges, indeed. Though my past behavior has betrayed arrogance, even my abhorrence of others at times, I have never been a man of corruption. It pains me to think that my reputation suggests that I would be induced to accept a bribe in any situation. No doubt the misinterpretation of the man I once was will shadow me for years to come." He looked into her eyes. "But you do not deserve to be dragged into such slander. I'm sorry my past has spilled over onto you and stained you. However, you always give the gracious reply. I should not be surprised to discover that you gained her friendship at the end of it. Don't keep me in suspense, Alex. Tell me your response so I might know how to answer such an accusation am I ever to hear it."

"Actually, for the first time to my recollection, I had no reply. I could think of no words that would either respectfully defend you or turn back her anger. So, I let you come to your own defense."

Roman's brow wrinkled in curiosity.

"I happened to have in my pocket the last letter you wrote to me. I simply handed it to her and said, 'Let this be my reply.' I never wished to bring pain upon any person, but her willful blindness and false accusations had to be confronted somehow. And your words tore the veil from her eyes. As she read your closing sentiments, her anger reached a pinnacle. She hurled some less-than-ladylike phrases at me and tore your letter to pieces, throwing it into the air before storming back to her coach."

Roman laughed, then grew serious. "Alex, I swear to you upon this book in my hand, I never gave her reason to hope for any future with me. I'm so sorry she chose to believe falsely all these years. And I'm certain her parents will be at the ceremony tomorrow. Mrs. Landly is a dear friend of Mother's, but surely Caroline will not be present." He reached out and lifted her chin. "Let's put the past behind us. Now she can move ahead...and so, too, can we."

"I saved the pieces of the letter. Your first assignment as my husband is to rewrite it, every word, so I may keep it forever."

His eyes twinkling, he nodded. "I will do that—during our honeymoon even. Now concerning the potential guest list, we need not worry that Gregory Westcliffe will make an appearance to mar our otherwise perfect day."

"Now there's a name I haven't heard for a while. To what do we owe the pleasure of his absence?"

"I'm surprised at you, Alex. That could almost be considered an unkind statement."

She grinned. "Such a remark is most appropriate in this particular case, I believe. But you didn't answer my question."

"At this point I'm not sure even his family will come. Nor am I certain they were invited. Gregory has been located by Scotland Yard and will soon be serving a lengthy jail sentence."

"So it seems that Mr. Westcliffe is at last reaping what he sowed."

"It does indeed." Roman smiled. "I must go now. And since we both need some sleep, I must insist that you forego that ride in the dark." He took her into his arms. "From tomorrow night onward, you are a Winterfield." He kissed her gently and longingly before vanishing behind the bushes.

The night air felt chillier, and she looked up to see that a mist had covered the half moon.

Chapter Forty-Eight

"What if she doesn't come, Roman?" Andrew paced the perimeter of the Persian rug in Winterfield Manor's billiard room.

"Of course she'll come." Roman leaned over the felt-covered table and gave the cue ball a gentle tap. It rolled into the solid green ball, which dropped into the leather net at one corner.

Andrew now had the door ajar, peering out toward the Indoor Garden. He closed it again. "Already the guests are arriving." He pulled his watch out of his pocket. "Roman, it's six o'clock. She has thirty minutes."

Roman wore a double-breasted ivory vest over his white cotton shirt. The neat cravat knotted at his chin was tucked in a 'V' under the vest. His sleeves billowed when he leaned over for the next shot. Several wooden balls clacked together.

"How can you play at a moment like this? What will the guests think to hear a billiard game in progress?"

Ignoring his brother's concern, Roman crouched, one hand on the frame of the heavy mahogany table, the other holding the straight cue stick as he examined the alignment of the balls atop the golden felt. The black satin stripe running the length of his black slacks from waist to ankle glistened in the glow of the bright oil lamps.

"Really, Andrew, one would think you were the groom. I care not how those people out there feel about me. Let them hear our celebrating. Nothing and no one will dampen my joy this night."

At a quarter after six the door to the billiard room swung open. Richard Winterfield strolled into the room, accompanied by Antoine and young John Viana.

"Well, don't you all look dashing in black," Roman said. Although finding his father outwardly calm, Roman was quick to note concern in his expression.

"It's snowing," Richard reported. "I'll go in search of them if the carriage hasn't arrived by half past."

"At last someone's concerned," Andrew blurted.

"Not to worry. Her father's with them," Roman said.

Ten more minutes elapsed. Roman joined Antoine at the door, peering out at the room filling with guests. The orchestra played quietly, awaiting their cue. The candelabras threw an orange glow about the ever-darkening room. Above, the glass ceiling wore a blanket of snow. The guests whispered amongst themselves, their backs toward the billiard room.

Roman closed the door.

Just as his father reached to pull the watch from his pocket, the side door joining the billiard room with the grand dining hall opened and in rushed a flustered Olivia Winterfield. "She's here! The bride has just arrived. Apparently there was some problem with the harnesses, but they're all safe and sound. Andrew, assist your brother with his jacket."

Andrew obliged by lifting the black jacket from its stand.

"Antoine, John, come with me," Olivia ordered. She stepped over to Roman and placed her palm on his cheek. "Please forgive me for attempting to intrude in your life these many years. I should have trusted your ability to choose the perfect wife. I could never have loved Caroline as I do Alexandra."

"Thank you, Mother." He knew the great effort it must have taken for her to own up to the error.

"I could not have asked for more honorable or handsome sons," she said. "And you have chosen as wives the most wonderful and beautiful women in all of England."

Before exiting the room, she touched her fingers to her lips and held them out toward her sons.

Richard, Antoine, and John followed behind her into the dark dining hall.

Moments later, the door opened again. Roman was surprised to see Alexandra's two sisters, dressed in rosy satin dresses.

"Ah, there is the most beautiful woman in the entire assembly," Andrew said, placing a kiss on his wife's cheek.

"You may change your mind when you catch sight of the bride," Jessica said. "She's nothing short of a work of art." She glanced at the groom, whose smile broadened upon hearing her words.

"Roman," Grace said, her gaze dropping to the floor. "I know we've not all been the best of friends in the past—"

"That's about to change, Grace," he interrupted.

"I wish to congratulate you," she said. "You have won the heart and the hand of an extraordinary woman."

"I know that. And I also hope to win the heart—and trust—of all her family."

Grace nodded. "I believe you already have."

The guests sat in the soft glow, impatient murmurings rising from their ranks.

"Look at the time, dear," Roman heard a woman near the back complain to her husband, who hushed her.

"This is Roman Winterfield we're talking about here," he murmured in reply. "He's renowned for his lateness. Why would his wedding be any different?"

Roman smirked from the room behind them.

At ten minutes to seven the guests quieted as the small orchestra began a soft ballad. The mother of the bride appeared and was escorted by her son down the few white marble steps to take their seats before the guests. They were followed by Richard and Olivia Winterfield.

One by one, the guests turned back to where Andrew stood in the doorway of the billiard room, the groom behind. Warm light from the candelabras stationed between several tall windows to their left illuminated the walkway along the indoor garden. An intricate iron banister to their right overlooked the open, sunken room. With all eyes upon him, Roman followed his brother in a slow pace toward the front of the room.

His eyes were drawn momentarily to the high windows, where large white flakes fluttered to the ground outside in quiet respect for the vows about to be exchanged. Frost had begun to etch its good wishes at the corners of the glass. Seconds later, they reached the front of the indoor garden. Andrew stepped aside and allowed his brother to pass and stop a few steps ahead.

The parlor door at the opposite corner opened.

Catherine Aramis emerged first, smiling as she approached her brothers and pausing a few feet before Roman. She was followed by Alexandra's sisters, who advanced and stood beside Catherine. The three turned back toward the parlor.

John Viana stepped from the room and moved to one side as the bride appeared in the doorway, taking her father's arm.

Roman's pulse pounded in his ears and drowned the sweet sound of the orchestra.

Alexandra's dress was white satin. The bodice hugged her form down to the waist, where the skirts flowed simply and softly to the floor, trailing several feet behind across the marble tiles. The entire bodice shimmered under a layer of lace, which rose above the satin to cover her otherwise bare neck, shoulders, and arms. Her radiant chestnut hair had been pulled up into a mound of soft curls, surrounded by a short diamond tiara. As she drew closer, Roman noted the sparkle in her crystal blue eyes. A lace veil flowed the full length of the long train.

One of the guests noted, "Someone said they've not set eyes on each other in over three months." The bride must have heard the whisperings, for she responded with a broad smile, her rosy lips glistening against the silk of her cheeks. Roman winked as if to say the secret of their meeting the night before had been kept safe with him.

In a few steps, she and her father stood before him.

"She's no longer my little girl, Roman," John said in an undertone. "I know that."

"And to me she will always be a precious gift—from you, John."

"Four years ago, I told your father I dreaded the day I would be replaced by the men I would be forced to call 'son.' Today I can honestly say I could not have found my replacement in any greater men."

Unable to resist, Roman hooked one arm around John's neck, patting his back in a quick and grateful embrace.

John held Alexandra's hand out to him and kissed her cheek before descending the steps to take his seat beside his wife.

The bride and groom received their guests in the grand ballroom, their parents to either side of them. The bride was greeted by each guest with a kiss on the cheek, followed by a congratulating handshake for the groom. She received warm wishes from many whom she did not even recognize.

However, not all expressed approval of the union.

"Some felt he would never marry," commented one regal woman to the bride, "while others were simply surprised by his 'particular selection,' shall we say." She eyed Alexandra from head to toe. Dressed in gold satin with a feather propped in her hair, she towered several inches above her.

Although conversing with another guest, Roman turned to the woman. "Perhaps it was that all society was surprised to find that I had acquired such good taste, hmm, Mrs. Landly?" He put an arm around the waist of his bride.

The woman's gaze dropped, though her nose remained in the air.

When she stepped away, he whispered, "Have I not proven myself a fine student, Mrs. Winterfield?"

Contemplating what his response might have been just a year before, Alexandra covered her grin with one white glove.

Roman stepped closer to his wife when a handsome man approached her to take her hands in his and place a tender kiss on her cheek. Without a word, he moved to Roman, allowing Alexandra to greet the next guest, and extended his hand. "I should never have allowed that dance at the summer ball."

Roman accepted the hand. "Ah, but her heart had been stolen long before then, Preston."

"Yes, the 'Hideous Ogre' had somehow shed his repulsive shell." Preston's voice lowered as he leaned forward. "According to her sister, that's the nickname your bride once bestowed upon you, you know."

"It's not as though I was undeserving of the title. There must have been an uncanny resemblance."

Preston laughed and moved away.

When the guests had all migrated into the ballroom, the families followed. The orchestra began the evening with a waltz. The crowd flowed to the perimeter when the groom escorted his bride to the center of the dance floor. She gazed up at the eight magnificent portraits of the Winterfield family members, her eyes resting upon the confident, yet charming image of her husband—a perfect likeness that revealed his new personality. Even the lips betrayed the slightest hint of a smile, and the dark eyes a whisper of true contentment.

Roman took her into his arms as they danced alone, only the second dance they had ever shared.

Soon the floor filled with couples dancing alongside them.

Outside, the estate sparkled under a blanket of fresh white snow.

Chapter Forty-Nine

"Paris is beautiful in the springtime," Alexandra said, filling her lungs with fresh, fragrant air.

She strolled alongside her husband, arm-in-arm, through the park she had visited a full year before. Pink and white petals drifted from the trees to decorate the path beneath their feet, and Alexandra laughed to find several settled atop Roman's dark hair.

"I can't wait to introduce you to Germany's Black Forest this summer," he said.

"The only visions I have of that part of Europe is a place of dark and cold, of trudging through snow knee-deep."

"No wonder. The letter I sent you from Frankfurt in December had no warmth to offer. But a very different experience awaits you. You'll love it."

"Each season brings its own beauty," she said. "I'm no stranger to the cold. Don't forget the many childhood winters I spent at Brentwood. Or those awaiting us when we settle in at Muir Ceann."

"What a beautiful country, Scotland."

"I've always wanted to see it in autumn."

"Unfortunately, our travels will keep us away until winter," he said.

"Yes, but we will have the opportunity to see the secret meadow in its autumn attire. My parents will love it. How kind of you to invite them along."

They stopped briefly to listen to a young man practicing on his lute. Roman wrapped his arms about his wife and brushed his lips against her hair.

Alexandra allowed her thoughts to drift to her memory of the previous spring. Indeed, she had been correct, for there was now a different song in the air, and a change in the aroma on the breeze. The young woman who had gazed upon the park the previous year, alone and uncertain, now stood secure in the arms of the man she had come to so dearly love. The hopes and dreams she dared devise in her mind while he had been away those months were now coming true one by one. They traveled together, lived, loved, and laughed.

Before long, they left the park for the city streets, having a destination in mind. She saw the familiar blue awning of LeFigaro's come into view.

He asked for a table on the patio.

The late afternoon proved to be reminiscent of the day they had shared the meal alone together the previous year. The one exception was the light rain through which Alexandra had hastened with the young Frenchman.

After ordering a bottle of wine, Roman placed his elbows on the table and rested his chin atop his fists. "Recall the story you told me from that very chair? The one about the beggar?"

"I do."

"Was it true?"

"Somewhere, in some place, I'm sure it is."

"This time I've a story to tell you. A true story."

"All right."

"Let's see, how did you begin? Oh, yes. I've recently heard the tale of...a Hideous Ogre who once wandered the countryside throughout all of Europe. Are you familiar with the tale?"

"Perhaps." She raised an eyebrow, wondering how he had learned of the nickname she and her sisters had concocted for him years before. "Tell me more."

"I've heard it said," he began, "that the ogre didn't realize his most basic need, that of finding happiness. Nor had he the knowledge to obtain it. So along he went, terrorizing the unwary and humiliating the rest. One day he found himself in the company of a beautiful princess who showed him a pathway. Her kindness was neither solicited nor deserved on the part of the ogre. Though she did not tell him so, he suspected there would be a valuable treasure at the end of it. Any recognition yet?"

"Do go on," she urged.

"Since all other paths had led to disappointment, the ogre decided to take this last one to see where it would lead him. As he traveled along day by day, he noticed a transformation taking place. Somehow his shoulders felt a bit lighter, and he began to smile now and then. He even found that others would approach to walk beside him for a time; they actually appeared to enjoy his company. On occasion, even the princess would appear and walk with him. But then she would depart again. Though he stumbled on that path many times, he picked himself up and continued onward."

The waiter returned with two crystal wine flutes and poured a sample into Roman's, who tasted the red drink and nodded his approval. The waiter filled both glasses and excused himself.

"Tell me more about the ogre," Alexandra said.

"He took note of the surrounding forest and began to see things that had before gone unnoticed by him. The sun felt warm upon his face and the rain refreshing on his tongue. He took pleasure in the breezes and watched with curiosity the creatures of the forest. It was along the road that the princess had so graciously shown him that he finally recognized the true happiness he had unknowingly been seeking. He became grateful to her, for he had indeed found a great reward. Yet a terrible sadness overshadowed him because he felt he had seen the princess for the last time. Surely, her prince awaited her elsewhere, and she would not appear to walk beside the ogre ever again. So he sank to the ground and began to think about his situation. He even considered leaving the path."

Alexandra watched the dark eyes of her husband, absorbing his every word.

"But his senses told him that to do so would show great disrespect for the gift with which he had been entrusted. So he stood and continued on the path, striving to remain upon it. How difficult it was without her, but he bravely pressed on. Soon, the forest opened to a clearing, and the ogre found that he had come to the end of the path. He turned and looked back at the forest, knowing then he could never return to the place where he had originated."

She stared into his eyes, rightly called the windows of the soul. Her heart pounded in steady rhythm to the pace of the story.

"He wondered where his lonely life would next lead him. But as he looked ahead, he found something truly remarkable. There, at the end of the pathway, a priceless treasure appeared before him. The princess was there, smiling at him. She told him she had loved him ever since the beginning. She had been watching his progress and wishing for his success in the journey. To his exquisite delight, she agreed to marry him, and they found a new path had opened to them. The ogre, gruesome as he had been, found his happiness complete. And the two would travel side by side forevermore."

"Ah, but perhaps the ogre had overlooked something."

Roman looked at her curiously, his eyes compelling her to continue.

"Had he stopped along the way to gaze into the surface of a pond at his own reflection," she said, "he would have discovered what the princess had already seen. The one who approached her at the end of the path was no longer a hideous ogre, but a charming prince. Never again would anyone call him The Ogre or gaze upon him and recall his previous ways—the princess most of all."

Just as the year before, a violinist approached to play a soft ballad for them. Roman reached across the table and took her hands into his own.

She studied his face. Here sat a true gentleman, nearly perfect in features and now in personality, as well. He was, to her knowledge, the only man whose very name was found in the word 'romance.' And she had the priceless privilege of being the recipient of his unbounded love.

Suddenly, she realized her childhood dreams had been fulfilled in this most unlikely person—Roman Winterfield. At the end of his long journey, he had indeed become her prince.

The End

Other Fine Books by L. Katherine Dailey

Fruits of the Famine (Oct. 2004) Driven from her home after her father dies, Amanda Darby leaves her native Ireland and sails to America under an assumed name. She doesn't expect to fall in love— nor does she expect to be the subject of a criminal investigation— but life is full of the unexpected.

Afraid to tell her wealthy suitor her awful secret, she learns by accident that he has one of his own, one that can destroy any chance they have for happiness. And just in case it doesn't, his scheming brother will.

This beautifully written coming-of-age novel begins during the Irish famine that destroyed or dislocated one-quarter of the population between 1845 and 1851 and continues in 1875 when the daughter of a famine survivor seeks to make sense of the devastating tragedy that forever altered their lives.

The Navigator (2005) is a tale of of husband and father's endearing love, a friend's enduring search, and the lessons learned through the heartache and victory of true love.

A young stranger, lying unconscious on the roadside, is found and cared for by the daughters of John Viana, keeper of the Brentwood Lighthouse. When he reports the disappearance of a valuable ring,

they fear he will suspect them of taking it...but never suspecting that its later discovery will impact them in a way they could never have imagined.

This romantic adventure takes the Viana family from the serene life of the lighthouse into Victorian London's high society. Then past and present collide to change their lives forever.

Couple that with love *before* first sight, and you have Volume I of the exciting Viana Memoirs, a story that will rivet you to its pages from beginning to end.

Coming Soon
from L. Katherine Dailey ~

Once a Thief

Don't miss this exciting new adventure!

Chapter One

When their gazes met, Vanessa froze.

What is he doing here?

Stunned at his boldness, she turned away, but not before detecting a note of recognition in his expression. Had he also noted the fear that sent her heart into furious action?

She moved among the people—ignoring their glances—into an adjoining room. Whether her sudden flush came from the afternoon sunshine burning through the high glass ceiling to light the vast hall or from her racing heart, she knew not.

With the focus of so many upon her, she could not just leave the exhibit. Surely they were surprised to see her out at a time that must have seemed somewhat premature; yet it was her keen interest in sculpting—and this artist in particular—that had coaxed her from her compulsory isolation and back into the public eye.

Departure from the event was certainly no option now that she had made such a statement in attending.

Who is he anyway?

It wasn't until their eyes locked on the second occasion awhile later—this time from a greater distance—that she knew a confrontation was inevitable and possibly imminent.

"Vanessa!"

She turned at the soft pitch of a familiar voice. "Sandra." She embraced her friend.

"I can't say I'm surprised to see you here, but are you sure you should be out so soon?"

"I had to get out of that house, Sandra. I thought I would go mad from the solitude. I was flattered to have received the invitation for the exhibit. He must view me as a competitor, you know."

Sandra reached up to pull the black netting from the top of Vanessa's petite hat and back over her eyes, a pleasing smile passing over her lips. "Well, at least you're dressed appropriately."

"As I always am." Vanessa cast a light sneer her friend's way and began walking, her lips settling into a casual smile.

"True, you are always ladylike; but I know your response— to put up a fight before conforming."

"You know I underwent that battle in private. It lasted but a few hours and, as usual, I conceded. Eventually I always conclude that I'm no match against society *or* tradition. But as long as I may live, I shall never understand why either should so often defy logic."

Strolling along with her friend, Vanessa peered behind them, the edges of the layered black crepe and wool cloth of her skirts dusting the floor. "I feel I may faint. All this fabric." She fanned her face. "Black in the middle of summer—a *man* must have made these rules."

"Can I get you some water?"

"I'll be alright," Vanessa said as they moved into the shadow of a balcony above. "I suppose such a reaction would command a certain respect from onlookers. It would add such drama to my situation. Really, Sandra, they may tell me how to sip my tea or hold my parasol, but can one not mourn in one's own way? I assume only after the prescribed time will it be acceptable to enjoy life again." Pausing, she held her index finger before her friend. "But pity the wretch who grieveth a minute more, lest the wrath of society fall upon her." Her words, delivered in a dramatic hiss, drove both ladies into a giggling fit.

"Oh, how I've missed your company, my dear friend," said Sandra. "To be in your presence is to be at the theatre."

"Always entertaining, am I?" She smiled, but then forced it away, thinking others would view the expression as uncouth. "Thank you for your visit last week and for your letter. What ever would I do without my friends?"

"And how are you coping?"

"Oh, I do miss him dearly. But I think I can face moving ahead now. It has been several weeks, you know. It's so strange being in that enormous house with only the servants; it was Father and me for so long. He was a good man, a good companion."

The two settled into a spot behind the base of an immense sculpted bronze bear, its form looming tall and horrible. It seemed out of place among the white marble swans and deer in graceful poses.

As Vanessa studied the details of the bear's heavy coat, she could feel several pairs of eyes discreetly studying her.

"What about the gallery?" Sandra spoke in an innocent and interested tone, provoking a smile from Vanessa. "Do you think you'll be able to keep it?"

"Father paid the rent through October. At least I'll not be forced to make any quick decisions about the business. However, I know it won't be long before I will have to close it for good. And the house…I've already had to release all but two of the servants. Duncan, my house servant and Paul, the gardener, are still with me, but only half of their regular hours."

"Well, if I know you, a plan is already underway to save both house *and* gallery."

"I can only see one option, Sandra." Her gaze dropped to study the taupe veins marbling the white tiles beneath their feet. "Selling Father's remaining pieces is what will be required to keep the house. Offers keep pouring in. But I can't envision it; they'll be cherished, yes, but scattered, hidden from the eyes of his public. Yet neither can I imagine selling the house and moving father's pieces into storage, to be forever forgotten beneath dusty sheets in some old warehouse.

Graham Ambrose was one of the greatest sculptors in all of England and perhaps Europe itself. His work deserves so much more. Yet, nor can I afford to donate them."

"Then *what*? What is your strategy?" Sandra's sweet voice was barely a whisper among the echoing murmur of the crowd, now increasing and filling the exhibit hall.

"You'll think me unreasonable, or insane from grief."

"It was *your* ideas that earned your father the reputation he enjoyed. He may have brought them to fruition, but you were the one prompting him. What is your thought?"

"I want to be certain that all people will be able to view his work for decades, if not centuries to come." Vanessa bit her lower lip and then blurted, "I want to buy the gallery. But not just that one suite, the entire building."

Her friend gasped.

"It would make a fine museum, not just for father's work, but many artists."

"How will you do it?"

"Well, I thought I knew a way, but that plan has now failed. Short of selling the house and property, I'm not sure how it will happen. Father left very little in the way of monetary funds; he was a good spender, you know. He left me everything he owned; everything, that is, but his talent. Had I only inherited that…"

"Well, you'll come up with some clever idea. I know you. You'll not stop until it's accomplished. Speaking of talent, what do you think of this exhibit? Is this local artist any comparison?"

"Sandra, I'm surprised at you." Vanessa gazed back up to examine the frightful bronze creature standing poised on its hind legs above them. "Come with me."

Grabbing the hand of her friend, she pulled her to the wide opening of the room. Before stepping back into the main hall, Vanessa peeked around the corner.

No sign of him.

Suddenly a hand touched her shoulder. Jumping, she spun around.

"I didn't mean to startle you," said Sandra, who stood beside a man in a black jacket.

"Would you like an hors d'oeuvre?" The servant held out a silver tray piled with dainty sandwiches.

"No, thank you." Her palm pressed to her chest, she released her breath. "But would you please bring me some water? I'll be in the front hall."

The man bobbed his head and stepped away.

Vanessa led her friend to the exhibit's centerpiece, a true-to-size sculpture encircled by a heavy crimson rope of satin. Several guests surrounded it, studying it, pointing and whispering to their companions.

"Look at her, Sandra." Stepping up to the draping rope, Vanessa's gaze settled upon the white marble figure. "Did you see her when you first entered?"

"Who could miss it?"

"She is...*magnificent.* Now really look at her." Vanessa once again lifted the black netting from before her eyes. "See how her skirts flow? You can almost feel the breeze that ruffles them. And her hand so lightly grasps the rope of her swing. Did you even notice that it abruptly ends just above her fingers? No, one doesn't perceive that. In fact, you can practically see the shadows of the leaves on the tree that suspends her, though the tree is absent. And look at her expression. Her face is an open book. Though her eyes are downcast, the face says so much. She is obviously in deep contemplation over some critical decision." She stepped around to view it from another angle. "There is no wedding band. Perhaps someone has just proposed marriage and she is trying to reach a conclusion, possibly someone other than the one she truly loves. It would suit the title well."

"Yes, 'Forbidden Love,'" her friend whispered.

"But..." Vanessa studied the marble face. "...perhaps the greatest aspect of this work is not the girl's grace at all, not the feeling in her countenance or the emotion she draws from deep within her observer. It's not her contemplative expression, or the wonder she evokes from her viewer."

"Then what?"

"Did you notice, Sandra, what is *anchoring* her?"

They stepped around to the back to examine the block base from which the sculpture had been carved.

"Only the toes from *one foot* grace the ground as they rest so gently in the grass, which is not even there. No, your imagination sees the grass, too. The toes of one bare foot. Look! The other foot is tucked behind the ankle." Vanessa crossed her arms, a smile of amazement forming on her lips. "Do you know how heavy that marble is, Sandra? It's ever so precisely balanced." After a moment, her hands moved to the black fabric covering her hips. "This is nothing short of perfection in every aspect. I stand in awe."

"Do you know what I thought when I first saw her?" Sandra asked. "Imagine her hair auburn with more curl. I would think I was gazing at you, Vanessa."

Her friend looked over at her and then back at the carving. "You flatter me. And to answer your earlier question, there is no comparing this man's work to father's. Just look around at all his creations. And such a variety of materials: nostalgic bronze, pristine marble, humble cedar. Where did he acquire this talent? Where has he been hiding all these years?" Gazing again at the statue of the woman, Vanessa felt herself drifting away, into another world or a different time. "This talent is *far* superior to Father's, Sandra."

"How can you say that? He's your father."

The statement brought Vanessa back to her senses. "Loyalty should never supersede honesty. The honest person will not be blinded to the truth."

"Have you met this artist?" Sandra asked.

"I have not yet had that pleasure."

"Well, I have. You must do so at once. I dare say, the two of you have quite a bit in common. But he is not so open as you just described his work. His face is stern, expressionless."

"Well, I perceive then that he must be a snob," Vanessa stated as the two strolled into another room.

"Do I detect a hint of jealousy in your tone?"

"Perhaps. But just his name alone, *Arlyn James Pierce*." Mockery tinted her words. "Whoever would boast such a name? What kind of name is Arlyn, anyway?"

"I believe I heard someone say he's Scottish."

"How can such talent possibly emanate from a Scotsman? It seems to me—"

"Excuse me, Miss Ambrose." A deep voice from behind interrupted her thought. "Please allow me to introduce you to AJ Pierce. He has expressed a desire to meet you."

Vanessa's eyes flew open wide as her lips clamped closed.

"I'll get your thoughts later," Sandra whispered and ducked away.

As Vanessa turned to meet the artist, her heart stopped. Standing in front of her was the man from whom she'd earlier fled.

"Miss Vanessa Ambrose, please meet AJ Pierce."

"It's my pleasure to finally meet you, Miss Ambrose." The sculptor extended his hand to her. "I've heard much about you."

The velvet sound of his voice— so soothing it was almost comforting—did not match the cold iron of his eyes. She wondered if he'd overheard her snide comment. After discovering that he was the artist, she silently wished he had indeed. It was all she could do to settle her hand into his, but she said nothing in return.

The man who made the introduction nodded and stepped away. If their introduction had been noticed by the other guests, she remained oblivious.

It seemed an eternity before he released her hand and before she was able to breathe again. She chastised herself for not preparing for the moment she knew full well was impending.

"Miss Ambrose, it would seem that your manners have escaped you. Our eyes met twice earlier, and you turned the other way. Is not the proper response to offer some acknowledgment to a stranger with whom one's eyes have linked? A simple nod would have been sufficient."

Manners? A stranger? How dare he say such things! Though almost paralyzed with fear, she lifted her chin. The reply had hardly formed in her mind before it was on her tongue. "Mr. Pierce, pardon my frankness, but your sudden appearance in the darkness of my room the other night would hardly deem us strangers."

Her words stunned even herself. What was she thinking? Where had she found the courage for such a confrontation? "Your warm breath on my throat as you slipped your hand beneath my pillow and your silhouette in the moonlight of my window as you escaped will forever haunt me."

His broad lips eased into an amused smile, his dark eyes narrowing. "If you were awake, why did you not stir to defend yourself?"

"It's hardly a secret that I now dwell alone in that house. Who would have heard had I called out? To attempt a defense would surely have meant my injury."

"It's a brave soul that can maintain her composure under such circumstances. Though you were unaware of it, it was not my intent to harm you."

"Perhaps not, but simply to *rob* me. And now you would make me a fool." He had not even the concern to deny the charge! And why should he? She couldn't even retaliate. "Mr. Pierce—if that is truly your name—I know not who you are or where you obtained this magnificent collection. But I do know *what* you are, which is nothing more than a loathsome thief. You now have what you came for, and there is nothing else you could *possibly* want from me. I'm warning you here and now to keep your distance, or at once I will have the authorities on your heels!"

Crossing his arms over his chest, his lips fell into a snide smile.

Waving away the servant that approached her with a glass of water, she backed away and hastened toward the exit.